HYDE

HYDE

A novel

CRAIG RUSSELL

Doubleday · New York

All rights reserved. Published in the United States by Doubleday, a division of Penguin Random House LLC, New York, and distributed in Canada by Penguin Random House Canada Limited, Toronto. Originally published in hardcover in Great Britain by Constable, an imprint of Little Brown, an Hachette UK Company, London, in 2021.

www.doubleday.com

DOUBLEDAY and the portrayal of an anchor with a dolphin are registered trademarks of Penguin Random House LLC.

Illustration © BestVector/iStock

Front-of-jacket images: cityscape © John Lawson/Moment/Getty Images; blood © nico_blue/E+/Getty Images; clouds © Oliver Strewe/The Image Bank/ Getty Images; scrolls: ANGELGILD © DigitalVision Vectors/Getty Images; texture © wepix/E+/Getty Images; cracked glass © naskami/Shutterstock
Jacket design by Michael J. Windsor

Library of Congress Cataloging-in-Publication Data
Names: Russell, Craig, [date] author.
Title: Hyde / Craig Russell.
Description: New York : Doubleday, 2021.
Identifiers: LCCN 2021010142 (print) | LCCN 2021010143 (ebook) |
ISBN 9780385544443 (hardcover) | ISBN 9780385544450 (ebook)
Subjects: GSAFD: Mystery fiction.
Classification: LCC PR6118.U85 H93 2021 (print) |
LCC PR6118.U85 (ebook) | DDC 823/.92—dc23
LC record available at https://lccn.loc.gov/2021010142
LC ebook record available at https://lccn.loc.gov/2021010143

MANUFACTURED IN THE UNITED STATES OF AMERICA

1 3 5 7 9 10 8 6 4 2
First American Edition

For Wendy

"It was a man of the name of Hyde."

"Hm," said Mr. Utterson. "What sort of a man is he to see?"

"He is not easy to describe. There is something wrong with his appearance; something displeasing, something downright detestable. I never saw a man I so disliked, and yet I scarce know why."

The Strange Case of Dr. Jekyll and Mr. Hyde
Robert Louis Stevenson, 1886

HYDE

PROLOGUE

He looked at his friend and wondered how he still lived. Such a strong character, such a powerful personality, such an irrepressible force of will and resolve confined in so small and fragile a vessel. He knew, as he took in the narrow-shouldered frame and the thin, birdlike face bleached yet paler by the bright sun, that his friend would not be long among the living. Even now, his presence in this world was attenuated, fading, like the image of a man unfixed and dissolving on an exposed photographic plate.

And all the time, as they sat on the bench looking out over the pale sand of the beach and the glittering shield of the English Channel beyond, he was aware how starkly his own robustness contrasted with his friend's infirmity. As could be gathered from the sometimes uneasy glances cast by passers-by, there was nothing attenuated about the larger man's presence in the world.

The conversation between the two was scant. Theirs was an acquaintance of long standing where companionship alone often sufficed. Also, the larger man was afraid of tiring the other. It had been years since they had last met, and the deterioration of his friend had alarmed him.

"We'll head back to Skerryvore in a while," said the gaunt man. "Fanny will have prepared something to eat." Despite the summer warmth, he wore an ill-fitting jacket of heavy velveteen draped over insubstantial shoulders. There had been talk of seeking out a more curative climate—less tainted airs and brighter suns; the American West or the South Seas, perhaps—and the heavy-set man wondered if his companion would still wear the same jacket under friendlier skies, and if those skies would at long last bring some colour to his pale complexion.

"It's this damned book as much as anything," said the frail man without moving his gaze from the sea but clearly having read his friend's concern. "It consumes me so, eats at me—yet I can find no clear framework for the telling of it. I know exactly what it is I want to write about, I know that at its heart must lie a tale of the duality of human nature, about the good within the bad and the bad within the good, but every day it confronts me with a blank page."

"The duality of human nature, you say?" asked the other.

"Although we pretend otherwise," said the frail man, "we are all manifold. There are bright angels and dark demons in each of us. It is a subject that has consumed me since childhood. You know I inherited that dresser—the one carpentered by Deacon Brodie—from my late father. It is such a beautifully crafted piece and, as a child, I would stare at it in daylight wonder—but at night . . . oh, at night the thought of it sitting there in the dark filled me with dread, thinking that the ghost of the other Brodie, the night-time Brodie, would steal into our house with his gang and murder us all in our sleep.

"As a boy, I became obsessed with Brodie's story, burned into Edinburgh's history—a prominent and respected member of Edinburgh society by day, the worst villain by night. I would have this nightmare where Brodie would be in my room; I would just and no more make out in the shadows this tall, dark figure wearing a tricorn hat. He would cross the room, the tools of his daytime trade rattling in his satchel against the pistols of his nightwork. He would lean down over my bed, his neck encircled by the steel band they say he wore to cheat the hangman. As he did so, I would see both Brodies as one: his smile would be courteous and benevolent and at the same time a malicious, cruel grinning." He paused for a moment. "I have it still, you know—the Brodie dresser, I mean. I brought it with me here to Skerryvore. Anyway, Brodie's tale fascinates me still and I want to tell something of the like. Something not just about good and evil, but about their coexistence in the same personality, and all the shades and contrasts between them. About the dualities and conflicts within the human soul." He laughed weakly. "Perhaps it's the Celt in me that leads me to such obsessions. Or maybe it's because our country itself has a divided personality: that Scotland's dual sense of self echoes in its sons. Whatever its source, I am driven to write something about the duality of man's nature." He sighed, the shrug of his narrow shoulders almost lost in his voluminous jacket. "It's just that I can't seem to pin my story to its page."

The larger man remained silent for a while, he too directing his gaze out to some unfixed point over the water.

"If you have want of such a story," he said eventually, "I can tell you one."

And under a bright but cheerless Bournemouth sun, Edward Hyde told his frail friend, Robert Louis Stevenson, his tale.

Part One

THE HANGED MAN

Two years before

1

It was a sound like no other.

High, shrill, raw, it stabbed the night with sharp, juddering, ragged edges. It was a sound somewhere between a wail and a scream, yet it was unlike a voice; spoke of no human origin.

Moonless night had already claimed the city: dragging itself around the flanks of the Mound, insinuating itself through the crenels and embrasures of the castle, creeping down into the Old Town and stretching dark fingers into its narrow wynds and cramped closes; in the grand terraces and crescents of the New Town it rubbed itself blackly against the prosperous panes of the broad, high windows. But as if possessed of some dark gravity, nowhere was the night blacker than where it had sunk into the depths of the gulley that creased the city, carrying pure waters from the heights of the Pentlands to where they became soiled dark and foam crusted in the effluent shadows of the clustering mills that lined the Water of Leith.

When the sound found her, Nell McCrossan was a slight, insubstantial shadow moving through a greater darkness. Small for her fourteen years, her frame meagre and birdlike, her skin in the scarce and insubstantial pools of lamplight as bleach white as the flour produced by the mill in which she worked.

Nell was a fearful soul. She feared the walk to her shift, feared the swelling darknesses between the lamps, feared the shifting elm shadows and the voices she sometimes thought she could hear in the tumbling waters of the river. She had learned to mistrust her ears: the thunderings and clashings of the machines in the mill had distorted her hearing, tinkling in her ears as spectral tintinnabulations and haunting the vault of her skull with booming ghosts long after she had left the mill.

A generation before, her people had come to the city from the Highlands, driven from the green quiet of strath, mountain and glen to make way for the greater profit of sheep. The only world Nell had known had been the clattering, cramped, smoke-wreathed clamour of the tenements, alleys and closes of the Old Town, and the harsh, guttural Sassenach tongue of Edinburgh, yet her childhood had echoed with her parents' soft Gaelic and tales of an unseen otherworld. So, as she made her shadow-haunted, brisk-paced way to her work in the mill, the mistrusted sounds of an ink-sleek river reached out to her from the gulley beside the path and conjured up remembered tales of selkies and kelpies and other malevolent water spirits.

But when the sound found her, all other fears, all other noises real and imagined, fell from her. The sound—that terrible wailing screech of a sound—seemed to penetrate her insubstantial flesh and ring in her bones. Nell gave a cry of her own as the fear within her welled up and spilled into the night.

The sound came again, a shuddering, ragged screech that seemed to swell and echo in the depression of the gulley, reflecting itself off the black flanks of the mills until it seemed to come from every direction at once.

Nell whimpered, a child lost in the night, desperately scanning the darkness to catch sight of the dread thing that issued such a fearful sound, to work out in which direction she should run.

Again. A third inhuman wailing.

Nell turned on her heel and fled, plunging into the darkness between the lamp standards.

She ran straight into it.

A mass unseen in the darkness but suddenly solid, as if the shadows had coalesced to form an obstruction to her flight. The force of her collision caused her to rebound and she landed painfully, her back slamming against the grease-slicked cobbles. The impact winded her, and she desperately sought to draw air back into her tortured lungs.

She had no breath to scream for help as the shape leaned down over her, its silhouette growing larger, darker yet against the black gathered night. Strong hands seized her, and Nell issued a strangled cry, still not yet possessing enough breath to shape a scream. And still her captor remained inhuman; she could make out no face, no feature.

The dark form lifted her to her feet as if there were no substance to her. It held her by her upper arms and she felt it would cost this monster no effort to crush her, to fold and crack her bones. She was helpless as he steered her into one of the pools cast by the gas lanterns.

The lamplight and shadow now etched a face for Nell to see. Her breath had returned to her but she found herself still unable to form a scream, to call out into the night for deliverance from the rough beast who now held her captive. The man in the gaslight had features that instilled terror. Heavy, brutal, harsh features that, while cruelly handsome, provoked revulsion. Fright. Terror. She felt captured by some monster; by the devil.

Then she recognized him. She knew exactly who he was and it did little to abate her fear.

"Are you all right?" His voice was deep and as velvet dark as the night. "Are you injured?"

Nell shook her head.

"Where did it come from?" he asked. Again she shook her head dully, still hypnotized by the bright blue eyes that glittered in the cruel face. "The scream, girl," he urged, his voice impatient. "Where did that scream come from?"

"I don't know, sir," she stammered. "It was like it came from all around. But the first time . . ." She pointed vaguely down into the gulley beside them.

"Do you know who I am?" he asked. Nell once more took in his face, the glitter of eyes from under the shadow of both hat and heavy brow, the wide, sharp-angled shields of cheekbone, the broad bulk of the jaw. It was like a face carved from some material harder than stone. She nodded, still fearful.

"You are Captain Hyde, sir."

"What is your name, child?"

"Nell, sir. Nell McCrossan."

"Do you work in the mill, Nell?"

She nodded again.

"Then run there now and tell your foreman I need men to help me search—and tell him to send someone to the Dean police office to bring constables."

She neither replied nor moved, instead fixed and immobile in her study of Hyde's face.

"Go now!" he urged with more severity than he intended, and the jolt of his words sent her running in the direction of the mill.

Hyde took a pocket lantern from his Ulster topcoat and scanned the path, the trees and the river around him. Its light gave menacing life to his surroundings: the rushing water glistened blackly and oil-sleek in the lantern's beam; the shadows of trees and bushes that edged the river writhed sinuously. Yet there was no sign of anything wrong.

He surrendered the path and took to the river's edge, following it in the direction indicated by the terrified girl. The river became a sleek-backed snake, writhing its dark way towards distant Leith and the sea, while all around the sounds of industry clamoured louder in the night. Hyde startled at a loud metallic clang as the buffers of unseen locomotives clashed in Balerno railway goods yard. As he made his way farther along the water's edge, the sounds beyond became lost. The currents of the Water of Leith drove the waterwheels of the mills along its course, and at intervals the tumbling torrent would cascade over weirs and cataracts. Hyde could hear he now approached the thunderous rush of water over a weir.

The tangle of branches and bush along the river's edge slowed his progress and he had briefly to retake the path. Over the roar of the waterfall he could just and no more hear the sound of voices calling him: the men brought from the mill. To indicate the direction he had taken, Hyde removed his service whistle from his pocket and gave three sharp summoning blasts.

He walked on, along the path in the direction of the weir, but the river was shielded from him by a screen of dense vegetation. He reached the cataract and the water's edge suddenly cleared of undergrowth. A short section of iron railing, rusted and time bent, offered the only security from where the river dropped twenty feet to the lower level. The darkness of the night and the thunder of the waterfall disconcertingly rendered him deaf and blind to anything outside this small theatre of his awareness. He shone the light from his pocket lantern along the riverbank on his side, then across the foaming edge of the waterfall to the other bank.

It was then he saw it.

It moved in the light, turning, twisting and shuddering: something sallow and fleshlike. At first, he could make no sense of it.

The bough of an elm reached out across the water as if offering Hyde its pale fruit. The form which hung from it was at first unrecognizable in the insufficient illumination of Hyde's hand lantern. What added to the confusion was the movement of the thing, as if alive. Then he made dark sense of it: close to the far bank, suspended by a long rope fastened around the tree's bough, a naked man hung upside down, his ankles rope bound. Hyde's lantern followed the pallid form to where a wound gaped lividly in the chest. A thick trail of blood, glistening black and sleek in the night, traced its way down to the man's throat, but his head was hidden, submerged in the frothing water of the river. It was the tugging of the impatient current on the unseen head that had given the form motion and the semblance of life.

Hyde again took the whistle from his pocket, turned in the direction he had come and gave three short blasts.

As if in response, it came again. The cry. Audible and no more over the roar of the waterfall. To start with, Hyde thought it was the echo of his whistle, but he recognized the same high, inhuman sound, this time more plaintive, mournful. He spun around but couldn't fix the direction of its origin. But wherever it had come from, one thing was sure: it had not issued from the dead man hanging upside down from the tree.

He gave another three blasts on his whistle and was answered this time with louder cries of mill workers hastening towards him. When they arrived, the young girl who had run into him earlier was with them, her face ghostly in the light of the lanterns. Hyde instructed the men to take her to one side, lest she see the horror hanging from the far bank of the river.

"Did you hear it again, sir?" she asked Hyde. "The *bean-nighe*."

"The what?"

"The *bean-nighe*." Nell's voice trembled with a fear sown not just into her fabric but woven through generations before her. "The washerwoman—her that laments by the water's edge."

"What are you talking about?" asked Hyde.

"The *bean-nighe* comes up from the Otherworld and wails while she washes the clothes of them about to die." The shaking of her voice was now a tremor through her whole insubstantial body. "That's what we heard. The *bean-nighe*—she's a *ban-sìth*, you see."

Hyde nodded. "I understand now. But I assure you what we heard was very much of this world, Nell." He turned to one of the men. "She's in shock. Take her back to the mill and have someone attend to her."

After the young Highland girl was gone, Hyde led the men to the nearest bridge across the water and back along the other bank toward where the naked man hung from the tree. They stood in silence for a moment, as men do in the presence of violent death. Hyde could see the body more clearly, but the head and face remained hidden in the rush of the river. The wound in the chest he could now see was deep and wide, like a gaping mouth. Someone had removed the man's heart.

"He's been murdered," said one of the mill workers at Hyde's shoulder.

"More than that," said another. "He's been three times murdered."

Hyde turned questioningly in the man's direction.

"Hanged, ripped and drowned . . ." explained the man. "Why would anybody do that to someone?"

"Get me a pole or anything with a hook on it," said Hyde. "I want to bring the body to the riverbank."

A third mill worker volunteered to run back to the mill and find something suitable.

As he waited with the others, Captain Edward Henry Hyde, superintendent of detective officers in Edinburgh's City Police, was greatly troubled by two thoughts. The first was that he had, by pure chance, uncovered a brutal murder through his entirely coincidental and fortuitous presence at the scene—yet he could not, for the life of him, remember why he was in this place, so far from his usual habit, or how he had got there.

The second thing troubling him was the earnest terror of a young, frightened mill girl haunted still by the distant Highlands and their myths. A terror founded on the belief that what they had heard had been the cries of a *ban-sith*.

A banshee.

2

Dr. Samuel Porteous sat by the fire in his study and awaited the arrival of Edward Hyde.

An energetic, handsome man of medium height, Porteous's almost boyish look belied his being in his forty-seventh year of life and twenty-first of professional medical practice. He was a man given to vanity, particularly about his auburn hair and emerald-green eyes, which were striking. This vanity had been given artistic form in the portrait that dressed the chimney breast above the fire. Now, five years hence from its commission, Porteous resented the portrait, envious of his younger image's immutability; its imperviousness to age.

Samuel Porteous's origins had been more humble than many of his profession and current station, and he tended to compensate for his social insecurity by spending more on fine tailoring than Scottish Presbyterian propriety normally dictated.

One thing that gave him no cause for insecurity, however, was the wealth of his intellectual gifts. From his first year studying medicine at Edinburgh University, Porteous had been recognized as a rising star of the science. To be considered such in Edinburgh, the world's capital of medical advancement, meant that no ambition could be too audacious—and Dr. Samuel Porteous was a man of audacious ambition. In the course of his career, he had established a reputation as a pioneering neuropsychiatrist. Over the last two years, he had become increasingly involved in the new disciplines of psychophysics and psychology. It was in this new direction, he was convinced, that the answers lay to so many of the intractable puzzles of modern psychiatry.

Porteous's main clinic was in the lunatic wing of Craiglockhart Hydropathic Hospital, but he also attended at the nearby private Craig

House Asylum, as well as maintaining consulting rooms in the New Town. In addition, however, he saw two patients—and only ever the two—at his private residence and outside normal consulting hours. These cases had their own and distinct reasons for seeking privacy— secrecy even—in their treatment. Each was totally unaware of the other's existence; equally ignorant of the fact that, while their personalities could not differ more, in Porteous's eyes they were paradoxically but two sides of the same coin.

These clandestine visitors were the cases of which Porteous kept no official record. The details of his impressions of both, and his treatment of them, were confined to the physician's personal journal, kept locked in his study safe. He had his own reasons for keeping their secrets: these two cases provided unique opportunities to pursue pioneering research. A great discovery waited to be uncovered; an even greater reputation waited to be established.

Added to which, Dr. Samuel Porteous had secrets enough of his own. Two packets of compound sat unopened in his medical cabinet, waiting to be pressed into service should the symptoms that slept within him reawaken. But that was a fear deferred: a challenge for another, hopefully distant day.

One of the two confidential cases was Porteous's friend Edward Hyde. Tonight, it was Hyde who would visit.

There was something about Hyde that confounded Porteous. The physician often struggled to understand what it was about the man, about his presence, that inspired unease on each new encounter. As Porteous had noted in his journal, though not tall, Hyde was certainly imposing. His build was broad but not exceptional, yet his *presence* was—as if he cast before him an oppressive shadow. Porteous often had the sense that there was something discordant about Hyde's proportions: his head a few ounces too heavy, his arms an inch or two too long, his shoulders possessing a fraction too much mass. Something about Edward Hyde hinted at a humanity surpassed, at some recent but lost Darwinian foreshadow of mankind. All impressions not so much observed or measured as perceived, as *intuited*.

Nor was Hyde an ugly man: indeed, he possessed a dark handsomeness, but something in his appearance was devilish, forbidding, encouraged distance; Hyde repelled without being explicably repellent. His manner, too, was oddly tranquil, with an economy of speech, expression and movement, yet this very calmness was in itself disconcerting, leaving the impression that it was but a veil drawn over an extreme and combustible volatility: that at any moment Hyde's stillness, which was great, could explode into an even greater violence.

Yet these impressions always dispelled completely and instantly the moment Hyde engaged Porteous in conversation. The sad truth of it was that the physician doubted he had ever known a better man than Captain Edward Henry Hyde. Every knowledge Porteous had of the man was that he possessed a heart vulnerable to the injuries and injustices suffered by others. And far from primitive, he was a gentleman of profound sophistication and learning.

Porteous had diagnosed in his friend a form of epilepsy, which, if known to Hyde's superiors, would debar him from his post as superintendent of detective officers for the City of Edinburgh Police. He had therefore promised Hyde secrecy—but there were other less noble considerations that bound Porteous to his silence. His friend's condition—strange absences from reality and the even more bizarre dreams that were in truth florid hallucinations shaped by Hyde's nocturnal seizures—offered the ambitious psychiatrist a window into hitherto unexplored levels of the human consciousness.

There was, Porteous knew, a great deal to be learned from the strange otherworld of Captain Edward Henry Hyde.

The night gathered at the windows and Dr. Samuel Porteous drew closed the heavy velvet curtains of his study, set match to the kindling in the hearth, and sat watching the flames spark into life, all the time seeking to remind himself that it was a friend, not something darker than the deepening night, that was making its way towards him.

3

It was full dark when Hyde arrived. Once more, Porteous's first impression was that his friend and patient had brought something of the night with him.

As was their agreed custom, Porteous dimmed the lantern at the rear door that opened from his study onto the garden so that no servant be alerted to Hyde's arrival. The servants all knew Captain Hyde, of course, from his frequent social visits, during which he arrived and departed as all other guests, through the main street door. And, naturally, the Captain's appearance made him memorable to all. But these clandestine visits often occurred when Hyde was not fully at himself, usually after a particularly bad episode, and sought no scrutiny or company other than that of his physician.

Additionally, Porteous's study in the converted garden room was a safe and secret place for them both. No servants were allowed in here other than Mrs. Wilson, the housekeeper, who came in to tidy and clean once a week, but only once Porteous had told her it was all right so to do.

When he arrived, Hyde was agitated. Porteous had expected him to complain that he had yet again had one of his vivid and lucid dreams, which would cast their spell over the following waking day, distracting his thoughts from his work. The haunted otherworld of his dreaming troubled Hyde greatly, despite the psychiatrist's assurances that it was the result of his epilepsy—sleeping seizures, not normal dreams.

This evening, however, Hyde's concern lay elsewhere.

"I attended a murder locus last night," he explained. "In fact, it was I who discovered the crime." Like some gathered shadow, he sat in the leather wingback chair by the fire, his mood dark as he gazed gloomily into the flames, as if some resolution were to be found there. The firelight etched the harsh-angled, hard handsomeness of his profile and again Porteous felt something akin to an instinctive revulsion.

"You found the victim?" asked the physician.

"I did. I heard . . ." Hyde paused, searching for the right word, "*screams*. Cries that led me to the victim."

"Did you apprehend the murderer?" asked Porteous. "If you heard the victim's cries, you must have been close."

"The cries I heard were not the victim's." Hyde shook his head in frustration. "This is no easy matter to explain . . . But no, there was no trace to be found of the killer. And that is exactly what troubles me."

"I don't understand."

"As I said, I discovered the victim's remains. I uncovered the crime. I, an investigator of murder, just happened conveniently to be in the locus of a homicide's commission."

"And that troubles you? Why?"

Hyde leaned forward in the wingback, elbows on knees, his heavy shoulders sagging. "I lost time again." He sighed. "The movements and events that brought me to that place are lost to me. I have no recollection of how I ended up there; I lost time from shortly before I left the station only to regain my senses at a scene of murder."

"Oh," said Porteous. "I see. Have you disclosed this to your superiors?"

"I have disclosed this to no one other than you," said Hyde, "yet. But I think you understand why I was so anxious to see you. In most cases I lose time for a matter of minutes. This time it was more than an hour . . . this time there was a *murder*. I was there at the scene and I cannot for the life of me remember how I got there. I cannot remember what I *did*."

Porteous rose from his chair and stood by the fire, leaning a hooked elbow on the mantelpiece. He took a paper packet from his smoking jacket pocket, removed a cigarillo and lit it. Knowing smoking was another habit that his friend eschewed, he did not offer one to Hyde.

"You think you had something to do with this murder—I mean something to do with its commission?" he scoffed. "That's ridiculous. You are no more capable of murder than I."

"How can you say that with such certainty?" Desperation crept into Hyde's tone. "Think about all the things we've discussed these last two years—the absolute *madness* of my dreams. The abnormality of my mind . . ."

"Edward, we have talked about this so many times before. There is no abnormality to your mind: what ails you is not a mental sickness, it is a neurological defect. Epilepsy, nothing more. In your case that epilepsy creates these extended absence seizures you call lost time and I call status epilepticus—as well as these powerful nocturnal hallucinations which, as I have again explained so often, are so much more than mere dreams. And, in any case, there is madness in everybody's dreams—they are spun in the deepest and darkest parts of our minds."

"But not dreams like these," said Hyde.

Porteous nodded and looked into the fire, the flames glittering in cold emerald reflection in his eyes. The truth was he struggled to imagine what it must be like to have a sleeping seizure that manifested itself as a dream so vivid it was completely indistinguishable from reality. An electrical storm in the sleeping brain that conjured up impossible, often terrifying, yet completely credible universes.

"Listen, Edward . . ." The doctor drew on the cigarillo, blowing smoke into the air and filling the room with its fragrance. "This is a new age of medicine: we more and more understand the mechanics of status epilepticus. I promise you that the sleepwalking murderer and epileptic homicidal maniac are the stuff of cheap chapbooks and other low fiction—they simply don't exist in reality."

"If what I suffer from *is* epilepsy," Hyde protested weakly.

"It is epilepsy, Edward, have no doubt. We now understand the nature of such absences—the detachment from reality that they cause. Believe me: no intent, no conscious or unconscious will can be expressed during such a seizure."

"There must have been will enough to propel me to that destination," Hyde insisted, "some two miles from where I last remembered being."

"That isn't will," countered Porteous. "It is nothing more than automatism. Only the simplest, near-autonomic functions can take place in such a state. You certainly could not have committed any act of real purpose during a seizure."

"But what if the will were not mine?" Hyde frowned, perplexed, as if trying to locate a thought that evaded him. "What if I was *led* to that place? What if someone put the idea of being there in my head? I mean while I was in that state?"

"Again, Edward, this is all the stuff of low fiction—or the lower fiction of stage mesmerism—without an ounce of science behind it. No person in an altered state of consciousness can be compelled to do that which he would not do when fully aware. John Hughlings Jackson—a pioneer in the field of epilepsy—has a name for the state of consciousness you enter during one of your absences: he calls it 'otherwhere'—because you are not consciously present in this world. You are not *here* to do any bidding, good or ill."

"I still cannot understand why I found myself so close to the scene of a yet undiscovered murder," Hyde said darkly. "It seems too much of a coincidence."

"Perhaps no coincidence. Not all of your lost time is automatism or pure seizure," said Porteous. "An element of amnesia adheres to events leading up to an episode. Before the seizure, you will have been fully yourself, functioning normally, but you just cannot remember those events now. Immediately before your seizure you may even have learned or thought of something that bound you for that destination."

"And that memory is gone? Lost to me?"

"Perhaps not. We are making discoveries all the time about how the mind works. It is increasingly clear that it is not of single dimension—instead there are many layers to it." Porteous paused, throwing what was left of his cigarillo into the flames and looking up at his portrait above the fireplace. "Think of it as a painting. Underneath lies a once-naked canvas. But the picture we all see was not flawlessly laid down on that bare canvas. All kinds of missteps, changes of composition, altera-tions of line and colour lie hidden beneath that which is presented to the world. The Italians have a name for it, *pentimenti*: layer upon layer of the artist's thoughts, worked and reworked until some are lost even to him. The mind is exactly like that: its blank canvas is the *tabula rasa* of the infant brain, upon which is laid layer after layer of experi-ences, emotions, memories. Scenes and personages are described in detail, then painted over. We can't see these figures any more, but that doesn't mean they are no longer there. If we look close enough, we can perhaps trace their outlines—or even gently remove some of the obscuring layers."

"So you think that my memories from before my seizure may still be there? In this deeper mental layer? How do I retrieve them?"

"I don't know that you can. There are hypnosis methods pioneered here in Edinburgh by James Braid, which can be used to try to reach into the subconscious. But, my dear Edward, you are an investigator by nature and profession. Perhaps that is your best way to answers. I would suggest you retrace your steps as best you can to the last place you remember before the seizure. Or maybe the answer is already before you."

"I don't understand . . ."

"In your otherworld, Edward. In your dreams."

Hyde stayed for another hour. They talked, Porteous drinking port and smoking cigars, as if the two friends were simply sharing a pleasant hour's visiting, yet Porteous could tell Hyde's mood had not improved.

Before Hyde left, Porteous dispensed his prescription, as was their usual custom. This latest episode had so unsettled his patient that the doctor felt it prudent to make adjustments to the formulation. He did not want Hyde, the professional investigator, to become too curious about every component of the mixture.

It was near twelve when he saw Hyde out through the rear door of his study and watched as he disappeared from view, a shadow merging with others in the midnight garden. Porteous puzzled at his feelings as his patient and friend departed. Feelings of pity, sorrow, concern. Guilt, even.

And relief.

4

Outside, dawn was breaking. Edward Hyde lay still and quiet in closed-curtain darkness, suspended between the universes of sleep and wakefulness. He had dreamed that night—but he had dreamed as others dreamed, not the kaleidoscopic hallucinations of a night-time seizure—and the dream endured behind his closed eyes, time remaining folded in on itself. He had dreamt of himself young and carefree, lost in bright juvenile play, of still-light late-summer evenings painted gold and green with the vibrant palette of childhood; of his mother and the bedtime tales she would tell of brownies and fairy folk; of the heroes Cú Chulainn and Fionn mac Cumhaill, of demonic villains and fantastical beasts.

For that sweet hypnopompic moment, the dream lingered, Hyde neither asleep nor awake. And something else lingered: a feeling that hung in the air like a long-forgotten scent that awoke clear remembrance of a distant time. A feeling he had not felt for so very long: Hyde was, in that vanishing instant, truly happy.

The waking world called: outside, beyond the drawn curtains, iron-shod hoof and iron-banded wheel rang unmusically on the cobbles of Northumberland Street and stirred him fully. And with wakefulness came metamorphosis: Edward, the happy, light-footed child of the dream, changed in mass, conformation and appearance, took on rough aspect and heavy form; became Hyde.

He listened to the slow swell of the day: more wheels on the cobbles outside; the wax and wane of indistinct voices as people passed on the pavement below. The smoke-grey city stirring into smoke-grey life. The images of his dream were replaced by memories of two nights before: the hanged man, head and hands trailing in the soiled current of the

Water of Leith. The inhuman, wailing cry of what must undoubtedly be an insane murderer, for surely only insanity could lead one human being to inflict such horror on another.

However, other, more distant memories came back to trouble him too: memories of a long-ago and distant, bright and scent-laden land—and cruelties performed under a sun-blazed sky in the name of Empire and without the exculpation of insanity. Memories of a man, driven by duty, who had become known by the dread epithet *Jaanavar*. The Beast.

It had been a different world, back then; he had been a different man, back then.

Hyde rose earlier than usual, his mood darkened further when he thought of the appointment he had to keep that morning. His large and moderately grand townhouse was mostly unoccupied, its many closed rooms reflecting the man habitant within. He bathed, as he did each morning, then dressed. Of a class, though not a profession, where it was expected he should have a manservant, Hyde instead valued his privacy too highly to have a professional intimate. His episodes, he had guessed, would be confusing, even alarming, for another to witness. And if one did, and shared their witnessing, then Hyde's competence to serve as superintendent of detectives could be called into question.

Edward Hyde therefore served as his own bootblack, own presser, own dresser, own man. He set his own table and own fireplace. He prepared his own breakfast and consumed it in solitary silence. His early mornings were encapsulations of self-contained rituals: sealed from the world and seclusive. His preparations for the day were systematic, habitual; his mind on the detail and never, ever on the knife edge of loneliness that would often pierce his life.

For the coming workday he donned a black three-button sack suit with a grey silk waistcoat. He stud-fastened a down collar of the new style, rather than a winged collar, to his shirt, and chose a four-in-hand tie rather than a day cravat. Over this he wore a black tweed Ulster coat, bought in Lockwood's store on Princes Street, chosen that its short cape should disguise the bulk of his shoulders, and a broad-brimmed dark grey Homburg that might cast his features in shadow. He sheathed thick fingers in hand-made pigskin gloves.

Were the hour not so early, and the figure beneath the fine clothes not so robust, Captain Edward Henry Hyde would have looked as if he were about to start the business of the day in one of Edinburgh's banks or financial institutions. But the business that was to take place that morning, the settling of accounts that Hyde was to witness, was a much darker affair.

The carriage awaited him outside as the morning fumed, rippling soot-black columns of smoke from ten thousand wakening fireplaces rising in the cold, breezeless air.

"Morning, Captain Hyde," said the custodian-helmeted coach-man atop the police carriage. "I take it we are not for the station this morning?"

"Good morning, Mackinley," said Hyde. "No, not yet. I have two appointments to keep . . ."

When he gave Mackinley the address of the first, the constable-coachman nodded grimly, then said: "Very good, sir."

It was, paradoxically, a place of brightness, of light.

The white room.

The walls were distempered and all the woodwork—the doors, the small table set against the wall, the frames of the roof-light windows, the balustrade that sectioned off the part of the room in which Hyde and the others stood, the vertical wooden beam and even the trapdoor—was painted white. The walls were unbroken by windows, but the large skylights in the roof filled the space with the morning's light.

It was also a place of quiet: Hyde and the others, some six of them, stood behind the balustrade and waited in silent expectation.

Morrison, a young man yet to see his twenty-second year, entered the room and looked around it with urgency, as if needing to fill eyes hungry for impressions, for sight of the world. He was tall, lean and broad-shouldered, his skin ruddy and his uncombed hair the colour of rust. His rubicund complexion seemed more vivid in the white quiet of the room, accentuated further by the collarless bleached-linen shirt he wore. He saw Hyde where he stood with the others and nodded in acknowledgement, an uncertain smile quivering briefly on his lips. One of his two escorts touched his elbow in encouragement and Morrison turned to him, almost in apology for his inattentiveness, then stepped forward.

"Drink this," the second uniformed escort commanded brusquely, and handed him a small tumbler filled with a clear liquid. Morrison did as he was bidden, grimacing as he swallowed the liquor at a one. A small, moustachioed man, a head shorter than Morrison and dressed in a dark serge suit, stepped forward from behind the balustrade and towards the youth. His swift, decisive movements spoke of well-practised, professional habit: he pinioned Morrison's elbows with a leather strap, dropped to his knees behind him and clasped D-form shackles around his ankles. Morrison looked again in Hyde's direction and seemed to be about to speak, but the short man snatched a white cotton hood from the table and placed it over Morrison's head. With equally workmanlike deftness, he looped the noose over the hood, around Morrison's neck and tightened it. In what seemed a single, swift and continuous movement, he stepped back, grasped the lever and pulled. The silence was broken by the loud clatter of the trapdoor opening, and Morrison dropped through it. The loop in the rope slipped its leather sleeve and the hangman's hemp snapped taut.

Morrison's head was still just visible above the trapdoor. The hanged man twitched, as if giving a small shrug of his shoulders, then was still save for a brief, muffled mumbling sound and the narrow pendulum swing of his body.

It had taken less than thirty seconds from the young quarryman's entry into the white room till his exit from life.

The governor of Calton Gaol nodded to the small group of witnesses: Hyde stood with Abercrombie, the police surgeon; with them were two newspaper reporters and two representatives of the procurator fiscal's office, the younger of whom looked as if he was about to be sick. All left the white room of the hanging shed in silence, breaking only into speech once they were in the green-and-cream-tiled prison hallway.

"No matter how deserved," said Hyde to Abercrombie, "it is always a sad sight to behold. I can't put my mind to the rightness of it."

"We all must have our rituals," said Abercrombie absently, as he checked his pocket watch for the time. Hyde knew the physician would take some tea with the governor while he waited for the prescribed hour's hanging time to pass; thereafter he would descend into the brick-lined execution pit beneath the white room and check that life was extinct from the remains of the condemned.

"Rituals?" asked Hyde.

"A hanging is a rite as religious as any other," said the doctor. "A sacrifice to the greater good. To the religion of the law, of order. To the gods of justice. A small act to return the universe to its correct motions. And let's be honest, if anyone deserved to hang, it was Hugh Morrison. That poor child . . ." Abercrombie left the thought unfulfilled.

It was a story all knew: Mary Paton, who had lived all her eight years in tenement squalor, had disappeared from her play on the street. Her body had not been found until a month later, half buried in a ditch on a disused lane on the edge of Gypsy Brae. Someone had gathered branches and twigs and carefully woven them together in an improvised nest, like a crude baby basket, before laying her remains in it and covering them with more branches and leaves. The public had heard of the manner of her rest and Mary Paton became known as the "Gypsy Brae Bairn" or the "Bairn in the Witch's Cradle."

Her remains had been discovered by Hugh Morrison, employed nearby as a stone-hewer at the Duke of Buccleuch's Granton Sea Quarry. Morrison had run to the quarry and told of his dark discovery to his foreman, who came with him to the scene before in turn alerting the authorities.

The impression Morrison had made on Hyde was not so much a simpleton as a child in a man's body: someone trapped in a private universe, unable to understand the mechanics of society, of companionship. He had been separated from his fellows by habit and personality, but also by origin: Morrison carried in his speech the lilt and cadence of the Highlands. To others, particularly his workmates, he had simply been regarded as "touched" or odd. He would often sing or talk to himself while working, and seemed unable to engage his fellows in any meaningful way.

He had also been known to keep company with children much younger than himself.

Most telling, however, was that the young stone-hewer had been unable to explain why he had been on a lane that had fallen into disuse a decade before and was so overgrown as to be almost impossible to navigate. A strange man discovering the strange resting place of a murdered child.

It had been inevitable that suspicion should fall on him. Such suspicion had been unsupported by evidence, but before Hyde had had a chance to question the young quarryman, a confession had been obtained. In truth, the condition of the dead child had stirred the Granton constables to determined violence, and a confession of sorts had been beaten from Morrison. A confession the young Highlander would later vehemently retract.

Hyde had questioned why Morrison should voluntarily expose the hiding place of his victim, or why the supposed murderer did not seem to know the location from which the girl had been abducted. Both were attributed to the youth's idiocy, and Hyde's concerns were dismissed and overruled. In truth, Morrison's case had been injured further by his bizarre ramblings: he had claimed in both English and Gaelic that the girl must have fallen victim to *cù dubh ifrinn*, the great black hellhound, some mythical beast from Highland lore.

"He swore to me he was innocent," Hyde said to the police surgeon.

"Don't they all?" said Abercrombie. "I myself would choose protestation over confession were I faced with the noose."

"Yes," said Hyde. "Yes, they do. But I can usually see through their lies—I don't know if it is a feature of my nature or a skill acquired over the years, but I can normally see the truth behind the lie, see the shadow of the other nature they try to hide from the world."

"And your insight failed you with Morrison?"

"It did. Or perhaps it didn't. Perhaps there was no dark side to find. In any case, I believed him. I did all I could to find evidence of his innocence, but I failed."

"Your reputation for unearthing the truth is unequalled—it could be his claim offered no truth to be unearthed."

"Perhaps," said Hyde. "But I cannot help but think we have just killed an innocent man."

They made their way in silence through the carbolic-rinsed halls of Calton Gaol. Mackinley waited with the coach outside, in the shadow of the governor's residence with its castellated towers. Abercrombie paused before saying goodbye.

"What of this other hanging?" he asked. "Yon inverted one down by the Water of Leith. One of the strangest things you've ever brought me. It's been passed on to Dr. Bell to carry out the necropsy, I believe."

"This morning, yes."

"A strange thing, Hyde. A strange thing indeed."

5

It was a place of diversion, of entertainment, a space designed to ring with laughter and applause. Yet when Hyde came in from the bright day, and after the bleak, achromous simplicity of the execution shed, it seemed to him he was entering some red hell.

Perhaps his reaction had something to do with his knowing the theatre's temporary function.

As in all auditoria, the theatre's focus was the stage, and the building's architecture seemed to cluster expectantly around it. The auditorium was three tiered; the empty flap-stall chairs were gilt-framed and lavishly upholstered in cherry-coloured cloth and arranged in serried, stepped arcs. The stage was flanked by box balconies, three stacked ranks of three to each side, their swollen bone-coloured bellies adorned with crimson glass details, like droplets of blood. Everything else was red: claret-coloured vines of acanthus sinuously coiled and twisted their flocked way through the wallpaper; the heavy stage curtains were carmine; the folds and velvet drapes that decked the proscenium arches were dark scarlet. Above the ornate sconces, the shades that shielded the unlit gas mantles were fashioned from red glass. Coming in from the daylit street, there was something anatomical, organic, in the enveloping crimson dark.

The only brightly illuminated part of the theatre was the stage itself. Just two players were onstage, in the sole pool of bright light: a bloody-handed Dr. Joseph Bell, and the man lying on the portable surgeon's table and under the pathologist's scrutiny. It was clear the supine man had no further part to play in any drama of this world.

"Ah, Hyde . . ." Dr. Bell straightened himself up and smiled broadly. The anatomist and pathologist was a tall, clean-shaven man of around fifty with a bristling mane of prematurely white hair swept back from a broad forehead. His shirtsleeves were rolled up clear of his elbows, and his waistcoat and trousers were protected by a rubberized apron. "An audience at last for my performance."

"I knew you were fond of the theatrical, Doctor, but . . ." Hyde smiled and waved a hand in the air to indicate their surroundings.

"In my time I've done autopsies in many places, from army field tents and deserted churches to barrooms or the deceased's home. But I grant you that this is somewhat . . . *grander*. You know about this blasted fire at the infirmary, I take it? Our dissecting hall and examination rooms are out of commission for at least three weeks. Unfortunately, in the interim, we are itinerant players . . ." Bell waved the long, slim fingers of a bloodied hand in an echo of Hyde's earlier gesture. "We have the theatre for only one week, then we must yield the stage to Shakespeare. *Macbeth*, I believe. All in all, a gorier enterprise than this."

"In the meantime, I see yours is a solo performance," said Hyde.

"What? Oh, no . . . My assistant has stepped out for a moment to fetch more equipment."

"Dr. Conan Doyle is assisting you today?"

"No, not today. Sadly, young Arthur has left us to take up general practice on England's south coast. To be honest, I think my former clerk's passion is more for scribbling than prescribing—his parting gift was a promise to make me the detective hero of one of his stories, no less. So, today, I am assisted by Dr. Burr." Joseph Bell smiled. Hyde, aware of his own coarse robustness, often envied the easy, gentlemanly grace of the pathologist. "Have you met Dr. Burr? No? Remarkable young physician. Anyway, we are in something of a guddle at the moment. Damned inconvenient having to vacate our usual environment, where everything was always at hand." Bell paused to nod to the body on the examination table. "This gentleman is one of yours, I take it?"

Hyde looked down at the corpse. Death, he knew, designed its own patterns, paling skin here, darkening it there, as blood robbed of its motive pooled where gravity demanded. Death also by its very nature stilled vigour. The effect was to age, to rob youth. For that reason, as he had stood shining his pocket lantern on the inverted and pendulous form dangling above the torrent at Dean Village, Hyde had had the impression of an older man, of life-wearied flesh. But now, seeing the victim laid on the dissecting table, it was clear that he had been reasonably young. There was a firm muscularity to the body.

The head had been the lowest part of the hanging inverted corpse, and consequently the face remained sickeningly dark with post-mortem lividity. Some of the captured blood had drained from the face, but the lips and eyelids were still empurpled and swollen, and the skin was laced through with spidering, inky capillaries. The face's darkness was accentuated by the man's pale blond hair, side whiskers and moustache. Despite death's dark palette, Hyde could see the face too was youthful.

"Unfortunately, yes, he is one of mine," he said. "He was hung upside down from a tree with his head under the water. Did he . . ."

"Drown?" Bell looked down at the corpse, pursing his lips and shaking his head. "There's no evidence of water in the lungs. Nor did he die from the damage to his chest. The removal of his heart and the head's immersion in water were both post-mortem."

"So what did kill him?" asked Hyde.

Joseph Bell's answer was interrupted by the echoing thud of a door · slamming in the wings. "Ah," he said, " 'noises off,' as they say in the theatre. That will be my assistant. Dr. Burr carried out the initial examination and can answer your questions."

A young woman emerged into the pool of light, carrying a large Gladstone bag. A nurse, Hyde assumed, and looked past her to seek out Bell's assistant. The young woman was alone.

"Allow me to introduce Dr. Cally Burr," said Bell with a broad smile. "Dr. Burr, this is Captain Edward Hyde, formerly Indian Army, now superintendent of criminal officers for the City of Edinburgh Police. He is the source of question, we the providers of answer."

"I rather think my gender has taken Captain Hyde aback," said Dr. Burr. Hyde thought he could detect the trace of an Irish accent in her intonation.

"Not at all—" he began, but checked himself. "Truthfully, yes. One does not encounter many female physicians, and I was guilty of an assumption that should have been beneath me."

Dr. Burr smiled, but not warmly, then unpinned and removed her hat. Her gathered-up hair was raven black, and her honey-toned skin, Hyde thought, was a shade darker than fashion preferred. She was undoubtedly a woman of considerable and vaguely exotic beauty, and he sensed about her the defensiveness of an intelligent woman whose appearance, and gender, were obstructions to her intellect being taken seriously.

"Thank you for your honesty, Captain Hyde," she said. "My choice of profession means I experience everything from confusion and amusement to disdain and outright hostility. What are your feelings on women becoming physicians?"

"Truthfully? I have not given it any thought. But now that I have, I see no reason why not. What is more important is that you clearly have Dr. Bell's confidence, which is a considerable achievement for any physician, whatever their gender."

"Well said!" Bell again smiled broadly. "Let me tell you, Hyde, young Dr. Burr here is one of the most capable and dedicated physicians I have ever encountered. And that includes young Conan Doyle—and Samuel Porteous, who I believe is a close friend of yours. I value those who value knowledge, those who prize it. And Dr. Burr has had to fight harder than most to win her knowledge."

Dr. Burr placed her gloves, hat and coat on a side table. A large ring, set with sapphires and emeralds and of a pattern Hyde thought he recognized, decorated her right hand. She removed the ring, carefully placing it next to her gloves before donning a white dustcoat that protected her clothing from neck to floor. The whiteness of the coat accentuated the golden tone in her complexion, and Hyde wondered if there was something more distant than Ireland in her ancestry.

The female physician stepped forward to the table without hesitation, and with quick and assured movements grasped the cadaver by its shoulder with one hand while supporting the head with the other, lifting and tilting it upwards so Hyde could see the dead man's neck and back. Much of the skin on the back was purple-black where dead blood had settled, but the neck remained pale except for a faint bluish stripe running laterally across the nape at its axis with the skull.

"A blow to the neck?" asked Hyde.

"That is your fatal injury, Captain Hyde. The spinal cord has been severed or irreparably compressed by a fracture of the second cervical vertebra. Instant quadriplegia and paralysis of respiratory function. Everything else you see, the damage to the chest and excision of the heart, was all done post-mortem. But this wasn't caused by a blow. You know what this kind of fracture is called?"

Hyde frowned. "The hangman's break." The memory came to his mind of earlier that morning: a young and bewildered Hugh Morrison looking at him across a white room, about to form words that would never be uttered.

"Exactly. There are rope burns under the jaw, and I'll wager we find a compressed trachea when we open the throat up."

"He was hanged? I mean hanged the right way up?"

Cally Burr nodded. "Except this was very clearly an extra-judicial hanging."

"Then why all this?" Hyde indicated the devastated torso.

"Ritual?" Dr. Burr held him with dark, disturbing eyes. Hyde was used to people avoiding his gaze, intimidated by either his appearance or his office. There were those women who were franker in their study of him, who seemed stimulated by his presence, but Cally Burr's regarding of him was empty of any emotion, base or otherwise. "You think this is some kind of ritual?" he asked.

"It would appear so, but such speculations are beyond my brief. My work here is to establish the corporeal realities and factual, not speculative, causes of death."

"Oh, come now, Dr. Burr," said Dr. Bell, good-naturedly. "I have taught you better than that!" He indicated their surroundings. "Inconvenience has brought us and our work to such a strange setting. But it is, in a way, appropriate." He looked down at the cadaver on the table. "This—these mortal remains—this is our true theatre: a theatre of flesh and bone. There is a drama to be discovered in this dead man's bones, in his blood and tissue. We are the audience to that drama—we interpret that drama. And no audience should be without imagination. A pathologist—a *good* pathologist—should observe with clinical dispassion, take note of the physical proofs of death. But then his—or her—professionally informed imagination should interpret, extrapolate and expand that which the eye perceives. Please, Dr. Burr, tell us what dramas have unfolded in this fleshy theatre . . ."

Easing the cadaver back to a supine position, Dr. Burr held up the dead man's arm, the hand still blood-blackened with post-mortem lividity. In stark contrast, the skin of his forearm was chalk white, causing a rough, sand-coloured patch to stand out.

"Solar keratosis," she explained. "Not unusual for someone of his pale colouring, but unusual in someone so young. It suggests that he has spent some considerable time exposed to much fiercer sunshine than Scotland experiences, but that he has been removed from such climes long enough for tanning to fade."

"You see!" said Bell enthusiastically.

"All it tells us is that he spent time abroad," said Hyde. "It yields no wisdom about what took him to that climate. Many young men take advantage of the opportunities the Empire offers. He could be anything from a merchant seaman to an engineer or a soldier. Anything else would be speculation. Guesswork."

"But educated guesswork, dear Captain," said Dr. Bell. "Informed speculation. It could yield at least a direction for your inquiries to take. But young Dr. Burr has more to reveal."

The female physician eased an arm out from the dead man's side to allow them to examine his flank. There was a long, indented scar, pale and perfectly straight, almost like a furrow in the flesh, running from front to back.

"Earlier in his life, our friend was luckier with an encounter with potential mortality," she said. "A large-calibre bullet creased his side some considerable time ago. I can just and no more palpate a bone callus on his sixth rib where the transit of the bullet caused a fracture that then healed. A few inches to the left and there would have been organ damage."

Hyde was about to say something, but Dr. Burr held up her hand. "There's more . . ." Hyde could see Joseph Bell beaming with pride at his protégée's accomplishments. "On his lower left abdomen . . ." She smoothed the skin between forefinger and thumb, revealing a two-inch-wide ridge of puckered flesh.

Hyde leaned in to inspect it more closely. As he did so, his nostrils filled with the odours of death. The fabric of the dead man's flesh was already beginning to unravel. He pulled back. Cally Burr saw his reaction and frowned.

"Another wound," she continued. "Again not a recent injury, given the fading of the scar. But this time caused by penetration by some form of thick blade. Given the age of the deceased, I would guess both the bullet graze and this stab wound date from broadly the same period in his life."

"He seems to have been in the wars," chipped in Dr. Bell. "Perhaps literally."

"You think he was or has been a soldier?" Hyde frowned.

"You are the detective," said Dr. Burr, "but my guess is that injuries such as the deceased has sustained in the past point to that conclusion."

Hyde remained silent for a moment. He braced himself against the sway he felt in his body. The smell of death, the stark light of the stage, the crimson dark of the empty theatre beyond—all combined in a surge of light-headedness. There was a nauseating tingling in his tongue. He recognized the foreshadows of one of his episodes.

"Are you staying for the full necropsy?" asked Cally Burr. "We may discover more when we open him up." She looked down at the gaping wound in the dead man's chest. "Open him up *more.*"

Hyde thought for a moment. He found post-mortem examinations unpleasant, nauseating. He somehow could not separate the dead flesh on the table from the spirit, the personality, that had departed it. Added to that was the growing feeling of an impending episode. Yet there was something deeply disturbing about this case and he wanted as much information as quickly as possible. He nodded.

"Then why not take the best seat in the house?" said Bell and indicated the empty stalls. "We will talk you through our discoveries as we make them."

Hyde thought he detected a warmer smile on the young female doctor's face. He stepped down from the stage and took his seat, placing his hat and coat on the vacant stall next to him. It seemed so bizarre, so dreamlike, so unreal to sit enveloped in the crimson dark of a blood-and-bone-coloured theatre and watch the systematic dissection of a human being take place on the stage.

His pulse throbbed in his temples and he felt a dull ache behind his right eye. A deeper level of unreality settled on him. Fearing the onset of another episode and that he would soon slide from one already bizarre reality into an even more counterfeit world, he surreptitiously eased the small paper packet from his waistcoat pocket and slipped one of the tablets prescribed by Porteous under his tongue.

"Please," he said with a weak smile. "Proceed."

While he waited for the symptoms to subside, Edward Hyde looked around the theatre, then settled his gaze on the beautiful dark-haired woman on the stage as she peeled back a man's face from his skull.

6

"I am dreaming," said Hyde.

"You are dreaming," said the voice over his shoulder. "You felt the symptoms begin to search you out in the theatre, and now they have found you."

"I am in my bed."

"You are here. This is your reality."

"Where am I going?" he asked.

"You must return to the white room. You know that. After all other things are resolved, you must return to the white room and remember a truth you have forgotten."

In his dream, Hyde spun around at the sound of a jangle-edged wailing.

"The banshee . . ." he muttered.

"You have to rediscover the white room," said the voice. "But first, there are other things to find."

Hyde dreamed as another.

As always, he knew he was dreaming; as always, the dream constructed a universe that was utterly impossible yet as real to the senses, as credible, as that he inhabited when awake. In his dream, his surroundings seemed to unfold before him, as if this world took form only when he looked in a particular direction.

He walked through a green world, surrounded by emerald forests that seemed to spring from the earth wherever he looked, the grass beneath his feet thick, lush and verdant.

Ahead of him he saw her. He watched the young woman from a distance, but never saw her face, as her back was always turned to him, the blaze of her black hair loose in the breeze of a conjured world.

Suddenly he saw the dream through her eyes, inhabited her body, felt the emotions and sensations that she felt. He was almost overcome by the lightness of the body he wore, of the ease and grace of movement. He was no longer in his own heavy, dense form. The sense of liberation was intoxicating.

"This is not at all uncommon." The voice came from behind him and he turned as the girl and saw Samuel Porteous standing at his-her shoulder. The doctor was distracted as he struggled with arms full of leather-backed books, some with German titles, some Latin. Each step over the uneven grass threatened a landslide of volumes. "I explained this to you before, during one of our sessions. With sleeping seizures, the dreamer often occupies the body of another. We don't yet understand why . . ."

"Where is this place?" asked Hyde and was again startled, this time by the lightness, the musicality of the female voice with which he spoke.

"Otherwhere," said Porteous. "An otherworld of limitless potentiality. A landscape you navigate not by the movement of muscle, but by the movement of mind."

Hyde looked around the unfolded, viridescent world. It was a land he knew with his blood, but not with his experience. He stood above the treeline at the head of a widening river valley, the mountains on each side stretching apart like arms opening to embrace the distant shimmering sea at the valley's mouth. The mountains and the valley were cloaked thick with forests, unlike the glens of Scotland or Ireland. Unlike but like, as if the same body had been dressed in the vestments of an earlier time.

"But *where* is this place?" He turned to Porteous but the physician was gone. Hyde's voice and form had returned to his own. The girl whose form he had occupied only an instant before was now again some distance ahead of him, walking down into the valley and about to be swallowed by the verdant embrace of the forest. He ran after her, but though he ran and she walked, he could not close the gap between them.

Suddenly he found himself in the forest without having traversed the distance between, and realized he once more inhabited the girl's body. He felt a pounding in his chest and an unaccustomed tightness in his throat. He recognized the feeling as fear, but an intensity of fear he had never before experienced. It seemed such a strange place to feel such terror: the forest was rich and green, yet not so dense as to block out the sunlight that cut through the trees and dappled the forest floor. A river sparkled in the same light to the girl's left, and it was there that Hyde saw the object of her terror. A naked man hung inverted, suspended from a bough, his head immersed in the river's flow. The chest had been sliced open and Hyde could see the heartless chasm gape darkly. It was the same body he had found at the Water of Leith, transported to the otherwise pleasant landscape of his dream.

"Don't be afraid," he tried to tell the girl, but it was her words that sounded. Then, as he watched, the hanged man twitched and twisted, not because of the water's movement, but because some terrible animation had possessed the corpse. There were sickening cracking noises as elbow and shoulder joints disarticulated and the spine bent beyond possibility. The head, the hair dripping, emerged from the water and the neck twisted horribly. Dead eyes in a blood-blackened face held Hyde's gaze and he could feel the girl's terror rise.

"Why do you come here for answers?" The dead man's voice was moist and crackling, as if the death rattle had been spun through every word. "Can you not see that which is in front of you?"

"I don't understand," said Hyde in the girl's voice.

"We all must have our rituals," said a voice to Hyde's right. He turned, still inhabiting the girl's body, and saw that the short, sullen and dark-suited form of Abercrombie, the police surgeon, had taken Porteous's place. "A hanging is a rite as religious as any other." Abercrombie repeated his words from the white room. "A sacrifice to the greater good . . ."

"More than that," said another voice to his left. Hyde turned and saw the mill worker from the Water of Leith murder scene. "He's been three times murdered. Hanged, ripped and drowned . . . Why would anybody do that to someone?"

"We all must have our rituals," repeated Abercrombie, but when Hyde again turned to him, he was gone.

Another sudden series of crackling and tearing sounds drew Hyde's attention back to the pendulous form over the river. The corpse had folded itself completely double at the waist, pale skin tearing like paper and bones snapping as they were stretched beyond nature. Wet, sleek coils spilled from the rent abdomen and splashed unmusically into the stream. The corpse clambered, hand over hand, climbing up its own legs as if they were ropes. The body was now hideously bent back on itself like a snapped twig: the head and torso upright, the legs still upside down. It laughed, and the sound was sickening to hear. "You knew all this already," it said. "I have been hanged, I have been ripped, I have been drowned. I have been thrice killed. And we all must have our rituals."

"The Threefold Death . . ." muttered Hyde, still with the girl's voice. "The Celtic sacrificial rite."

"The ritual of the ancients," said the corpse. "And the tree from which I hang is an elm tree."

"The tree that connects the living world with the Otherworld . . ."

"I told you," said the dead man. "You knew the answers to all of this already."

"But why did I find my way to you that night?" asked Hyde in the girl's voice. "How did I get there?"

The corpse did not answer, but collapsed like a deckchair, falling back into the hanging position, its artificial vitality gone as quickly as it had come.

"Wait . . ." Hyde began to protest, but he no longer spoke or moved as the girl. Nor did he find himself returned to his own body. Instead there was a moment of confusion as the world around him frothed and bubbled. When he realized he now occupied the corpse's perspective and his head was underwater, he tried to scream. But there was no air in his dead lungs.

Hyde awoke.

He found himself sitting upright in bed, gasping for breath. He sat so for a few moments, gathering himself and taking in the shadows of his room, the distant sound of hooves and iron-shod wheels on cobbles, the geometry cut on his bedroom floor by the moonlight through the gap in his curtains. With trembling fingers, he ran his hands over his face, over the bulk of his arms and shoulders, reassuring himself that he was fully returned to his own form.

Only once he was convinced that he was in a real and waking world did he rise from his bed, cross to the escritoire and, before the seizure dream faded from his mind, start to write in his notebook.

7

One of the consequences of a nocturnal seizure was that it robbed Hyde of both quantity and quality of sleep. It meant that the following day was usually measured in leaden-limbed steps and fogged, slow thoughts. Added to that was the strange detachment of spirit: a feeling of unreality and disconnectedness from the waking world. When in this state, he would feel the world illusory, counterfeit, as if he had simply fallen into another level of dreaming.

At times, the dream would fade from his memory and remain only as vague impressions, like the ghost wisps of a dissolving cloud drifting across the clear sky of his waking consciousness. At other times, the bizarre imagery of his nightmare would flash like lightning into his recall, unbidden and with startling vividity.

Occasionally, Hyde would even doubt the certainty of the world around him: he would see things and people, or recall having seen them, and be unsure whether they had really been there or were spectres conjured up by his seizure-injured mind.

Porteous had once explained this after-effect to him: the postictal state, as it was known. In most instances it lasted no more than minutes, or an hour, but in rare cases, such as Hyde's, the seizures cast a longer shadow into the day beyond.

It seemed to Hyde that Porteous was skilled at offering explanations of his condition, but not remedies. He had been taking the doctor's prescribed compound for six months, without betterment of his condition. Indeed, he could swear his symptoms, particularly his "lost time," were becoming more frequent and prolonged. Yet whenever he raised his concerns with Porteous, the physician would simply make slight adjustments to the formula, which continued to lack efficacy.

In the meantime, until a true remedy was found, Hyde sought hard to conceal his condition—particularly the strange, haunted state that persisted after an attack—from his fellows and superiors. He hoped that if on such occasions any did notice a lethargy or detachedness about him, they would assume that he had perhaps overindulged the night before and was now paying the cost. However, he knew, such an assumption was unlikely: Hyde's abstemiousness with alcohol was well known among the City of Edinburgh Police.

As he prepared to engage the new day, Hyde was haunted by the images of the seizure-induced dream of the night before. One image eluded him, however, its faded memory jangling in his mind, like an itch that could not be scratched: he had seen the girl's face clearly, had occupied her form, had been familiar with every aspect of her appearance—yet now her face refused to reveal itself to the daylight.

Yet the other images persisted sharp and clear—as did the revelation about the nature of the hanged man's murder. Edward Hyde had grown up with the tales of the Celtic Otherworld, through the bedtime stories told him by his mother. It had been a rich tapestry sewn into the fabric of his infant mind, later elaborated by his own studies into the subject. So, with his knowledge of Celtic legend and custom, why had it been only in his dream that clarity had come? Why had it only been then that he made the connection between the Water of Leith hanged man and the ancient ritual of the Threefold Death?

The thought troubled him but also offered comfort: perhaps Samuel Porteous was right to say that it was possible his lost memories lay in the same place, the same otherwhere realm, waiting to be retrieved.

Mackinley, the constable-coachman, picked up Hyde as normal and took him to the station. Like so many in Edinburgh, this particular morning was one of joyless brightness. A surgeon blade of chill wind sliced its way up from the River Forth, excising any warmth from the sunlight. A clutching grey-gloved hand of rising smoke from a thousand morning chimneys stretched thick, leaden fingers into the sky; bright, hard-edged shafts of sunlight piercing the spaces between and etching the outlines of the soot-dark buildings. It made the city look like an artist's creation, sketched in charcoal, adding to Hyde's sense of unreality.

At the best of times, Edinburgh was for Hyde like an imagined city: an improbable collision of the Georgian symmetry and measure of the New Town with the clustering mediaeval chaos of the Old Town, all built in the shadows of the Castle Rock, the Calton Hill and Arthur's Seat—once titanic volcanoes, now long extinct and ground down to stump ghosts twenty millennia ago by mile-thick glaciers.

People had lived in this landscape for nearly nine thousand years, speaking different tongues, living different lives, laying down different identities in the strata of the city's confused personality. In the dream-haunted days that followed one of his nocturnal seizures, Hyde often had the odd sensation that he was sensible to the layers of their presence, to the usually invisible traces of their passing. It was, he knew, nothing but a fancy brought on by a neurological event.

For Hyde, it was like the scent in the air after a fall of fresh rain. As if the storm in his sleeping brain had left its taint in the Edinburgh air.

Hyde's offices were at the extreme west end of the New Town, in Torphichen Place. The station looked for all the world like any of its neighbours: a Georgian-style townhouse set over three floors and a basement, distinguished externally only by the gas-lit blue-glass lantern above the main door that announced in bright white letters that it was a police station. It was from here that Hyde ran the city's criminal investigation squad of twelve detective officers, five uniformed constables and a desk sergeant. What distinguished it internally was the suite of four cells set in the dense stone of the station's cellar, where prisoners awaiting interrogation would be held.

The journey by carriage from Hyde's home to the station normally took ten minutes—in the summer, he often walked to his work in less than half an hour—but this morning the carriage was delayed.

"It's the electrification, sir," explained Mackinley through the hatch. "They've got half of Princes Street dug up. I don't think anything good will come of it, if you ask me. Lightning through wires . . ."

"Progress, Constable Mackinley," said Hyde. "An electric dawn to a new age, to a new century just around the corner. I'm afraid there's nothing we can do to halt it."

They came to another stop where the road and part of the pavement had been dug up, narrowing the thoroughfare to allow passage in only one direction at a time, a ruddy-faced Irish navvy conducting the traffic with a red flag. From a distance, and for less than a second, the road worker's form and complexion confused Hyde into thinking that he was looking at Hugh Morrison.

Through the carriage window, he saw a group of four children on the pavement looking into the freshly dug trench and talking animatedly, huddled in the urgent conspiracy of childhood. A fifth stood apart from them, seemingly unconnected. Hyde started at the feeling of sudden recognition, but knew it could not be the child he had in mind. She was a young girl, no more than eight—too young to be alone and untended—dressed in poor and dirty clothes. Her unnaturally pale face was grimed with soil and dust, as if she had just clambered out of the excavation. With large green eyes, she stared back at Hyde and shook her head slowly, her expression one of sorrowful admonition.

The carriage started forward with a lurch, and Hyde called through the hatch for Mackinley to wait. But when he turned back, the girl was gone. Only the four other children remained, and turned their attention to the carriage.

"It's all right, Mackinley, I just thought I . . ." He paused, shook his head and sighed. "Never mind, let's get to the station."

Hyde had hoped to be able to sit alone in his office for a while and allow his mind some ease; a gift of time to dispel the image of the small girl who had, impossibly, reminded him of another. However, when he arrived at the stationhouse, the two officers who were permanently assigned as his deputies awaited him. Sergeant of Detectives Peter MacCandless, a good-natured man of thirty-four whose thinning blond hair aged him prematurely, handed Hyde a buff-coloured folder.

"The initial police surgeon's report from Dr. Abercrombie and the full post-mortem results from Doctors Burr and Bell."

"Thank you, Peter," said Hyde.

"But you will maybe get all the intelligence you need from this . . ." MacCandless handed Hyde a copy of a newspaper. The *Edinburgh Expositor* declared in strident newsprint: *THE HANGED MAN OF DEAN: RITUAL WITCHCRAFT MURDER . . . OR THE WORK OF THE DARK GUILD?*

"That was quick." Hyde sighed and handed the paper back to Mac-Candless. "I can well do without the *Expositor*'s fictions about the Dark Guild." He sat behind his desk, placing the file on the blotter and flicking it open, nodding for Sergeants MacCandless and Dempster to sit opposite. Through the high windows, the same Edinburgh sun, cheerless and cold, divided the office into hard-edged light and shadow, and Hyde resisted the temptation to rub at his eyes.

He read through the documents while MacCandless and Dempster, used to their superior's diligence, sat silently until he was finished. Most of the autopsy report was as Dr. Burr had explained. The only surprise had come back from the laboratory at the Royal Infirmary: the man's stomach contents revealed he had been fed a meal of grains and mushrooms no more than half an hour before his death, the food not having had time to be fully digested.

There was also a mention of an unusual substance in the victim's blood. Blood testing was a resource that was both new and limited, and was largely mistrusted by Hyde's colleagues. In this case, Hyde struggled to understand any significance to the findings. He made a note to ask Dr. Bell about the comment but checked himself as he wrote: it was Dr. Burr who had been the principal author of the report, and it should be she he consulted.

"There was a message first thing for you, sir—from the chief constable," said MacCandless when Hyde closed the file. "He asks that you see him at ten this morning at Parliament Square." The sergeant referred to the City of Edinburgh Police's headquarters.

"Any indication what the meeting is about?"

"None, sir."

Hyde turned to the other officer. "I want you to go this morning to the city library and fetch these volumes for me." He handed a foolscap piece of paper with ten items written neatly on it to Sergeant of Detectives William Dempster, an earnest-looking, dark-haired man of forty. The ever-serious Dempster frowned, puzzled, as he read the list.

"Mythology, sir?"

"Do as I ask, William." Dempster was known to all as Willie; all except Hyde, who almost always addressed him as Sergeant Dempster or, when the occasion demanded emphasis, William. "There may be a connection to the murder at the Water of Leith."

"What? He was done away with by kelpies?" MacCandless turned to Dempster and laughed. Dempster remained serious, as was his custom. Not for the first time, Hyde noted the contrast in personality between the two detectives. They could not have been more different, yet somehow they worked together extremely well, and were even friends beyond their work.

"I'll have them here by the time you return from headquarters, sir," said Dempster.

Hyde turned back to MacCandless. "There is something I would like you to pursue, Detective Sergeant."

"Sir?" asked MacCandless, still smiling at his own witticism.

"I would like you to find me a good photographer."

8

Something dark like a shadow stirred in its sleep.

The sleep in which it stirred was not its own, but the sleep of another. Another mind. Another ocean of consciousness that lay dark, cold fathoms deep, weighing down upon it.

It yearned to return to the far-distant surface, the light and air of the world. Like some monstrous leviathan, it lay in abyssal depths dreaming of liberty. It knew the surface. Before, many times before, it had risen upwards and broken through, taking its turn to suppress that other, before sinking once more into the dark.

To start with, its time in the light had been limited, brief and sweet. But with each return, it had grown stronger, walked the world for longer, set its dark strategies in motion. There had been one particularly glorious time when it had occupied the light and occupied more fully than ever the body it shared with that oblivious other.

During that shining time it had made its will known, and the medium of its will had been murder: it had extinguished the light of another and cleared a path for further glory. And it had relished in the killing.

Then it had returned to the dark, forced once more to occupy the abyss of a shared mind. The other walked the world in its stead, perplexed with forgetfulness but still ignorant of the shadow's existence.

But the shadow was getting stronger. Its times in the light, in the world were becoming more frequent, more sustained.

Soon. Soon it would again be able to slouch darkly into the sunlight.

9

Robert John MacGregor Rintoul had never walked a beat in his life, nor had he ever personally made a single arrest.

The Rintouls had, originally, been a family of Fife-shire farmers who, at exactly the right moment in history, had changed from tilling the surface of the earth to burrowing deep into it. The infant Rintoul Coal Company had, almost by accident, found itself struggling to feed the ravenous appetite of a monster to which Scotland just happened to be a parent: the Industrial Revolution.

A rapidly growing and forever coal-hungry family of foundries, factories, shipping lines and railways had demanded constant feeding as they, in turn, fed the machineries of Empire.

Across the Central Belt of Scotland, communities, even entire towns, had grown up around the Rintoul pits, populated by miners' families compelled to purchase all their daily needs from the company's stores. A vast fortune was made, but not by those who toiled—and often died—deep in the earth.

Robert John MacGregor Rintoul, belonging to the fourth generation of the family, was far distanced by class, education and social standing from his forebears' humble origins. He had not, however, inherited his father's position as head of the family concern—that had gone to an older, more capable brother—but he had retained major shareholdings in the company and a substantial private income. Much of what men struggle for in life had been handed to Robert Rintoul without his effort.

Rintoul was an unexceptional-looking man of fifty-seven, tall, lean and balding. Like Hyde, he had served as an army officer. Unlike Hyde, however, not once during his service had he been promoted through merit. In the days before the Cardwell reforms had outlawed the purchase of British Army commissions, Rintoul's father had bought him a starting rank as a major for £4,000, later paying a further increment for his son to be promoted to lieutenant colonel.

As far as Hyde knew, Rintoul had never seen combat of any significance and, on retiring his commission, his family connections had secured him the post he now held and for which he similarly offered no qualification: Chief Constable of the City of Edinburgh Police.

Robert John MacGregor Rintoul now commanded the city's uniformed and detective officers. Everything about his background made him exactly the kind of man Hyde resented. It had been the purchase of commissions—and the consequent bad leadership in battle—that had led to the greatest disasters in British military history. Hyde had seen its results for himself in India. Given the man's background, he had no reason to believe that Robert Rintoul would fare any better leading a peacetime police service.

Except he did.

For some odd reason, the post of chief police officer was perfectly suited to Rintoul. Despite the privilege of his background, there were no pretentions about the man, no arrogance—indeed, Hyde had detected on first encounter that Rintoul was embarrassed by the ease with which he had been able to navigate both career and life. He never pretended to be a policeman, nor to have any skills as an investigator. He was, however, a highly capable administrator and someone who listened to those in his command who possessed the capabilities and experience he lacked.

Hyde had put aside his prejudices—after all, when he gave it sufficient thought, there were perhaps many under his own command who resented a man of his background and social standing leading more experienced officers.

Hyde had already been heading the detective force when Rintoul had taken over as chief constable, and despite his preconceptions, he found he respected, liked even, his new superior. For Rintoul's part, he had made it very clear from the start that he intended to invest absolute autonomy in Hyde and his detective branch, so long as Parliament Square was kept informed and consulted on major investigations. It was not that the chief constable was abdicating responsibilities and duties—Hyde had been surprised at just how assiduous an administrator Rintoul was—more that he recognized the boundaries between supervision and interference, something his predecessor had failed to do.

Despite their mutual respect and the closeness of their working relationship, Hyde knew that Rintoul's adherence to regulation meant he could never share the details of his condition with his commanding officer. He had therefore greeted with some trepidation the news that his superior sought an interview with him the very morning after a seizure.

The chief constable's office was in the top floor of the police headquarters in Edinburgh's Old Town, looking out over Parliament Square, another of Edinburgh's ghosts, this time the ghost of a nation's self-determination. Until the Act of Union, the governance of Scotland had been conducted from these buildings, specifically Parliament Hall, now subsumed into a larger cluster of later, post-Union buildings.

Rintoul greeted Hyde warmly, as was his custom, but once he had asked the chief of detectives to sit, he settled down to the matter at hand.

"This is a bad business, Edward," he said with gravity. "This murder down in Dean Village, I mean. Are we getting anywhere with it?"

"It is very early days, sir," explained Hyde. "But I agree it is a particularly troubling homicide. As you know, the vast majority of the cases we deal with are within a certain milieu—fall-outs amongst the criminal classes, drunken brawls turning deadly, or murders within a family. But this . . ." He shrugged his heavy shoulders. "This is something else entirely."

"And that's what I don't like about it. There is already unrest and disquiet—which as you know can turn so easily to hysteria. I take it you've seen the headlines in the *Edinburgh Expositor*?"

"I have, sir. I don't think anyone with any intelligence will believe this was the work of modern-day witches or of a mythical Dark Guild, led by the ghost of Deacon Brodie."

"I think you credit the great unwashed of Edinburgh with more intelligence than they deserve. Notwithstanding the *Expositor*'s wild speculations, people are talking about some homicidal maniac roaming the streets. Do you think it *is* a maniac? Do you think we will see more of these grotesque murders?" Rintoul posed the questions as if beseeching Hyde to reply in the negative.

"My concern is that it may be the work of more than one man," said Hyde, and he could see it had failed to assuage Rintoul's concern. "Maniacs or otherwise. It would appear that the dead man was killed elsewhere and brought to the Water of Leith, then suspended from the tree. The physical management and effort of such an undertaking suggests more than one perpetrator. At least in that respect the *Expositor* got it right."

"More than one killer?"

"More than one person acting in consort to display the body the way it was found. How many hands were involved with the actual murder is impossible to know. More than that I'm afraid I cannot say at the moment. What concerns me most is that there seems to be an element of symbolism to the whole affair. We have yet to establish the identity of the victim, but should he turn out to be involved in the city's underworld, then the symbolism may simply be one gang sending a message—a particularly gruesome message—to another."

Hyde's thesis seemed to give Rintoul some ease, so he decided not to share the findings about the man's stomach contents. It was too early to attach significance, if there was any significance to be attached, to the man's final meal of grains and mushrooms.

"Was it about this case you wanted to see me?" he asked the chief constable.

"Yes . . . well, partly." Rintoul reached into a drawer and placed a file on the desk in front of him. "I have had a strange request, Edward. More a demand, I should say, and I don't care for its provenance."

"Oh?"

"I don't like interference in the policing of this city. Particularly when that interference comes from Scotland Yard."

"What interest has Scotland Yard in Edinburgh?" asked Hyde.

"The request has come from a Superintendent William Melville, of the Special Irish Branch. Apparently the Special Irish Branch is to be renamed simply Special Branch, with a wider remit to investigate insurrectionists, anarchists and anyone else seeking to destabilize the Empire."

"That sounds suspiciously like a secret police," said Hyde.

"Maybe so, maybe so," said Rintoul, "but the fact is we have to be seen to take this request seriously. Melville—I believe the man is an Irishman himself and previously headed the Royal Irish Constabulary's detective branch in Dublin—is a specialist in hunting down Fenian Brotherhood and fellow Irish nationalists, as well as other anarchists." The chief constable turned the file around and pushed it across the desktop to Hyde. "I have been asked to provide him with all knowledge we have on Jacob McNeil Mackendrick."

"Cobb Mackendrick?" Hyde frowned. "The painter? The one who paints society portraits?"

"And fervent Scottish nationalist," said Rintoul. "I believe Superintendent Melville is more concerned with Mackendrick's politics than his artistic abilities. However, the truth is that we have nothing on him. We have no reason to have anything on him—he has never committed an offence or encouraged the commission of one. He certainly has never advocated any form of armed insurrection in Scotland or even support for the insurrectionists in Ireland. In any case, there is currently little or no support for Home Rulers here. He is an eccentric, politically, intellectually, socially and, I have heard, personally. What interest Scotland Yard could possibly have in him is beyond me."

Hyde nodded. "I know very little about Mackendrick, sir. That which I do know relates to his artistic talent, which I believe is considerable."

"I think Special Branch is responding to—or perhaps for its own purposes fanning the flames of—public anxiety. There was that terrible Phoenix Park business in Dublin last year, and the recent spate of mainland Fenian bombings—including January's Glasgow explosions. Ever since, I think much of the establishment see Clan na Gael and the Irish Republican Brotherhood lurking around every corner."

"But, as you said," said Hyde, "Mackendrick is a Scottish nationalist and has never voiced any support for the Fenians . . ."

"I suspect the fear is that we might see such a movement arise in Scotland. We have no Special Branch here, Edward. The idea of a political police concerns me as much as it does you, but the Empire has many enemies who make such policing necessary. I rather fear that any such investigations in Edinburgh fall under your purview."

"You want me to investigate Cobb Mackendrick?"

"I wouldn't say investigate—perhaps more enquire generally about him. All I want is enough to satisfy this Melville that we are not blind to or ignorant of any potential political intrigues within our jurisdiction.

I'm talking about paying little more than lip service to this request, Edward: I know you have much more pressing matters, not least of which is this murder. Perhaps you could assign one of your officers to the task?"

Hyde nodded. "Yes, sir."

The matter settled, Rintoul turned to a new subject. "I believe you attended Hugh Morrison's execution," he said. "Does that judgement still trouble you?"

"I cannot honestly say it does not," said Hyde. "It is not that I am convinced of Morrison's innocence, but I equally cannot say with any certainty that he was guilty. I fear we may have made an error. And in capital cases error can cost an innocent life."

"I thought the man was clearly insane, was he not? Blaming the murder on some mythical wild dog . . ."

"He wasn't insane, he was desperate. You know I pride myself on seeing through the guises of others—of seeing the misdeed through the protestations of innocence—but with Morrison . . . with Morrison I was convinced he had no knowledge of the killing of Mary Paton. And as far as the beast he spoke of, he simply sought some other explanation for a crime he vehemently denied. I think the animal he referred to is merely some kind of Gaelic metaphor for all the evil in the world, but because of his simplicity he took it literally." Hyde sighed.

"Yes," said Rintoul. "You told me all this on Tuesday: the *cù dubh ifrinn* you said this mythical beast was called."

"I did?" Hyde frowned.

"Well, you know my feelings on the matter," said Rintoul. "I think it's a fool's errand for you to pursue the case further; as far as this city is concerned, justice has been served. And the Dean Village case should take all your attention. I was prepared to allow you some licence with the Morrison thing, as we discussed on Tuesday, but I take it nothing new came out of your meeting on Tuesday night? I dare say the events at the Water of Leith took your mind from it."

Hyde felt a chill run through him. He had no recollection of discussing Morrison with Rintoul two days before, nor of expressing his intentions for that evening. He had no recollection of what those intentions had been.

"I'm sorry, sir, my meeting?"

"The night of the murder . . ." Rintoul frowned, confused. "You informed me that afternoon that you had a lead that may cast further light on the Morrison case. What's wrong, man? Can't you remember a discussion from the other day?"

"Of course, sir. Sorry." Hyde struggled to compose himself. Here was one of the trails that could lead him to where he had been immediately before coming to himself at the Water of Leith. But it also meant he was in danger of revealing his memory loss to Rintoul, who was already looking puzzled by Hyde's confusion.

"So nothing came of it?"

"Sir?"

"Your meeting, man—the one in Dean Village. The whole reason you were there in that area when the body was found. Was this woman you were meeting helpful?"

Hyde paused for a moment, his mind still racing. He took a breath, then said calmly, "No, I'm afraid not, Chief Constable. I cannot recall anything from it that can help us now."

10

After his meeting with the chief constable, Hyde returned to his office and sat, using every effort of his will to recall the conversation to which Rintoul had referred.

It had clearly taken place on the afternoon he had lost time, and during their discussion he had given his superior some indication of his destination that evening. It was so frustrating to be so close to knowing why he had been down by the Water of Leith that night—but to have asked Rintoul directly to remind him would have ignited the chief constable's suspicion and inspired questions to which Hyde would have no comprehensible answer.

No matter how hard he tried to illuminate the darkness of his memory, no fragment of what had been discussed yielded to light.

He knew there was nothing logged in his daybook about where he had gone that evening—he had checked it before, along with station logs and messenger slips. The absence of any record surprised him: he knew that many of his men kept their informants' identities close secrets, but Hyde was a man of method, driven to contain in a web of careful record the chaos that his condition brought. It was particularly important on occasions such as these, where he had to account for lost time. His sedulous written accounting of his days allowed him normally to fill at least some of the gaps in his memory.

His journal for that afternoon, however, confounded him with a page as empty and blank as his recall.

It was at times like these that Hyde felt most isolated: he trusted both Dempster and MacCandless, the latter especially, but knew he could never reveal to either that there were times he lapsed from this world and could not account for his actions.

Robert Rintoul had revealed some of what Hyde had said, and that had provided a location for the meeting: Dean Village. It offered Hyde at least some relief: it proved that there had been a reason for him being in the vicinity that night—a reason unconnected to the murder he was later to discover.

The coincidence, however, still troubled him.

He questioned Mackinley. The constable-coachman confirmed he had not conveyed Hyde to Dean Village that afternoon. Hyde had told him he would not need him for the rest of that day and Mackinley had instead been conscripted by the station sergeant into conveying evidence boxes from Torphichen Place to Parliament Square. Mackinley seemed not to be confused or troubled by Hyde's questions. It occurred to Hyde that he perhaps worried too much about arousing the suspicions of others by asking to be reminded of events. Everyone, after all, had lapses of memory.

His thoughts were disrupted by a knock on his office door and the entrance of Dempster, who announced that a lady had called and wished to speak to Hyde.

"She claims she is a doctor," he said, with no attempt to hide his scepticism.

"Then she is, Sergeant Dempster," said Hyde. "In fact, she is the Dr. Burr whose post-mortem report you have just read."

"A pathologist?" Dempster's scepticism turned to incredulity.

"Dr. Bell's assistant."

"I thought Dr. Bell's assistant and clerk was Dr. Conan Doyle."

"Dr. Conan Doyle has moved on to private practice in England," said Hyde. "Dr. Burr now assists Dr. Bell on occasion. And, I have to say, she is almost as skilled as Dr. Bell at forensic detection and could prove an invaluable resource. She yielded much about the possible history of our victim. Please show her up."

When she entered his office, Hyde was again struck by Cally Burr's beauty. She was dressed in a black skirt and a high-collared waister jacket of the new fashion, her glossy black hair swept up and gathered under a hat. There was something about her, about the golden tone of her skin, that made her seem, in the achromic Edinburgh light, like a creature from another world. For some reason, Hyde found her presence soothing.

He bade her sit and offered her tea, which she declined.

"Probably advisable," said Hyde with a smile. "Perhaps you have had the misfortune of experiencing police station tea before."

"I was passing and I thought I would call in on the off-chance that you had any questions regarding my report," she said, ignoring his witticism, her tone businesslike.

"As a matter of fact," said Hyde, "I was going to contact you because I have, indeed, some questions. You have saved me the time."

She smiled, her smile, like her tone and entire demeanour, again businesslike, almost cold. Hyde surmised that Cally Burr, as a woman in a man's profession, had learned to suppress any hint of femininity or warmth in her demeanour.

It had been, after all, only thirteen years since the Edinburgh Surgeons' Hall riot, where the Edinburgh Seven—seven women, Britain's first female medical students, attending an anatomy exam—had been mobbed by their male fellow students and a general Edinburgh rabble, infuriated by the idea of women entering the profession. But enter they had, though every effort had been made by the Edinburgh medical establishment, led by Sir Robert Christison, to exclude them as much as possible. Those who had qualified found themselves restricted to gynaecology and obstetrics. No man would submit to the indecency of a female doctor's examination, it had been claimed.

Perhaps, thought Hyde, that was why Cally Burr had become a pathologist: dead men were in no position to object.

While her visit was a pleasant surprise, he guessed her motive: ensuring that he directed any questions about her findings to her, not her superior.

"What questions do you have, Captain Hyde?" Again she held him in a disconcertingly frank gaze.

"The laboratory results—I don't really understand why they are significant, but I know you would not have included them had you not considered them so."

"I have a particular interest in a new branch of medical science, pharmacology," said Dr. Burr. "Indeed, I would claim to have considerable understanding of it. You may or may not know that the few women physicians in Scotland have often had to resort to foreign universities for at least some of their medical education."

"I'm afraid I did not."

"I myself was lucky to have the opportunity to study briefly under Dr. Oswald Schmiedeberg at the University of Strassburg. Have you heard of Dr. Schmiedeberg, Captain Hyde?"

"I'm afraid I have not," said Hyde.

"Dr. Schmiedeberg is a pioneer in pharmacological research. While at Strassburg, I read his ground-breaking *Outline of Pharmacology*. One of his first discoveries was how to isolate and measure chloroform levels in blood. About fifteen years ago Dr. Schmiedeberg made another discovery: that muscarine has the same effect on the heart as when the vagus nerve is galvanically stimulated."

"Doctor, I'm afraid I don't—" Hyde began to say.

Impatiently, Burr held up her hand to halt him, causing Hyde to smile. He was used to people being intimidated by his presence—an effect clearly not experienced by the young female doctor.

"Often found present along with muscarine, Captain Hyde, is muscimol. I followed Schmiedeberg's analysis protocols and found traces of both muscarine and muscimol in the dead man's blood."

"He was poisoned?" Hyde's smile waned.

"In a manner of speaking. Muscarine and muscimol are indeed highly toxic and occur naturally in specific members of the mushroom family."

"The stomach contents . . ." The significance dawned on Hyde.

Cally Burr nodded. "The stomach contents. Muscarine and muscimol are found in high quantities in *Amanita muscaria*, commonly known as fly-agaric. If the fly-agaric mushroom is cooked—usually boiled—it mitigates its toxicity without reducing its other effects. Have you read the Irish writer Oliver Goldsmith's *Citizen of the World*?"

Hyde shook his head.

"It mentions the revolting habit in some quarters of drinking the urine of someone who has eaten fly-agaric. A less pleasant processing method to reduce the toxicity." She again held Hyde in her frank gaze as if defying him to be offended by her indelicacy. Hyde's thoughts were elsewhere.

"Other effects?" he asked. "What kind of effects?"

"We know that either muscarine or muscimol, or both acting together, is psychoactive—meaning it affects the mind, perception and consciousness. Consumption of fly-agaric induces a state of euphoria, a feeling of increased strength, but most of all it causes powerful, vivid hallucinations. In primitive societies, it was and remains widely used as an entheogen—a substance used in witch-doctor or shamanic rituals to open the doors to new levels of consciousness, allowing the living to commune with spirits, with the dead, for example, or revealing another realm of existence. The truth is, of course, that all it really does is simply change the physical chemistry of the brain and cause delusion and hallucination. Nothing mystical to it in reality."

For a moment, Hyde considered what Dr. Burr had said. He tried to clear from his thoughts the idea that he had no need of such substances to access an alternative reality—his epilepsy delivered the same effects.

"But that clearly wasn't the case with our victim," he said at last. "I doubt a corpse found in Edinburgh was poisoned by some African savage. A witch doctor or the like."

Cally Burr smiled, and there was something about her smile, though beautiful, that he did not like. "I'm afraid you're guilty of a common arrogance, Captain Hyde. A British arrogance. We think ourselves as at the pinnacle of civilization—that British racial and cultural superiority and freedom from savagery is what has entitled us to take command of a quarter of the world's surface.

"The truth is that the history of the British peoples is more prosaic and infinitely more savage and uncivilized than we allow. The shamans and witch doctors who specialized in the kind of intoxication I've described were our very own Celtic ancestors. Our fairy tales, our folk customs are not as innocent as we would like to think. There is a fashion at the moment for so-called 'fairy painting.' The tales we tell our children are filled with illustrations of fairies, of elves, of the Irish leprechaun. And what, Captain Hyde, do you most commonly see them sitting upon?"

"Toadstools." Hyde had said it before the significance struck him.

"Specifically a red-capped, white-spotted toadstool," Cally Burr said, "and a toadstool is simply a poisonous mushroom. The red-capped toadstool portrayed in Celtic mythological scenes or in fairy paintings is the fly-agaric. There is a very good reason for its presence in such representations: our ancestors would use fly-agaric to open the doors of the Celtic Otherworld, to see into another universe. It was the key to Celtic dreams. Believe me, Captain Hyde, if you were to consume any significant quantity of fly-agaric, you would see leprechauns too."

Hyde nodded, feeling unease. Again the thought struck him that he personally required no hallucinogen to experience another realm of the senses.

"This troubles you, Captain Hyde?"

"It fits with a theory of mine."

"Oh?"

"The manner of the victim's murder," he said. "It looks very much to me as if he suffered the Threefold Death. It was an ancient Celtic ritual of human sacrifice. The victim was hanged, drowned and had his or her heart cut out. They were always hung upside down. It's as ancient as the Celtic peoples and found its way into other beliefs: the Norse god Odin hung upside down from the world tree Yggdrasil—Yggdrasil means 'Odin's gallows'—to suffer near-death and gain wisdom of runes. You see the image on the tarot card the Hanged Man."

"You are well versed in folklore, Captain Hyde. Something I wouldn't expect from a policeman." Cally Burr smiled, this time with warmth, and Hyde felt the room light up.

"It is something of an interest of mine," he said, suddenly awkward. "Since childhood. Particularly Celtic mythology. I don't know why I didn't think of the Threefold Death when I first saw the body. He was hanging from an elm and over moving water—both considered by the ancients to be connections between our reality and the Otherworld. I knew nothing about the significance of the toadstools."

"You believe that there is some kind of occult connection to this murder?" she asked.

"During the autopsy you said yourself that the manner of the victim's death smacked of the ritualistic. This city is crawling with insane beliefs: theosophists, hermeticists, spiritualists, occultists, religious fanatics . . ."

Cally Burr nodded. "I see your point. I find it perplexing that in a scientifically enlightened age such as ours, people still seem to need such superstitions. I can understand why these beliefs prevailed before science was there to offer rational explanations of the world. But now . . . now we are living in an age of unprecedented scientific advance, yet these fashions for bizarre occult beliefs flourish. It seems to me that the more science illuminates, the more suspicion obfuscates." She rose and held out her hand. "Anyway, I hope I have helped. And if I can be of any further assistance, Captain Hyde, please let me know."

Hyde thought for a while, then said, "As a matter of fact, I think you can . . ."

11

He felt that the house had been waiting for him, or they had been waiting for each other. This was a place steeped in dark history and darker legend; he was a man steeped in dark deeds and darker ambition. That was why he had come to this place, this house.

Crunnach House lay far beyond the city boundary. A glacial whim ten millennia before had carved out a bowl-shaped depression in the Lothian landscape, and the house stood, flanked by ragged and insubstantial clumps of elder and ash, in dark vigil on a low drumlin hill that swelled on the depression's rim like a bruise on a lip.

The house as it was now had been there since the early eighteenth century, but an earlier structure had occupied the same spot for centuries before. Some said that the mound on which it stood was in fact the ghost of a Stone Age hill fort.

Whatever its nature or the specifics of its history, the great antiquity of habitation in the location was attested by the presence of a roughly man-shaped standing stone in the bowl of the depression. The menhir was known locally as the *Feardorch*, or the Dark Man, and decorated with eroded cup-and-ring petroglyphs. Some seven and a half feet tall, the stone was unevenly conformed and its base was twice the width of its upper part. Some primaeval violence had sundered the rock from its matrix and had formed a concave ledge of sorts halfway up the menhir.

The effect was that of a figure holding forth a dish, as if in offering. A fissure, its edges eroded, traversed the ledge from front to back, forming something akin to a drainage channel. All this was mere geological happenstance, but the dished ledge was, like the rest of the menhir, decorated in prehistorically carved rings and spirals. For as long as anyone could remember, the legend was that the Dark Man stone had been a place of past and present evil, that the ancients had performed sacrifice there, and the channel in the ledge had been used to drain the blood of offerings.

Not all the evil associated with the place was distant primaeval wickedness. The hill at the far side of the depression, directly opposite that on which the house stood, was crowned by a vast, crooked and ancient yew—rumoured to be a dule tree—thrusting gnarl-knuckled fingers skywards.

The hill was known locally as Witchknowe. In the early seventeenth century it had been said that the Dark Man and the depression in which it sat had been sequestered enough to be used as the place of assembly for witches from all over Lowland Scotland. It was even claimed that the name of Crunnach House derived from the Scottish Gaelic for gathering place, *áite cruinneachaidh*—though others said it referred to the house's position on the crown, *crún* or *crunnach* of a hill. Some even believed it got his name from *Crom Dubh,* the Dark Crooked One of Scottish mythology, who demanded human sacrifice and whose form had been trapped in the black stone of the Dark Man menhir.

Whatever the origin of its name, it had become synonymous with the basest evil.

There had been committed there, according to accounts of the time, blasphemy on an unprecedented scale. All forms of carnal and spiritual sin had been performed before the Dark Man, whose shadow had been cast large and vivid by the witches' balefire. The channel on the menhir's ledge had, it was claimed, lived up to its legendary purpose and drained the blood of all forms of sacrifice, including human. The witches had apparently felt secure in their isolation, as at that time the house was enduring one of its frequent periods of abandonment.

This had all taken place, however, during the great turmoil of the Wars of the Three Kingdoms, and a company of Cromwellian soldiers, armed with muskets and puritan certainty, had hidden in the vacant house and witnessed the debauchery. Such was their outrage on seeing a stolen babe placed on the altar of the Dark Man that they had surged forth, mowing down with musket ball, backsword and pike many of the witches where they stood. The others, without charge or trial, were bound and confined in the abandoned house while on the hill opposite the soldiers built execution pyres—eschewing the quick death offered by the natural gallows of the hill's ancient yew tree.

The kindling had, however, been meagre, with only the scant and ragged copses of ash and elder to provide fallen wood. The pyres had in turn been sparse and supplemented with green timber cut down by the Cromwellians.

The burning had therefore been slow. As many as thirty were put to the flame, it was said, and it had taken half a night for them to expire.

And in that cruelty another legend had been born: that the keening, whining wind often heard in the Crunnach valley was the tormented cries of the executed witches—either the echoes of their tortured death throes or the laments of their spirits, doomed to wander the valley as banshees.

And from that time onwards, the hillock became known as Witchknowe; its ancient yew also given a name. The Lamentation Tree.

For all of these reasons and many more, the house and its lands had been shunned. There were no extant villages, hamlets or other habitations of note anywhere near, and the house had stood empty, yet undisturbed, for some fifteen years.

And it was for all these reasons and more that a new occupier came to Crunnach House. Someone who had sought out exactly such a place. A man with a night-dark soul to invest in its stone flesh.

It was already twilight when the coach approached; the house, the Lamentation Tree, the Dark Man menhir and the dark green landscape tenebrous against the sky's fading light.

The coach arrived first and alone: the removers had stated they would not deliver to the house until it was occupied, so the new owner attended with just one retainer, who acted as both manservant and coachman. A little under five feet in height, the servant who dismounted was too tall for a dwarf, but there was something peculiar in his build and features, his shoulders and arms full and heavy, his eyes set apart on a wide face, his mouth a recessed, lipless slash between arched nose and jutting chin.

The stunted servant held open the door of the coach and his master alighted, smiling as he took in the dark, irregular form of Crunnach House. He was a man of average height, too powerfully built and too immaculately dressed for a gentleman, and would have been handsome if not for the fact that one eye was hidden beneath a black silk eyepatch. He removed his hat to reveal crow-black hair and with his one unshielded eye looked up appreciatively at the building before him.

Crunnach House stood dark and mute in expectant welcome for its new master.

Frederic Ballor.

12

Henry Dunlop was a small, wiry man of about fifty, his height shortened by the bow in his legs that added a sway to his gait. The effect of poor nutrition, no doubt, thought Hyde. But as Dunlop walked towards him across the mortuary hall, it looked as if his legs bent under the weight of the burdens he struggled to carry: a large rectangular wooden box tucked precariously under the same arm that carried a bulging carpet bag, and a bundle of wooden rods bound together by leather straps propped, rifle-style, upon the opposite shoulder.

Adding to the precariousness of his bandy-legged progress were the remains of a badly rolled cigarette pinched between Dunlop's tight lips. With no free hand to remove it, he had to compress his face into a cramped grimace against the eye-stinging smoke. It was clear, even at a distance, that Henry Dunlop was not one to care for his appearance. His suit was bagged and unpressed, the front of his Norfolk jacket speckled with cigarette ash.

When he reached where Hyde and Cally Burr stood waiting for him, Dunlop set the bag, bundle and box carefully down on the polished floor of the mortuary hall, removed the butt from his lips, extinguished it with a pinch of thumb and forefinger and tucked the remains behind his ear. Hyde could see where the grizzled grey-white hair on the temple above the ear was discoloured yellow from the clearly long-standing habit.

"Mr. Dunlop?" he asked, and extended his hand. Dunlop hesitated for a moment, taking in Hyde's features. Hyde was accustomed to the caution of strangers on first encounter with him, but there was something different about Dunlop's reaction. The small man had the weary mien of someone who had seen so much of the world there was little left to surprise him, and his response to Hyde was almost as if he were appraising him, working out where the policeman fitted in his experience of the world and its people.

"Aye, I'm Dunlop, and you would be Captain Hyde."

"I am. And this is Dr. Burr. Thank you for coming."

"No thanks needed," said the small man drily, "merely payment for my time and materials." Again he paused, tilting his head slightly as if to change the angle of his scrutiny of Hyde's face. "Have you ever had your photograph taken, Captain Hyde?"

"I have not," said the other, self-consciously.

"A most interesting face," said Dunlop almost absently. "You possess a unique physiognomy—I would very much like to take your photograph some time, if you would allow. I take photographs of interesting faces. Interesting people." He examined Cally Burr in the same insolently candid manner. "Indeed, you would both make excellent subjects, if I may say. But it is particularly your unusually striking bone structure that would play well with light, Captain Hyde. Not for profit, mind, but for my art—my profession is also my hobby—so there would be no charge."

"You know why I asked you here, Mr. Dunlop?" enquired Hyde, ignoring the invitation. The truth was, the little man's interest in and candour about his appearance had disconcerted him.

"I do. Sergeant MacCandless explained it to me. Where is the subject?"

There were two mortuary attendants, in shirt sleeves despite the chill of the unheated, stone-walled morgue, waiting beside the double doors at the far side. Hyde nodded to them and they left the hall for a moment before returning with a trolley, on which lay the corpse of the Hanged Man. The gaping wound in the chest had been coarsely sewn closed with horsehair sutures, and in face and form the dead man's appearance had, after the ravages of murder and post-mortem examination, been roughly restored. A sheet covered the body from the waist down.

"I know you have taken many custody photographs for us, Mr. Dunlop. Today is somewhat different. Your subject is not a living one, I'm afraid," said Hyde.

"Aye, I can see that," said the photographer. "But I'm used to such things."

"You are?" asked Cally Burr.

"Aye, I am," said Dunlop. "I take a good many portraits of the dead. There's a particular fashion for it, you could say. Especially bairns. When a wee one is taken too soon by consumption or the scarlet fever, the parents often get me to photograph the child with its living family. Even the living need to be absolutely still for the time it takes to expose the plate, so I already have the stands and braces that can hold the dead in any position. They're my most patient subjects, you could say—and there's no problem with them blinking in the middle of an exposure." He revealed a smile of gaps and diseased teeth.

Neither Hyde nor Cally Burr returned his smile, and the photographer seemed not to care that his humour had not been appreciated. He reached into the soiled and aged carpet bag and brought out a large volume, bound in fine red leather. It was a surprise to see an item of such quality emerge from the bag. Dunlop carefully held it open, the leather binding against his chest, and turned the pages for Hyde and Cally Burr to see. On each page, held in place by gummed corners, were photographs. Some were portraits, and Hyde reluctantly had to agree that they really were works of art. The faces were all striking, and Dunlop had used angles of light to emphasize their features. He turned these pages quickly until he got to what looked like more standard portraits of children, or group pieces with a family. In one, a girl in her early teens, her dark hair loose and cascading over her shoulders, gazed out candidly from the photograph. She sat on a chair, her hands crossed and resting on a book on her aproned lap.

"Such a beautiful girl, don't you think?" asked Dunlop.

"Is she . . . ?" Hyde started to ask.

The photographer nodded. "A heart weakened by scarlet fever in infancy and stilled by influenza at fourteen. She was an avid reader, according to her parents, which is why she is posed with her hands upon a book. You would think she was about to recommence reading, would you not? And here is another . . ." He turned a few pages. The photograph he stopped at was of a young boy, about five or six. He sat on a sofa, his legs not long enough for his small feet to reach its edge, his arm around a stuffed toy in the shape of a horse. He too stared out at the camera, but there was something about the eyes—the drooping of the lids and the shadows around the sockets—that hinted at the lack of true vitality. Hyde decided the previous photograph, with its convincing verisimilitude of life, troubled him more.

"It is strange, is it not," said Dunlop, "that we feel the need still to pose the dead? To surround them with things from their living days? Science has given us the innovation of photography, yet there is no difference between these photographs and the burial sites of the ancients, where we interred our dead with the items they treasured in life."

"That was different," said Cally Burr. "Grave goods were believed to be of use to the dead in the otherworld. Your photographs are mementos, a comfort for the living."

"Aye, perhaps so." Dunlop shrugged. "Or perhaps my photographs do represent an otherworld—a place where their deceased loved ones live on in eternal youth. In any case, you can see I have an established relationship with the dead, so to speak, so this present task causes me no difficulties. And, may I say, Dr. Burr, that should you or your colleagues ever require my services, I would have no trouble taking photographs of surgical record. I earnestly believe there is a place in medicine for photography—perhaps pathology in particular. It means a better record than word alone. Should you ever need me, Dr. Burr, please let me know." He offered her his visiting card.

Cally Burr nodded and took the card without comment. Hyde sensed her distaste for the small man and could not deny his own growing antipathy. Peter MacCandless had, however, assured him that Dunlop had a reputation for accuracy and reliability and was probably the best photographer the City Police used.

The small man unfastened the leather-strap-bound wooden staves which revealed themselves to be a tripod, which he set up at the foot of the mortuary trolley. The wooden box opened into a bellows camera, its mahogany and brass lens and plateholder boards connected by the bellows, a concertina of red leather. Everything about the camera, in contrast to its owner, was immaculate, as if the glass lens, wood and brass had been polished and the leather waxed immediately before being brought to the mortuary. Dunlop took the other items he needed from the carpet bag. Its fabric was that of an oriental rug, its crimson and aquamarine colours darkened and time-worn, but Hyde could make out the repeating pattern of a stylized eye.

"Can the gentleman be encouraged to sit upright?" asked Dunlop.

Hyde nodded to the two attendants, who raised the corpse into a sitting position and held him there. Dunlop took a collection of metal rods, again gleaming as if new, from the old carpet bag. With the swift ease of the practised hand, he interlocked the rods to form a pyramidic structure, capped with a stouter rod holding a wide U-shaped clamp. He slid the assembled brace into place behind the corpse's back and tightened the clamp on the neck.

"Very well," said Dunlop. "Now our subject is comfortable . . ."

He positioned a second stand next to the propped-up corpse and fixed a large mirror, again produced from the carpet bag, close to the dead man's head. "To capture full face and profile at a once," he explained.

He next brought the camera closer to the mortuary trolley, measured with a tape the distance from the camera to the lifeless face, adjusted the lens and the extent of the bellows; then he placed a finger on the camera trigger and took his watch from his pocket. He flicked the trigger and Hyde could see his head move as he silently counted the seconds. He repeated the process, with minor adjustments, three times more, with different plates.

"It is my way of making sure we are guaranteed at least one perfect image," he explained. "I pride myself on my thoroughness."

After Dunlop was finished, he packed up his equipment, asking the attendants to hold the dead man in place while he disengaged the clamp from his neck and dismantled the brace. As he did so, when he reached out his hand and his wrist extended beyond the grubby shirt cuff, Hyde could see a mark on his wrist. A tattoo. He only saw it for an instant, but the pattern seemed to be of three connected spirals.

Dunlop caught him looking at the mark and smiled his ugly, gap-toothed smile. "I see you're admiring my tattoo, Captain Hyde." He extended his arm, pulling the cuff clear for Hyde to see the mark.

As Hyde had thought, it consisted of three connected spirals. Each spiral had been fashioned to give the impression of an eye.

"It is my trademark, you could say," explained Dunlop. "My professional—and personal—motif. I think of myself as an eye. I believe I see things differently from others—I see things, see moments, in greater detail than most. More than that, I believe I see another reality that others fail to notice."

"What do you mean, another reality?" asked Cally Burr.

Dunlop shrugged. "A second reality, if you like. A hidden aspect. It is surprising how the eye of the camera is more difficult to deceive than the eye of a man. A person's true nature—the other nature they hide from the world—tends to be laid bare by the photograph." He tugged his sleeve down to cover the tattoo and tapped the polished mahogany of the closed bellows camera. "And I use this to record those moments. In that way, others can see as I do: experience a place, a face or a moment fully, the details that they otherwise would have missed. Without this invention, I would struggle. I have no gift as a painter of pictures, but had I lived in earlier times, I would have had to try to record on paper or canvas that which I can now capture in a photograph."

"But the design," said Hyde. "The pattern of your tattoo. That is the triskelion, is it not? The ancient Celtic symbol."

Dunlop shrugged again. "That I cannot say. All I know is that it contains three eyes, and to me it signifies that additional vision that the photographer needs. I'm not aware of any symbolism of the mark other than my own personal one." He straightened himself up as much as his bow legs would permit. "Well, Captain Hyde, how many copies of the photograph do you want? I can produce as many as you wish, but it will cost, mind."

"At least a dozen," said Hyde. "Ideally twenty."

"Then you will have twenty. I shall deliver them tomorrow, but not before lunch." Dunlop again tilted his head in examination of Hyde. "A really most interesting face. Please do consider allowing me to take a portrait of you."

13

Elspeth Lockwood constantly made great effort not to surrender easily to her anxieties, but the coachman made her nervous.

He was the strangest creature, neither dwarf nor full-grown man, with eyes set too far apart beneath a broad, heavy brow. Though small, he gave the impression of great strength and his complexion was dark, despite his hair being sand coloured. There was, Elspeth thought with distaste, something utterly alien about him. Un-British.

Furthermore, though he had removed his cap and bowed respectfully when she spoke to him, he had responded to her commands with short, breathy grunts. It dawned on her that he may be some form of congenital degenerate and be incapable of articulate speech. Most disturbingly, there had been something about his mien that had suggested familiarity; that he knew her, or she should know him, despite this being their first encounter.

As arranged, he waited with the carriage, a closed-cabin brougham with curtains drawn, on the corner of Great King Street and Dundas Street. When she entered the carriage, she was surprised to find it empty: Frederic had not come to meet her. She would make the journey alone. At least, in the cabin, she was separated from the strange creature who served as coachman.

The subterfuge, she knew, was a necessity: she could not travel to Crunnach House using any mode of transport where her identity was known or her movements could be traced. Any connection with the notorious house or its even more notorious occupant would cause an immediate scandal and irreparable damage to her reputation—and reputation was all a gentlewoman of her station had in Edinburgh's stifling, narrow-minded society.

Elspeth Lockwood was the daughter and, since the death of her brother Joseph, sole heir of James Lockwood, who in turn had been the son and sole heir of William Lockwood. Elspeth had always been a woman of enormous drive and vision, who resented the constraints placed on her by her gender. In contrast, her father's ambition for her had been limited: it had always been his desire that she find herself a suitable husband from one of the more established Edinburgh families. There was, she knew, no snobbery greater than that of the recently socially elevated. But it was her grandfather William, not her father, who had been her exemplar, her model. She was aware that it was his traits—his single-mindedness, his ruthless ambition—that ran in her blood.

Elspeth's grandfather had been a simple draper in the Burgh of Leith. Perhaps not so simple, because he had had the prescience to recognize the advantage of dealing directly with the shipmasters and company men who docked cargo in the port, often employing common bribery to secure the best goods. He also had had a particular sense of style and quality, unusual for someone of so humble a birth station.

A reputation for value and quality had spread, and the more bargain-conscious Edinburgh burghers—of whom there famously were many—had overcome their reluctance to enter Leith and sought out his store. Soon the founder Lockwood had saved them the incommodity of travelling to Leith by setting up a store in the Old Town. Even that compromise was spared his customers when he moved once more, this time into the solid respectability of Georgian stonework and Edinburgh's New Town.

Since then, Lockwood and Son had become the city's premier department store. The company's home now was a seven-floored building that commanded Princes Street. There was, indeed, a cachet of petty snobbery in being seen to shop in the store, which, while remaining true to its founder's principle of quality, had long since abandoned that of value.

It had been Joseph, Elspeth's beloved brother, who had been chosen to take control of the store. Joseph had, in contrast to Elspeth, been a gentle, fragile soul, and he had confided in her that he intended her to be his equal partner and driving force in the business when his time came to inherit the store. Unfortunately, Joseph's fragility had ultimately cut short his season on earth.

Elspeth had been distraught, and remained damaged, by her brother's untimely death. The strength and vigour that had exemplified her had diminished, and she was now given to attacks of blind existential panic.

With no son to take the business into a third generation, she was set to inherit her father's position. It made her potentially the most powerful and influential woman in Edinburgh, and there were many keen to court her. She knew that her father sought out some groom for her who could be measured by his business acumen more than his suitability as a husband. Elspeth, however, would allow no man to hold sway over her or a business that was rightfully hers. If she were ever to marry, it would be on her terms and no husband would ever displace her at Lockwood's.

She knew she could never marry Frederic.

Whatever it was she felt for him was not love; it was a dark obsession, a passion of the body and mind, not the heart and soul. In any case, he was a man of the blackest reputation, and Edinburgh society would never tolerate such a union. Not that she cared about their mores; she was free of that—Frederic had freed her of that—but she could not risk Lockwood and Son being shunned by its clientele.

Frederic had eased her pain after Joseph's death. His beliefs and philosophies had offered succour and his shameless physicality had opened up for Elspeth a new world of senses.

When she had first encountered him, Frederic Ballor had resided in the West End of the New Town, in a large end-terraced mansion which he had rented from an unsuspecting absentee landlord. There he had carried out séances—a not uncommon and innocent distraction among Edinburgh's gentlefolk. However, there had been an increasing whiff of sulphur about Ballor's invocations, and rumours of drug-taking and worse. Word had reached his remote landlord and his lease was brought to a premature end.

It was then the news had broken that Ballor was to take up residence in the infamous Crunnach House—and details of the man's history before his arrival in Edinburgh had become whispered gossip in the city's grandest parlours.

So now Elspeth travelled in secret into Edinburgh's hinterland to meet with a man who had courted scandal and intrigue wherever he had gone. An occultist and black magician, an adventurer, a gunrunner to the Irish Republican Brotherhood, some said. There was a rumour that, in France, he had stood trial for the murder of a rival.

For Elspeth, however, Frederic had been a liberator. Instead of her sex being an impediment to her ambitions, he had shown her that it was her strength. Women, the feminine, he had explained, had two characters, two aspects, and society had striven for centuries to suppress her sex. He had revealed to her the other side of her muliebrity; he had shown her why society feared the feminine, feared the power and strength of women. That power lay within her, he had told her, waiting to be awakened.

And he had revealed the lies imposed on her race in the name of Empire. He had told her the truth of her history, of her race and kind, of the blood that flowed through her veins; he had spoken with passion of the Celtic chieftainesses and war goddesses. He had held her in the golden gaze of that single eye and had talked with huge passion of the Morrígan, of Bríg, of Macha, and of the mother of winter and the world herself: the Cailleach.

Frederic Ballor's seduction of Elspeth Lockwood had been both forceful and worshipful. Complete. And it had been a seduction of her mind and will as well as her body. She had given herself to the man and she had given herself to his beliefs. A new world was being revealed to Elspeth Lockwood. A world as wondrous in its shadows as it was in its light, full of great secrets to be discovered, dark knowledge to be unlocked.

As the city around her gave way to open countryside, she considered just how dangerous a game she was playing. And the thought of it frightened her and thrilled her to the core with dark anticipation.

The ceremony was to be tonight. Tonight there was to be the greatest revelation of all.

14

As promised, Henry Dunlop had delivered the photographs to the Torphichen Place police station the following afternoon. Hyde had sat staring at the face of the dead man as if challenging it to yield his name, his origin, the nature of the life taken from him.

It was around three p.m., shortly after the back shift had relieved the early shift, that Hyde summoned MacCandless and Dempster to his office and handed them eight photographs each.

"Keep one for your own use," he instructed them. "Distribute the others among the uniformed officers I have requested and who will report here this afternoon. Our only potential line of investigation at the moment is the belief that the victim may have been a soldier. I have additional photographs should you need them, although I am keeping one myself. I intend to visit the garrison at the castle and see if anyone can identify him. I want you to organize the uniformed men into two teams and to go into every public house, inn, whorehouse and doss house in Edinburgh and show this picture. If our departed friend has set foot in this city, then someone must recognize him."

Once he had dismissed MacCandless and Dempster to their tasks, he asked that another officer, Constable Iain Pollock, be sent to see him. Pollock was barely twenty-two and still officially a uniformed officer until completion of his plainclothes probation. Hyde had always thought him too slender and youthful looking to be a police officer, which was exactly why he had encouraged the young constable to join his detective force: Pollock's divergence from the appearance expected of a policeman, and the lack of exposure he had had to the city's criminal classes, meant he could potentially go unnoticed in situations where a police presence would not be welcome.

And that was exactly what Hyde had in mind.

Standing before Hyde's desk, Pollock's demeanour was, as always, a combination of eagerness to please his superior officer and vague trepidation in his presence. Hyde liked Pollock, but often felt annoyed with the young policeman's near-fearful reaction to him. It felt as if he were innocently holding up a mirror to Hyde's rough-hewn form and intimidating appearance.

"I need you to observe a political meeting," said Hyde. "Not attend, mind, just observe." He handed Pollock a printed leaflet. "There are to be three speakers, one of whom will be Jacob McNeil Mackendrick, otherwise known as Cobb Mackendrick."

He handed a second item to Pollock: a newspaper cutting with a lithograph illustration, clearly copied from a photograph, of a shock-headed, heavily bearded man. The subject posed looking slightly to the left, his densely whiskered chin jutting pugnaciously.

Pollock took the leaflet and the cutting from Hyde and studied both eagerly—he was a man young enough and unsullied enough by the world to engage a task eagerly.

"I want you to make sure you go unremarked, unnoticed. Simply observe from a distance, Constable Pollock, and report back to me."

"Am I looking for anything in particular, sir?" asked the young plainclothesman.

"Report everything back to me. I just want a general picture of Mackendrick, his habits, his associates. Watch out particularly for anything resembling rabble-rousing or incitement. If possible from a safe distance, also take especial note of any Irish with whom you may find him associating."

"Very good, sir."

Pollock was at the door when Hyde halted him. "Iain, I see no reason to assume that Mackendrick is involved in illegality, but take care not to make yourself conspicuous. Political types are famed for violent passions and may take ill to having a police spy in their presence."

"I will take great care, sir. And thank you for trusting me with this mission. I shall not disappoint you."

"Of that I am sure, Constable Pollock," said Hyde.

—

A hard-edged, uncompromising skyward thrust of impenetrable volcanic dolerite, the Castle Rock dominated Edinburgh. And the castle dominated the Castle Rock.

A thousand years of history, and the strategic importance of the rock and its stronghold, had made this soil the most contested and blood soaked in Britain; and Edinburgh Castle had earned the reputation of being the most besieged fortress in the island's history.

There had been a military garrison at the castle for six hundred years, and, since the Acts of Union, if anything exemplified Scotland's collaboration in the concept and adventure of Great Britain and its Empire, then it was the body of men that guarded the capital's citadel.

Hyde was expected. An NCO in scarlet tunic and tartan trews, his bearing and sleeve insignia marking him as a colour sergeant, escorted him from the castle gatehouse. A small man around forty, the colour sergeant had that compact robustness of many soldiers, and Hyde had noticed that his face on the right was creased deep from forehead to jaw by a sabre scar. It brought to Hyde's mind that military service leaves its mark, and he began to have more faith that the murder victim, with his healed wounds, may have had some military connection.

Perhaps this excursion would not turn into the fool's errand he had anticipated.

The colour sergeant conducted him to the castle garrison officers' mess, a large oak-panelled room populated with leather club chairs and low tables, where he was told Brigadier Lawson would attend shortly.

A steward bearing a silver tray came over and placed a glass of whisky and a small jug of water on the table next to him. Hyde smiled and thanked the steward but left the liquor untouched.

The late-afternoon light outside the tall windows was dimming and the steward placed another log in the fireplace at the mess's far end. The fire blazed but its warmth did not reach Hyde, and he sensed long centuries of accumulated chill loitering in the thick stone walls behind the oak panelling.

A tall, lean man in civilian clothes entered the mess and made his way across to Hyde, his face breaking into a broad grin.

"How are you, Edward, it's been ages since I saw you."

Hyde stood up and shook hands with Brigadier Allan Lawson, and the two men exchanged small talk for a while before settling down to the matter behind Hyde's visit.

"I heard about the murder," said Lawson. "Terrible business. Sounds like the actions of some crazed lunatic."

"It does indeed," said Hyde. "What the motive was we are still far from establishing, but I fear there may be some symbolism behind the manner of the dead man's discovery. But that's not what brings me here. We have no idea of the victim's identity: no one has made enquiries about a missing relative or acquaintance remotely fitting his description. But I do believe there is a chance that he may have been a soldier, or at least has at one time seen military service."

"And you want me to check if we are missing anyone? I can ask the provost to look into it."

"I was hoping that you could perhaps circulate these . . ." Hyde flipped open the leather portfolio that rested on his lap. He took out two photograph cards, each with the image taken in the mortuary of the Hanged Man.

"This is he?" asked Lawson. He studied the photograph for a moment. "I'm afraid I don't recognize him, but there again, that really doesn't mean anything; we have a complement of five hundred men here. May I keep these for a while?"

Hyde nodded. Lawson pointed to the untouched whisky on the side table. "Still teetotal, I see, Edward." He waved to the steward and ordered two coffees of his "usual type."

"I'll give one photograph to the provost and another to Warrant Officer MacAllistair. MacAllistair seems to know everyone and everything."

"I appreciate it, Allan," said Hyde. "Is this suiting you? The castle, I mean?"

"Well enough," said Lawson, but a grudge lingered in his tone. "I have always been one for soldiering, not pageantry. And God knows the Empire needs all her units active and in the field at the moment. I'm afraid I'm tiring of being a shortcake-tin warrior."

He sighed deeply. "We're stretched too far, Edward. This latest Irish Coercion Act, the continued deployment in Egypt and the despatch of reserves to Bulgaria—all on top of this mad rush to seize territories in Africa before the French and the Belgians get there first. And the Fenian dynamite campaign means we have to have soldiers ready to deploy on British streets too. Two bombs in Glasgow alone this year—so much for Celtic fraternity. And India—well, you know from personal experience just how much a powder keg that is."

The steward arrived with a coffee pot, two cups, and a jug of cream. He poured a thick, viscous dark liquid into the cups and the air fumed with a hazelnut-like odour. Hyde laughed.

"So you still have the taste for chicory coffee?" he asked. "I haven't had any since India."

"The only two things I brought back with me from India: Camp Coffee and malaria."

"I'm not sure which is worse," Hyde said, smiling. The smile faded. "Is that all you brought back. Do you ever think about it, Allan?" he asked. "I mean, what we did in India?"

"No." Lawson answered with the vehemence of the self-lie. "I do not. I find it's best not to dwell on such things. What had to be done had to be done. And anyway, we were different people out there. It was a different world and we were different men to those we are here."

"Does that excuse us?" asked Hyde.

"I seek no excuse. We did our duty. We were soldiers." Lawson sighed again. "And, my friend, it does not benefit us to dwell on the matter."

"I can't help dwelling on it," said Hyde, gloomily. "I discovered a part of me out there I wish had remained unfound. Some of what we did . . . I can't seem to get it out of my head."

"You were a good soldier, Edward. A good officer. You did what Queen and country demanded of you. Sometimes, well, I admit those demands were onerous. Unpleasant." Lawson drew a deep breath, forced a smile across his features, and slapped Hyde heartily on his heavy shoulder. "Let's talk about today, if yesterday troubles you. How is the battle against crime in this fair city?"

Hyde and Lawson talked inconsequentially for little more than a further half-hour, the castle commander promising to report if anyone recognized the face of the Hanged Man. Hyde was then escorted out by the same colour sergeant. When they reached the gatehouse, the sergeant held open the outer gate, and Hyde hesitated for a moment, causing the colour sergeant to frown slightly. Hyde gathered himself and smiled, thanking the soldier and stepping out onto the Castle Esplanade.

As he climbed into the hansom that awaited him, he reflected on the cause of his earlier hesitation: when the colour sergeant had held open the gate for him, Hyde had caught sight of a small dark mark on his wrist.

A tattoo he had seen before.

15

It was as if the universe entire was contained in that small bowl-shaped depression. The darkening sky above it seemed now an enclosing dome, coiled around them and streaked deep silk-blue and crimson. Standing there as the night huddled closer, Elspeth suddenly found it difficult to imagine any other world, any other place. Edinburgh, her family's store, her place in society became abstract, even absurd concepts. Everything around her seemed unreal, she felt herself unreal, yet it was all more credible, possessed more truth, than that absurd life she thought she had lived until now.

It was just as Frederic had promised: she was dreaming herself awake.

They were assembled in a semicircle facing the megalith. The Dark Man stood in screaming stone silence, mocking the flickering insignificance of their lives in the context of the millennia-long span of its vigil. Elspeth knew it had not been waiting for them: it waited for something beyond them, after them, greater than them, just as it had waited for a thousand unnoticed generations before.

She was cold beneath the flimsy scarlet fabric of her gown; she felt she should shiver, but something about the drink she had been given earlier in Crunnach House seemed to stretch and weaken the connections between her mind and her body. They had all taken the drink served up by Frederic's strange servant while they had still been in the house. It had been an odd, thick, viscous fluid with an unpleasant texture and flavour that was simultaneously musty and sweet.

There were thirteen of them.

All were dressed the same, man and woman, gowned in a single layer of scarlet satin, with no other clothes to protect them from the chill of the late-autumn evening. Only Frederic was distinguished from the others by his black gown and his silk eyepatch of the same colour. Elspeth had recoiled at the idea that her identity—and her involvement with Frederic and his beliefs—would be revealed to others. But then she had seen those assembled there and had recognized most: among them figures even more prominent in Edinburgh society than Elspeth herself, each with arguably much more to lose if their association with Frederic became public. It had shocked her to see so many establishment figures, the last people on earth she would have expected to be part of Frederic's dark cabal.

One face in particular was known to her. Its presence here, in this context, made no sense to her, but the effects of the bitter brew put working out its significance beyond her.

Through the fog of the drink's intoxication, she vaguely wondered if each of the assembled had donated the same small fortune as she had, or perhaps even more, to Frederic; and if each had been promised the same revelation, the great unfolding of truth. The drink's effect seemed to be to make thoughts slick and untenable and this one, too, slipped from her mind almost as soon as it had formed.

She was aware that all the assembled acolytes had taken the same drink from the servant and, with vague disinterest, she recognized in each of them the same detachment and disconnection from their bodies. Whoever they had been in the waking world, here they were other. Different. The shadow sides of each revealed.

Elspeth felt sick for a moment, but the nausea passed and she became aware that the night, the dark of the night, was filled with colour: hues and shades she had never before noticed. Something in her universe was changing, she realized, just as Frederic had promised.

She looked at her lover, yet felt he was not *there*; that there was no substance to him. In contrast, the *Feardorch*, the Dark Man standing stone, seemed the only thing of substance, of solidity. Her gaze was drawn to the menhir as if guided by a will other than her own. The stone seemed blacker, darker, sleeker than she had noticed before. As she gazed at it, she felt pulled towards it. She did not move, the stone did not move, yet Elspeth felt that part of her was drifting towards its darkness—the part separated from her body by the concoction she had imbibed. The Dark Man was graven all over with spirals and circles.

Impossibly, as she watched, she saw the patterns start to move: to ripple and writhe nauseatingly over the menhir's stone skin.

Her gaze was broken by something intervening between her and the stone. It took her a moment to make sense of the dark shape that obstructed her view, then she recognized Frederic. The strange, small servant, unlike the others dressed normally, stood mutely at his side, his expression as he looked at her again one of insolent recognition, holding out before him a large, thick volume, its leather binding worn and stained as if by great time.

Elspeth knew what it was: the treasure Frederic had obtained by unknown means. An ancient grimoire of histories and secrets and spells, written in Ogham script and hidden from the world for centuries. It was *Leabhar an t-Saoghail Eile*. The Book of the Otherworld. Their bible.

Her gaze shifted to Frederic. He was holding a large chalice, cradling its base with a white cloth. He took it from one to another of the acolytes, commanding them to drink, which they did. He came to Elspeth last, and she felt she was being singled out, as if there was an added significance to her turn.

"He waits in the Otherworld . . ." Frederic wiped the rim of the chalice and held it out to her. "The festival of Samhainn is close, ever closer. The year as measured by our ancestors ends and another is born. The veil between the worlds grows thin. He waits in the Otherworld, our dark lord . . . waits to be summoned into this world . . . waits to serve us and to be served by us. But first we must have knowledge of him. First we must have sight of him. Drink . . ."

Elspeth took the chalice and sipped the contents. It was the same as before but stronger, the unpleasant flavours more intense; this time the mustiness was truly bitter, the sweetness sickly. She hesitated after the first sip.

"Drink!" commanded Frederic, pushing the chalice once more to her lips. "Drink! *Deoch!*"

She drained the chalice and fought back the nausea it brought. Frederic Ballor smiled and took the empty vessel from her hands. "Soon," he said. "Soon you will be ready. Soon you will have the gift of true vision."

Elspeth swayed a little. The feeling that swelled up inside her was one of intoxication, but not drunkenness. Instead she felt she could see inside herself and there was nothing to see. She was as false, as devoid of real existence as everything else she had thought real beyond this bowl-shaped depression. Again her gaze was drawn to the Dark Man. The carvings writhed and rippled across it with increased vitality, as if its surface crawled with a thousand small serpents.

She looked up at the enclosing sky, which now also writhed with the same serpentine carvings, star-etched into its dark blue.

Frederic stood in front of her once more, placing his hands on her shoulders and forcing her focus onto his face. "Are you ready?" he asked. "Are you ready to look into the eye of Balor? *Balor Birugderc*— Balor of the Piercing Eye?"

She nodded.

Frederic Ballor lifted the eyepatch from his covered eye. "This is the window to the Otherworld, to the realm of the Formorii and the Tuatha Dé Danann, to where the Great Dark King of the Formorians scours the world with his gaze and leaves it burned. Behold! Behold!"

The assembled others murmured in drugged anticipation and watched Elspeth with dull intensity. All they could see was that she stood unchanged, staring into Frederic Ballor's dead eye. They would not even have noticed that all expression had been washed clean from her face. They certainly could not have seen nor heard that deep inside herself, insensible now to her surroundings, Elspeth Lockwood was screaming with inhuman terror.

She gazed into Ballor's exposed eye: an eye devoid of a white, simply a black glassy pupil filling it from lid to lid. She gazed into the eye and through it, for Ballor's eye served as a black-glazed window, beyond which she stared straight into the depths of some dread place.

There was no time, no moment, and she spent a second and an eternity watching the twisting torment of a billion souls. She saw great palaces of pain and endless plains of fire and torment. A great vortex of flame, like a burning whirlwind, scoured the desolate landscape and made a deafening, screeching, high-pitched noise. The flames of the vortex were mottled dark with numberless flecks, and she saw that each fleck was a human body, burning without being consumed, tormented without the relief of death. And the whirling, screeching, high-pitched noise was the sound of their endless shrieking.

Knowledge reached her through her own silent screaming, through her motionless struggling to be free from her fastening to the eye. She knew that this dread place she saw was not some Celtic Otherworld. It was true hell; a place, she now also knew, from which she would never escape.

At the heart of the hellscape stood a monstrous creature: a colossus and master towering above it all. This, she knew, was Balor of the Piercing Eye. The monster's body was flaked red and black like a burning ember, and it raked at its victims with the talons of its three-fingered hands. It turned its head in Elspeth's direction and she could see it had for a mouth a hideous hooked black beak; above the beak was a massive round, glossy black eye, exactly the same as Frederic's, except on a titanic scale. But this eye, in turn, was a window through which she penetrated another hellscape, similar but not identical to the first, in which other countless souls were tortured. At the heart of this scene too stood a giant, monocular beaked demon, and through its eye she saw yet another level, and another, and another . . .

And somewhere in this eternity of hells, Elspeth Lockwood lost every last shred of her sanity.

Part Two

A TIME OF VISIONS

16

The shadow awoke.

It awoke because its counterpart slept. It knew itself to be a shadow because it was a thing of coalesced darkness that took its form as the shade reflection of another; because it came from the deep blackness of unbeing and brought with it the night. A great dark shadow stirring to consciousness.

The shadow did not fully understand its own nature—how it could be a mind complete yet was forced to share the face and body, to speak with the same voice, of that other: the weak one.

Unlike its counterpart, it knew itself to possess memories beyond the span of the life that held it captive. It knew part of itself to be timeless, immortal, condemned in the darkness to dream the dreams of its ancestors; causing the vast, dark ocean of its memory to roil with the remembrances of the generations before it.

But now, the dreamer was awake.

The main challenge, it knew, was to navigate the days and the world as that other, to concern itself with the dull mediocrity of that other's existence. It knew that it would be easy to arouse suspicion, but if it were exposed, uncovered, then they would ascribe its existence to something else.

If it were discovered, they would say it was a madness hidden inside the mind, a mental aberration, and the body that hosted it would be confined in some asylum. So, the shadow navigated the world with care and pretended to be that other.

There was already one who called it insanity: a man blind to his own vanity and ambition; a professional inquisitor who had coaxed it out of hiding, who had tricked it into coming to the surface, into confiding in him; who had bade it reveal its true nature.

The shadow had explained that, while trapped in the darkness of the mind it shared, it had unravelled the tight-coiled memories of all those who had preceded it. It had told its interrogator how it carried the memories of its people since the earliest days, and how the burden of those remembrances weighed so heavily. It explained how its coming into being was the anamnesis of an entire race since its beginnings in Scythia, since the traversing of desert and mountain; since the crossing into Spain and the centuries spent among the Celtiberians; since the invasion of Ireland and the conquest of the mighty Fir Bolg. It had told its inquisitor of memories of crossing into the land of the Picts and Britons and Angles, all of whom too would yield to the might of its people, and that land would come to bear its people's name.

The Scots.

It remembered. It remembered it all.

And among these remembrances, dense and tight bound in its recall, there had been the bitterest memory of all: of how the Scots had come to betray their ancestors; how they had forgotten the glory and power of their blood.

It had explained how it would now use the fire of pain and death to remind them.

This one man who knew where the shadow lay hidden had listened, had nodded, had written notes. He had denied the truth of its nature and had talked of delusion, of a personality in fragments, of a fractured mind to be healed. Of a plural to be made singular. He had given medicines that the shadow knew would be poison to it and strengthen its host's will to overcome it.

The shadow had been weak then, its counterpart stronger. It had let the meddler live with his knowledge of the shadow's existence. But now it was stronger. Now it must silence him before he told others.

Its coming into the light was always brief, so it knew it must use its wakefulness well. It planned and devised and schemed.

It was ready to kill—kill again—and it rejoiced at the idea of it, thrilled at the joy of watching another die with that strange, uncomprehending, beseeching expression on their face. It was at that point of life-taking that the shadow felt its power, knew its true nature. It was then that it gained strength. Through killing it would eventually hold permanent sway over this form.

And now, it stepped once more from the darkness and into the light.

This world seemed hard-etched dark and bright. The city was grey, the sky bleach white, and the shadow was filled with contempt for this place, for the people who lived in it, and it longed to colour the grey city with their bright red blood.

They were all pathetic, and as it walked the streets, the truth of its shadow nature hidden, it had to resist the temptation to laugh out loud, laugh in their faces, and mock them for their mundanity, for their stupidity, for their blindness to its true nature. For their treachery.

It would bring them death; would bring them bright-dark fears and make them bow before it.

But first it had to gather more strength, take more control, so that it was the shadow, and not the host, who was awake the longer, who steered the course of this shared life. One day, it knew, it would be all that was left; it would be in sole command of this form. No longer the shadow of the other, but the caster of shadows.

Until then, it had to protect itself.

It must kill the one who knew of its existence; who already feared it and might tell the world not of its being, but of its hiding place. It intended the world to know and fear its being—but no one must know where it hid, the identity of its host.

So, with the cold, sharp edge of its intellect, the shadow schemed and planned. Its host bore a face and form well known in the city, so it disguised itself as well as it could and went to Leith. It was there, in Edinburgh's grubby, chaotic port, that it had set its lair in a squalid tenement.

It was growing dark when it reached the tenement and climbed to the top-floor room. Inside, there was nothing of human habitation: no bed, no chair, no comfort. The only furniture was the single plant stand that stood in the centre of the room, bearing upon it the dark fruit of the shadow's labour, which filled the attic with the sweet odour of putrefaction.

The faltering light outside was dimmed even more by the grimed glass of the naked windows, and the shadow took one of the cathedral candles from the tray by the stairs and lit it, placing it on the floor. It prised up a stained floorboard, reached into the rat-scurrying void and pulled out a leather bundle, fastened with two buckled straps. With almost religious ceremony, it laid the bundle on the floor, unfastened the straps, unwrapped and stretched out the leather pouch across the wooden boards.

It thrilled at their beauty: its tools. Even in the dim light they shone sharp and eager. They were three: the sacred number of Celtic faith, the number of faces of the Morrígan. Three blades, keen and sharp. The shortest was a *sgian-dubh*, the longest of the three was the Highland battle dirk. It selected the centrepiece, the mattucashlass, the hidden weapon of the Gaels: double-edged, ten inches in length, designed to be hidden in sleeve or shirt. Its edges were honed to razor sharpness and it carried enough weight to bite through skin, muscle and sinew to bone. This, the mattucashlass, the *biodag-achlais*, would sever and silence the tongue that denied the shadow's nature; that would speak out against it.

Soon.

17

The morning of the next day did not start well for Hyde. Having spent the previous evening poring over volumes on Celtic mythology, both his own and those Dempster had brought from the library, his sleep had burned with such strange dreams, but he was unsure if they had been ignited by a seizure or the normal turmoil of a mind perturbed.

It was not the sleeping but the waking that troubled him more. He was woken by a noise: a noise that stirred him from sleep not with its volume, but with its quiet out-of-placeness. He lay still in the half-light for a moment, listening intently to make sure that it was a sound of the waking world.

The noise, so faint that he had to strain to hear it, was of breathing. Breathing that was not his own. The dying night lingered in the far corner of his bedroom, the dim pre-dawn light that seeped around the edges of his curtains not reaching that far and leaving it in darkness.

Hyde sat bolt upright with the realization that the sound came from that shadowed corner. From his bed he peered into it. There was something there. Something moving.

Again, the quiet sound of a small breath being taken.

He felt his heart hammering in his chest and held his own breath for a moment as he strained to listen.

Another breath. Small, quiet, shallow. He heard more movement from the corner and scanned the half-light for a weapon, anything that could be used against whatever creature lurked in the corner.

Then he saw it move.

Slowly, a figure unfolded from the shadows, as if taking form from their darkness. It was the girl again. The same girl: the same ragged clothes, soiled with the dust and mud of a shallow grave; the same reproachful look. She moved, she breathed, yet he knew that this was no living thing. The shadow-hewn apparition was both pathetic and baleful: hers was a sad horror, and Hyde knew she was a thing of death and darkness.

And he recognized her. Mary Paton, the murdered girl. The Bairn in the Witch's Cradle.

Pitifully small and fragile, she stepped towards him, and he smelt the odour of stale earth and fresh decay. She moved closer, still silent except for the slow, quiet sound of her breathing.

"You don't exist," said Hyde. "You are an illusion."

She stepped even closer. Her complexion was pallid, and Hyde could see a network of blue-black veins and capillaries spider their inky way across the parchment of her skin. She was so close now that her breath spilled onto his face, each exhalation chill and tainted with the odour of her body's corruption.

"You don't exist," he repeated. "You are an image projected from my mind."

"You have forgotten," she said, her voice small and high. "That night, you looked for the truth and you found the truth, but now you have forgotten it. You deny my murderer his name."

Hyde drew back from the apparition. He squeezed his eyes tight shut, clamped his hands over his ears and took a long, slow breath. With it came the sweet, sickly odour of death and the corruption of human flesh.

"You have to remember." The girl's voice rang in his skull, clear and unimpeded despite his efforts to block it out. "You must remember that which you have forgotten." The voice paused, then said breathily: "It is here."

Another sound reached Hyde. Faint, distant, unworldly. For an instant he was convinced it was the banshee wail he had heard the night of the Hanged Man, but then the sound changed, its tone and pitch shifting. He recognized the sound of a hound baying somewhere in the distance. He heard the closer noise of the girl taking a frightened gasp.

"It comes . . ." she said, her voice tight with fear. "It comes for me."

Hyde reopened his eyes; she was gone. No shadows, no sounds near or far. The bedroom was brighter, the corner unshadowed. Even the gloom had been a hallucination.

Hyde sighed: it troubled him greatly that the hallucinations were persisting so long after a nocturnal seizure, unless a second had lain hidden in the tumbling dreaming of the night before.

Or perhaps these hypnopompic mirages were the prelude to another, even more profound, seizure: the clouds gathering before a greater storm.

He felt frustration that Samuel Porteous had never been fully explicit in his diagnosis of the root cause of his strange symptoms. What hidden deformity of brain caused him to conjure up the reproachful ghost of a murdered child?

Edward Hyde rose from his bed. Before he dressed, he walked over to the corner where the apparition had taken shape and, cursing the illogic of his actions, made sure there was nothing lurking there still.

18

Having sent a messenger first, Hyde met again with Samuel Porteous, this time calling at his clinic at Craiglockhart Hydropathic Hospital. A nurse led him through whitewashed halls and along burnished linoleum floors. Despite the corridors and halls being open and spacious, there was something about the unyielding carbolic brightness of the place that reminded him of the white room at Calton Gaol.

Every now and then he would hear the sound of running water—the medium of physical and mental remedy at Craiglockhart—from rooms off the hall. The nurses were all dressed in pale blue blouses with starched white caps and aprons, and any patients Hyde caught sight of were gowned in white. These, he knew, were the alcoholics, the neurotics and the neurasthenics, whose main therapy was the hydropathic cure. Some would spend hours at a time immersed in water, others would be plunged into alternatingly hot and ice baths.

Hyde knew they had reached the lunatic wing when the brightness was broken by black-enamelled iron bars and gate, which the nurse unlocked with a set of keys she produced from her apron.

She led him into a large room that doubled as Samuel Porteous's office and consulting room. Porteous rose from behind a huge mahogany desk and came around to shake his friend's hand. Hyde was struck by the doctor's youthful handsomeness and the near flamboyance of his dress. To his eyes, Porteous looked more like a bohemian than a physician, and not for the first time, he found his manner a little effeminate. Porteous also, Hyde noticed, looked tired, and his usual ebullience seemed a little forced.

"Good to see you, Edward," said Porteous. "I got the feeling from your message that this is a professional visit." He turned to the nurse who had conducted Hyde to the office and asked her to bring some tea.

"More a personal motive concealed in a professional one, if I'm honest," said Hyde when the nurse was gone.

"You've had more trouble?" asked Porteous, his welcome yielding to a frown.

"I had a nocturnal seizure, but I thought myself quite recovered from it," said Hyde. "Nevertheless, I find that I suffer more persistent and . . ." he struggled for the right word, "*distinct* after-effects."

"Such as?"

"Visions. Hallucinations. I see things, Samuel, and people, who are not there. I have to be frank and say that were I not a man of reason and not given to such fancies, I would describe them as ghosts." Hyde shook his head in frustration. "Or, at other times, I see real people and mistake them for someone else, someone dead. I know I've had these before, but they have always been random and vague. There is a specificity about these latest episodes that troubles me."

"In what way specific?" asked Porteous, indicating that Hyde should sit.

"My ghost is that of a child, a little girl. Just occasionally and fleetingly, but it's the same little girl each time."

"Do you recognize this little girl?" asked Porteous.

Hyde sighed. "It's Mary Paton, the murdered girl from Gypsy Brae."

Porteous nodded gravely. "Oh, I see. The murder for which this man Morrison was hanged, about whose conviction you have reservations. The hallucinations are fleeting, you say . . . How long do they persist?"

"Moments. Never more than a few seconds. To start with they were no more than a passing impression. But her last appearance, just this morning, was more persistent. And she spoke, for the first time."

"Any other effects? Have you lost time again?"

"No, not lost time. Just what we have discussed before: déjà vu, feelings of unreality, disconnectedness . . . And, as I said, occasionally I mistake someone I see for someone other they cannot be: like when I caught sight of Hugh Morrison in the street only to realize it was a road worker."

"But no amnesia? No time you cannot account for your actions?"

"No, I told you." Hyde failed to keep his frustration from his voice. It was not the first time that he had noticed Porteous seemed to disregard his other symptoms and focus on the lacunae in Hyde's memory—as if that were where the psychiatrist's true interest lay.

"And you have been taking the new prescription I gave you?"

"Yes . . . but sometimes I feel it makes things worse, the lethargy, particularly. As if my mind is clouded, foggy. And these waking hallucinations plague me more often than before."

"All right, I will adjust the dosages again. But try not to worry too much about the hallucinations. I suspect they are more to do with your state of mind than the medication. You have been under considerable stress lately, and both the hallucinations you've described are related to a matter that has weighed heavily on your mind for some time. Seeing the girl is perhaps merely the fulfilment of a wish that she still lived."

"But if I am so concerned about the wrongful hanging of Hugh Morrison, then why is it not his spectre who visits and talks to me?"

"That I cannot answer, Edward." Porteous's tone was of weary indulgence and it annoyed Hyde more. "But try to rest more. If your nights are disturbed, try to catch up on your sleep during the day."

"What would be changed in the prescription?" asked Hyde.

Porteous smiled, again indulgently. "Nothing significant, Edward. Just a recalibration of the components to see if we can increase the efficacy of the compound."

"I'm sorry, Samuel, but I see no efficacy. In fact, I would swear that my symptoms have worsened since I've been medicated. I wondered what you thought about me ceasing the compound—perhaps just keeping the pills I take when I feel a seizure coming on."

"You must not!" Porteous's vehemence took Hyde aback. "To stop the medication suddenly could have very serious repercussions."

"Such as what?"

"You could seriously exacerbate your symptoms. Your nocturnal seizures may spill out into your waking life."

"But that's exactly what is happening now. These . . . these *visions* I'm having. The lost time. I have no real sense of getting better; quite the reverse."

Porteous stood up. "If you have no faith in my care, then I suggest you consult another physician." His voice was raised now, his face flushed. For the first time Hyde saw the traces of age in his otherwise youthful face. "Although I doubt you will find another who would so willingly conceal your condition from official record."

"What is wrong with you, Samuel?" Hyde too rose to his feet. "All I'm asking is that you consider the possibility that the combination you have prescribed is having an adverse effect. Surely that is not unknown in medical science?"

"If there were any risk, then I would not prescribe as I have. I suggest you rely on my knowledge of medicine and not your uninformed theories."

"You may be right that my theories are uninformed. That was indeed another matter I wanted to discuss with you. Why have you never given me a clearly explicatory diagnosis of my condition?"

"What?" Porteous shook his head irritatedly. "Of course I have. Repeatedly. You have a form of epilepsy."

"That's not what I mean. I mean what is the root cause of my epilepsy, if that is what it is."

"So now you call my diagnosis into question?" The ember of Porteous's anger now blossomed into full flame.

"I just want to know what it is that is causing these effects. And why they are getting worse. Is that so much to ask?"

The door opened, and the nurse, carrying a tray laden with a tea service, started to come in, but halted in the door frame. Hyde realized that his voice had been raised and he was still standing, leaning on Porteous's desk in a posture that could have looked intimidating, aggressive.

Both men, seeing the nurse's uncertainty and guessing its cause, resumed their seats and their composure.

The nurse carried in the tray with the tea service laid out for them. She placed it on Porteous's desk. As she did so, she stared at Hyde. It was a scrutiny to which he had become accustomed, and he could read in her eyes that strange combination of repulsion, fear and physical attraction he seemed to inspire in women.

"Thank you," said Porteous, and smiled.

After she had left, he said, with regained calm, "I'm sorry I got heated, Edward. I would like to think you know I always have your best interests at heart." He sighed. "The truth is, I don't know what causes your symptoms—or at least specifically. And because of that, I have sought not to concern you. It could be—and this is the worst possible scenario—that you have a lesion in your brain, in the temporal lobe, that is growing and making your symptoms worse."

"A tumour?"

Porteous held up his hands in a halting gesture. "And this is exactly why I haven't wanted to speculate on the cause—it *could* be a tumour, it could be a venous anomaly, it could simply be a minor congenital deformity in a structure. We have no way of looking inside your brain without opening it up, which is infinitely more dangerous than trying to treat and manage the symptoms. I promise that is my only hesitation in ascribing these symptoms to a specific cause."

"So not a tumour, or not definitely . . ."

"Like I said," answered Porteous, "I cannot offer a definitive cause. If it were some kind of lesion, then it does not necessarily follow that it is growing or malignant. In any case, the vast majority of epilepsies are idiopathic—unique to the patient and not attributable to any discernible cause."

"Of course," said Hyde. "I quite understand. So you recommend I stick with the prescription?"

"I do."

The conversation turned to the effects of fly-agaric. Hyde explained what Cally Burr had told him about the significance of the autopsy report on the Hanged Man.

"I find it strange," said Hyde, "that others use artificial means to achieve the same condition of which I seek to be cured."

"I wouldn't describe it as being the same."

"No? It seems so to me. They actively seek to reach an otherworld, a different plane of being. A different reality. I actively seek to be released from it. My 'otherwhere,' as your colleague describes it, sounds pretty analogous with their otherworld."

Hyde left twenty minutes later. The rest of their meeting had been the awkwardly polite, inconsequential talk of two men attempting to recover friendship after disagreement.

After they finished their tea, Porteous walked Hyde through the secure gate, along the whitewashed, carbolic-sanitized corridors, and out through the hospital's main doors. The day had grown colder, and grey-white sheets of cloud hung like damp linen over the city, threatening rain.

As they stood on the steps, Hyde looked out across the expanse of the hospital grounds.

"You say it was Cally Burr who told you about the effect of fly-agaric?" asked Porteous.

"It was. She works in the pathology department with Dr. Bell and Dr. Conan Doyle. Do you know Dr. Burr?"

"I do indeed. To tell the truth, many of my younger colleagues are smitten by her. She is quite the beauty."

"I suppose."

"Oh, come, Edward, don't tell me you haven't noticed!" Porteous scoffed.

"I have noticed," said Hyde. "But my interest in Dr. Burr is professional. She has a powerful intellect and keen insight."

Porteous's handsome face broke into a wide grin for which Hyde did not care. "I do believe you are smitten yourself, my dear Edward!"

"As I say, my interest in Dr. Burr is purely professional," Hyde protested, but felt the heat of a flush in his cheeks.

As Hyde walked out through the grounds of the hospital, there were still so many questions left unanswered. One had been comprehensively resolved for him, however; something of which he was now certain.

Samuel Porteous had lied to him.

Porteous may have had the advantage of a medical education and career, but Hyde had another skill: the policeman's ability to catch the lie.

Sometimes the lie stood alone, a false answer to a specific question; other times it would lurk, half hidden, behind an entire conversation: a strategy of general distortion rather than a specific falsehood. It had been the latter Hyde had detected in Porteous: the intent to mislead about the nature and purpose of his treatment.

Hyde had not been entirely truthful himself: he had not told Porteous that he had already ceased taking his prescription.

Consumed by thought, he walked through the hospital grounds and the main gates to the omnibus stop on the main thoroughfare. As he stood at the kerb's edge, he reached into his pocket and took out a small dark-blue glass bottle and the paper packet that contained the pills.

As approaching hoof-falls heralded the arrival of the omnibus, Hyde dropped the bottle and the packet into the gutter storm drain at his feet.

19

Night had already cast its shadow over the port by the time he arrived.

According to the leaflet Captain Hyde had given him, the meeting was to be held in Leith: a clustered place of warehouses, distilleries, soapworks, glassworks, woollen mills and ship chandlers, all huddled close and dark around where the port's harbour, piers and jetties cut the stone geometries of commerce into the broad waters of the Forth. It was here that the Water of Leith finally spilled out into the wide estuary, itself already mingling with the brackish chill of the North Sea.

Leith was the basest of places, yet the whole world was here to see, smell and hear. Its warehouses were filled with the vibrant colours woven into lush carpets and tapestries from Anatolia, Afghanistan and Persia. Its air was tinged with the aromas of tobacco and tea leaves, still moist and fragrant from the humid climates of the West Indies and the highlands of Assam and Nilgiri. Its docks and boarding houses rang with a cacophony of curses and songs in Cape Dutch, Bengali, German, Hindi, Danish, Punjabi, Urdu, and French.

Leith was Edinburgh's port and important to the commercial life of the nation's capital. So important that it had its own heavily fortified citadel and garrison—a strategy inspired when, a century before during the Revolutionary War, the Kirkcudbrightshire-born, Scotsman-turned-American naval adventurer John Paul Jones had sailed three warships into the Forth on a mission to visit the land of his birth and seize the port of Leith. It had been the intemperate humours of the Scottish climate, and not the nine-gun battery hastily brought in as defence, that had deflected Jones's advances. The lesson had been learned, however, and a heavily garrisoned fort had been built at great haste and enormous expense to replace the old Cromwellian citadel.

Probationer Detective Constable Iain Pollock, as all others with any acquaintance of Leith, knew it now to be a low place of ale houses and bordellos serving the merchant sailors and stevedores from the docks, the soldiers from the fort, and the occasional fisherman from Newhaven. It was an environment where violence hung like mine dust in the air, waiting for a spark to bring it to combustion. This was a place where arguments quickly turned deadly, where a throat could be cut for a few pennies, where a human being could be purchased for all forms of depravity.

Although directly connected to the north-east extremity of Edinburgh, Leith was a burgh in its own right and had its own police force and technically lay beyond the jurisdiction of the City of Edinburgh Police. That was reason enough for a young Edinburgh plainclothesman to feel ill at ease in the port, but the truth was any policeman, whatever his origin or jurisdiction, in uniform or civilian clothes, would have good reason to be cautious in Leith. Worst of all would be to be mistaken for an exciseman from the Customs House, spying on the traffic of smugglers.

Great care, Pollock knew, had to be taken.

The address of the meeting place had been given on the leaflet but was nonetheless difficult to find. It turned out to be a small wooden hall near the railyards. Faded lettering arcing above the entrance and only just visible in the light of the lantern set above the door informed that the shabby building had once been in the service of the old *Edinburgh, Leith and Newhaven Railway Limited*. The building's long retirement had not been kind to it and its oaken flanks were rot-gapped in places, and the windows soot-stained dark.

Iain Pollock had arrived early, having been instructed by Captain Hyde to take the train from Waverley to Leith Central with enough time for him to find an observation point from which to reconnoitre the hall and take note of any arrivals.

This area of Leith was poorly lit and afforded him many opportunities of concealment nearby. Conversely, other than the lantern immediately above the hall's entrance, there was insufficient illumination for him to make out any details of those attending the convocation. All he could see from his initial vantage point was that a female figure stood in the pool of light at the entrance, greeting each new arrival and handing something to them as they entered the hall. He estimated five people had arrived while he watched, but it was impossible to see them clearly. He knew he needed to get closer, and moved from one shadow to another. He was nearer now, and when some new arrivals appeared, he stepped back into the dark between two warehouse buildings.

As he did so, a figure emerged from the shadows behind him and gave him a start. The wraith which emerged was dreadfully pale in the dim lamplight, a badly applied smudge of rouge, like smeared blood, on each cheek, another a gash across her lips. Her large eyes sat empty and blank in the sunken sockets and the rouged cheeks were gaunt. The importuning ghost was, Pollock estimated, no more than fifteen and opened her bodice jacket to reveal breasts as pale and undernourished as her face. The entire soliciting was done silently and joylessly, and when Pollock, regaining himself, dismissed her with an abrupt shake of his head, the wraith-prostitute shrank back, dissolving again into the shadows from which she had taken form.

Leith, Pollock realized, was a place of dark transaction in all its forms.

He moved on to the next warehouse corner, the next shadow, closer still to the shabby hall. He waited until there were no more arrivals, and cursed silently when he contemplated delivering such meagre intelligence to Captain Hyde.

He hesitated for a moment, then decided the only course open to him was to gain personal admittance to the hall. It was in direct contradiction to Hyde's instructions, but he could see no other way of gaining anything worthy of report.

Taking a deep breath, Probationer Detective Constable Iain Pollock strode with purpose towards the pool of light that illuminated the hall's doorway and the female figure standing in it.

20

Elspeth Lockwood rose early and prepared for the day. Her father, who always departed for the store before dawn had broken, had arranged for her to meet later that morning with the managers of each department, and she was determined to make a good impression on both parent and staff.

It was, she realized, the first step in her father's acknowledgement that Elspeth was, after all, to be heir to the family business. With no marriage prospect immediately presenting itself, James Lockwood had been forced to accept that it would be Elspeth's that would eventually be the sole hand on the tiller of the family's commercial destiny.

Her maid, a small, dark Irish immigrant called Deirdre, helped her dress, having laid out the dark navy skirt and jacket and the cream chenille blouse for which Elspeth had asked. Her chambers were bright, with high Georgian windows flooding the rooms with light, capturing bright motes suspended in shafts of morning sun.

Elspeth comported herself with a quiet grace and ease, and to any observer, of which there were none, the scene would have appeared an unremarkable one: the maiden daughter of a typical upper-middle-class household preparing for her day. Inside, however, her mind was consumed by a roiling, convulsing torment. Second by second she struggled to keep her emotions, her terror, under control. She must prevail, she told herself. Today of all days, she must prevail.

It had been so since the night at Crunnach House.

In a life so deprived of colour and excitement, Elspeth Lockwood had sunk herself into the hedonism and abandon of her relationship with Frederic Ballor. It had, she had known all along, been a charade: an excuse to cast off—if only temporarily and secretly—the prohibitions enforced by her gender, and the mores imposed by her class, and surrender to lasciviousness and sexual adventure. So much of what Frederic had taught her was liberating, exciting, vitalizing; much of it—the politicized pan-Celtism, the arcane pseudo-philosophies and religiosity—had, she had thought all along, been ridiculous. The rituals, the paganism, the whole thing with the *Leabhar an t-Saoghail Eile*, the supposedly forbidden Book of the Otherworld, had been preposterous.

But then she had seen it for herself: the otherworld Frederic had promised. Except it had not taken the form he had said it would. Elspeth had looked deep into that dread place and had seen another reality, another, horrific truth.

And now she could not get it out of her mind. It was as if the door to that world had not been properly closed and parts of it had followed her into this.

Every now and then, in the solid architecture of the real world, something of that other place would take sudden and unbidden shape. Only ever for a second—for less than a second—but enough to distract her from speech and action, to cause her to stumble; to cause a lightning bolt of terror to course through her.

She would see things. The pattern on the wallpaper would mutate and contort, taking fleeting form as serpents writhing across the walls, as had the petroglyphs on the Dark Man standing stone. A reflection of a lamp or of the evening sun, caught in a window's glazing or a wine glass's crystal, would for an instant burn a malevolent crimson, as if that terrible monocular monster's eye had been reflected. Occasionally she would start when, in broad daylight, a shadow cast by the sun would suddenly darken, become denser, hint at independent motion, as if taking solid and organic form and preparing to reach out and drag her into the darkness.

All of these things would last but the briefest moment, fleeting impressions that lingered not long enough to be captured fully by her mind. Yet they were enough to torture her, deep tremors to shake the solidity of her waking world.

Elspeth Lockwood found herself faced with two possibilities: the first that there really was such a thing as the Otherworld, a place, a universe that existed in dark parallel to this one, and she had opened up some kind of portal to it; the second was, quite simply, that she was going mad—that the drug with which she had been plied had distorted the functioning of her mind. Of the two, the former frightened her more, because there was no remediation, no escape from it. The latter was something for which she could seek help, discreetly.

She drew a deep breath, causing her maid to pause in her dressing of her mistress.

Elspeth smiled. "My hat, Deirdre. I think I shall walk to the store today . . ."

As she made her way through the New Town, Elspeth welcomed the chill breeze that cold-etched the regulated geometry of its streets and squares. The sky was clear and the late-autumn sun hung bright but warmthless. The chill brightness reassured her. Cold was her season, her climate, her nature. She knew hers was a soul in winter; her personality was *cauldrife*, as they said in Scots. She had seen Frederic as her liberator from that eternal chill. But instead of warmth, he had brought fire.

She crossed George Street, the wind tugging at her, encouraged by the boulevard's ambitious breadth. Once on the decline of Castle Street, she looked down towards Princes Street and its gardens; beyond them, the castle and its rock thrust upward into the pale blue silk of the sky, dominating the scene. Another reassurance of Edinburgh's solidity.

Then something changed.

Elspeth stopped suddenly, robbed of her breath. It seemed that everything around her had come to a complete halt, that she herself was frozen, mid step. In that instant the sky above the castle darkened suddenly and unnaturally, taking on alien, nauseating hues of dark vermillion, copper and crimson. Black columns sprang upwards, twirling and twisting, speckled as if with soot, and once more she heard the same screeching, whining sound, sharp and shrill, that she had heard when she had looked through Frederic's dead eye into the hell beyond.

It rose up from behind the castle, a massive dark unfolding filling the tortured sky. She saw him there, for a second and for an eternity: his skin blistered and bubbling as if burning, the monstrous single eye glaring red above the hooked-beak mouth. Balor. The one-eyed demon king.

Edinburgh lost all sense of solidity and looked vulnerable and fragile beneath the titan's malevolent gaze. Elspeth knew that in an instant she, and all around her, would be excoriated by that eye—her skin seared and flayed and her undying flesh bubbling and blistering as she was swept up into the endless spiralling of an ever-burning whirlwind.

As quickly as it had appeared, the vision vanished. She had not had the chance to scream, nor to call out, before it was gone. The impression had lasted a time too small to be measurable, the space between steps, the silence between breaths, so fleeting that she could have doubted she had seen it at all—that it had been a false impression created by a passing cloud. Yet the sky was cloudless, and despite its evanescence, that dread image had burned every detail vivid and clear in Elspeth's mind.

She staggered slightly and pressed a gloved hand to the railings of one of the buildings to steady herself. A passer-by frowned his concern and took a step towards her, but she froze him with a glare of her own and he walked on.

She straightened herself and looked up at the castle. All was normal. All was as it had been. No one around her seemed perturbed by the frightening vision of a demon filling the sky above castle and city.

"I am going mad," she said to herself. "I am losing my sanity."

Elspeth Lockwood took a moment to gather herself, to quieten the pounding in her chest and ears, to slow her breathing. She steeled herself to stride purposefully down Castle Street towards Princes Street and Lockwood's store.

When she began walking, however, she found her steps determined her to a different destination.

21

Every official meeting Hyde had conducted with Chief Constable Rintoul had taken place in the latter's office within the Parliament Square headquarters. He was therefore taken aback when Rintoul arrived unannounced at the Torphichen Place stationhouse.

When he did arrive, the chief constable was not alone. His companion was in late middle age, of average height and unexceptional looking save for his clothes, which were of the highest quality. He was also someone Hyde instantly recognized: James Lockwood, owner of Lockwood's department store on Princes Street.

"I'm sorry to call by unannounced," said Rintoul, but Hyde could tell the apology was a formality. "And I know that you have a great deal to keep you occupied at the moment, but I fear this is a matter of some urgency."

"That it most certainly is," interrupted Lockwood, clearly irritated by Rintoul's diplomacy. "My daughter has gone missing, with no trace of her whereabouts."

"Please, gentlemen . . ." said Hyde, gesturing to the chairs opposite, "please take a seat."

They both did as he suggested, and it gave him a moment to study Lockwood. He mentally excused the older man's brusqueness: it was clear Lockwood was deeply troubled, and his face bore the electric weariness of a man deprived sleep through great worry.

"When did your daughter go missing, Mr. Lockwood?" Hyde asked, opening his notebook and setting it on the desk before him.

"Yesterday morning. She was due to attend a management meeting at the store, but failed to turn up. Her maid, Deirdre, was the last to see her."

"Did the maid notice anything different about your daughter's demeanour, her mood?"

"Nothing out of the ordinary, other than Elspeth seemed keen to walk to the store."

"So she left home intending to attend this meeting at Lockwood's?"

"I had arranged it. Since the death of my only son, it is Elspeth who will eventually step into my shoes and take over the running of the family business. She was most keen to attend the meeting—excited, almost. It makes no sense that she should disappear into thin air betwixt home and store."

Hyde wrote some details into his notebook. "This was yesterday morning, you say?"

"I did, yes." The tired, agitated impatience was creeping back into Lockwood's tone.

"Why, then," asked Hyde, "have you only come to us today, rather than yesterday?"

Lockwood sighed. "Because Elspeth is and always has been strong-willed. Independent-minded to the point of stubbornness. It means she does not always inform me of her movements. I was hoping she would return with some explanation for her failure to attend the meeting. You see, to start with I could not be sure that her disappearance was unwilling."

"Oh? Why so?"

"Elspeth does not know this, but I am aware of some of the company she has been keeping. Unsavoury company."

Hyde set his pen down and looked at Lockwood directly. "What kind of unsavoury company?"

"Frederic Ballor."

"The occultist?"

"The charlatan." Lockwood almost spat the word out. "My daughter has been meeting with Ballor in secret."

"If she has been meeting him in secret," asked Hyde, "then how did you come to find out about it?"

"As I said, Elspeth is strong-willed and independent, but she is also a young gentlewoman and possesses the vulnerabilities and sensitivities of her gender. She was very close to her brother, and he to her, right up until his death. In many ways, he was much more fragile than she and Elspeth was very protective of him. When he died, it affected her terribly. She had a sort of nervous breakdown. I did all I could to help her through that time—sought treatment for her, paid for her to see a specialist and even sent her abroad for a while. When she came back, however, she started to consult spiritualists, go to séances, that kind of thing. As you may know, there is a strange fashion for that sort of occult nonsense these days. Although her involvement in that world made me uneasy, I indulged her, turned a blind eye to it in the hope she would find some kind of peace through it."

"But that was how she met Ballor . . ." Hyde anticipated.

"Ballor had . . . well, it was like a salon in the house he rented in the West End. He had all kind of bohemian types hanging around the place and he funded his degenerate lifestyle through these occultist gatherings. I knew Elspeth had attended a couple of his séances. See-ing spiritualists was one thing, but I could not tolerate her comporting with a deviant like Ballor—I told her to sever contact with the man, that he was a scoundrel and a fraud and that her reputation could be ruined by association."

"But she did not give him up?" asked Rintoul.

"She promised me she had, and I believed she did, for a while. Then the scandal about Ballor's activities broke and he left Edinburgh. I thought that was an end to the matter, but Elspeth became secretive— or more secretive than normal. I found out—and it's best not to discuss the means—that she had paid out near on six hundred pounds from her personal account, so I hired this . . . *gentleman*, a kind of private policeman, an investigator, to find out what she was up to, to follow her and see where she went."

"Who was this gentleman you employed?"

"His name is Donald Farquharson. He was a non-commissioned officer in the army and then became store detective at Lockwood's."

"Is he still in your employ? Can he not tell you where she has gone?"

"He left the store a year ago to go out on his own. He deals with all kinds of unsavoury business, I believe. But he remains a consultant to Lockwood's. He is a reliable and diligent man, good at his job."

"Have you heard of him, Edward?" asked Rintoul. Hyde shook his head.

"When I got his report, about two weeks ago," continued Lock-wood, "I paid and dismissed him, unfortunately. I intended to con-front Elspeth with the particulars of the report after the meeting at the store—to place before her a stark choice: a future as head of the family business, or one of scandal, disgrace and dependency on an allowance. Of course, I never got the chance."

"May I see this report?" asked Hyde.

"The gist of it is that Ballor has removed himself to some dilapidated pile outside the city. Farquharson expressed some real unease about the man and his circle. He has some kind of mute servant whom Farquharson described as a Cagot, whatever that is. But I'll have a copy sent over to you. In the meantime, what do you intend to do?"

Rintoul's expression suggested it was Hyde's decision.

"I'll put a man on it right away," Hyde said at last. "I have this murder case which is most pressing, but I will see your man Farquharson and find out what I can from him. Then I'll visit Ballor personally."

"I'll come with you," said Lockwood.

Hyde smiled and shook his head. "You have placed this in our hands, Mr. Lockwood. It is a police matter now. We shall deal with it."

22

After the chief constable and James Lockwood had left his office, Hyde sent for Iain Pollock. The young constable looked uneasy as he stood before his superior's desk, as if giving careful thought to how he should frame his report.

"What is the matter, Iain?" asked Hyde.

"Sir?"

"I sense you have something to tell me that you don't think I am going to like, so spit it out."

Pollock drew a breath. "I was unable to secure a vantage point from which I could get a clear view of those attending the Cobb Mackendrick meeting, sir."

"So you have nothing to report?" asked Hyde.

Again the young constable hesitated. "I wouldn't say that, sir. Because I could not find a suitable observation point, I was forced to enter the meeting. I'm sorry, sir, I know you instructed me to keep my distance, but I would have nothing to report otherwise."

"But you do now?"

Pollock took out his notebook and read from his notes. Cobb Mackendrick had appeared as advertised in the leaflet; there had been some twenty-five people in the hall, of the broadest range of social class and background—unusually so. Mackendrick's address had concerned the Declaration of Arbroath, the origins of the Scottish race, the Act of Union being "Scotland sold for English gold"; the oath in the Declaration that England would never hold sway over Scotland as long as even as few as a hundred Scots remain to resist.

He paused and took a pamphlet from his jacket pocket and handed it to Hyde.

"These were handed to each attendee."

Hyde examined the pamphlet. The title read:

THE DECLARATION OF ARBROATH:
AN OATH FORSWORN
Or how the Scottish Nation sold its Sovran Soul for
the Stolen Baubles of Empire

"These were handed out to everyone, you say?" asked Hyde.

"There was a young woman at the door—a gentlewoman, and very striking in appearance—and she handed one to all who arrived."

Hyde nodded. "Sit, Iain," he said, and set about reading the tract.

We Scots as a people are become as travellers stricken with amnesia: bereft of recollection whence and whither we travel. Our origin and the destination we promised ourselves are forgotten. We misremember who we are, in ignorance denying the ancient verity of our race.

We have entered into a devil's compact with another nation and have sold our true soul for an invented and fallacious identity. We have been bought with the baubles of Empire, stolen from lands and peoples unskilled, unequipped and unprepared to defend against technologies and machineries of war they do not themselves possess.

The amnesia of the Scottish race has made us collaborators not only in this global plunder, but in the surrender and subsumption of our very own identity. The dominion to which we are now subject was not achieved through invasion of our land nor subjugation or dispossession of our peoples, but through deed and contract delivered by our own hand. These instruments, however, remain adventitious; the Acts of Union supervenient. Only one document remains the true native expression of the Scottish nation, our statement of liberty and sovereignty as a land and a people: the Declaration of Arbroath.

For those of you who need reminding, it states:

We know from the ancients we find that among other famous nations our own, the Scots, has been graced with widespread renown. It journeyed from Greater Scythia by way of the Tyrrhe-

nian Sea and the Pillars of Hercules, and dwelt for a long course of time in Spain among the most savage peoples, but nowhere could it be subdued by any people, however barbarous. Thence it came, twelve hundred years after the people of Israel crossed the Red Sea, to its home in the west where it still lives today. The Britons it first drove out, the Picts it utterly destroyed, and, even though very often assailed by the Norwegians, the Danes and the English, it took possession of that home with many victories and untold efforts; and, as the histories of old time bear witness, they have held it free of all servitude ever since.

Yet now, in this new age, we have abandoned this history, abjured these pledges to ourselves. We have voluntarily surrendered our liberty and embraced the servitude of which we were so proud to be free. And, most of all, we have abandoned the sovran pledge of the Declaration:

As long as a hundred of us remain alive, never will we on any conditions be subjected to the lordship of the English. It is in truth not for glory, nor riches, nor honours that we are fighting, but for freedom alone, which no honest man gives up but with life itself.

"Interesting," said Hyde, setting the pamphlet down on his desk. "What of the man himself: did he make much of an impression on you, Constable?"

"Truthfully, Mackendrick makes a considerable impression," said Pollock. "He is physically imposing and a very powerful speaker. One might also say he possesses a magnetic personality. But when one takes away all of that, what he had to say was really rather predictable."

"I take it you were not swayed by his arguments?"

"I feel we—I mean the Scots—are something other than he described. Or at least we are now. I see no appetite here for home rule, as there is in Ireland, far less independence. The Empire he so despises has given Scotland much."

"Mmm," said Hyde. "He also has a point in that we have indeed *taken* much, and history may judge us through a similar lens. Tell me, is this as far as his rhetoric went? Was there talk of insurrection or disobedience to achieve nationalist aims?"

"None," said Pollock. "He merely called for supporters to spread the word, to convince through argument so that some foothold may be gained through the ballot box . . ."

Hyde again read something in Pollock's pause. "Go on, Iain, what is it you have to say?"

"It's just that I got the feeling there was something more going on than a gathering of political malcontents or fringe nationalists. The mix of people was strange. There was a man—a gentleman, clearly—whom I thought I recognized, but I couldn't place from where. The truth is that he had his back to me most of the time and I did not get a clear enough look at his face. I have some idea—I'm not sure why—that he may have been an artist or writer. And as I said, her manner and dress suggested the young woman at the door had a background of some rank. I really got the idea that the meeting would have followed another course had I not been present."

"You think they suspected you were a policeman?"

Pollock frowned thoughtfully. "Not necessarily; more that I was a strange face. I came with the announcement leaflet in hand, which was an open invitation to all to attend, but I just got the idea that if there had been no strangers, then a different evening would have unfolded. I could be wrong, and I have no rational basis for my feeling—more an instinct than anything."

"There is nothing wrong with an instinct, Constable Pollock. Anything else to report?"

"Yes, sir. What struck me most was that there were three men at the rear of the hall who seemed to pay little attention to Mackendrick's oratory, but who remained behind when the others left."

"Why did these men in particular attract your attention?"

"I don't know, sir. They looked . . . well, they looked *purposeful*, as if they were there for a specific reason. And they looked tough, dangerous."

"Criminal types?"

"Could be, but my feeling was more that they had a military background, I suppose. One of them had an ugly scar on his face, and it looked something more likely to have been picked up on a battlefield than in a barroom or back alley."

Hyde nodded, smiling. Pollock had exactly the instincts, and the penetrating observational skills, that he had guessed he might have. "And these three men remained behind?"

"They did," answered Pollock, "as did the well-dressed gentleman. I waited around the corner, out of sight, until they all left the hall. They exchanged a few words then went their separate ways: Mackendrick and the gentleman left together in one direction, the three men in another. I followed Mackendrick and the gentleman back to the harbour, where they took a cab, meaning I lost them."

"That cannot be helped," said Hyde.

Pollock smiled. "But I did wait at the harbour cab rank, thinking that it would be the hansom driver's usual station. It was. He returned some forty minutes later. I told him I was a police detective and asked where he had taken Mackendrick and the other man. I'm sorry, sir, I know there's a danger of alerting Mackendrick to our observation of him, but I thought it was worth the risk."

"And you got their destination?"

"A corner townhouse in Stockbridge. Or more exactly, the basement of the house. The cabbie told me that the other man had a key to the basement, but it wasn't as if he lived there. Just before he returned to Leith, the cabbie noticed a third gentleman let himself into the house through the basement with a key. It struck him as odd that they used the basement rather than the main street door."

"And you have the full address?"

"I have the street address, sir, but the cabbie told me he would be able to point out the specific building, should we so require. I have his details."

"Good. Write it up in your report when we get back."

"Get back, sir?"

"We're going for a trip out of town."

23

"What do you know of Frederic Ballor, sir?" asked Pollock. He and Hyde sat in the brougham carriage, glazed to the front and sides, allowing them to watch the cityscape beyond the windows open out and yield to countryside. It was raining, a thin mizzle that dulled the light and muted the colours of the Lothian landscape.

"As far as can be ascertained, he has no criminal record," answered Hyde. "But if his reputation is to be believed, that is merely a matter of good fortune, rather than compliance with the law. According to the reports supplied to James Lockwood by his private investigator, Ballor has been involved in several scandals, mainly sexual adventures dressed up in counterfeit mysticism. But there have been darker deeds associated with the name Frederic Ballor; suggestions of criminal activity. The rumour that concerns me most is that he is said to have been at one time involved in gun-running for the Republican Brotherhood. There again, there are so many tall tales circulating about the man, it's difficult to know which carry any credence."

Hyde was halted by the jolting of the carriage, a signal that they were now beyond the boundaries of smooth-cobbled Edinburgh.

"Our concern, however," he continued, once the carriage steadied itself to its course, "is more immediate and lies within our jurisdiction: that of Elspeth Lockwood's disappearance. The house in the West End that Ballor was eventually forced to quit seems to have been little more than a brothel, and the séances or mystic gatherings—or whatever he dressed them up as—were little more than orgies. There were some allegations of gross indecency and unnatural acts between individuals of the same gender. More than a whiff of larceny, too—a hint of blackmail being mixed up in the black magic. But never enough in the way of direct accusation or actual evidence to provoke police intervention. It was at that time, while Ballor was still in Edinburgh, that Elspeth Lockwood got involved with him."

"Do you think he really has had something to do—either directly or indirectly—with Miss Lockwood's disappearance?"

"That, Constable Pollock, is what I intend to find out . . ."

The drizzling rain had stopped but the clouds hung sullen and lumbering in the grey graceless sky. They were now out in open, empty countryside, unbroken by habitation other than the occasional cottage. The carriage stopped twice while the apologetic coachman checked his map.

"Don't worry, Mackinley," Hyde said through the glass to the coachman. "I believe our destination was specifically chosen by its occupant exactly because it is so hard to find."

The landscape around the carriage changed again: the occasional bristling of trees grew less frequent, the hedgerows more sparse, the aspect ever more cheerless. There was something austere, forbidding, bleak about the countryside here; and it was forsaken: they had passed through the tooth-stump ruins of a long-deserted hamlet, and the only other habitations were the now even more scattered cottages, low-walled and deep-roofed, most of which lay abandoned. Eventually, Mackinley called down to Hyde.

"We have it, sir . . ."

Through the brougham's windows, Hyde saw that they passed through long-gateless stone piers, crumbling and overgrown, on one of which was a grimy plaque etched with the name *Crunnach House.*

The tumbled, soot-stained ruins of a gatehouse lay like a black-boned skeleton just beyond the gate pillars. The lane became uneven, and Hyde and Pollock were jostled as the suspension was tested while the carriage jolted and jounced its way along the driveway.

A strange, powerful feeling came over Hyde as soon as they drew near to their destination. It was a feeling of deepening unreality and darkening threat, but he knew it was not a result of his condition nor the onset of an episode. There was no interiority to its source: Hyde knew it came from without—from the place in which they now found themselves—and not from within. Though not normally given to such fancies, his instincts told him that they drew close to some place of great evil.

The feeling intensified as the situation of Crunnach House and its grounds was revealed.

The track followed by the carriage had arced around the side of a larger hillock, atop of which stood a huge yew tree, twisted and gnarled as if arthritic. It imposed not just with its size and great age, but with the fact that it was the only tree of any note or substance within view.

Hyde tapped on the cabin's front glass and called to the driver. "Halt here a moment, please, Mackinley."

"What is it, sir?" asked Pollock.

"Come with me, Iain," said Hyde as he swung open the carriage door and dismounted. "I want to have a look . . ."

He climbed up the small hill until he reached the foot of the tree, Pollock following. They looked down and across the valley, which was more like a large dish-shaped depression, edged with a vaguely tumulose rim. Directly opposite the hill on which they stood, a large house sat on another hillock on the far edge of the valley.

The house was clearly of some considerable age, a newer stable block at its side. At a distance, Crunnach House—imposing and desolate-looking as it was—appeared to Hyde less remarkable than he had imagined. It was tall and narrow, unevenly conformed as if added to through the years. Its corners were rounded by towers, only one of which was capped with the witch's hat of a baronial-style conical roof; the others were topped with box garrets, consistent with the period of the house's original construction.

It was, however, something other than the house that drew Hyde's attention: centred in the valley's bowl-shaped depression, equidistant between his vantage point and Crunnach House, stood a dark monolith. He noted with unease that the standing stone seemed to be the centre point—as if the depression's edge, the house and the yew tree were all arranged around it, waiting attendance upon it.

"It's ancient," said Pollock. Hyde turned and saw the young policeman resting his gloved hand on the ridged and knotted bark of the tree's trunk, looking up into its branches.

"It looks like a dule tree," said Hyde, "and I suspect we may be standing upon a moot hill."

"A what, sir?" asked the constable.

"A dule tree is a tree that has stood in some special place for centuries, millennia, even. Usually alone like this, or separated from other trees by some natural happenstance, springing from some lost windborne seed finding elevated ground fertile enough only for a single rooting." Hyde moved around the tree, examining its branches. One stout limb reached out at right angles to the trunk.

"What are you looking for, sir?" asked Pollock.

Hyde sighed and gave a small laugh. "A coincidence, Iain, a coincidence. You see, *dule* means sorrow or grief—grief from the fact that a dule tree was most often a gallows tree. Men were hanged from them and left to dangle while they rotted."

"Judicial hangings?" asked Pollock.

Hyde nodded. "In times gone by—in the days before more civilized and balanced justice came to prevail—a moot hill was a place where matters were mooted, or debated. And often the matter of moot was that of a man's life. Even before that, dule trees were used in Celtic rituals. If some disaster befell a clan, they would gather in the shadows of a dule tree to lament it."

"You're thinking of the Hanged Man murder?" asked Pollock.

Hyde shrugged. "He was long hanged somewhere before he was taken to the Water of Leith—maybe somewhere like this." He looked up at the branches that reached crooked fingers into the sky, then shook his head dismissively. "I'm just clutching at straws." Hyde nodded to the waiting brougham and both men made their way back to it. He pointed down to the standing stone in the depression. "It would appear this has been a gathering place since before even this ancient yew first took root. Anyway, I think it is time we met the master of Crunnach."

The house was more forbidding closer up than it had been when viewed from across the depression. As the carriage had passed along the arcing drive, Hyde had been able to see the standing stone more clearly, and it did nothing to abate the feeling of dark malice that the location inspired.

Before Hyde and Pollock had reached Crunnach House's portico, the main door swung open and they were greeted by a servant. Pollock started slightly at the sight of the man. Although the servant was in no way similar to Hyde in build or appearance, Hyde recognized in Pollock's reaction the same instinctive recoiling his own presence seemed occasionally to inspire.

Clearly some kind of foreigner, the servant was abnormally short, yet powerfully built, with the strangest features. He did not speak, instead silently nodding his head in a half-bow, then standing to one side and gesturing that the two detectives should enter.

"We are here to see your master," said Hyde once they were in the reception hall. "Could you tell Mr. Ballor that Captain Hyde of the City of Edinburgh Police is here?"

The strange little man shook his head, then tapped his lips with his fingertips; he held out a hand and Hyde passed him an official visiting card.

"A mute?" asked Pollock, once the servant had left them alone.

"It would appear so." Hyde looked around the hall. If there was a grandness to it, it was a strangely austere grandness. The pale plasterwork was time-dulled and yellowed. An imposing oak staircase swept down from the upper floors, and the walls were dressed with oil paintings. There were no gas mantles for lighting; instead, wrought-iron candle sconces punctuated the walls at regular intervals and a large oil lamp sat centred on the oval reception table. In contrast to the time-worn feel of the house, a large, striking armoire of the Gothic style stood against one wall, its rich red-gold mahogany burnished to a sheen.

The paintings that dressed the walls were not what one would expect in such a setting yet were strangely accordant with it. Some were of dubious taste, nude studies of women, yet even these were skilfully executed and seemed to have something other than an erotic intent. All the compositions were dark and menacing, where naked human flesh stood out vividly vulnerable against backgrounds in crimson and black.

One painting in particular caught Hyde's eye: a naked man was suspended impossibly in the air, his back arched and his face contorted in an expression of horror. Malevolent figures, flying winglessly, reeled all around him, as if closing in on him. Each of the floating man's tormentors wore the long, conical *coroza*—like a stretched dunce's cap—of witches condemned by the Spanish Inquisition.

"My God," said Hyde, to himself as much as to Pollock. "It's a Goya . . ."

"Sadly not." A rich, cultured voice, tinged lightly with either a Highland or Irish accent, spoke behind them. Hyde and Pollock turned to see the servant had returned. At his side stood the man who had spoken, dressed in a black velvet smoking jacket over a blood-red waistcoat. He was a handsome man in his mid forties, but one eye was concealed behind a black satin eyepatch. Hyde was struck with the almost unnatural blackness of his hair.

"It is the work of a copyist," continued Frederic Ballor. "In fact the original, *The Flight of the Witches*, is much smaller; it was commissioned by the Duchess of Osuna originally and remains in that family's possession. I would not have expected an Edinburgh policeman to be familiar with Goya."

"And I would not have expected to come across such a skilful copy in a country house in the Lothians," responded Hyde.

Ballor smiled. "We are both men of surprises, it would seem. And I thank you for your compliment on behalf of my man, Gorka Salazar," Ballor gestured towards his servant, "for he is the copyist whose skills you so admire."

Surprised, Hyde nodded towards the servant, who returned with an impassive gaze.

"You see," continued Ballor, "Salazar is a Cagot—sometimes referred to in the Basque country, where he comes from, as an Agotak. As such he was a member of an untouchable caste, forbidden to live, worship, eat, socialize or work with any other than his own kind."

"Your manservant is a gypsy?" asked Hyde.

"No, not at all. The origin of the Cagots—and the origins of their exclusion from society—is very much a matter of debate, but they are certainly not related to gypsies. There are Cagots in northern Spain, western France and Brittany, but nowhere else in Europe and certainly not in the east—and in all of these places they are shunned, forbidden even to drink from the same fountains, or use the same doors to a church, as the rest of the population."

"For what reason?" asked Pollock. "Why are they so shunned?"

Ballor gave a small laugh. "It is prejudice for prejudice's sake, it would seem. No one can remember why it started, but it has been so for a thousand years. Some believe the Cagots descend from leper families; others claim they are descendants of marauding Visigoths, or conversely Saracens. Some even say their lineage is that of an autochthonous race of dwarves who once were the sole inhabitants of Europe before the arrival of the Celts—and as such they became part of our myths and legends." He looked at Salazar, whose strange features remained empty of expression. "Moreover, Cagots are forbidden from all but a few occupations, skilled artisans in stone, wood or iron. Imagine what it must be like to possess an artistic talent such as Salazar's and be forbidden its practice. That is why I am his liberator, patron and benefactor, as well as his employer."

"How did he come into your employ?" asked Pollock. "If he is a Spaniard?"

"Gorka Salazar is neither Spaniard nor Basque—he is of a people denied the right to call the land of their birth theirs. It is something with which I have particular sympathy. I spent some time in the Basque country—similar in so many ways to the Celtic lands—and it was there I encountered Gorka. Don't let his disability in speech fool you; his is a considerable intellect. He understands and can read Spanish, French and English perfectly."

Ballor paused and extended an arm to indicate the drawing room. "But I am sure you did not come all this way to discuss art or ethnology. Please, gentlemen, come take a seat and tell me how I can be of assistance."

24

Elspeth Lockwood awoke into darkness and into fear. Her sense of place, of time, of herself was lost to her. Her disorientation was compounded by her emerging from sleep to wakefulness in total, impenetrable darkness. Pulling herself into a sitting position, she stretched tremulous fingers into tenebrous space. Beneath her she felt rough sacking, on which she had clearly slept. The eyes of her fingertips perceived that the floor beyond the sacking comprised uneven and grimy flagstones; the wall to her side was chill, sleek stone, damp and slimy to the touch. The unstirred air hung frowsty and heavy around her with the smell of damp old earth.

She was seized with a greater panic upon the realization of a single fact: she was underground. She could be in a cellar. She could be in a tunnel.

She could be in her tomb.

For that moment, there was no thought, no remembrance; there was no recollection of how she had fallen into the bonds of darkness, no speculations of what fate awaited her beyond it nor plans to escape it. For that moment, all there was was the moment, and the darkness, and the terror.

She peered into the dark but it refused to yield to perception. She could have been in a space the size of a crypt, she could have been in a space the size of a cathedral. She could be alone and forsaken, left to perish from hunger and thirst in a crow-black dark desert, or she could be surrounded by others, hungering for blood and flesh.

Another dark, cold thought intensified her panic: she might already be dead. She might be condemned to the sepulchral dungeon of her final thoughts and fears. Or this, she thought with cold terror, could be hell.

For now she would not move. She determined to gather her thoughts, her wits; to recollect the events that brought her here. She had been drugged, of that she was convinced: she had woken in this darkness with no immediate memory. When she tried to remember events further back, she found there was no clear demarcation between light and dark in her recall: the memories were neither present nor absent, but remained tattered fragments that refused to stitch together into coherence.

She remembered walking to Lockwood's; she remembered the hallucination she had experienced, but also her recovery from it. She remembered her change, of course, of destination, of her purpose. But then the shadows came. She met someone. A man. That memory was clear, yet his face would not form in her recall, but she knew it had frightened her—frightened her terribly. She had become subject to his will and he had taken her. Whence and whither, however, were lost to her.

Nonetheless, she somehow knew it had been that man who had brought her here, who had some dark purpose in his confinement of her. She forced herself to think, to reason. For her to be in this place meant she had had to enter, to have been brought into it. That meant a door: a way in.

A way out.

Elspeth did not know what lay in the vaulted darkness. A few steps into it could bring collision with some unseen obstacle that would injure her; or it could take her over the edge of some precipice and to her death. The floor she felt around her could even be nothing but a ledge in the wall of some bottomless well.

She had heard there were places in Edinburgh, *under* Edinburgh, that were hidden. Some said the whole city was undermined by tunnels and catacombs. Underground caves and passages were said to stretch out like hidden fingers from Gilmerton Cove and reach far beneath the city. During the time of plague, alleys, closes and whole streets had been sealed off and built over, confining the infectious to perpetual dark. According to Edinburgh legend, cut-throat thieves, grave robbers and night stalkers of all kinds had haunted the city's hidden underground ways.

Perhaps that was where she now found herself. Perhaps she was deep beneath the city she knew, in its subterranean shadow.

She decided she would crawl, keeping her left shoulder to the wall and using her hands to test the solidity of the unseen floor as she went. That way, if she followed the wall, she would ascertain the geometry of her confinement.

That way, she would find the door.

25

The drawing room was huge and the windows along one wall reached almost from floor to ceiling, looking out across the shallow valley to the standing stone and the moot hill beyond. Hyde noticed that when Ballor dismissed his servant, the Cagot retired to a corner of the room, instead of leaving it, and stood silently with his hands behind his back.

"This aspect allows me to watch my guests as they arrive," said Ballor, nodding towards the windows. "I noticed you stopped to admire the Lamentation Tree."

"I did," said Hyde. "So I was right to think it is a dule tree?"

"It is indeed. And it is truly ancient. Some say as old as, or even older than, the three-thousand-year-old Fortingall Yew in Perthshire. And the *Feardorch*, the Dark Man standing stone you see, is perhaps twice as old again. This house, the standing stone and the Lamentation Tree are all in perfect alignment—a syzygy, one could say."

"Is that why you chose this place?" asked Hyde. "Does it *align* with your beliefs?"

"I detect some scorn in your tone, Captain Hyde, if I may say. But yes, this house—this situation—is perfect for my purposes." Ballor smiled, indulgently. "Anyway, I suspect you were brought here by more than an interest in my home and habits. What is it I can do for you, Captain Hyde?"

"Do you know Elspeth Lockwood, heiress to the Lockwood's department store fortune?"

"Why do you ask?"

"Do you know Elspeth Lockwood?" Hyde repeated the question with force.

"I know Elspeth, yes."

"Is Miss Lockwood here? Now?"

"What?" Ballor's expression suggested he found the question ridiculous. "Why would Elspeth be here now?"

"Is she here, Mr. Ballor?" Pollock repeated his superior's question.

"No," Ballor laughed as if confused, "she is not."

"Then you would not mind if we looked around the house, just to confirm that?" asked Hyde.

For a moment, Ballor looked as if he were about to protest. Instead, he sighed and called to where his manservant attended in the corner.

"Gorka, please escort the officers around the house." He turned back to Hyde. "I will await you here."

"You will come with us, Mr. Ballor," said Hyde. "We may have questions and your manservant is incapable of providing answers."

A dark fury flashed across Ballor's face, burning for an instant in the one unshielded eye. Then it was gone. He rose to his feet.

"Very well, Captain Hyde. I am at your disposal. Shall we?"

As they moved from room to room, it became clear that in its time, Crunnach had been a grand house. Hyde and Pollock were led through four more reception rooms on the ground floor, each equal in size to the drawing room. Of these, two were unused to the point of dereliction, the plasterwork, like decaying flesh, having flaked from the wooden bones of wall joists and timbers. It was clear to Hyde that Ballor had moved the furnishings of a much smaller abode into these grander appointments, and in doing so had chosen to dress certain rooms lavishly while leaving the others shut up and derelict. It allowed him, Hyde suspected, to suggest to such guests as visited that his station and wealth were more robust than in truth.

The kitchens were large, but again only one part of them was in use, which made sense to Hyde, given that Ballor had only one servant. The pantry was full, however, and Hyde could smell garlic and other exotic herbs and spices.

Spread over the upper three floors were a total of ten bedrooms, of which only four had been furnished. Each floor had a lavatory and bathroom in a corner tower room; all but one was in a state of desuetude, the porcelain of the furniture and tiles stained and cracked. The four furnished bedrooms were lavish—almost garish—in their decor, and again the art on the walls was either darkly erotic or menacing in theme and execution.

Nowhere was there any sign of Elspeth Lockwood's current or recent presence.

"All my secrets are exposed to your scrutiny, Captain Hyde," said Ballor as they stood in the second-floor hall. "But, as you can see, none of them is that I have stolen Elspeth Lockwood away from the world and hidden her here."

Hyde looked up the final flight of stairs. No cupola admitted light and the uppermost floor sat in darkness, impervious to the grey day outside.

"What is up there?" he asked.

"Nothing other than the servants' attic quarters. Salazar only occupies a couple of the rooms."

"Then we shall see them."

Ballor shrugged and nodded to Salazar, who led the way. The hall at the top of the stairs was floored with naked boards, covered only with a patina of dust and grime accumulated over decades of inoccupation. The walls and vaulted roof, too, were undressed wood. It was, as Ballor had indicated, an attic with several small rooms. Salazar had obviously taken occupation of one of the rooms in the cone-roofed tower, and Hyde noticed that it was the only space in the attic that had been cleaned. In fact, the Cagot's chamber was scrupulously clean and tidy, his few possessions and items of clothing neatly arranged.

"What's in here?" asked Pollock when they reached another tower room, its door closed. He put his hand on the doorknob and Salazar made a sudden move forward.

"Gorka . . ." Ballor's warning checked his servant.

Pollock swung open the door, and he and Hyde entered. As everywhere else, there was no sign of the missing Edinburgh heiress. But what did await them caught both policemen by surprise. This tower room, unlike the conically roofed one occupied by Salazar as a bedroom, was one of the box garrets that topped off three of the towers. At some time the south-facing wall and part of the roof had been opened up to accommodate a huge window of multiple panes. The window flooded the room with light and cast across the floor the shadow geometry of the lead muntin grid that held the panes in place.

Several canvases of various sizes stood on the floor, leaning against the walls, and a long army trestle table was covered with artists' paints, brushes, palettes, and bottles of linseed oils and varnishes. All were arranged with the same care for order that Salazar's belongings had been.

On the wall to their right, illuminated by the large window to their left, a vast canvas, too big to be accommodated on an easel, leaned against the wall, weights along its base holding it in place. It was in the same style, but on a much grander scale, as the other paintings throughout the house. The figure of a young and vigorous woman strode across a landscape like some warlike Amazon, naked except for a woven girdle around her waist and a leather sack thrown across her shoulder. What was most striking about the painting was the contrast of scale: the striding woman was of titanic proportion compared to the landscape. Entire forests bristled insignificantly like lawn grass beneath her unshod feet and vast lochs appeared as puddles. Wisps of cloud coiled around her shoulders and neck like a gossamer scarf. Rocks tumbled from her leather sack, as if shaken free by her prodigious striding. The painting was nearly, but not completely, finished, the face incondite and waiting for the woman's features to be defined.

"This is Gorka's studio," explained Ballor. "Which I hope excuses his protectiveness towards it. And this magnificent painting is no copy—it is my commission for an original work that he fulfils."

"What is its subject?" asked Hyde.

"Its title is *Cruthachadh na h-Alba—The Creation of Scotland*. The figure is that of the Cailleach, the Queen of Winter and the creatrix of Scotland. The rocks you see tumbling from her sack are what formed the mountains of the Highlands."

"I thought, according to legend, the Cailleach was an old hag, a monstrous aged crone. This figure is a young woman."

"That she is," said Ballor. "The Cailleach is neither and she is both. She represents the duality of nature. As Queen of Winter she is old, haggard and bent. But on the Winter Solstice she bathes in and drinks from the Well of Youth and grows younger every day thereafter. This shows her in her prime, robust and strong enough to give shape to the nation of Scotland."

Their search of the house complete, they descended to the main hall on the ground floor. Hyde paused at the armoire.

"This is a distinctive item. Did you bring it from Edinburgh?"

"As a matter of fact, I didn't," said Ballor. "It was here, in the hall, when I moved in. It was in quite a state, but Gorka has restored it almost to its original glory."

"May I look inside?"

"Do you believe I have hidden poor Elspeth therein? Come now, Captain Hyde."

"Indulge me, Mr. Ballor."

Ballor sighed and swung open the armoire's double doors, revealing a set of drawers and a hanging rail. Upon the rail hung fourteen garments, all save one of satin and crimson red, the fourteenth black silk.

"These look like ceremonial garb," said Hyde, examining the material of one between finger and thumb. "I take it they are used in your rituals?"

"Captain Hyde, I feel that I have been as cooperative as I can be. You clearly are concerned about Elspeth's safety, and I commend you for that and have done all I can to help. However, it is clear to you that Miss Lockwood is not here, and it has been over a week since I last saw her. I fear your inquiries are now becoming intrusive and impertinent."

"I'm afraid it is I who decides what is pertinent, Mr. Ballor. Who takes part in your rituals?"

"I am not at liberty to say. Our society is founded on confidentiality— but I warn you that among our number are figures of considerable influence."

"And Elspeth Lockwood is one of them? She takes part in these rituals you conduct here?"

"As I say, Captain Hyde, I am not at liberty—"

"Allow me to make myself clear," interrupted Hyde, leaning closer in to Ballor. "This is a very serious matter concerning the safety of a vulnerable young woman. Time is of the essence in finding her hale and safe, if indeed she remains in that condition. If she does not, then it becomes a yet more serious matter. So, if you do not answer my questions fully and frankly, you will find yourself 'not at liberty' in the most literal sense—and we will continue this interview through the bars of a cell. Have I made myself clear, Mr. Ballor?"

If Ballor felt the weight of Hyde's words, he did not let it show. Instead he nodded slowly, an arrogant smile creasing his handsome face.

"Elspeth has attended some of my gatherings, yes," he said. "Not often, but she occasionally takes part in our rituals of honour."

"Honouring whom?"

"The kings and queens of the Otherworld. Our rituals are Celtic and druidical, the true faith of these islands before the incursion of Roman or Angle."

"And what do you do in these rituals?"

"Through prayer, meditation and incantation we seek to stretch thin the veil between our world and the other. At this time of year, as you may know, that veil grows thinner, culminating in Samhainn, or All Hallows Eve, when the gods and beings of the Otherworld, along with the souls of the dead, can commune with us."

"Ridiculous." Hyde gave a small, scornful laugh. "Do you really believe this nonsense, or is it merely a ruse to gain wealth at the expense of the rich and gullible?"

"I believe in it with passion and dedication. And I find it infinitely less ridiculous than believing a Nazerene Jew could multiply loaves and fishes and walk on water. What's more, your faith gives you not just one, but three otherworlds: heaven, purgatory and hell. All of which sound much less believable than another realm of the senses coexisting in parallel with ours."

"So you believe in pixies and elves, that sort of thing?" asked Pollock.

Ballor turned to the young policeman. "I believe that there are other measures, other dimensions to our reality. I believe that there are things we cannot see but are nevertheless present." He nodded towards the doorway. "Out there, by the Dark Man, I am convinced those dimensions meet. That there the veil is stretched thinnest."

"Well, what I believe," said Pollock, "is that if you cannot see, hear, feel or smell something, then it does not exist."

"Then you do not believe in atoms? You do not believe in germs that bring disease?" Ballor shook his head. "Sometimes, I go out to the Dark Man at night, when there is a clear sky and I can look up at the stars. If we were to go out there now and look up, we wouldn't see stars, even if the sky were cloudless. During the day, the sun has the sky to itself. But that does not mean the stars are no longer there. It just means we cannot see them—that we are blinded to their presence by another, brighter presence. That is what the Otherworld is like. It is hidden from our view because we are blinded to it by the noise and glare and clamour of our physical world. The truth is, darkness and light share the world, but sometimes it is the darkness that shines brightest."

"Do you know where Elspeth Lockwood is?" asked Hyde, clearly impatient with Ballor's philosophizing.

"No, Captain Hyde, I do not know where Elspeth Lockwood has gone. But I do know she is a woman infinitely more *complex* than her father could ever imagine. Complex and fiercely independent. There are two sides to Elspeth, just as there are two sides to everyone. That she has disappeared from view, like a star in daylight, does not mean she has ceased to exist. I suggest you are looking in the wrong place."

As the brougham made its way back along the drive and circled the hill crowned by the Lamentation Tree, Hyde turned to Pollock.

"What do you think, Constable Pollock?"

"Of Ballor? I'll be bound that he knows more about Elspeth Lockwood's whereabouts than he has admitted. And there is something very strange in the relationship with his manservant. And heaven knows what transpires during these rituals."

"I agree with you. We need to think very carefully about how we handle Mr. Ballor. I would very much like to place him under close observation, but, as he himself pointed out, he can see from the house anyone approaching at a distance, and there is no natural cover from which to observe. And it is so damnably far from anything."

"So what should we do?"

"That will take some thought, Constable. But I would give anything to have an hour in that house alone and undisturbed. In the meantime, I suggest we talk with this man Farquharson." He tapped on the window and handed Mackinley the address James Lockwood had given for the investigator.

Part Three

HELL'S BLACK HOUND

26

There were two Samuel Porteouses in the room, facing each other in silence: the man and the reflected man.

Standing before the large gilt-edged mirror in his bedroom, Porteous examined his image. The curtains drawn, the lamplight did him a kindness and softened where time had begun to etch, smoothed where it had started to crease. He still possessed much of the comeliness of his youth, but the years had begun their irrepressible advance across the battlefield of his skin. His auburn hair, too, seemed to have yielded some of its lustre, as if clearing the field for occupation by the grey already heralded in his temples.

The magic of mirrors, Porteous reflected, was to hold the truth of a moment. He found himself wishing that that moment could be captured and taken away with him when he turned from the glass; that it would be his reflection that would age, not he, and the accumulation of disease, injury and sin would gather mirror-bound, allowing him to stay as he was. It was the most unscientific of fancies; Porteous the physician knew that there was no remedy, no potion nor medicament, to halt that most pernicious and deadly of diseases: age.

And Porteous the physician also knew that there was another reckoning that must come with time. Another secret that slept, locked in his cells, in his blood, whose dark awakening was inevitable and spurred him to achieve his aims, establish his reputation, before it was too late.

Downstairs, the hall clock chimed midnight; time's inexorable momentum mocking his fears.

There were other things about his reflection that held him in his study of his mirrored self: it was another he, a reversed image, sinister and dexter exchanged, symbolic of the inversion of nature he kept hidden from all.

Almost all.

Again he wished that that other Samuel Porteous, that secret life and inverted nature, could also be held captive in the silvered glass.

But secrets could not be bound up in reflections. That other nature sought its expression in the real world, and all it would take would be for him to make one mistake, to be careless in any aspect, and his secret would be revealed to all.

He took the leather fob and its key from his waistcoat pocket and examined it, rubbing his thumb over its symbol and embossed legend.

Duo in unum occultatum.

He sighed, replaced the fob in his pocket and finished changing into his smoking jacket and silk-embroidered slippers, before going downstairs to his study. He had dismissed his servants for the evening, and Mrs. Wilson, his housekeeper, had instructions never to enter the study without his prior knowledge.

The garden room that served as his study was untidy, which was unusual for Porteous, whose need for order and neatness often bordered on the obsessional. That evening had, however, been one of unusual intellectual turmoil for the doctor as he had searched desperately for some kind of resolution in his research notes.

As a result, papers lay scattered across the desk, books and files sat carelessly stacked on the chair in the corner. A copy of Ernst von Feuchtersleben's *Principles of Medical Psychology* sat beneath a pile of the medical journal *Brain*, edited by James Crichton-Browne, who had been one of Porteous's fellow students at Edinburgh University but had then gone on to build a reputation that eclipsed even that of his former classmate.

That, Porteous had promised himself, was about to change. But only if he could solve the problem.

His private journal, the one he normally kept locked in his safe, lay exposed on the paper-strewn desk, open where he had left off writing his notes from earlier that evening. With weary resignation, he took a glass and a decanter of brandy and set them on a clear space on his desk, then sat down and began to read, once more, through his notes.

In this journal lay the fundaments of a great discovery—and of a scientific reputation to match. It remained, however, an incomplete discovery, and he could not share it with his peers. Yet.

There was so much that troubled him about his research. So many questions left unanswered—not all of which were his own. Edward Hyde was now agitating for a more precise diagnosis of the source of his symptoms. Porteous had fobbed him off with generalities once too often, and the time was coming soon when the physician was going to have to face his patient with unwelcome truths.

In the meantime, Porteous had more pressing questions begging answers. And he felt the pressure of time upon him: others were examining the same subject, the same aspects of human psychology, and it was only a matter of time before someone else achieved the goal he aspired to and published their findings. Already, another psychiatrist had defined the condition. Porteous sighed as he picked up the piece about the French case reported by Pierre Janet, a rising star in the world of pioneering psychology.

Porteous's French was not the best, but with some effort and the aid of a dictionary he had been able to translate most of the article. In it, Dr. Janet explained how he had been researching and treating cases of female hysteria—a field of research pioneered by his mentor, Professor Jean-Martin Charcot. Dr. Janet's research had been focused on a minority of women who seemed to undergo a complete change of personality during a hysterical fit.

However, it had been a male patient who had revealed the most intriguing example. Pierre Janet reported that this patient had for some years been confined to a wheelchair, left paralysed by an event in youth that had delivered a profound physical and psychological shock. The patient in question was possessed of a gentle, pleasant nature, to the point of being meek and compliant. Placed in a sanatorium, he was well liked by his doctors and nursing staff.

However, every now and then, he would suffer profound headaches, preceded by bouts of disorientating déjà vu. These headaches would herald a complete change of personality—not just mood or demeanour, but personality and identity in every aspect. The patient would rise from his wheelchair, the full power of his legs restored, and attempt to leave the sanatorium. When prevented from doing so, he would, in complete contrast to his usual disposition, become aggressive and heap all forms of curse and profanity on those charged with his care. During these episodes, he would claim no knowledge of his true identity nor recollection of his paralysis. Most intriguingly, he would have different memories of his childhood, unshared with his "normal" self.

Eventually, these episodes would pass; the patient would retake his wheelchair, suddenly exhausted, and fall asleep. When he awoke, his usual placid personality would be restored and he would have no recall of what had transpired, nor that he had recovered the use of his legs. Indeed, according to Dr. Janet, the patient would become most upset at the suggestion that such occurrences had taken place.

In the article, Pierre Janet posited that the same emotional and psychic shock—a *trauma*, as such events were becoming known—that had paralysed the patient in his youth had sundered his personality in twain. He proposed that it was possible for two distinct and independent personalities—perhaps even more than two—to coexist within the same body.

One body, two minds.

Porteous had been overwhelmed when he read the article—a direct corroboration and substantiation of his own findings. He believed—he knew—that a great shock or psychological injury could cleave a single mind into separate, independent personalities. He had been excited and encouraged by the piece, but also concerned that Janet or some other researcher would prove his theory definitively before he himself could do so.

What Porteous was dealing with, however, eclipsed any other case he had read about in the literature. The subject of his case study, whose schism of identity was even more profound and remarkable than the French case, had revealed an alternative personality so dark, so violent and corrupt, that Porteous feared the public risk in not confining the patient. But there lay the paradox: confinement to an asylum would condemn not just the dangerous, insane personality, but the innocent, unknowing personality as well.

Porteous knew that what he was doing was wrong, neglectful of his responsibilities to the public as a physician. He knew his motive was his furious ambition and desire for professional acclaim and aggrandizement. His name in this field would rise above all others—and if there was haste and ruthlessness in his pursuit of that aim, it was because, he knew, time was against him. A reckoning was on its way.

But he was determined that his reputation would not be founded upon advancing the work of others, or simply defining further the nature and causes of the syndrome; his fame, instead, would be established by developing the means to control it.

The key.

The aim of Porteous's research was to develop a pharmacological agent to control the switching of personalities in afflicted patients: a key with which to liberate the desirable personality and confine the other.

The problem—the danger—of course was that the reverse could occur: his compound could cause a switch in dominance in a fractured mind, allowing a malicious, base personality to take hold.

And he feared its misuse, to control others not exhibiting harmful traits. What injury, he thought, was there in the more gentle dualities? The sentiment inspired him to once more take the key fob from his pocket and examine it.

Duo in unum occultatum.

With a sigh, Samuel Porteous replaced the fob, poured himself a brandy from the decanter on his desk and lit a cigarillo. He sat and read through the notes he had made: his less than objective and professional comments about the horror he felt when confronted with his patient's alternative personality.

Instead of stimulating him, the brandy seemed to add to his tiredness, and he leaned back in his chair and rubbed weary eyes with the heels of his hands.

It was at that moment that he heard someone quietly ring the bell outside the garden door of his study.

He rose, walked over to the door, drew back the bolt, and opened it.

"Oh," he said in unwelcome surprise at his revealed visitor. "I wasn't expecting you . . ."

27

The darkness had not remitted. There had been no adjustment to it, no accustoming of her eyes. So total and so impenetrable remained the blackness that another fear gripped her: that the reality was that she was in a place of light, that all was visible to those capable of seeing. That it was, in fact, Elspeth who was blind.

And it seemed that time had been lost with the light. She had no idea how long she had shuffled along on hands and knees, timorous fingers exploring the floor ahead and checking she remained close to the wall: it could have been minutes, it could have been hours. One thing had become certain, however: in this place, whatever this place was, there were no corners, no angles to the wall; rather she had formed the impression that she traced a single continuous wall, almost imperceptibly curved, leading her to the conclusion that she was confined within some circular structure.

And it was vast. She knew she had not yet come full circle because she was still to regain the sacking that had formed her bed. Most disheartening was the fact that her exploration had thus far failed to uncover any door, any shuttered window, any breach in her immurement to offer hope of escape.

Her skirt formed a continuous impediment to her progress, repeatedly being pulled taut by shuffling knees and causing her to pitch forward. She was aware that the material of her skirt had been shredded by the gravel that seemed to coat the broken flagstones of the floor, and it was now biting into her skin with every forward crawl. She was surprised that anger began to supplant the terror her confinement had brought. She became determined that she would overcome this captivity, overcome her captor, and take her place again in the world of light.

She felt herself pitch suddenly forwards and downwards. She had become less timid in her exploration, more impatient in her quest to find some escape, and she had hastened the pace of her crawling. Her outstretched hands had moved to brace her against the flagstones, but none had yielded to her touch. Blind panic seized her for a second, until she realized her hands had dropped onto more stone, but at a level some six or seven inches lower than her progress thus far. Tentatively, she felt forward and discovered another drop of roughly the same measure.

Steps.

Bracing herself against the wall, she rose to her feet. She eased herself slowly upright: Elspeth had no idea whether the headroom in the blackness above her was that of a low mine roof or a cathedral vault. Once she established that she could fully stand without hitting her head, she eased her foot forward and down, taking the first step.

Then another. Then another.

28

Edward Hyde had slept well. Unusually well. He had felt the call of no world, real or other, to stir his sleeping mind to dream. He awoke feeling fresh and reinvigorated in a way he had not done for months, years even. Just as his sleep had been dreamless, so had his waking been free of the ghostly heralds of murdered children.

When he arose, he navigated the tasks of breaking fast and dressing for the day with an unaccustomed lightness of spirit and ease of movement. He puzzled briefly as to what had so transformed his spirits. Had it been, perhaps, that he had not taken his prescription for several days? If that were the case, he thought, then what game had Samuel Porteous been playing with him?

As he sat over his breakfast, Hyde read through his notebook.

There remained several threads to be followed. He had been able to read once more the report supplied to James Lockwood by his private investigator Farquharson. Though Hyde disdained unofficial investigators, and had dismissed Farquharson as a store detective most likely out of his depth, he had to admit the man's report was methodical and professional. What had been frustrating had been Hyde's failure to speak directly with the investigator: he had not been at home when Hyde and Pollock had called at the Stockbridge address that served as Farquharson's abode and business premises.

Their knocking had, however, brought to her door the upstairs neighbour, a middle-aged woman of stern demeanour, who insisted on examining both policemen's warrant cards before answering their questions. She was, she told them, proprietrix of the whole building; Mr. Farquharson was her tenant, and a good one at that. She further explained that his work frequently took him away from the city, often for protracted periods. This, she explained, was one such period. Some two weeks before, Farquharson had left her an envelope containing the next month's full rent, along with a note explaining that he would be away on business for some time.

"Do you know where he has gone? An address where we might contact him?" Pollock had asked.

"I did not speak with Mr. Farquharson directly," the landlady had explained. "He pushed the envelope through the letter box, which he has done before."

Again, working his way through his notes, Hyde was surprised at how little such frustrations troubled him; how light were his spirits. He determined to confront Samuel Porteous once more about what active agents had been in his prescription, the absence of which had seemingly so invigorated him.

There was another course to which he resolved himself: he had increasingly found himself thinking of Cally Burr. He had been aware of his feelings towards her, but had always dismissed any possibility of her developing a romantic association with such a creature as he. But in the brightness of this new day, everything seemed possible—and he resolved to ask her to take tea with him.

He had just tidied away his breakfast items when the front doorbell rang with urgency. He checked his watch and saw it was seven fifteen, too early for Mackinley the coachman, who in any case always waited at the kerb for Hyde's arrival.

He hastened along the hall, and when he swung open the street door, he found Peter MacCandless and Willie Dempster framed in it, standing on the doorstep.

"Whatever is the matter?" asked Hyde.

MacCandless said: "You are to come with us, sir. Chief Constable Rintoul's orders."

Their transport had not been a carriage but rather a Black Maria custody van—heavily constructed and drawn by a team of four horses—usually employed in the conveyance of prisoners. The suddenness of his summoning, added to the incapacity or unwillingness of his deputies to disclose the nature of their mission, had dulled the edge of Hyde's earlier good spirits. What blunted it completely had been when, through the small barred window of the van, he recognized their destination: an impressive Georgian townhouse facing onto Queen Street Gardens.

A house Hyde knew well.

When they entered, the hallway, from which rose the three-flight staircase crowned with a glass cupola, was crowded with uniformed policemen and three servants, all of whom Hyde recognized.

"Oh, Captain Hyde!" Mrs. Wilson, the housekeeper, clearly distraught and in shock, clutched his arm earnestly. "Who could have done such a terrible thing? To such a kind and gentle man too . . ."

Hyde frowned, confused, but spoke to her soothingly in vague reassurance.

"This way, sir," said MacCandless and conducted him into the garden room study.

Hyde saw his friend first, the focus of all activity in the room. Samuel Porteous lay on his back, sprawled across his desk. His silk smoking jacket and shirt had been ripped wide open, exposing his naked chest. The crumpled cloth of both was encrimsoned, sodden and dark with blood. Someone had used a bladed weapon on Porteous's thorax and abdomen, which were rent open with livid gapes. Some kind of rough hemp rope had been bound around his neck and tightened, forcing his tongue to protrude hideously from forced-apart lips. Porteous's handsome, boyish face had also been disfigured: where once had been his striking emerald-green eyes were now only black-red sockets. Rivulets of blood, like crimson tears, streaked the dead man's temples.

The hideous mutilation had also been repeated in effigy: whoever had gouged out Porteous's eyes from his head had sliced their canvas representations from the portrait above the fireplace, which now gazed blindly out at the scene.

The sight of his tortured and murdered friend sent a pang through Hyde's chest and he gave a small gasp.

Waiting for him in the room was Chief Constable Rintoul and the police surgeon Abercrombie. Abercrombie conducted himself with his usual professional matter-of-factness, but Rintoul, unaccustomed to the immediacy of murder, or any other crime, looked wan and nauseated.

Abercrombie nodded acknowledgement to Hyde. "Another strange one, Hyde," he said. "As is obvious to anyone, the victim has been stran-gled, stabbed and has had his eyes cut out."

"The Threefold Death," said Hyde.

"What?" asked Rintoul.

"The Threefold Death," repeated Hyde. "Thrice murdered, like the victim down at the Water of Leith."

"Aye?" said Abercrombie. "Well this time the victim is a member of the Hippocratic profession. One of our own. This kind of barbarity, and the fact that he was a psychiatrist . . . well, just make sure you don't let whatever fiend did this escape the hangman by claiming insanity."

"You think he was murdered by a patient?" asked Rintoul. He cast a meaningful glance in Hyde's direction before turning back to the police surgeon.

"That's not my business, rather yours. But it would seem pretty obvious to me that this is the work of someone severely mentally deranged—and it was Dr. Porteous's business to treat the severely deranged." Abercrombie shrugged. "Anyway, have the body removed to the mortuary for autopsy and I shall ask Dr. Bell if he will oblige. I think this is a case where nothing should go undiscovered."

"On that we are agreed," said Rintoul. He nodded over to the cor-ner of the room. Hyde followed his indication to a large mahogany cabinet, a piece in the aesthetic movement style. Despite his familiarity with it from countless visits, the cabinet now struck Hyde as cumber-some, alien and ugly. But what impressed him most about it was the secret it now revealed: its doors thrown open, a heavy cast-iron safe was exposed. He could see the safe's door was also open and the inte-rior was naked of content.

"Robbery?" asked Rintoul.

"What?" Hyde looked at his superior in confusion for a moment. "Robbery? If this were a robbery, then why . . . ?" He nodded in the direction of the mutilated body. "Whatever was taken from this safe was no doubt taken to confound us—to remove material evidence that might give us a clue to the murderer's identity. But whatever dark motive brought the killer to Samuel's door, it was not larceny."

"That's rather what I thought," said Rintoul, dully. He turned to the others. "Gentlemen, I would like to have a moment alone with Captain Hyde."

The police surgeon already having departed, MacCandless and Dempster nodded and left, indicating to the uniformed sergeant at the door that he should follow them out into the hall.

"Sir?" asked Hyde when he and Rintoul were alone, save for the mute presence of the dead doctor.

"I am at a loss as to what to do," said Rintoul. "You knew this man, didn't you?"

Hyde sighed, and nodded. "I knew him."

"In fact, would I not be correct to say that you were more than an acquaintance?" Rintoul held up a thick journal, bound in red leather. "Do you know what this is?"

Hyde shook his head.

"Sergeant MacCandless was on early shift and attended the locus when the report came in. While surveying the scene, he found this journal and, on reading what he could from it, thought it prudent to summon me, where normally he would have first notified you." Rintoul examined the red binding. "This, it would appear, was Dr. Porteous's private journal. It seems that rather than personal reflections, he used it for keeping detailed notes on a particular patient and a project that he kept hidden from everyone else. My guess is that its usual home would have been the corner safe." He handed Hyde the journal.

Hyde examined it. Most of the pages had been ripped from it, not in haste, but with care not to leave a telltale fragment. What remained attached to its binding would have amounted to no more than a third of the original. As he flicked through the remainder, he saw his name repeated several times. Something cold and heavy coalesced around his heart.

"The missing pages?" he asked.

"I am assuming that the murderer tore them out and took them with him when he fled the scene, presumably with other contents from the safe." Rintoul held out his hand, indicating that he wished the journal returned to him. Hyde returned it.

"I have been able to give this only a cursory examination," said the chief constable, "but those pages that remain seem to discuss you and your treatment by Porteous. I need you now to make clear the nature of your relationship with the deceased, and the nature of the condition that brought you to his door."

"I see," said Hyde. He looked again at his dead friend and physician, his heart still heavy. "I consulted Samuel because I was suffering from lost time: brief periods—sometimes very brief—for which I could not account for my whereabouts or actions. Additionally, I am plagued with a form of dreaming that occasionally leaves me enervated mentally and physically. I used to suffer from these symptoms when I was a boy and into young adulthood, then they diminished. Over the past two or three years my condition seems to have returned, and Samuel, who diagnosed it as epilepsy, was medicating me for it. That is all."

"I'm afraid that is most certainly not all," replied the chief constable. "Before we discuss why you have hidden from me facts that have material bearing on your fitness to serve in your current post, I have to tell you that we sent men this morning to Craiglockhart Hydropathic Hospital, to examine Dr. Porteous's consulting rooms there. The staff confirmed that you visited him there the day before yesterday. They also say that you had an argument with Porteous; indeed, that you were in something of a rage. The nurse who witnessed the incident was not on duty, but I have sent someone to her home to obtain a statement."

"Are you leading this investigation, Chief Constable?" asked Hyde. "Not I?"

"That," said Rintoul, "remains to be seen."

"It's not true." Hyde shook his head in frustration. "I mean, it's not true I was in a rage. I *was* angry with Samuel, but it was a disagreement, not an argument. You know that some people—I don't know, because of the way I look—some people see threat in me where there is none."

"What was the nature of this disagreement?" asked Rintoul. "Or am I to find the answer to that in here?" He once more held up the leather journal. "At least what is left of what Porteous wrote in here."

"I don't know what Samuel has written about me." Hyde sighed. "Samuel Porteous was my friend, my confidant. He was also my physician. He agreed to keep my treatment confidential, and I suppose he will have kept note of the details of my condition."

"And you say he was treating you for epilepsy?" asked Rintoul.

"He was. But I believe he had some other purpose."

"Other purpose? What nature of purpose?"

"I believe I was some form of experimental subject, and the treatment he prescribed was having a detrimental effect. Making my condition worse."

Rintoul frowned. "May I see the prescription so that we may know its components?"

Hyde shook his head. "He always dispensed it himself. Either gave me the medicine in person or had it made up and sent to me by messenger."

"I see." Rintoul thought for a moment. He turned in the direction of the corpse and once more his face blanched. Hyde guessed that the chief constable had never, during his military experience, set foot on a battlefield. He turned back to Hyde. "Do you have any of this potion left, so that we may analyse it?"

"There were two elements to his prescription: the suspension—the potion, as you call it—and tablets to be taken whenever I felt . . ." Hyde paused. "Whenever I felt I was becoming *unwell*. I'm afraid I have neither: I threw them away some days ago."

"And why would you do such a thing?" asked Rintoul.

"Because, as I've already told you, I believed they were making my symptoms worse. Actually *causing* me to have episodes."

"I see."

"Do you seriously suspect I have anything to do with this?" Hyde waved a hand in the direction of his dead friend. Rintoul followed his gaze.

"Perhaps we should step out into the garden and discuss this," said the chief constable.

Hyde followed him through the door he had used so many times and out into the small garden. In the grey day, under a cloud-fumed sky, the green of the bushes and the small square of gravel-edged grass seemed muted and dull. Hyde thought how distant his good spirits of little more than an hour ago seemed.

"Captain Hyde," said Rintoul, "you have placed me in the most invidious position. You were known to and actively involved with a murder victim with whom you were seen to be arguing. On top of this I discover, as a result of this murder, that you have been concealing a condition from me and from the City Police that seriously compromises your ability to serve as an officer of the law."

"Am I dismissed?" asked Hyde. "Or under arrest?"

"For the moment, neither." Rintoul held him in a steady steel gaze. "The invidiousness of my position is compounded by the fact that this murder, above all, demands the skills of the best detective I have at my disposal—a detective who is now a potential suspect. How can I have you investigate it when, for all I know, you could be obscuring the truth of the matter instead of illuminating it?"

Hyde thought for a moment. "How much of this have you shared with MacCandless and Dempster?"

"MacCandless read enough of the remaining journal pages for it to awaken concern—and for him to realize he could not involve you without first contacting me. I have told him to discuss the matter with no one else."

Both men were temporarily distracted by the sound of sobbing from a window on the second floor of the house. One of the servants; probably Mrs. Wilson, guessed Hyde.

"May I suggest," he said, turning back to Rintoul, "that you allow me to conduct this inquiry as I would normally—particularly as it smacks of the Hanged Man murder. My knowledge of the victim may be a benefit, rather than a complication. If you do not trust me, then I suggest further that you keep me under constant surveillance, on and off duty. Tell whomever you charge with the task that you are concerned that my life, too, may be in peril. As I am a friend of the victim, such an instruction does not lack credibility. I know both MacCandless and Dempster to be steadfast in their duty, and believe they would not be swayed by any loyalty to me. If you instruct them to report directly to you, and in full, you can trust them both to do exactly that."

Rintoul did not answer right away, instead looking up at the milk-coloured sky as if resolution might lay written on its cloud page. Then he shook his head. "It's absurd to believe you had anything to do with this murder. And the best way for you to exculpate yourself entirely would be to catch the true villain in this deed. Conduct this investigation as you would any other. I want these murders resolved and young Elspeth Lockwood found."

"Thank you, sir," said Hyde.

"Don't thank me too quickly. You have misled me—hidden from me that which has a significant bearing on your fitness for office. I must be candid and admit that, at the moment, I cannot see your tenure stretching beyond this investigation. In the meantime, I commend you to your duty, Captain Hyde. Find this monster."

29

Hyde watched as Porteous's remains were removed to the same Black Maria that had brought him to the scene. It stung him to see his dead friend, his clothes sodden and dripping with gore, unceremoniously hoisted into the unvarnished pine coffin used by the police for transporting the suddenly or inexplicably dead. He tried not to think about the chill porcelain destination of the mortuary, nor of his friend's face being sliced open along the jawline and peeled back like a mask, as the Hanged Man's had been by Cally Burr in that strange, theatrical autopsy.

The thought of her distracted him for a moment and he found himself aching for her company, for the sight of her; for the peace her presence seemed to bring him.

"Make sure his clothes are preserved," he called to the constables carrying the coffin. "I'll want to examine them later."

He watched the coffin as it left the room, a peal of woe swelling in the hall as Mrs. Wilson caught sight of it. Hyde himself felt a rising surge of panic: despite their recent disagreement, Samuel Porteous had been the only person helping him overcome his condition; now he would have to face it alone, as he had been forced to since adolescence.

Once the body had been removed, Hyde set MacCandless, Dempster and two uniformed officers to separating out the blood-glued papers that had lain beneath it. As he had requested, all contents from Porteous's pockets had been removed and set in the physician's wicker desk tray. Hyde studied each item closely; some of them were blood-tainted, but none bore him any intelligence.

Then he came to the pocket fob with the key attached. There was something discordant about it that Hyde could not explain. The leather fob showed much wear, as if worried at between finger and thumb, but the emblem and legend, both embossed in faded gold, were still legible. The emblem was of a classical design and showed the laurel-wreathed head of a twin-faced, double-bearded man. Identical profiles looked in opposite directions but shared the same head.

"Janus," muttered Hyde.

"Sir?" asked MacCandless, who was closest to him, but Hyde dismissed him with a shake of the head.

He read the motto beneath the emblem: *Duo in unum occultatum.* Two concealed in one.

"William . . ." he called over to Dempster. "I want you to find the lock this key opens. From the size of the key, it must be a door, rather than a casket or press."

"Sir," said Dempster, and took the fob and key.

Along with his men, Hyde spent three further hours in his friend's home. Intrusion, he knew, was a policeman's function, his duty; but he felt uncomfortable in his invasion of his friend's private life. Drawers and cupboards locked against the world's scrutiny were either unlocked for them by the distraught Mrs. Wilson or unceremoniously broken open. Letters and papers were read, diaries examined, pockets turned out. Every private corner of a man's life was exposed to dispassionate scrutiny.

And it told them nothing.

So much so that it perturbed Hyde. They had been through everything, examined every scrap and item, yet nothing of Porteous, of his movements was revealed. It indicated a man clearly guarded about his privacy, his personal life. But, Hyde thought, no man is without secrets; whatever Porteous held back from the world's eye had been kept in the torn-out pages of his journal, or sequestered in the study safe. In either case, those secrets had been taken from this house at the same time as the life of its owner.

Something else troubled Hyde. Their search of a tall, narrow burr-walnut medical cabinet that stood like a sentry on guard next to the door into the hall revealed equipment for mixing compounds, as well as several vials and bottles of powders and liquids, all labelled with their contents: potassium bromide, lithium, strychnine, laudanum, arsenic, sweet spirit of nitre, and various others that were the staples of a modern doctor's cabinet. There were also, unopened, two packets marked as calomel, mercurous chloride.

But nothing out of the usual; nothing that suggested experiment or research.

Furthermore, all the bottles, vials, beakers and flasks were either of clear, green or amber glass; none was the dark blue of the bottle Porteous had ready each time Hyde visited, and from which he had dispensed Hyde's medication.

Hyde's guess was that whatever compound it was that Porteous had concocted to treat him, its exotic constituents had resided in the hidden safe, and the murderer had removed them also.

Dempster returned the key and fob to Hyde. "It looks to me like a main door key—a house key—but I can promise you there isn't a door, store or press in this building that possesses the lock to match it."

"Thank you, William," said Hyde. "Tell the others to gather all the evidence, such as it is, and place it in boxes for the court productions store. There is no point in lingering here longer." He examined again the fob and its key. "I suspect our answers lie elsewhere."

30

That evening, Hyde assembled all the officers of his detective force in the muster room of Torphichen Place station. The room fumed with cigar smoke and speculation, and when Hyde entered, he called for quiet, pausing to open a window. After the lightness with which he had greeted the morning, he was now weary from carrying the weight of the day, and a headache throbbed malevolently behind his eyes.

At Hyde's command, the detectives methodically outlined such facts as were at their disposal.

It became something of a forlorn effort: in none of the cases had anything of significance revealed itself to their scrutiny.

No one had been seen by any of the servants, nor neighbours, arriving or leaving Samuel Porteous's home the night of his murder. Two lists of patients, however, had been acquired: one from Craiglockhart Hospital, the other from Porteous's private consulting rooms in the New Town. A quick check of the first had revealed that almost all of his hospital patients were confined to the lunatic wing; the second list would take longer to check, as it comprised wealthier patients, mostly women from the upper echelons of Edinburgh society seeking discreet treatment for hysteria, and great delicacy would have to be employed in conducting any interviews.

Similarly disheartening, there had still been no identification from the photograph of the Water of Leith victim, despite every insalubrious haunt in Edinburgh being visited.

"We will have to widen our search—visit hotels and guesthouses," Hyde commanded his men. "It could be that our victim moved in circles more exalted than those we have explored thus far."

Hyde shared with his men that he had also received a message from the castle: Allan Lawson, the commanding officer of the garrison, had informed him that his provost marshal had been unable to identify the dead man as either a serving or former soldier.

Acting Detective Constable Pollock confirmed that no trace of Elspeth Lockwood had yet been found, other than that a man had come forward to say he had seen her in Castle Street the morning she disappeared and he had thought she looked distressed, but she had recovered herself and walked on briskly. "With some purpose, as if late for an appointment," Pollock quoted the witness as saying.

"I am beginning to worry that Miss Lockwood has come to harm," he added. "And not just because we cannot trace her. I looked into the death of her brother, the event that had such a profound nervous effect on her. Do you remember the incident, sir?"

"Lockwood's son's death? I do," said Hyde. "I think everyone in Edinburgh remembers that tragedy. He fell from the roof of the store."

"Exactly. As you say, sir, his death was treated as a tragic accident, but Joseph Lockwood was in truth a severe neurasthenic, and a discouraged but nonetheless widely held belief is that he did not fall but jumped, his nerve trouble causing him to take his own life. I fear that Miss Lockwood is perhaps no less prone to nerve disorder."

"You worry she has committed suicide?"

"I do, sir. If not, I fear she has come to harm by a hand other than her own. I was not reassured by our visit to Crunnach House. I am not at all convinced that Frederic Ballor is not implicated in her disappearance."

"Nor I," said Hyde. "I want you to focus your attention solely on the Lockwood case and report directly to me." He noticed MacCandless and Dempster exchange a look, but ignored it: now was not the time to concern himself with hierarchical protocols.

"What about the Cobb Mackendrick observation, sir?" asked Pollock.

"We have no time at the moment to concern ourselves with possible political intrigues to entertain the whims of Scotland Yard." Hyde turned to the rest of the assembled team. "Gentlemen, I wish you to continue to view the murders of our still unnamed Hanged Man and Samuel Porteous as separate cases. Detective Sergeant MacCandless will lead the team investigating the Hanged Man murder, Detective Sergeant Dempster will take charge of those of you engaged on the Porteous case. Let's treat these as separate evidential paths—but, given

the brutality and the Threefold Death element common to both homi-
cides, I anticipate the paths will converge before long. I have a feeling
that both are the work of the same maniac."

It was after ten when Hyde left the station for home. Night had fallen
without its usual chill, the air strangely and unseasonably humid, and
the sky had drawn cloud curtains across the stars, the moon's presence
only evident as a dull, milky blooming.

Nevertheless, and despite the late hour, Hyde decided on a whim to
walk home to Northumberland Street. Perhaps it had been his tiredness, the musty, smoke-filled air of the muster room, or a combination of both, but his head pounded and, for the first time since he had
stopped taking his medication, he felt the strange foreshadows of an
episode.

A carriage awaited him at the kerb and he stood for a moment,
vaguely confused and consumed by the dreadful but familiar feeling
of unreality that preceded an attack. Perhaps, he thought, the twenty-
minute walk through the night air would help, and he dismissed the
carriage.

It did not entirely surprise him when Edinburgh began to pull a
cloak of fog around its shoulders: the night's unusual humidity con-
densing in the chill air drifting up from the Forth and combining with
the lingering soot and smoke from the day's industry. As he reached the
west end of Princes Street, however, he *was* surprised at how quickly
the fog densified, turning the gas lanterns into muffled, pale blooms on
the barely visible black stalks of their standards.

By the time he reached the corner of Princes Street and Hanover
Street, the halfway point in his journey, the brumous night had rendered him almost sightless, and he had to stop several times to attempt
to establish in which bearing lay his destination.

Something else halted him in his uncertain tracks, sending a chill
through his bones. It was a far-off sound, incongruous in this setting,
of baying. It was as if some howling beast was calling from the distant
wild into the city. He held his breath for a moment: there was a second
howling in the distance. Then silence.

Hyde moved on, slowly, unsteadily. He had only gone some twenty
yards when another sound reached him, this time closer.

"Can someone guide me?" a male voice called out, from somewhere ahead, lost in the grainy murk. "I cannot see my way."

Hyde felt a chill of recognition at the sound of the voice and, arms stretched before him, pressed on in the direction from which it had come.

"I cannot see my way," the voice repeated.

Hyde hastened his pace towards the voice's origin and was rewarded with a forward stumble as he stepped off the unseen kerb. Regaining both his stability and the pavement, he saw a figure, little more than a charcoal shadow insubstantially limned in the graphite gloom, and moving away from him.

"Wait!" he called to the figure and, running his outstretched hand along the cold railings to keep his course true, pursued the spectre.

"I cannot see," said the voice again, plaintively. "Can some soul lend me a hand in guidance?"

Hyde's heart hammered in his chest at recognition of the voice, the pulse reverberating in his ears. He rushed forward and closed the distance between himself and the figure, which he could now see was hooded and cloaked.

He placed his hand on the figure's shoulder, and it came to a halt but did not turn, keeping its back to him. It reached up and eased the hood from its head, still facing away from him.

Hyde suppressed a cry when he was confronted with Samuel Porteous, gazing at him with his striking emerald eyes restored to his face—but a face unnaturally positioned on his neck and looking backward.

"Samuel?" Hyde asked, confused through his horror. The figure spun around. Another countenance, another Porteous, now confronted him: the figure had two faces on a single skull. The one that now faced Hyde had, where the eyes should have been, two black-red chasms weeping blood down the death-paled cheeks.

"Please, Edward, be my guide—I cannot see."

Hyde shrank back in horror, but the apparition seized him by the wrist with inhuman strength and pulled him towards it. It pushed its gory face into Hyde's.

"*Duo in unum occultatum,*" it hissed. "*Duo in unum occultatum.*" Then, with great force and clarity: "I am JANUS!"

Summoning all his strength, Hyde snatched his wrist from Porteous's grasp. The violence of the act sent Hyde staggering, and he fell onto his back with a cry. He waited for the ghost to seize him again, but instead, it turned away from him. The backward-looking face glared malevolently at him with its emerald eyes, then was hidden when the creature replaced its hood. It stepped into the fog and disappeared in the miasma.

As Hyde rose to his feet, he again heard the faraway howl of a beast. The fog, impossibly thickened and darkened, seemed to be alive with black shapes, shadows that coalesced into an impenetrable darkness. He reached back, seeking railing or stone masonry against which to lean, but none yielded to touch, only the brume-laden but otherwise empty air.

He was, he knew, somewhere else, in some other realm.

For some reason he could not explain, every inch of his being was seized with terror. He had never felt so alone, so isolated.

Like the breath of some titan, a scouring wind picked up in an instant and began to blow the fog away, shredding it into ragged grey scraps that dissipated as they tumbled and fluttered across the revealed landscape.

Hyde was no longer in Edinburgh.

He stood in a broad, wind-scoured strath braced by bald mountains on either side. There were no trees here, no green. He recognized the vista from his previous dream, but this time the landscape was denuded of trees, and every colour was inverted: that which should have been green had become shades of scarlet and crimson, the heather on the flanks of the mountain black scabs. The sky was a nauseous yellow, scarred by the too-fast scudding of rust-coloured clouds.

In the far distance, he saw a titanic female figure, her back turned and her head and shoulders wreathed in blood-red cloud, striding away from him. Despite the great distance between them, the ground beneath him still shook with each of her footfalls, and as the rocks of mountains tumbled from her satchel.

"The Cailleach," he muttered.

It was cold. An unnatural, dead cold. But Hyde no longer wore the vestments of winter: he found himself dressed only in a loose linen shirt and threadbare trousers, his feet naked on the black-red grass. A chill wind bit through the insubstantial cloth and into his flesh.

"I am dreaming, I am just dreaming," he repeated, needing to assure himself that he occupied a world of imaginings, not of his real senses, despite its raw, visceral reality. "I took the carriage from the station. I did not walk to my house. There was no fog. I took a sleeping draught and I now lie in my bed, at home."

His reassurances to himself did no good. He knew he was in the throes of a nocturnal seizure—that this was all a dream—yet his body was there with him: feeling, experiencing physically every dimension of this world. His fear, he knew, came from this knowledge: he could be injured here. He could feel great pain here.

He could die here.

The chill air around him, the miscoloured sky and land, suddenly seemed charged with some dark intent. He sensed something evil coming.

Beneath his naked feet the earth trembled, then shook. He looked up to the mountainside and saw its flank sunder. A great chasm glowing crimson and gold and white appeared, and Hyde's chill was replaced by a sense of a searing heat in the air. There were screams and cries, as if of great angers and great agonies, and the clashing sounds of battle, spilling out from the chasm. One voice rose above all others, roaring in inhuman fury. It lasted only a moment, then, slowly, the chasm closed itself, cleaving into an ugly scabrous scar. The silence and chill returned to the glen.

He heard it again: a deep, bestial howling, still distant, but closer than before.

"He is loose. He has escaped the Otherworld . . ." said a child's voice. Hyde turned and saw, standing behind him, the girl who had haunted the fleeting moments and dark bedroom corners of his days in recent weeks. She stood staring up at him with the same blank admonition. She was so small, he so large, yet she terrified him.

Behind her was the shallow grave from which she had emerged, its soil and dust clinging to her ragged clothes. Hyde could see, pressed into the bowl of her grave, interwoven branches and twigs, arranged like an animal's lair or nest.

She was Mary Paton, the Bairn in the Witch's Cradle.

"Who is loose?" he asked.

"The Black Hound. *Cù dubh ifrinn.* The monster. He was left behind when the mountain closed. He is coming. He comes now. Will you save me?" Mary's small voice was empty of fear, of any passion. "He comes for me now."

Hyde looked up to the mountain, and when he turned back another figure stood beside Mary Paton's.

"*Cù dubh ifrinn* is coming and he will take us both," said Hugh Morrison, his expression as blankly open and childlike as the girl's. "We are both his victims, but you know that. You understand that. You know it was he, not I, who killed Mary."

"It was *cù dubh ifrinn*—the Black Hound of Hell," confirmed Mary.

It was then that Hyde saw it. In the far distance at first, but growing larger, blacker, with every bound.

"Run!" yelled Hyde. "For God's sake, run!"

But both Mary and Hugh Morrison stood mute and empty faced, looking at Hyde.

"You have got to run! Now!" yelled Hyde. "Please! Please run! It will take you. It is coming!"

In the chill of the red glen, he felt the heat of tears on his face. Frantically, he searched the valley floor for a branch, a rock, anything he could use as a weapon. And all the time the beast bounded ever closer. It was now only two hundred yards from them, and already he could see that its proportions were beyond that of any wolf or hound.

One hundred yards.

"Run!"

Fifty yards.

Hyde picked up a rock, the largest he could find, and ran forward, placing himself between the advancing beast and the two victims, who still regarded Hyde with dispassion and disinterest.

He had never known terror like it. The beast was a huge black hound, at the shoulder the height of a man. Its coat was as sleek and black as obsidian, its eyes fire red. It departed from normal conformation not only in its huge size: the massive foam-flecked jaws, jutting from an ugly, heavily muscled neck and head, were over-filled with teeth: a double row of long, pointed white blades.

Hyde threw the rock with true aim and it struck the beast on the snout. Without any effect. It was upon them now and he knew there was nothing he could do to stop it slicing through his flesh and crushing his bones in its huge jaws.

But the beast swung its heavy head and, as if swatting away a fly, knocked Hyde sideways and off his feet with a blow of its muzzle. He fell to the ground and found himself lying in the grave of woven branches. He tried to rise from it, but the dead black branches stirred to life, growing and stretching, closing round him to hold him captive.

Edward Hyde looked on helplessly as the monstrous hound walked without haste across to where Morrison and Mary Paton stood, holding hands, their faces empty of fear. It raised its great head to the yellow and rust sky and gave a bellowing howl. Its call was answered from some shadowed part of the glen by a screeching cry of lament, and Hyde recognized it as the banshee call he had heard at the Water of Leith.

The Black Hound leaned down over the small girl in the ragged clothes and opened wide its great maw of clustered teeth.

While the demon hound's breath stirred her hair and its drool dripped onto her shoulders, Mary Paton continued to look at Hyde and with the same dispassion said: "The great beast is still loose in the world. You leave it loose in the world."

Still held captive in the witch's cradle, Hyde watched on helplessly as the demon jaws snapped shut.

Once more a shrill, screeching sound like a banshee's cry filled the strath and echoed against the mountains, but it became lost in the sound of Hyde's own screaming.

Edward Hyde woke into the darkness of his bedroom, the sounds of teeth clashing and bones crushing still ringing in his head. He thrashed his arms and legs desperately until he was assured he was not still bound to the earth by clutching twigs and tendrils.

For an instant, while he breathed deep and slowly to calm the racing of his pulse, Hyde believed he could still hear the hound's howl and the banshee's response resonating in the stonework of his home.

31

The following morning, Hyde was again summoned to Rintoul's office. It was too soon after the discovery of Porteous's body for Hyde to have anything worthwhile to report, so he guessed there was more bad news to hear. Despite Rintoul's new knowledge of his condition, Hyde decided he would not, for the moment, tell the chief constable about his nocturnal seizure, and its bizarre imagery, of the night before.

There had been much in his visit to that dream otherworld that he needed to think about. He had remembered Samuel's advice that the answers to his questions may lie in the dark imagery of his seizure dreams: there was something about this most recent dream that seemed laden with significance. To Hyde, it was like mastering a different language: there was a symbolic vocabulary and grammar to the images that had flashed through his sleeping brain. He just needed to learn them.

Rintoul sat grim-faced at his desk, the journal centred and alone on its leather-panelled surface. The chief constable's hands rested on either side of it.

"Sit down, Captain Hyde," said Rintoul. "You will need Dr. Porteous's journal to continue your investigation into his murder."

"You have read through it?" asked Hyde. At Rintoul's waved invitation, he sat down opposite the chief constable.

"I have, or at least as much of it as has been left by the murderer. It makes troubling reading. Much of which concerns your afflictions."

"I'm sorry, Chief Constable," said Hyde. "I should have disclosed my condition to you from the start."

"Yes, Hyde," said Rintoul. "You most certainly should have. To be frank, you should have disclosed it to my predecessor. But that is the least of the matter."

"I don't understand."

"Now that I have been able fully to decipher what remains of Porteous's notes, it leads—or at least it could lead—to a disturbing conclusion."

"What conclusion?" asked Hyde.

"I now understand the focus of Dr. Porteous's research. According to what has survived in his journal, Porteous was treating two patients at his home, both in secret, one of whom was you. Both these patients had their needs for that secrecy, but so did Porteous. From what I can see, both were also unknowing subjects of study, experiment, almost, to prove a theory Porteous was exploring."

"Who was the other patient?"

"That is the thing." The chief constable gazed down at the red leather journal. "The only information left in the journal pertains to you—and much of that has been removed also. The other patient is left shrouded in mystery—no name given; Porteous refers to him only as 'the Beast.' Such mentions of this Beast as remain suggest that Porteous feared him. He describes him as monstrous and sadistically violent, as black a human soul as can be imagined. But all other references have been torn from the journal, including the name of this other patient."

"What I do not understand," said Hyde, "is why any of the journal remains. Instead of painstakingly removing only those pages that give a clue to the killer's identity, why did he not simply steal the whole journal? Why not take it somewhere it could be destroyed, burned? From what you say, it would seem to be clear that it was this other patient, this Beast, who murdered Samuel, so why leave any reference to his existence?"

Rintoul's expression darkened. "You are the detective, not I, but I believe it was done very specifically with one intention in mind."

"Which was?"

"To incriminate you."

"Me?" Hyde gave a small, confused laugh. "How so? If anything, it puts me in the clear, identifying me as the other patient."

Rintoul handed Hyde the journal. "I think you need to read through such as survives of Porteous's notes. All that remains refers only to either you, or this Beast; no name is given to any other patient. There is more gap than substance, but one interpretation is that the truth lies in Porteous's secret research."

"Which was?" asked Hyde, taking the journal from Rintoul.

The chief constable sighed, as if what he was about to impart was burdensome. "Samuel Porteous was hoping to make a huge break-through in the identification and treatment of a particular psychiat-ric condition. A condition he had named Alter Idem Syndrome. Alter Idem means—"

"A second self," said Hyde. "I know the phrase from Cicero."

"Quite . . ." Rintoul's expression suggested he had not understood Hyde's reference. "Porteous also makes much use of the terms 'ego' and 'alter ego,' which I gather are related to this concept. And here lies the problem, particularly as it applies to you, Captain Hyde. You see, from what I've been able to establish, this Beast did not exist indepen-dently—it was not a man, but a *part* of a man."

"I don't understand . . ." said Hyde.

"In truth, nor do I," said Rintoul. "And nor do I believe such a thing possible, which is why you remain at liberty."

Embers of anger started to glow in Hyde's confusion. "At liberty? Why would I not be at liberty?"

"Because . . ." Rintoul said slowly and deliberately, as if adding weight to each word, "according to Porteous, this so-called Beast was not a patient, but a *part* of his patient: a monstrous personality that existed *within* the man he treated but was not the man himself. He states in the journal that this patient had some kind of divided mind, and the identity of the so-called Beast would occasionally take over, unknown to its host. As Porteous described it, the patient was the ego, the Beast the alter ego. Once in control, the Beast would perform all kinds of evil that his host would never contemplate."

Hyde felt a chill penetrate his bones. "So you think that there was only one patient, not two? That this Beast Samuel referred to is *my* alter ego?"

"That is indeed the inference that can be drawn. Indeed, the implica-tion engineered by the individual who left only those pages for scru-tiny." The chief constable sighed. "I'm not a psychiatrist, Edward. I am not even an investigator, but it seems to me that if this Beast exists within you, then it would have sufficient instincts of self-preservation to make sure you would *not* be implicated. If you hang or are confined in an asylum, then the Beast also hangs with you or shares your confinement. In any case, I cannot believe for an instant that such a mental aberration really exists: how could a man have two identities, each totally independent and ignorant of the other?"

Hyde held Rintoul in a steady gaze for a moment, then said: "I have something to tell you . . ."

"You cannot seriously believe," said Rintoul when Hyde had finished, "that when you have one of these amnesiac periods you describe, you become this Beast of which Porteous wrote?"

"Think about it," said Hyde. "I cannot account for my actions during these episodes, I have no recollection of where I've been or what I have done. As I said to Samuel, it is too much of a coincidence that I found myself at the scene of a murder—the night I discovered the body of the Hanged Man—with no recollection of why I was there or how I got there."

"So what would you have me do?" asked Rintoul.

"At least put me under observation; ideally have me in custody for that observation."

Rintoul looked perplexed. "This is the stuff of cheap fiction. Two personalities within one body, each unaware of the other . . . Again I say I cannot believe a word of it."

"That is exactly what Samuel Porteous said—that it was the stuff of cheap fiction—when I challenged him that I perhaps committed evil acts during my lost time. And now he is dead. He said I could not do in an altered state that which I would not do normally. But I know that of which I am capable: I have seen it, in India. In any case, from what you say, this Beast is the antithesis of its host's personality. And once more I have to return to the fact that I found myself at the scene of the Hanged Man murder, with no recollection of how I got there."

Suddenly, the chief constable's expression lit up. "But that's the thing!" he exclaimed with uncharacteristic animation. "You weren't there by coincidence. Remember you told me you were meeting someone in Dean Village that night—someone with information about Hugh Morrison and his guilt or innocence. You told me yourself."

"I can't remember—I mean I can't remember because I lost time. I can't even remember our conversation about it prior to me leaving the station."

"But I can," said Rintoul, brightly. "I remember the name you mentioned. I remember exactly who you said you were going to see . . ."

32

The descent seemed endless. Elspeth had started to count each step, but had descended so far, for so long, that she gave up. It was exhausting, for each step was a testing, a probing with the toe of her shoe to ensure there was indeed a step to take her weight. Other than the knowledge that she was descending in a wide stone spiral, her progress yielded no intelligence of the nature of this place.

It must, she thought to herself, have been hours now since she had first recovered her senses—all but one of her senses, the caliginous nature of her prison keeping her blind. Or had it been days? Had she slept, her body moving as an automaton while her mind slumbered? The strange effects of the deprivation of her sight and the solid concentration required by her descent had bent her conception of time. She was aware that she felt no hunger, nor thirst, and wondered if her fear and her efforts had exaggerated the chronology of her confinement.

It was a shock to Elspeth when she failed to find another step, instead striking level ground. She inched her foot forward: still no step. Pressing her back to the wall, she slid down its chill, slime-sleek stone until she sat on the ground.

She took to her hands and knees and once more began crawling.

The scale of the place must be vast, she thought to herself. Once more she traced a route along the wall that seemed endless, her progress painful, her skirt and stockings torn by the sharp edges of gravel and broken stone.

Then she felt something different. Something softer.

Something familiar.

Elspeth screamed—a prolonged, wailing, desperate scream as a sudden hopelessness, as dark as the world around her, suddenly welled up and burst forth. As she wailed into the dark, rocking back and forth, she clutched to her breast with desperate hands that which she had found.

The sacking that had been her bedding.

33

They made the strangest partners, thought Hyde, as he walked to Dean Village, escorted by Chief Constable Rintoul, who had insisted with some force that he accompany him.

As they made their way out of the West End and down towards the Water of Leith, the personality of the city around them completely transformed. The planned and measured grace and generous proportions of the New Town suddenly gave way to the cluttering, cramped chaos and darker character of Dean Village. The air grew thicker: granular with smoke and soot leaking from fissured chimneys; damp with the humid humours from the mills and factories that lined the Water of Leith.

As they entered Dean Village, the foetid odours of boiled cabbage and raw sewage blended nauseatingly with the other smells. This was one of the poorest and most unsanitary areas of the city: a cluster of huddled, run-down tenements for those who laboured in the mills. Entire families lived in two rooms, more often than not a single room. Many had come here in hope of work after the clearances of Highland communities and rural Lowland villages to make way for sheep grazing, factory or sporting estate. Those who now lived here often did so in a state of bewilderment, disorientated and perplexed by the cramped, contaminated claustrophobia after the large-sky, clean-air openness of their forsaken homes.

Dean Village's deplorable conditions had become something of a bête noire among Edinburgh's liberal classes, and there was now talk of demolition and renovation. The owner of the *Scotsman* newspaper, Sir John Findlay, had purchased vast tracts of land along the banks of the Water of Leith and had talked of his vision of a new model village, cleared of derelict tenements and offering a new standard of housing for those who toiled in the nearby mills.

For now, however, Dean Village remained blighted by poverty, disease and violence. It struck Hyde that it would be from here that frightened little Nell McCrossan, the mill girl who had run into him that night, would no doubt have been making her way to work.

They found the address they sought. A ramshackle wooden building, three storeys high, leaned uncertainly against a more stable and more ancient stone neighbour, like a drunkard seeking balance from his partner in carouse.

"Does this bring anything back to your recall?" asked Rintoul.

Hyde shook his head.

"This is the address, more or less, you mentioned. You said you had been asked to attend an old, wooden-structured apartment house in this street. There is no other that I can see."

Hyde shrugged, then knocked on the door. A small woman, meagre and pale, with a lifeless expression and straw-coloured hair, came to the door. She could, he thought, be any age from thirty to sixty. Life for these people, he knew, was hard and passed at an accelerated pace.

"I am looking for a woman who goes by the name of Old Flora," said Hyde. "I believe she lives here."

"There is naeb'dy o' that name at this address." The woman made to close the door, but Hyde wedged his booted foot into its jamb.

"This is a police matter, madam. I demand your full attention to my questions."

"Yous are polis?" the woman of indeterminate age asked suspiciously.

"That we are," said Hyde's companion. "I am Chief Constable Rintoul, and this is Superintendent of Detectives, Captain Hyde."

The woman sighed and swung open the door, which creaked and clunked on its hinges. The lamplight from within spilled over Hyde's features and he saw the woman's suspicion deepen.

"I came here on the night the man was found murdered nearby, down by the water," he said. "I was in Dean Village that night because I had arranged to meet with a woman called Old Flora."

"Aye? Well she's no' here now. She was here like, but she's awa' hame, tae the Heelands. She was only here for a while."

"Where does she live?"

"Far in the north. The north-west coast o' Argyll. She was only a lodger here with us—temporary like. She only stayed until her business in Edinburgh was done with."

"What business?" asked Rintoul.

The woman looked from one to the other in sarcastic confusion. She snorted a scoffing laugh. "You sure yous are polis?"

Hyde sighed and removed his warrant from his pocket and held it out for her to see.

"Then yous should ken," she said.

"Why should we know?" asked Hyde, his patience growing thin.

"The business she was here for was the hanging."

"What hanging? The one by the river?"

Again the woman scoffed; this time the confusion in her expression was genuine. "No. No' that hanging, the proper one. The one yous did. Why is it you cannae remember if you were here that night? You could-nae forget yon terrible racket . . ."

"What racket?" asked Hyde.

"Her and a' those other Heeland women. Like screechin' cats they was. Because her son was going to hang, and they widnae be able to bury him, him having tae be buried in the prison grounds, an' that. That was why they had it here."

"Had what here?" asked Hyde, struggling to control his frustration.

"The keening. They had the keening for her son here."

Hyde felt a dark thrill course through him. A keening. Now it all made sense, now he knew from where the banshee wails had come.

"Old Flora . . . She was Hugh Morrison's mother?" he asked.

"She was his mother, all right," said the woman. "Yon poor simple boy yous hanged—that was her son. Old Flora is Old Flora Morrison."

Hyde and Rintoul exchanged a meaningful look.

"So that's it," said Hyde to Rintoul. "For some reason, I came here that night to meet with the mother of poor Hugh Morrison. She must have had something important to tell me." He turned back to the woman. "I shall need an address for Mrs. Morrison . . ."

"I told you," said Rintoul as they climbed Dean Path's shadowed and cobbled incline and out of Dean Village. "You had a good reason for being down here. I had no idea that the Old Flora you talked of meeting was Morrison's mother—but that now makes sense."

"It does. And we can now discount the banshee wailing I heard that night. It had nothing to do with the Hanged Man—it was a keening."

"I don't understand," said Rintoul.

"Banshees are supposed to keen for the dead, coming from the old Gaelic tradition of women keening at Highland funerals. It is such a significant tradition that there are professional keeners—women who take pay to attend a burial or a wake and keen for the deceased. That is what I heard that night—Highland women keening for the boy we were about to hang." Hyde turned to look over his shoulder, thinking he had heard footsteps behind them. There was no one there.

"So what now?" asked Rintoul. "I mean, about the Morrison case?"

"There's nothing I can do at the moment—for now, this matter must rest. I do not have the time to travel up north to find out the reason for our meeting. I shall do so, but I have more exigent matters to which I must attend. In the meantime, a man has hanged for Mary Paton's murder, so, right or wrong, justice has been seen to have been done. If the wrong man hanged and I try to prove his innocence, then the case will consume much of my time. And, with these other cases demanding my immediate attention, time is a currency in which I am a pauper. I will return to this matter, but at the moment it is difficult to see when."

Hyde halted, turning in the direction whence they had come.

"What is it?" asked Rintoul.

Hyde did not answer, instead scanning the shadows behind them.

"I thought . . ." He paused. Again he had imagined movement some distance behind them, in the darkness between the wide-spaced gas lamps, as if they were followed. But, as he knew, the shadows of his days had been haunted by spectres, not least the dual-faced ghost of his dead friend. He decided to say no more to Rintoul. "It's nothing, sir."

They walked on and up into Belford Road and the New Town. As they did so, Hyde resisted the temptation to look over his shoulder and into the shadows behind.

34

Hyde slept fitfully that night, beleaguered by dreams that tumbled and jangled in his slumberous brain. When he awoke, however, he was aware that his dreaming had been natural: simply the day-gathered knot of thoughts and suspicions, worries and desires seeking disentanglement. The images of his dreams evanesced upon waking, unlike those of a seizure dream, which would linger in his recall. One dreamed image, however, persisted a moment longer than the others: that of Cally Burr's face.

He smiled at the memory of her visit to his dreams and he knew he must see her soon. However forlorn they might be, he must tell her of his feelings.

It was a bright, cool day and Hyde apologetically dismissed the waiting Mackinley, explaining that he would walk to the office that morning. The truth was he wanted to use the time further to unravel the events of the last few days.

The images from his seizure dream still haunted him. The remembered spectre of a Janus-faced Samuel Porteous goading him to discover the significance of the strange key fob found among the murdered psychiatrist's personal items—and to identify the lock the key unbound.

So many priorities craved his immediate attention. Like Pollock, Hyde now began to have serious concerns about Elspeth Lockwood; with each new day that passed, his confidence in finding her safe and well diminished that little more.

The morning traffic of carriages, omnibuses and commercial waggons was lighter than usual as Hyde made his way through the New Town morning and onto Princes Street. The reason, he suspected, was the continued disruption of the thoroughfare by the digging works as the ever-expanding web of electric cable was woven through the city's fabric. A steam shovel clanged behind him as he passed one of the sites and he turned to the sound.

There was, he knew, an instinct in all humans. Charles Darwin, renowned alumnus of the University of Edinburgh medical school, had exposed the verity of man's nature and its evolution from distant savannah plains where danger constantly lurked—and where survival depended on keen awareness of a predator's stalking. It was this vestigial instinct that was awoken in Hyde when he saw the two men. They neither walked together nor looked of the same class or type, but he instinctively knew they were united in common purpose. He had become distrustful of his instincts, even of his vision, because of the strange distortions woven by his epilepsy and the shadows that had haunted his days. But these men were real; Hyde's instinct was real.

Keeping his pace steady, he walked on along Princes Street, which became busier with pedestrians as managers and clerks, draughtsmen and secretaries, shop girls and floorwalkers bustled their way to nine o'clock store or office. At no point in his progress did he again look back, but the same instinct told him with a prickle of the hairs on the nape of his neck that his followers were still there.

Hyde was Superintendent of Detectives in the City of Edinburgh Police; he was not going to brook being followed in the street. If Rintoul—to whom he had offered to become subject to voluntary supervision—felt they could put men on his tail without his knowledge and as if he were a common suspect, then they were in for a surprise. Alternatively, if these men were following him with illegal intent, they were bound for a gaol cell. Hyde, who knew the face of every plainclothesman in Edinburgh, determined to find out who his stalkers were and challenge them face-to-face on who had charged them to their task.

When he reached its corner, he casually turned up Hanover Street. Once around the corner, he halted abruptly and stood just out of sight of Princes Street. He measured in his head the distance the first of the men had been behind him and waited until they would be approaching the corner, before stepping out abruptly to face them.

Nearly walking straight into him, and clearly startled by the suddenness and nature of his appearance, a young woman shrank back in shock. Hyde lifted his hat and apologized, and she circled past him. He checked the other pedestrians as they flowed past, then scoured Princes Street as far as he could see along it. There was no sign of the two men.

Perhaps, he thought, with all of the shocks and injuries inflicted by my epilepsy, I am developing a persecution mania. He checked again, but there remained no sight of them.

He sighed and resumed his westward progress along Princes Street towards Torphichen Place and another day of dark discovery.

The autopsy report arrived on Hyde's desk at ten o'clock. It had been handed to him by Peter MacCandless, whose manner had struck Hyde as oddly guarded—indeed, many of his men seemed to behave differently around him after the Porteous murder, his entrance to a room often stilling conversation. There would be, he guessed, much conjecture about his association with the murdered psychiatrist. It was only a small speculative leap to the inexplicable coincidence of his seemingly prescient presence at the Hanged Man murder locus.

It was a situation he would have to address. For the moment, however, Hyde had more pressing things on his mind, and he set the report on his desk. Before he settled to its study, he had a visitor.

James Lockwood was a man beaten down. He looked no more rested than he had the last time he had visited the station, but Hyde suspected predictive grief had insinuated itself into his anxiety. Lockwood had already lost a wife and a son, and the man, despite himself, was clearly anticipating another bereavement. When he was conducted into Hyde's office, the latter felt it essential that some tea be fetched.

"You did not need to call here, Mr. Lockwood," said Hyde when his guest was seated. "I would have called at your office or home to save you the inconvenience."

"It is no inconvenience," said the older man wearily. "And it is better that we meet here. The less this matter is the subject of gossip, the better. Or at least gossip amongst my staff. Elspeth, when she is restored to us, remains my heiress and successor. I think the less her future employees know about this business, the better."

"I'm afraid I tend to the other," said Hyde. "The more who know about your daughter's disappearance, the more likely some fragment of fact may come to light and point us in the right direction. In any case, I am glad you are here."

"I have brought the photograph you requested," said Lockwood, handing Hyde a foolscap envelope. "It is the most recent I have, going back a couple of years. I know it is all the fashion now, but photographs are not something we have gone in for much."

"Thank you," said Hyde. He slipped the photograph, fixed to a grey card mount, from its envelope and examined it. An unsmiling Lockwood senior sat on a frame chair, Elspeth and her now-deceased brother Joseph flanking him. There was something about the set of the jaw that united Elspeth and her father, along with light-coloured hair, the red of which was lost in photographic monochrome. In contrast, Joseph was dark haired, soft featured, with a pale complexion and large, dark and vaguely melancholic eyes.

"This will be most helpful," said Hyde. "Until now we have had to rely on written descriptions of your daughter. We can have her image enlarged." He turned over the card mount to examine the back. The photographer's name and address were embossed into the grey card. "Ah," he said, surprised to recognize the name, "the photographer is Henry Dunlop—he does work for us and I can have him produce enlargements."

He replaced the photograph in its envelope. "What more can you tell me about Elspeth?" he asked. "I mean her personality, her habits, rather than the specifics of her disappearance, which we possess already."

"Elspeth is much like her grandfather—my father—were I to seek any family member as sharing her characteristics. Strong-willed, stubborn even. Not someone easily to be moved to fright."

"Are you close with your daughter?"

"We are close, I would say. But it is a closeness born of circumstance rather than natural affinity."

"I don't quite understand . . ." said Hyde.

"I am not a demonstrative man, Captain Hyde. I recognize the flaws in my character but there is little one can do to change what nature has designed. Elspeth shared much of my lineage, yet she was closer to her mother. Devoted, one could say."

"Her mother is deceased, I believe," said Hyde.

"She died seven years ago, but Elspeth had not seen her for five years before that."

"Oh?" Hyde frowned. "Why was that?"

"My wife was ill for that period. She was confined to a hospital."

"And Elspeth did not visit her mother during that time?"

"That would have been most distressing. You see, Captain Hyde, my wife went quite mad. There had been signs of it throughout our marriage, but then things became intolerable, unmanageable. I would find her talking—sometimes raving—at empty space. She became intemperate with the children, sometimes claiming they were not hers, but changelings. Margaret became subject to the darkest delusions and most extraordinary obsessions. She became a danger to the children, to me—even to herself. The hospital to which she was ultimately confined was Craig House."

"I see," said Hyde. He knew Craig House—it was an expensive private lunatic asylum, directly adjacent to but independent from Craiglockhart Hydropathic Hospital. For most, insanity was a tragedy; for Edinburgh's upper classes, it was an embarrassment. Craig House was the discreet and convenient solution. Samuel Porteous, in addition to his private practice and work at Craiglockhart, had consulted at Craig House.

"I'm sorry, but I have to ask," said Hyde. "Has there been any hint of similar mental aberration in Elspeth?"

"Other than this strange rebelliousness expressed through her involvement with Frederic Ballor, none whatsoever. Even that I see as the same kind of wilfulness and independent nature as her grandfather. As I say, Elspeth takes after my side: practical, forthright, businesslike. You see, Captain Hyde, I always thought there was something deficient in me. A lack of the romantic, or the imaginative. Perhaps that was why I was so attracted to Elspeth's mother. She was from the Western Isles and saw the world . . . well, differently. She was a creature of imagination and romance who seemed to find poetry in the most mundane." Lockwood gave a sad smile. "It made her the most captivating storyteller. She would enchant the children, even practical little Elspeth, with her Highland tales. But it was Elspeth's brother, my son Joseph, who inherited their mother's tendency to fancy. I fear I pushed him to adapt to the family business when all he wanted was to be a painter. Unfortunately, his creativity was not all he inherited from his mother."

"He was a neurasthenic, I believe," said Hyde.

"Of the greatest severity." Lockwood's expression dimmed further with sadness. "As I am sure you are aware, there are rumours that his death was suicide. That may be the case, though I doubt it. The truth is, his delusions were so vivid that it is entirely possible my son threw himself from the store's roof in the firm conviction he could fly. Those who saw him fall said he uttered no scream or cry—simply fell with arms outstretched."

"I'm sorry, Mr. Lockwood," said Hyde. They paused while the tea was brought in by Pollock. Hyde introduced them to each other.

"Would you mind if Detective Constable Pollock joined us?" asked Hyde. "He is working with me on your daughter's case—in fact he is engaged in no other duties at the moment. It might be useful for him to sit in on our discussion."

Lockwood examined Pollock coldly, perhaps disheartened by the constable's youth, but seemed too weary to protest. "Very well."

Pollock diplomatically did not take a seat but stood to the side, by the wall, notebook and pencil in hand.

"I take it that is what you meant by being close to Elspeth through circumstance rather than affinity?" asked Hyde. "That it was these tragedies that brought you close?"

"It was. I do believe Elspeth sees herself in me, though I think that, if anything, tended her to distance herself from me. Perhaps even inspired her rebellion. But after her mother was taken away, and particularly after Joseph's death, we became sole support, one to the other. We are all the other has." Lockwood's voice cracked with emotion quickly stifled. Hyde waited a moment before continuing.

"Elspeth has never blamed you for her mother's asylum committal?"

Lockwood shook his head. "Towards the end, my wife's behaviour was . . . *extreme*, one could say. The children were very much witness to those extremes, and became most distressed. By the time my wife was committed—which was a very last resort—though both very young, Elspeth and Joseph were aware of the full scale of her derangement."

"What about interests and hobbies?" asked Pollock. "Does any activity consume her time?"

Lockwood turned to Pollock as if he had forgotten the young constable was there. He then turned back and addressed his answer to Hyde.

"Elspeth is involved in many societies, charitable and otherwise. She is very active in the Edinburgh Gaelic Society—she speaks Erse well, her mother having taught her and Joseph as children. There were, of course, the associations of which you already know. And some others."

"Others?" asked Hyde.

"My daughter is independent of nature, as I have said—she believed that independence should extend to all of her gender."

"She is involved in suffragism?" asked Pollock.

"She is—or at least has been. She believes property-owning women should be given the vote. I understand she had some other strange political beliefs, but she chose not to share those with me. I suspect there was an element of anti-Unionism, inspired by that scoundrel Ballor."

"Your daughter was politically active?" asked Pollock.

"I wouldn't say active . . ." Lockwood replied, again without turning from Hyde. "But she did have some strange interests and involvements."

"May I see the photograph?" Pollock asked Hyde, who handed it to him.

Hyde noticed but did not react to the sudden change in Pollock's expression. Lockwood had his back to Pollock, and would not have seen the sudden animation in the young constable's face.

"What is it, Iain?" said Hyde after Lockwood had left. He had asked Pollock to escort the business-owner to the exit, and had heard his bounding steps as he had run back up the stairs and into Hyde's office without knocking.

"I have been describing Elspeth Lockwood, in every detail, to all and sundry, yet never made the simplest of connections myself." Pollock shook his head as if in wonderment at his own stupidity.

"And what connection, Acting Detective Constable Pollock, would that be?"

"The red-haired young woman who greeted me at the door of the Cobb Mackendrick gathering in Leith . . . sir, I would swear under oath that it was Elspeth Lockwood . . ."

35

Hyde ordered Pollock to ascertain Cobb Mackendrick's whereabouts and bring him into the police office.

"Should we inform Scotland Yard?" asked Pollock. "Seeing as Mackendrick is of interest to them."

"This is our investigation, Iain," said Hyde. "A missing person inquiry. Special Branch's interest is subordinate to that. Bring Cobb Mackendrick here for questioning."

As the day wore on, Hyde began to feel a throbbing in his temples and a tingling sensation in his mouth. "Not now," he muttered to himself. "Please, not now . . ."

He told the desk sergeant he did not want to be disturbed for an hour and, obtaining aspirin powders from the first aid locker, mixed them into a glass of water, sipping it as he sat in the quiet of his office with the autopsy report on his desk.

It made troubling reading.

Samuel Porteous had been subject to a sustained and brutal knife attack. The injuries to the thorax and abdomen had been incurred ante- and peri-mortem. There had been no mercy of a direct blow to the heart or aorta to offer instant release; instead he had died from the effects of blood loss and shock.

It was, Hyde realized, a significant difference from the Hanged Man murder. One similarity remained: that the mutilation of the corpse—in Porteous's case the removal of the eyes—had been performed post-mortem.

It had been Joseph Bell who had carried out the autopsy, and the report was full of small details. Dr. Bell had included a covering note to Hyde with the report. He wrote that Porteous had been one of his brightest pupils, and he wished Hyde every good fortune in finding his killer. He also promised to assist in any way he could; if he could be of further service, all Hyde had to do was ask. In his note he also explained that he had made mention in the autopsy report of all observations, no matter how trivial and irrespective of their relevance to the causes of death, just in case they should prove helpful in a wider investigation.

One such observation was that Porteous had shown some limited signs of developmental anatomical abnormality, probably due to diminished bone mass. Dr. Bell postulated that this was consistent with a poor or restricted diet in earlier life. Hyde realized that he knew nothing about his late friend's early years, and that Porteous had never discussed with him anything prior to his university and professional career.

He took the report over to the window and, standing in its light, continued to read. There was much that was lost to him in medical terminology, but one thing stood out: Bell reported that, on examining the brain, he found evidence of cerebral arteritis, particularly stenosis of the basilar artery. This, he stated, combined with other meningeal indications, pointed to a specific meningovascular disease.

Samuel Porteous had had syphilis.

The disease was in latency, Bell stated. For years Porteous would have been symptomless, without rash or lesion or other visible or palpable signs of its presence. But during that long latency, the disease had been accumulating damage and danger in his brain. He may already have been experiencing personality changes. Other neurological symptoms may have started to emerge: paresis and asthenia may have become manifest in physical weakness; he may also have suffered occasional mental exhaustion, dizziness or forgetfulness. Bell added a side note that Porteous, as a physician and psychiatrist, would have been fully aware of his condition and its inevitable outcome.

Hyde thought of how Porteous's typical good humour had begun to wane of late in his personality. Pausing from his reading of the unsettling details of the dissection of the body and soul of his friend, he happened to glance down into the street below.

He let the pages of the report fall from his hands onto the floor. He turned abruptly from the window and, violently throwing open his door, ran out of his office and down the flights of stone steps, forcing a shocked MacCandless, who had been coming up the stairs, to flatten himself against the wall and allow the barging Hyde to pass.

More surprised faces turned in his direction as he burst into the ground-floor reception area.

"You!" he bellowed at the young uniformed constable behind the reception desk. "With me, now!"

Hyde burst out from the station door and sprinted along Torphichen Place, the uniformed constable at his back. He ran to the end of the street, the leather of his shoes skidding on the pavement as he rounded the corner into Torphichen Street.

No one.

He had seen him from his office window. He *had* seen him. One of the men who had followed him earlier in the day had stood on the corner of Torphichen Place and Torphichen Street, watching the stationhouse.

Except now there was no one there.

He looked in every direction. It was an open space where the wide boulevards of Atholl Place, Torphichen Street and West Maitland Street formed a junction, offering no opportunities for hasty concealment or escape. A few pedestrians walked the pavements, none of whom were the figure he had spotted from the window. How could the man have disappeared so quickly?

Once more Hyde broke into a sprint, the constable in his wake, this time to the corner with West Maitland Street. He scanned the thoroughfare first towards Haymarket, then in the opposite direction towards the city centre.

Other officers had spilled out from the station and had now caught up with Hyde, who stood, turning his head in one direction, then another, in desperate search.

"What on earth is it, sir?"

"What?" Hyde turned around abruptly and saw it was MacCandless who had spoken and who now regarded his superior with confused concern.

"Whatever is the matter?" asked MacCandless. Then, with more insistence when his superior still did not answer but continued to search the streets desperately, "Captain Hyde?"

"I saw someone . . ."

"Who?"

"I'm being followed. I saw them earlier."

"Them?"

"Two men. I think they followed me the other night as well." Hyde shook his head in desperation. "I thought . . ."

Hyde read what was written in MacCandless's expression.

"Never mind," he said, and turned back towards the station, ignoring, as they cleared a way for him to pass through, the looks his men exchanged.

36

Elspeth had sobbed until there were no tears left in her and her cries echoed hoarse and empty in the black void. How could it be? she asked herself. How could she have descended the stairs so far, for so long, and ended up on the same level where she had begun? Whatever this place was, whatever dark design had shaped it, it was robbing her of such shreds of sanity as had been left her.

Was this reality no more real than the visions she had experienced that night at the Dark Man standing stone with Frederic? No more real than the hallucination of a one-eyed Celtic demon towering above Edinburgh?

She sat on the sacking, clasping one corner of it to her breast as a child might clutch a comfort blanket, in the hope it would dispel monsters lurking under the bed, waiting to vex to nightmare. She sat for a time measureless in the silent blackness, her mind as empty and dark as the void around her.

After a long time, or what seemed a long time, she made a decision. She would walk into the void. Her fruitless circumnavigation had told her her prison was vast yet had yielded no other clue to its nature. Perhaps if she walked out from the wall and across the space she would find something—there was of course danger in the strategy, but she was finished with crawling on her hands and knees. If she should plunge to her death at the bottom of some pit, then so be it: at least she would have met death on her feet.

She stepped forth with care, stretching her arms out into the darkness, stumbling on the broken and buckled flagstones. The uneven terrain slowed her progress, dampened her determination. After a while, however, she became aware that the ground beneath her feet became more even. Eventually her footfalls were regular and more assured, the sound of each echoing in the darkness. She walked on and on, never encountering an obstacle hidden in the dark, never reaching the opposite wall. If this was some vault beneath Edinburgh, then its sheer scale would threaten the stability of the city above. Nothing about this place made sense to her; its perplexing physics, its seemingly bound-less dimensionality defied logic.

She halted her step and her breath in the same instant. She strained the darkness for hint of the sound again. She was ready to dismiss it as the rushing of blood in her ears, or the wishful imaginings of her tortured mind when she heard it once more.

Footsteps.

She remained still to be sure it was not just the echo of her own walking. The sound of footfalls continued. They were distant, she could tell, but they were heading in her direction, slowly growing louder. Impossibly, the steps that approached were brisk and even, as if unhin-dered by the abyssal darkness.

Elspeth, who had hoped so desperately for rescue, clamped her hand to her mouth so as not to give away her location with a gasp. Some profound and powerful intuition told her that whoever or whatever was carried towards her by those footfalls was not determined to her rescue. Instinctively she knew they belonged to her tormentor.

Heedless of the blind danger, she started to run.

37

Cally Burr looked surprised to find Hyde on her doorstep; in truth, Hyde himself was surprised to find himself there. Her house was a respectable and stolid two-storeyed townhouse in a vaguely Palladian crescent on the northern edge of the city, where the New Town rubbed ennobled shoulders with areas of lesser gentility.

"I'm sorry to disturb you unannounced," said Hyde, weakly. "I needed . . ." He struggled for words.

"Come in," she said, frowning. "I'll make us some tea."

She invited him into her parlour while she prepared the tea. He did not know why, but Hyde was surprised by Cally Burr's choice of furnishings. Despite having a large window, the room was darkened by its decor. Perhaps because she was a woman of science, he had anticipated her home to be functional, bright and free of fuss. Here, the reverse was true: the dark enfolding walls were dressed in a satin-finished wallpaper, decorated with an ornate motif of interweaving leaves and vines, the sheening colours of which were dark greens, blues and turquoise. The sofa was low and exotic-looking, upholstered in a sinuously patterned satin material of a similar palette to the wallpaper and curtains.

Added to it all was an odour, a scent that stirred ancient memories in Hyde: the smell of sandalwood. The dark exoticism of the room, he realized, reflected that which was possessed but suppressed in its occupant.

The mahogany and glass display case that stood against one wall seemed disproportionately large for the room and was filled with objects fashioned from pottery, metal and wood. Even from across the room, Hyde could identify from the style of the items their provenance. He stepped closer and examined some of the contents: a large, elegantly tapered *surahi* flagon pot; an ornate betel nut box fashioned from beaten copper; an equally ornate *meenakari* box adorned with a peacock motif; two small brass claw bells impressed with crimson lacquer.

She wore the ring of sapphires and emeralds he had noticed before. Now he remembered where he had seen a ring like that. A polki ring.

"You have spent time in India?" Hyde turned to her and asked. Once more he found himself discomfited by her steady, unreadable stare, as if she were deciding to answer or not.

"I was born there," she said at last, some of the frost thawing in her eyes. "My father was an engineer—an Irish engineer." She paused. "My mother was Gujarati."

"I see," said Hyde, unsurprised. It was a revelation that he had already worked out from his impressions of Dr. Burr and the tone and content of her accommodations. "So what brought you to Scotland?"

"My mother died when I was young and my father sent me to live with his sister in Dublin. When my father returned from India, we moved to Edinburgh."

"Does your father live with you?" Hyde asked.

"He died, several years ago. He left me enough to live independently and complete my medical studies. All in all, I have learned to fend for myself."

"I am sorry to hear that. About your father, I mean. You live alone?" he asked.

"I do," she said defiantly. "Don't you?"

"Yes, I do," he said, and stopped himself from saying more.

They sat and chatted until Cally brought forth the matter at hand. "What brings you to my door, Captain Hyde?"

Hyde leaned forward, resting his elbows on his knees, in a pose of resignation. He started to talk. He told her about Porteous's gruesome murder, about his secret arrangement with the psychiatrist, about his condition and about his reasons for hiding it from the world, particularly his employers. He told her of the vivid, lucid dreaming, of his terrifying hallucinations of a small dead girl and his chance, out-of-the-corner-of-his-eye glimpses of a young man he knew to be innocent but who had been hanged nevertheless. He talked without pause, letting the tea sit untouched in its cup as he told Cally Burr about the journal with pages missing, but pages enough left to incriminate him.

He told her of the shadows, imagined and real, that had dogged his steps and darkened his days; about the men he was convinced followed him but could not be found. About the doubts of others about his sanity, about his own doubts.

He also told her of his argument with Porteous over the effects of his prescription; and how this had added to the vague cloud of suspicion that hung over him.

"What was in this prescription?" she asked.

"That I cannot tell you. Chief Constable Rintoul has already asked me the same. Samuel always had the compound made up for me and ready—if not, he would send it to my home. What is most strange is that there is no record of its formula among his notes. Whoever murdered him tore out a great many pages from his private journal, and I would guess they have taken other papers as well. And, as I've already explained to the chief constable, I threw out the last dose, so determined was I to be free of it."

"Be free of it? Why? What effects did it have on you?"

He told her about the lethargy, about the hallucinations on waking, about its failure to mitigate his nocturnal seizures.

"The truth is, my seizure-shaped otherworld and its dissembling inhabitants are most convincing in their guises. I cannot even be certain that these men who I thought followed me were as flesh and blood as they seemed. If you had seen the expressions on the faces of my men when I ran out onto the street to chase a ghost—staring as they would at a madman . . . I am also guessing that there were already rumours of my connection with Samuel."

Cally Burr sat for a moment, considering Hyde's words. The light was growing dim outside, and eventually she rose to turn up the gas mantles and the tabletop oil lamp. When she sat down again, the soft light emphasized the honey tones of her skin, and Hyde thought of the difficulties, the dislocation, her mixed parentage must have brought. For her then to pursue a career unfriendly to her gender suggested enormous inner resolve. He found himself understanding her combativeness and admiring her deeply. He also found himself thinking about how exquisitely beautiful she was and how she stirred in him feelings he had sought to deny.

"Why have you come to me with this?" she asked eventually.

Hyde sighed. "I need help. I need the help of someone capable of seeing through this mess. I just thought . . . I thought you would perhaps understand. You also told me about your interest in pharmacology. I thought you would have some idea of what Samuel had used to treat me."

"That's the thing," said Cally. "I cannot think what compound he would be using. Because your episodes do not involve tonic-clonic seizures, even an anticonvulsant such as potassium bromide would offer no real efficacy. I can only guess that Dr. Porteous was developing some kind of experimental treatment."

"That was my increasing concern," said Hyde. "One of the reasons I ceased taking the medication. I worried that I was perhaps more guinea pig than patient. Samuel was a very ambitious man, and I know that he often grudged the advances made by his peers. If there was any fault I could find in him, it would have been his vanity and overarching ambition. I had no idea he was hiding latent syphilis and was in a race against time."

Again she sat with poised calm as she considered Hyde's words. "Did Dr. Porteous offer an opinion on the cause of your symptoms?" she asked at last.

"That was precisely the source of our last disagreement: he remained vague about that. But he did suggest it might be a tumour, and its growth has made my symptoms worse."

"But stopping your medication has made no difference, one way or another?"

"If anything, it has made things better. I haven't had an episode since I stopped. But that isn't unusual: even before I started treatment, I could go weeks without one."

"When did you first start having these absences and nocturnal seizures? How old were you?"

"My first would have been when I was about ten. Eleven, perhaps."

"Then I think it is highly unlikely that your symptoms are the result of any form of malignancy, or even a benign lesion. And I'm not entirely sure why Dr. Porteous would suggest such a thing as a principal possibility, unless . . ."

"Unless what?"

"A trick occasionally employed by physicians—one that I deplore—is to try to dissuade an inquisitive patient by suggesting the answers they seek are so fearful that they are best left unexplored."

"Samuel certainly did seem to become agitated when I pressed him on the matter."

Again she sat thoughtfully for a moment before going over to the bureau and taking out a fountain pen and a leather-bound notebook.

"I want you to tell me everything about your seizures, about your strange dreams, about everything Dr. Porteous told you . . ."

Hyde's mood was much lifted when he left Cally Burr's home. She had sat quietly, patiently, kindly. She had listened and she had reassured. He had exposed his deepest fears, the secrets of his strange condition and even the isolation his appearance seemed to bring. In return, he had sensed her defences come down. Unspoken though it was, there emerged between them the mutual understanding of two people who recognized in each other the nature of an outsider. He even dared to believe there had been some hint of affection.

Most of all, he felt he was no longer alone in unravelling the mysteries of his condition, and what had happened to Samuel Porteous. He had been totally frank about his episodes of lost time—and the fears they had provoked in him that he had been responsible for some crime or other misdeed during their passage. Cally Burr had shared Porteous's opinion that no one was capable of committing an unconscious act that they would not brook while having their wits fully about them.

It was an autumn early evening and already the approaching winter was casting its foreshadow, pushing dark fingers into the day and promising longer nights to come. That had been the thing that had affected Hyde most on his return from India: after the dazzling brightness and the vibrant colours of the Indian days, it had been difficult to adjust to the opaque, mute melancholia of an Edinburgh winter.

He decided to walk to the corner and hail a hansom. He cast a glance back along the street whence he had come as he prepared to step off the pavement to cross the road.

It was then he saw him. A man walked along the pavement, some fifty yards behind him, his eyes neither on nor avoiding Hyde, his manner and pace of walking casual and without any attempt at concealment. There was nothing about the man's demeanour that suggested anything other than that he was walking along the street with innocent purpose.

Yet Hyde knew him. He was convinced it was the same man he had seen from his office window, waiting at the corner of Torphichen Place.

His heart pounded in his chest—not with fear of his shadow, but with the genuine anxiety that he was going mad; that this form, so convincingly solid and credible, was woven from the same stuff as the ghost of Mary Paton.

He trotted across the road and turned abruptly into a narrow street crowded in with tenements. He burst into a run until he found the entrance to a close and dodged into it, rendering himself invisible to his pursuer when he turned into the street. Hyde stopped and pressed his back against the china-tiled wall of the tenement close. He heard the sound of feet on cobbles, beating a rapid tattoo as his follower ran along the street, clearly now aware that the object of his surveillance had taken flight. The footsteps halted, but Hyde thought he could hear others further away, and he heard an exchange of oaths. More footsteps, some advancing, others retreating. He edged towards the close's entrance, his back still against the stonework, and stole a swift glance at his pursuer.

If this follower was real and not a phantasm, then he was not one of Hyde's men—and the only plainclothes detectives in Edinburgh were Hyde's men. It was therefore unlikely to be someone tasked by Rintoul to track Hyde's movements. In any case, a policeman watching a police station, where Hyde's movements could not be more obvious, would not make any sense.

He heard the footsteps grow closer and steeled himself to action. As the man walked past the mouth of the close, Hyde stepped out behind him. He grabbed the man, who was taller but leaner than Hyde, by the shoulder and spun him around. He now clearly saw his pursuer's face, wide-eyed in surprise, and it confirmed he was not one of his officers.

"Who are you and why are you following me?" he demanded.

The startled man's surprise dimmed instantly; the widened eyes narrowed, the face tightened into an expression of malevolent intent. Hyde saw gloved hand dip swiftly into coat pocket and produce a gleaming, narrow blade, about five inches in length. The blade flashed out and up towards Hyde's face, but he deflected the strike with his right forearm. He felt something had struck him just below the elbow and felt the warm wetness of blood gathering where the blade had sliced through coat, jacket and shirt.

Something like a dark fire ignited deep within Hyde and surged upwards into an explosion of violence. He launched himself at his assailant with a roar. His attacker swung the knife in an arc, this time aimed at the abdomen, but again Hyde successfully blocked the strike, this time getting a grip on the wrist of the hand that held the knife. The dark fire again surged upwards and he smashed his free fist into his attacker's face. The man staggered backwards and Hyde, still holding his assailant's knife hand, hooked his boot behind the man's calf, causing him to lose balance and fall onto his back. Hyde remained standing, twisting the arm with the knife until there was a sickening crack and the man screamed in pain, the knife clattering on the cobbles.

Hyde dropped down onto his now supine attacker, slamming his knee into his chest and emptying his lungs of air. Keeping him pinned to the ground with his knee, he struck his assailant in the face with his huge, heavy fists, over and over.

There was the sound of bone and cartilage snapping in the man's face, which became smeared with blood, but Hyde, blinded by black fury, did not stop in his attack.

When it was clear his opponent was unconscious, he halted, his chest heaving. The fire subsided and he looked at the man with concern, realizing he had come close to killing him. He had, for the duration of his attack, become that other Hyde, consumed by the same combat-ignited dark fury he had experienced a long time ago, a long way away. Suddenly Porteous's and Cally Burr's reassurances that he would not do during a seizure anything alien to his waking nature lost their potency.

Consciously or not, Edward Hyde knew he was capable of great violence.

He examined his unconscious attacker: his arm, clearly broken or dislocated, lay at an abnormal angle where Hyde had twisted it beyond nature.

It was then Hyde saw it again: between the wrist cuff of the man's glove and where his sleeve had ridden up, a small mark was exposed on his forearm. It was, he had no doubt, the same triskelion tattoo as possessed by the photographer Dunlop, and that he had thought he had detected on the wrist of the colour sergeant at the castle.

He was relieved to see his assailant begin to stir, moaning. Perhaps now he would have some of the answers he sought.

He had just started to ease himself up from kneeling on the man's chest and was reaching for his police whistle when something smashed into the back of his head and Edinburgh's greying evening turned suddenly to impenetrable darkness.

Hyde came round to the copper taste of blood, where it had trickled from his head wound into his mouth. He started to his feet, but checked the speed of his movement when it was met by a tenor of pain that resounded in the vault of his skull. Blood-blinded, he rose slowly and unsteadily to his feet, took a handkerchief and wiped the gore from his eyes.

A whining tone resounded in his ears, and the buildings and sky slowly spun around him, threatening to tip him sideways. He looked around himself and found he was alone in the mouth of the close.

It was slightly darker, but the night had not gathered fully during his senselessness and he estimated he had been unconscious for a matter of minutes. Time enough, it would seem, for his assailant to quit the scene, taking his injured partner in crime with him. The material of his coat sleeve was wet-stained where blood from the knife wound had bloomed darkly through its weave. He stood for a moment, gathering himself as much as he could from disequilibrium and confusion. He needed medical attention and he reached into his pocket and took out his police whistle to summon help, but checked himself before he blew it. With unsteady resolve, supporting himself on stonework and railings as he went, he retraced his steps whence he had come.

"Edward!" Cally Burr's expression was revealed naked of its usual defences when she saw Hyde returned to her door in such a condition.

"I'm sorry . . ." he said weakly as he stumbled simultaneously across the thresholds of her home and his unconsciousness.

38

His consciousness did not come back all at once, complete and lucid, but in frayed-edged fragments. At one stage he felt he had been drifting, as if floating on water, only to become aware of people around him, bearing him along on a stretcher. He had tried to stir to speech, but he remained too far detached from his body and slowly drifted further yet as he returned to oblivion.

In another fleeting moment of awareness, he thought he could hear Cally Burr's voice, soothing and sweet, close to his ear, but then it too drifted away and the darkness once more reclaimed him.

When he did recover his senses fully, he was looking up at a cream-coloured ceiling, the brightness of which hurt his eyes. The air was tainted with the same carbolic notes that he remembered from the hydropathic hospital. A nurse leaned over him and said something he did not catch, then she disappeared. By the time she returned, bringing a young man in a white hospital dustcoat, Hyde was fully restored to awareness.

"Can you tell me your name?" asked the young doctor.

"Edward Hyde. Captain Edward Henry Hyde. Where am I?"

"You're in the Royal Infirmary. Can you remember how you were injured?"

"I was struck from behind." Hyde made to sit up in the bed and was rewarded by a stab of pain through his skull and a sudden wave of nausea.

"You must remain still, Captain Hyde," said the doctor. "You are badly concussed and we need to establish if any other damage has been done."

"It is imperative that I speak with Chief Constable Rintoul," protested Hyde. "Right away."

"I'm afraid you are going nowhere; you must remain here under observation—"

"Then send someone to bring him here!" Hyde shouted at the physician, who took a step back. Hyde drew a breath, then calmed his tone: "This is a police matter—an urgent police matter. I must speak with Chief Constable Rintoul without delay."

The doctor nodded. "Nurse . . ."

The nurse left the room. The young doctor insisted on asking Hyde a series of questions, clearly formulated to ascertain how sensible he was to his surroundings and to test his memory. Hyde was able to answer them all without confusion.

A pain in his right arm competed with that in his head for his attention. He looked down to see where a bandage bound his forearm.

"You have a deep wound to your arm," explained the doctor, "from a bladed weapon. We had to stitch it. There may be some muscle and tendon damage, so I suggest wearing a sling when you are eventually up and about."

The nurse returned. "A messenger is on his way to police headquarters," she explained. "In the meantime, you have another visitor."

She stood to one side and Cally Burr was revealed. She was wearing a brocade jacket and matching bonnet in the same peacock blues and greens that graced her parlour. In the ivory and cream tones of the hospital ward, she seemed the most exotic of creatures. Despite his injured state, her beauty stirred him.

"How are you, Edward?" she asked.

"Relieved that I'm not going mad," he said. "Phantoms cannot inflict wounds like these. The man who slashed me with the knife was the one I told you about—the same man who had watched the station. It was his accomplice, I am guessing, who ambushed me from behind."

"I never doubted they were real," she said.

"Didn't you? I did." Hyde smiled weakly. "Thank you."

"For what?"

"For taking care of me. I take it it was you who arranged for me to be brought to hospital?"

"Dr. Burr did more than that," said the young doctor. "She attended to your wounds before summoning help. Without her intervention, you would have lost a great deal more blood."

"I did what any physician would do," said Cally.

"Well, I'm most grateful for it." Hyde smiled. "I have sent for Chief Constable Rintoul. I need to talk to him about all this."

"He was here most of the night you came in," Cally said. She rested her hand on Hyde's uninjured arm. "He has called regularly since to check on your progress."

"The night I was brought in?" asked Hyde. "How long have I been here?"

"Two nights. It's nearly noon of the second day. You have been drifting in and out of consciousness since the attack. We were worried that your skull was fractured and there was underlying brain damage."

"Cally," said Hyde, grasping her hand. "You know all I told you about everything that is going on at the moment. I cannot just lie about here—I need to get back on to these cases."

"That's impossible, you—" the young doctor started to say, but Cally Burr cut him off with a look. "I'll leave you with Dr. Burr," he said resignedly, and nodded to the nurse.

"Listen, Edward," said Cally, after they had gone, "you have a severe head injury—it's impossible at this stage to say how severe. We have no idea how much bleeding there is in your brain, and if you try to get up now, you could kill yourself."

"But—"

"There are no buts about it. You will have to stay here for twenty-four hours, perhaps longer. And when you do get out of here, there will be a period of convalescence."

"That cannot be, Cally," Hyde protested. "Forgetting the two murders I have to investigate, the trails of which grow colder with each passing hour, there is a young woman missing. Twenty-four hours could be the difference between finding her alive and finding her dead." He still had hold of her hand, small and delicate in his thick-fingered grasp. "Please, Cally, I need your help."

She held him in her unsettlingly frank gaze for a moment, then smiled. "I'll have them assess you again this evening," she said. "If you are still making progress, I'll ask about you being released into my care. But understand this, Edward, you *will* be in my care and you will follow my orders. And wherever you go, then there go I. Those are my conditions."

He smiled. "Conditions I would most happily accept in any situation."

Rintoul arrived shortly after lunchtime. Hyde's attempt to eat had resulted only in vomiting, and his endeavours to get out of bed rewarded him with severe bouts of vertigo and the ill humour of the ward sister. When Rintoul arrived, Hyde noticed that he looked tired and concerned, his face drawn and weary. The chief constable was clearly greatly relieved to see his chief of detectives restored to consciousness.

"Detective Sergeant MacCandless told me of the incident at the station, when you ran out after someone you said had been following you. Was the attack on you the work of the same men?"

Hyde told him it was, and went through all the details he had to give. He also advised Rintoul that he intended to be released from the hospital that evening.

"Is that wise?" asked the chief constable.

"Wise or not, it is necessary," said Hyde. "In the meantime, I need MacCandless, Dempster and Pollock to come here to see me. Time is of the essence, and I have tasks for each of them . . ."

Unpalatable as it was, the hospital's evening meal remained in Hyde's stomach, and he felt some of his energy return. He found he could stand without losing his balance, and walked the length of the ward and back, ignoring the officious protestations of the stout matron and the ward sister.

When the young doctor returned on his rounds mid evening, Cally Burr arrived at Hyde's bedside. She explained to the doctor that she would take charge of the patient, and that she would observe him for the next twenty-four to forty-eight hours.

"If you do not discharge me, young man," said Hyde when the houseman began to protest, "I shall discharge myself."

The doctor reluctantly agreed but insisted Hyde take the packet of powders he offered.

"What is in them?"

"Something to dull the pain, nothing more."

"Will they also dull my wits?"

"They may make you feel a little drowsy, but—"

"Then I have no use for them," interrupted Hyde.

"I'll make sure he takes them," said Cally Burr, seeing the young doctor was about to renew his protest. He sighed and handed her the package.

"Do you have time for this?" Hyde asked Cally as they sat in the hansom cab. He was bareheaded, his hat on his lap, to accommodate the bandage that bound his head.

"I seem to have more than enough time to spare. I'm afraid women doctors, particularly specialists, do not find themselves in especial demand. Were it not for Dr. Bell giving me hours whenever he can, I would either have nothing to do or be forced to work exclusively in women's medicine. So consider me your personal physician for the next two days."

Hyde smiled. "And consider me your obedient patient. I count myself lucky to be in such capable hands."

When they arrived at his townhouse in Northumberland Street, Hyde recognized Mackinley and the police carriage sitting outside at the kerb. As he and Cally Burr disembarked the cab, the door of the police carriage swung open and Chief Constable Rintoul appeared, followed by Iain Pollock.

"How are you, Hyde?" asked Rintoul. "I'm still not convinced you should be up and around."

"Nor am I," said Cally Burr. "But I'm afraid Edward is a most stubborn individual."

"About that, Dr. Burr," said the chief constable with a weary smile, "you will hear no argument from me."

"Shall we?" Hyde indicated his front door.

The architecture and internal modelling of Hyde's home was elegant, with a broad arcing staircase sweeping up from the hall. A chandelier suspended from an ornate central ceiling rose, and the walls were decorated with elaborate plasterwork cornices and details. It was easily the equal to Samuel Porteous's townhouse, but the elegance of the building contrasted with the comparative lack of furnishings and ornament. It appeared that only that which could be deemed functional had a place in Edward Hyde's life.

"You live alone?" asked Rintoul. "Without staff?"

"I have no need of them—most of the rooms are shut up. The house was left to me and is, if I'm honest, far too large for a bachelor without family. Please . . ." He held out his arm to indicate the drawing room, and winced in pain.

"That arm should be resting in a sling," said Cally Burr, disapprovingly, but Hyde merely nodded politely.

"Sergeant MacCandless took three constables with him to Dunlop's studio," said Rintoul once they were seated. "The only address we have for him. There was no answer nor any signs of life. MacCandless tried the door and checked through the windows, but Dunlop clearly wasn't there. Why is this so important, Captain Hyde?"

"The man who attacked me had exactly the same triskelion tattoo that Dunlop so proudly bore. I need to find out from him what its true significance is. I suspect we are dealing with some form of secret society."

"The Dark Guild—you are saying you think it exists?" asked Rintoul.

"I don't know, if I am honest. The tattoo clearly has significance—the triskelion is a universal Celtic symbol," said Hyde. "Wherever the Celts have held sway, the triskelion has appeared. It would, I suppose, make a fitting image for some arcane Celticist secret society. Maybe this has more to do with Mackendrick than we think. Or perhaps the Dark Guild does exist, after all."

Cally Burr frowned. "What is the Dark Guild? I saw the *Edinburgh Expositor* make mention of it."

"An old Edinburgh legend," said Rintoul. "A fiction, nothing more."

"It goes back to the time of Deacon Brodie," explained Hyde. "The Old Town is full of streets and closes named after particular trades: Candlemakers' Row, Fleshman's Close, et cetera. Each trade formed its own guild—formally called incorporations. The head of each incorporation is titled a deacon. On the Celtic festival of Beltane each year, the Kirking of the Deacons is part of formal Edinburgh tradition. The deacons of each of the ancient trade guilds proceed in full ceremonial garb from Candlemakers' Hall to the Kirk at Greyfriars. Once there, the authority of each deacon to lead his guild or incorporation is confirmed. There is an incorporation for all the trades, from hammermen to tailors, weavers, bakers and masons. Incidentally, one of the historical guilds was the Incorporation of Surgeons, until it elevated itself as the Royal College of Surgeons."

"And where does this Dark Guild fit in?"

"Deacon Brodie was the most famous of the deacons in Edinburgh history—or more correctly, infamous," said Hyde. "William Brodie was a wealthy cabinetmaker and deacon of the Incorporation of Wrights. The double life he pursued, and which ultimately led him to the gallows, is Edinburgh history—a matter of fact—but his ghost also haunts the city's mythology. Before being hanged, he cursed Edinburgh and swore to rise from the grave and bring a perpetual terror to the city. Some say he bribed his hangman to shorten his rope and ignore the steel collar Brodie wore hidden beneath his shirt. Others say he was executed but revived by a corrupt surgeon, or that his resurrection was a work of necromancy. Whatever his route to immortality, Brodie is said to have taken to the underground tunnels and sealed plague streets beneath the city. There he is said to have formed the Dark Guild, or the Shadow Guild, or the Dishonourable Incorporation, as some call it. According to the legend, an immortal Brodie still holds court as Deacon of the Dark Guild in some subterranean hall, where gather all the city's murderers, housebreakers, thieves, cutpurses and molesters."

"So it is nothing other than a myth?" asked Cally. "Pure superstition?"

"To an extent . . ." said Rintoul. "There has been a rumour for some time—credible enough for it to warrant our investigation—that this myth has been used as a model for a much more immediate and solid criminal enterprise. Nothing more than a glorified gang, headed by a mastermind who calls himself the Deacon and cloaks himself in the mystery of the legend."

Cally turned to Hyde. "You think these men who attacked you could be part of this Dark Guild?"

"All I know for sure is that there is some symbolic bond between them, and that symbol is the Celtic triskelion."

"If it is such a popular image," said Rintoul, "could it not simply be a coinci—"

"Trust me, Chief Constable," Hyde interrupted. "In these cases we have more than exhausted the possibilities of coincidence. We have two murders that seem connected, one of which was posed as a ritual Celtic Threefold Death. We have Scotland Yard asking us to investigate Cobb Mackendrick's possible links to Celtic nationalism. We have a wealthy Edinburgh heiress missing, perhaps abducted, which seems unconnected to anything else, until we discover that she was involved with Frederic Ballor, who also is reputed to have a shady political past—and she even has connections to our tattooed photographer friend Dunlop, who took the Lockwood family portraits. Added to all of which we discover she is involved with Cobb Mackendrick's nationalist group." Hyde paused, wincing slightly as he pressed the heel of his hand to his temple. "Did Dempster visit the castle?"

"He did exactly as you asked," said Rintoul. "Much to the displeasure of Brigadier Lawson, I might add. Alas, it was another fruitless errand. There was no colour sergeant with a battle scar such as you described; those he did find allowed him to examine their wrists, though with some ill grace. None had the tattoo."

"May I add something, sir?" asked Pollock tentatively.

"Go ahead, Iain," said Hyde.

"There may not have been anyone at the castle matching that description, but it does sound like one of the military types I saw at the Cobb Mackendrick meeting. If you recall, I mentioned a man with a battle scar down one cheek."

"I do," said Hyde. "I remembered you mentioning him and I had already thought of the colour sergeant I encountered that night. What concerns me at the moment is why neither Allan Lawson nor his provost marshal can remember someone with such a distinctive mark— and who was most definitely on duty that evening. It should be no more complicated than checking the duty roster."

"That was undertaken at Dempster's insistence," answered Rintoul. "He got the names of the rostered non-commissioned officers and there was only one colour sergeant. He was brought before Dempster and was most definitely not your man."

Hyde turned to Pollock. "What about Mackendrick—did you bring him in for questioning?"

"I'm sorry, sir," said Pollock. "I couldn't find him. I called at all the addresses we have for him—he was not present at any of them.

We have some constables in plain clothes taking turns to watch his home address and a couple that belong to his known associates. So far, nothing. Mackendrick has never had reason to hide away nor fear the police—I rather suspect he has taken flight and is more involved than we first thought."

"Or he has fled for his own safety, perhaps, given that anyone who can shed light on these matters has met a gruesome end. What about the investigator, Farquharson?" Hyde asked. "Did you get the landlady to open up his lodgings?"

"I did, sir. There was nothing to hint at where his current business took him. There was a collection of notebooks and some files, but we would need a removal warrant, and as Farquharson has committed no offence, we have no grounds. In the meantime, I have asked the landlady to let me know the instant he returns."

"If he does not return within the next two days, then we seize his files," said Hyde. "A young woman's safety is at stake." He turned again to his superior. "Chief Constable Rintoul, may I ask that you use all influence and press the exigency of the situation to obtain a search and seizure warrant from the sheriff?"

"I will have it by this time tomorrow."

"Thank you, sir. And MacCandless? How did his errand fare?"

"I doubt there is a locksmith or leathersmith in Edinburgh he has not visited, but so far none have identified the key nor recognized the fob as their work. But Sergeant MacCandless strikes me as a fiercely diligent man and seems determined to resolve the puzzle."

"And we are still no further with the Porteous case? No suspect has come to light from the patient lists?"

"Nothing of any note," said Pollock. "Dr. Porteous seems to have guarded his privacy jealously. Excessively so, one might say."

"Nothing else?" asked Hyde. "Nothing from his clinic at the hydropathic hospital?"

"Most of the cases he saw there are Craiglockhart inpatients. Only three were outpatients, of whom we've tracked down two. One had a serious relapse of symptoms while visiting family and is now permanently confined to Fife and Kinross Lunatic Asylum; the other can offer an alibied account of his whereabouts."

"The third?"

"The third we are still tracing, but she is a female patient being treated for psychotic melancholia following giving birth. An unlikely candidate as a murder suspect, I would say."

"All right." Hyde paused. "Constable Pollock—tomorrow you, I and Sergeant MacCandless shall pay our photographic friend Dunlop another visit."

Cally Burr had had to assure Chief Constable Rintoul that she would remain with Hyde until it was time for him to retire, and return early in the morning to ensure he remained in recovery. After Rintoul and Pollock had left, she prepared some tea and brought it into the drawing room. With the cup she handed Hyde was a glass of water into which she had stirred one of the powders supplied by the hospital.

Hyde protested, but Cally insisted. "I understand you don't want to dull your wits, but take it just this once. It's your first night at home and it will help you sleep."

Hyde reluctantly acquiesced and drank the dissolved powders.

As they sat in the drawing room taking tea together, their conversation turned again to Samuel Porteous.

"Do you honestly believe all this Alter Idem nonsense with which Samuel seemed so obsessed?" asked Hyde. "That two personalities can live within a single mind?"

"The truth is, I don't know. The article you found on Samuel's desk, the Pierre Janet case, is by no means the first discussion about this being a possible form of insanity. After you told me about Samuel's theories, I read up on the literature: there have been cases recorded and theories about their cause expounded since the end of the last century. I found a case study from 1791, from Tübingen in Germany. Eberhard Gmelin, who was a pioneer in mental medicine, described a striking case of what he called divided personalities."

"The same kind of thing as Samuel's Alter Idem hypothesis?"

Cally Burr nodded. "Almost exactly. Gmelin's patient was a local German woman of humble enough stock, but who would have episodes where she became a French noblewoman. The most bizarre element to this was that when she was in this state, her French would be highly cultured and absolutely perfect in grammar and accent, as if she were truly a French native—and when she did speak German, it would be limited and with a thick French accent. When she returned to her everyday self, she would have no recollection of the episode, nor could she speak anything more than a few broken phrases in French. One mind, but two identities, each of whom had no knowledge of the other or memory of the other's words or deeds. Exactly as in the current French case Janet described—and exactly like the patient Samuel discussed in his journal. Except in the latter instance the alternative personality is monstrous—bloodthirsty and base in every aspect. And that alternative personality is most probably Samuel's murderer."

"I am far from convinced," said Hyde. "I find it strange that this condition has only seemed to exist for the last hundred years or so. If it is such a common mental aberration, why is it only now we see cases?"

"But that's the thing, it has been known about since antiquity. The ancient Greeks described it and held it to be evidence of metempsychosis, the transfer or reincarnation of souls. And in the Middle Ages, such phenomena kept exorcists and witch burners busy. Think of it, Edward, we all have other sides to our natures—personalities we seek to deny. Is it so inconceivable that in some people the desire to deny them becomes so great that a schism occurs? That they completely disconnect from that part of their mind—in effect gifting it an independent life?"

Hyde sat and thought about what Cally had said.

"If this is true, and such a syndrome exists, that would mean Samuel's murderer may not even know he is the murderer. Concealed from justice in an unsuspecting mind . . ." He shook his head slowly, as if in wonderment. "I cannot think of a better place to hide."

39

Nothing in this place made sense. Elspeth had run, plunging headlong through the pitch blackness, repeatedly stumbling and falling painfully before getting up and running on. Yet no matter how fast she fled, how little regard she gave the blind risk, the steps behind her never picked up pace, but never faded. She ran while her tormentor walked, but still he continued to close the gap between them.

There was another noise, indistinct and far, far above her. She halted her flight for a moment and strained to listen. So very faint but nonetheless identifiable, it was the muffled sound of people's voices, of their chatter and clatter as they went about their daily business in a world so close yet so far away.

Her initial instincts had been right: wherever and whatever this place was, it belonged to the underground maze that was said to sprawl beneath Edinburgh and the land around it. She remained still, shutting out the relentless footsteps behind her and focusing on the faint, distant sounds.

Somewhere, in that universe so far removed yet so close to that which Elspeth occupied, a woman laughed; the sound sent a pang of remorse through her, recalling how seldom she herself had laughed when she had occupied the light. She became filled with an instant and all-consuming yearning to return to that world. More sounds came, even fainter this time: muffled hooves on cobbles, and again the faint buzz of chatter. The sound waxed and waned, as if carried on an inconstant breeze.

Then it was gone.

Elspeth remained where she was, stilling the rasping urgency of her own breath to listen, but there was no more to hear, except the relent-less approach of her tormentor's footsteps.

With a desperate sob, she ran on.

The footsteps behind her were now louder, closer. She puzzled as to why she still had not reached the opposite wall, why her even-paced but unhurried pursuer managed to grow closer, despite her breathless headlong flight from him.

She stopped again. It was the darkness, she had decided; the total, all-enveloping black velvet darkness. Senses became confused, time distorted, direction indeterminable. For all she knew, she may have been running in circles. Her descent down the stairs may have taken her not to even ground, but to a ramp whose incline was so gradual as to be imperceptible, but that had nonetheless restored her to her origi-nal level—cruelly returning her to her starting point at the sackcloth bedding. So spacious and directionless was the pitch darkness of this dungeon that anything was possible.

She stood still and held her breath. Perhaps the footsteps behind her, assured as they were, belonged not to her tormentor but to some other lost soul seeking redemption from the darkness. But she would not take the risk. Fleeing from him had not resulted in escape, and her own running footfalls only alerted him to her position. She would, she had decided, make friend of enemy: the darkness that had confounded her would now conceal her.

The footsteps were close now, so very close.

Elspeth stood still, but the sense-stealing darkness brought with it disequilibrium, and she swayed uncertainly. Slowly and silently, she eased herself down into a kneeling position, bracing herself with her palms stretched on the cold stone floor.

He was nearly upon her. The footsteps grew louder, and she could tell he was only a matter of feet away. They remained even, regularly spaced but still growing louder.

He is there, she thought. *He is right in front of me.*

The unseen walker's steps continued without breaking pace, and Elspeth feared he would hear her pounding heart over the sound of his own progress.

A second became an eternity, the steps like a hammer sounding on iron nails and resounding in her skull.

Pass. Please, for the love of God, walk past.

She dared not allow herself to hope, but she thought the steps were becoming quieter. Another breathless, pain-stretched moment. Yes— she was sure now: the footsteps diminished, grew fainter.

He had walked right past her in the dark. Her stratagem had worked. Elspeth felt a surge of sweet relief.

The footsteps stopped.

"Well, Elspeth," said the strangest voice in the dark. "Are you not going to follow me? I have so much to show you. So many dark wonders to reveal . . ."

40

Although nominally still a separate burgh, Portobello was the seafront suburb of Edinburgh and provided summertime diversion for the city's populace. For a place of entertainment, however, Portobello was, even at the best of times, dull and cheerless. On an off-season day such as this, it presented an especially dismal prospect. The two-mile stretch of sand that formed the beach sat bleak and deserted, the sluggishly restless sea beyond like liquid slate under a cloud-seethed sky.

The premises they sought were at the end of a short street that opened its mouth onto the promenade and the beach beyond. The studio was a large, single-storey wooden structure, like a low warehouse shed. Painted duck-egg blue with yellow detailing around the windows and board soffits, it presented its back to the street's end, its shopfront window facing seaward and onto the promenade, clearly designed to solicit custom from passing visitors in more clement weather.

"This is it?" asked Hyde.

"This is it," replied Detective Sergeant Peter MacCandless. As they came around to the promenade-facing frontage, MacCandless pointed to the sign above the door, upon which was emblazoned the name and motto:

HENRY J. DUNLOP
PHOTOGRAPHIC ARTIST
ENLARGEMENTS AND MULTIPLE COPIES AVAILABLE

Hyde remembered the studies of deceased children Dunlop had shown to him and Cally Burr. He could not imagine anything less appropriate than their small, dead bodies being conveyed into this garishly painted shorefront shed. There was a glass panel in the door, behind which a sign informed that the studio was *CLOSED*.

He knocked on the door. When there was no answer, he knocked again, this time slamming the heel of his gloved fist against it so vigorously that the door shook in its frame.

Again no answer.

"Force the lock," Hyde eventually ordered Pollock.

"But sir . . ."

"Force the lock, Constable. I shall bear full responsibility. I would do it myself were it not for my injuries."

Pollock looked from Hyde to MacCandless, then set his shoulder to the door and pushed. When it would not yield, he stood back and aimed a kick at the lock. The wood of the door frame splintered and the door burst inward, slamming against furniture within, the glass panel shattering.

The room they entered served as some kind of reception. It was small, its walls decorated with examples of Dunlop's work. A console table stood against one wall, a cash drawer sitting on top. Collapsed tripods leaned in a corner. Three large storage cabinets, their drawers lying open, stood in another corner. Double doors broke the wall and bore the sign *STUDIO AND DARKROOMS*. Hyde nodded to the two officers and they followed him as he swung open the doors to reveal a large room: so large it consumed the rest of the building's space.

This was clearly Dunlop's main studio. There was no ceiling, rather open access to the eaves of the roof, which on one side was glazed into a huge skylight window, casting full natural light into the space. On the other side of the room, a section had been curtained off as a darkroom.

There were more storage cabinets, next to furniture of different types—a chaise, a chesterfield, two wingback chairs and several wooden dining chairs—sitting along the opposite wall. The furniture had been arranged not for comfort, but clearly stored in readiness to be hauled into use, depending on the number of people in a group to be photographed.

A massive painted backdrop filled the whole wall beneath the skylight. It portrayed a Highland scene: mountains and loch arranged in golden section proportions, painted clouds filling the canvas sky. In front of the backdrop, green felt had been draped over trestles to simulate hillocks and was dressed with dried grasses, heathers and paper thistles. The centrepiece of the tableau was a full-sized red deer stag, sporting a magnificent set of antlers, its flank to the camera set up ten feet distant, its head turned to the lens, as if just alerted to the photographer's presence. The stag's convincing lifelikeness, however, was not that gifted by nature, but by a taxidermist's skills.

The tableau was the typical idealization of Scotland: Scotia the wild and majestic, in exaggerated simulation for seaside postcard or shortbread tin. Hyde was discomfited by the painted backdrop scene of strath, glen and mountain, something about it reminding him of the imagined topography of his seizure dreams.

A large camera, much larger than the one Dunlop had used to photograph the Hanged Man in the mortuary, stood on a sturdy tripod about ten feet in front of the simulated pastoral. The photographer, on an adjustable stool behind the camera, sat poised to capture the scene, leaning forward, his head and shoulders concealed beneath the camera hood of black lightproof cloth.

"Mr. Dunlop," Hyde called to him. "Why did you not answer our knocking?"

The photographer remained sitting on his stool, and did not remove the hood.

"Mr. Dunlop!" Hyde called again; and again the photographer ignored him.

Hyde strode impatiently across the studio to where Dunlop sat.

"Mr. Dunlop, it is Captain Hyde from the police. I want to ask you . . ." Irritated by Dunlop's continued wilful ignoring of him, he grabbed the camera hood and roughly threw the cloth off the photographer's shoulders.

Dunlop sat unmoving, his leaning forehead pressed against the glazed plate of the camera. Hyde noticed that his perpetual cigarette remained tucked behind his ear, nested among the yellowed and singed hair of his temple. One hand rested on a knee; the other, swollen and blackened where blood had pooled, hung loose at his side.

Hyde realized that Dunlop's pose had been staged with artfulness equal to that of the stag; he also realized that Dunlop was equally dead. He knelt down to examine the photographer and saw that his shirt was soaked in blood that had issued from the wide slash across his throat.

He heard Pollock gasp and straightened up.

"Damn," said MacCandless. "Another murder . . ."

"This one's different," said Hyde. "His throat's been cut, but I can see no other injury—there is no Threefold Death here. Dunlop's murder was practical and swift. Whoever did this did it with a specific purpose in mind: to stop him talking. Whoever did this knew we would be looking for him. What I do not understand is how his killers knew we were coming."

"But what about the pose?" asked Pollock, and Hyde saw the young constable's complexion had paled.

"It is a staged piece all right," said Hyde, "but there's nothing ritualistic about it. Indeed, although I very much doubt it, the pose could be accidental—his murderer perhaps cut his throat from behind, and Dunlop slumped forward. The blood loss, or comparative lack of it, suggests he died almost immediately. But I rather believe it is an act of whimsy on the part of the killer—arranging Dunlop's body thus for our benefit. Or his own amusement."

"Whimsy?" MacCandless frowned, incredulous.

Hyde stood up again, stepped back from the dead photographer and looked around the studio. "Don't you see? Dunlop was not photographing this tableau; he was *part* of it. This is all for our benefit. For all we know, it was the killer who set up the Highland scene. I have been struggling of late, for one reason or another, to interpret symbolisms. This . . ." he held his arms wide to embrace the scene, "this is symbolic. The killer has a message he wants us to understand."

"Then what kind of insanity," said MacCandless gloomily, "are we up against?"

Hyde did not answer, but turned to Pollock. "Iain, go into the street and stop the first carriage you see. Go to Portobello police office and arrange for the Burgh Police to come and attend. Peter, let us you and I search this place. But I suspect whatever would be useful to us is long gone from here."

He looked down again at the slumped figure of the bandy-legged photographer who had seen it as his calling to pose and capture the life-like dead so they might live on ageless in a photographic otherworld.

An immortality Dunlop had himself been denied.

—

The inspector from Portobello Burgh Police attended with four of his constables. A lean, dour man with a thick, blunt-vowelled Lothian accent, he was clearly not best pleased that Hyde had not informed the local station in advance of his visit to Dunlop's studio. But he made no complaint: Hyde was a far senior officer from a force with considerably more sway over events in Edinburghshire; added to which was the fact that the murder committed in the studio went far beyond the usual fare of the Portobello Burgh Police.

The local men, therefore, subjected themselves to Hyde's command and merely secured the locus while Hyde, Pollock and MacCandless searched the studio.

It was as Hyde suspected: evidence was conspicuous in its absence, rather than its presence. Whoever had killed the photographer had searched through the drawers of the studio's cabinets. Those that contained portraits, still lives and landscapes retained their contents.

"Sir . . ." MacCandless called. He was searching a cabinet of the type normally used for storing architectural plans, but when Hyde came over to it he could see that Dunlop had used it for flat storage of photographic plates and more prints.

"None of the other cabinets were locked, but these drawers were." MacCandless indicated where the locks of each drawer had been forced. The contents of the top three were still in place. "It would appear our bandy-legged friend had a sideline . . ." He handed Hyde several prints. Some were simple nude artistic studies of women, others more shamelessly posed, others explicitly pornographic. "Dunlop kept these under lock and key, for obvious reasons, but whoever ransacked this cabinet had no interest in them or any of his legitimate work. However . . ." MacCandless pushed closed the top drawers, exposing three lower ones, left open and empty, "they clearly found what they were looking for here."

Hyde nodded. "Collect everything into evidence boxes and have them brought to Torphichen Place." He turned to the local inspector. "Did you have any reason to know Henry Dunlop? Did he ever fall foul of the law that you are aware?"

"No, I cannae say he did."

"He did work for us at the City Police. Did your force ever use him as a police photographer?"

"Aye," said the inspector. "On occasion to record custodies, but no' that often. Our needs are less sophisticated here."

"Do you have a home address for him?" asked Hyde, ignoring the barb. "I mean other than this studio?"

"No' off hand, but I can have the Burgh records checked for an address."

"Thank you, Inspector."

Hyde turned to see the body being moved into a transport coffin. "If you don't mind, Inspector, we'll have him taken to the city for post-mortem examination by Dr. Bell. I have sound reason to believe this murder is connected to others in Edinburgh."

The inspector looked as if he was about to complain, pulling at the high serge tunic collar that rubbed at his neck. "I suppose. There'll be paperwork, mind . . ."

"I'm sure—" Hyde broke off abruptly and called over to the men hoisting the corpse into the coffin. "Hold on a minute!"

They stopped and turned to Hyde as he walked briskly over to the body. "Look," he said. "There's blood on his cuff—pull his sleeve up."

The uniformed officers did as they were bade. Dunlop's shirtsleeve and cuff were bloodstained. When they eased them up from the dead man's wrist, along with the coarse tweed of his cheap Norfolk jacket, it exposed a disc of exposed subcutaneous flesh, where the full thickness of the skin had been excised.

"Peter, Iain—come and see this."

MacCandless and Pollock came over and looked at the discovery.

"They removed his tattoo," said Hyde. "Either to further confound us so we had no record of it, or because his death was not enough—he was being stripped of his emblem of membership."

"Like being cashiered?" asked MacCandless.

Hyde nodded. "Except the insignia was not cloth, but flesh."

41

Henry J. Dunlop, artistic photographer, portraitist of the dead and occasional pornographer, had, it seemed, lived an empty life. The next two days' investigation into his affairs revealed little. Dunlop had been unmarried, had no issue, had few family connections of note. He had served in the army, as a sergeant, and had been a regimental photographer before his discharge, carrying his trade into civilian life. A sister had lived in South Queensferry, but had died three years before. Dunlop had frequented an inn in Portobello every Friday evening for the past ten years and was consequently acquainted to many, but known by none.

The Burgh of Portobello Police had provided a home address for him: a small, single-bedroomed flat on the second floor of a reasonable enough tenement on the Musselburgh side of Portobello.

Hyde attended with Pollock and they searched the apartment. The environment of his living was at odds with the untidiness and uncouthness of the man. The flat was scrupulously clean, the kitchen floor scrubbed, the grate cleaned of ashes and the ironwork of the fireplace black-leaded. There was care taken in the maintenance of this space, but it had remained exactly that: simply a space, with no real sense of a human spirit or personality ever having inhabited it.

It was the polished solitude of a former soldier, a routine Hyde recognized from his own life.

The only items of note revealed by their search had been kept in a desk set beneath the window that looked out seawards. In an unlocked drawer Hyde found the considerable sum of fifty-seven pounds, all in British Linen Bank notes; the search of another of the desk's drawers revealed a portfolio of photographs that, Hyde assumed, had been personally important to Dunlop.

Like the portfolio Dunlop had shown Hyde and Cally Burr in the mortuary, this personal volume was filled with images of considerable artistic quality. Unlike the hidden pictures in his studio, there was nothing prurient or vulgarly commercial in these photographs. They were, in fact, elevated in tone and execution and Hyde found himself reluctantly admiring the dead man's craft.

It seemed a varied collection—still lifes, landscapes and a few portraits—with nothing to connect them. Then Hyde realized that the common denominator to all of the images was a sense of Scottishness: the landscapes were all Highland scenes or Ayrshire pastorals; there was a collection of photographs of abandoned crofts, lying bleak and roofless beneath ruthless, cloud-fumed skies; the still lifes were all collections of Scottish items, many depicting household objects from rural Scottish life. He also realized that the people in the portraits were not the works' true subjects, but merely models representing figures from Scottish history. A tall, impressively built man represented Robert the Bruce, his head adorned with crown-crested helm, hand resting on the double head of his battleaxe.

Perhaps, thought Hyde, Dunlop really had set up the Highland scene in the studio, the murderer simply integrating his victim's body to the tableau.

Another image, this time of a model posing as William Wallace, caused him to start.

"Iain," he called to Pollock, who joined him at the desk. Hyde set the image separate from the others. "Recognize him?" he asked.

Pollock took in the thick, almost wild, curling hair and beard; the pugnaciously jutting jaw. "It's Cobb Mackendrick," he said.

"Exactly. So we can connect—" Hyde, who had been flicking through the rest of the photographs, broke off mid sentence. He examined the second image that had caught his attention: a study clearly meant to be that of Flora MacDonald, the Highland woman who had aided the escape of Prince Charles, the Young Pretender of the 1745 Jacobite Rebellion. He noticed that a canvas backdrop of an idealized Highland scene had been used—the same painted backcloth that had been hanging in the studio when they found Dunlop. But it had not been the coincidence of the background that had caught Hyde's attention.

"It seems we have an embarrassment of riches when it comes to connections," he said, as he held out for Pollock to see the image of a handsome young woman guised as Flora MacDonald.

Elspeth Lockwood.

42

Cally Burr called again at Hyde's house that evening to change the dressings on his arm and head. As she did so, Hyde apprised her of the events of the day.

"I cannot fully believe it," she said as she leaned over him, bandaging his head, he aware in their proximity of the warmth and perfume of her body. "It was so recently that we spoke with Dunlop. You believe he is tied up with this Dark Guild?"

"If such an organization exists," said Hyde dolefully. "Mind you, I have started to believe there may even be such a thing. Edinburgh drives me to distraction with its need for clandestine association. No one knows how many clubs, societies and drinking and gambling dens there are in this city—all frequented by fine Presbyterians of good birth and standing leading double lives and getting up to heaven knows what petty peccancies and grand sins behind closed doors. I tell you, sometimes I weary of the hypocrisy and duplicity of this city's privileged classes." He laughed apologetically and looked up at her. "I'm sorry, I'm raving. It has been quite some week."

"Sit still," admonished Cally. "I am nearly finished, then you may rave to your heart's content. Are you any closer to finding Elspeth Lockwood?"

"There is something strange about the prolonged absence of this investigator, Farquharson—young Pollock is going to visit his lodgings again tomorrow morning, this time with the authority to seize Farquharson's notes and files. But if I am totally honest, I fear the chances of finding Miss Lockwood safe and well diminish with the passing of each new day."

"Have you any idea what has become of her?"

"In truth, none. But I know young Pollock believes she may have succumbed to the same neurasthenic deliriums that beset both mother and brother, and that she has perhaps become a danger to herself. I doubt that, given what her father has told me about her."

His head re-bandaged, Cally turned her attention to his arm. She frowned when she eased the dressing from the wound. Blood had oozed from between the catgut stitches, but the puckered flesh was not inflamed with infection.

"You must take much more care of this, Edward," she said. "I have told you before that you could lose some use in your arm if you neglect it. I insist you put it into a sling."

Hyde made an indistinct noise of concordance and Cally lifted his chin with her fingertips so she looked him in the eyes. "Doctor's orders . . ." Their faces were close, the act of tending to him and the gesture of raising his head creating an inadvertent intimacy. There was a moment of awkwardness, then Cally straightened up. "I shall make some tea . . ."

When Hyde arrived at Torphichen Place the next morning, he had his arm in a sling, as Cally Burr had instructed. Working at his desk he however became irritated by the encumbrance and set it in a desk drawer. He had only just begun to go through the various reports that awaited him when he was disturbed.

He knew from the urgency of the knocking on his office door, then the energy that animated the face of the young plainclothes constable when he entered, that Pollock had something important to impart.

"Have you secured Farquharson's notes and files, Iain?" he asked.

"Yes, sir," said Pollock as he entered, "but—"

"Anything to report from them?"

"No. I mean not yet, sir," Pollock's tone was impatient. "I have not had an opportunity to go through them. But there is something more important—"

"I fail to see what could be more important than tracing a missing—"

"You don't understand, sir." This time Pollock interrupted his commander. "I have an idea." He shook his head in annoyance. "I really don't know why it did not occur to me before—something that has passed us by in our search. Somewhere we haven't looked."

"What are you talking about, Constable Pollock?" asked Hyde with strained patience.

"Cobb Mackendrick, sir. I think I know where we might find him . . ."

Hyde and Pollock had been waiting for thirty minutes at the shorefront cab station close to Leith Docks. The sun had broken through the clouds and cast a blank light on the drab, smoke-blackened dockside architecture.

The cab driver was a small, wiry man with the sing-song accent of a Fifer. When approached by the two policemen, he regarded Hyde, as so many tended, with a vague unease. However, he remembered Pollock from their previous conversation of the night the young detective had attended the meeting in Leith. He also remembered exactly where he had dropped Mackendrick and his companion that night.

"You have a good memory," said Hyde.

"Aye? Well y'have tae in this line of work, ken? No' just that, but wi' thon fellow bein' done away wi' like that, it stuck in ma mind that ah'd seen him afore. Ah was expectin' you tae come back again. Tae be honest, ah thought you'da been back afore now."

Hyde and Pollock exchanged a look. "What fellow?" asked Pollock.

"Thon man whit was murdered," sang the Fifer. "That doctor. It was him that was wi' the aither gentleman that night."

"Samuel Porteous?" asked Hyde.

"Aye, him. I recognized his picture in the *E'mbra Post*. That's why yous are here, eh?"

Hyde turned to Pollock, whose expression was a combination of revelation and annoyance. "The bohemian-looking gentleman I saw that night," said Pollock. "I took him to be a writer or an artist, but not a doctor. I'm sorry, sir, I did not get a good look at him and I never made the connection."

Hyde turned back to the cabbie with such an expression of determination that the Fifer looked taken aback. "I need you to take us," commanded Hyde, "right now, to the address you took them to that night."

Hyde ordered the cabbie to stop off on the way at the Torphichen Street station, sending Pollock to muster MacCandless, Dempster and half a dozen uniformed men. He also told Pollock to break out four service revolvers from the armoury for the detectives.

The Fifer cab driver looked on anxiously as a Black Maria, pulled by a team of four, clattered its way out of the stationhouse's yard and fell in behind his cab.

"All is well," Hyde sought to reassure him. "Just take us to the address and you can go about your business."

Stockbridge's character was a transition between the New Town's grandeur and Dean Village's squalor. There was much that remained from its origins as a village on the Water of Leith, while lower-middle-class aspirations and Edinburgh's grey expansion had taken more recent and staunch form as apartment tenements and squat stone houses. The townhouse they sought was a more impressive affair in an arcing terrace of similar properties. The terrace would have been no more than fifty years old, built in a style to echo the stateliness of the more prestigious addresses in the neighbouring New Town, but without the breadth of boulevard before it. All the townhouses in the crescent had three storeys above street level and a basement below.

The cabbie pointed out the basement, accessed from the street through a wrought-iron gate and down stone steps, into which his passengers had gone that night. Hyde knew that if this building remained, or had originally been, a townhouse, then the space below street level would have been devoted to either servants' quarters or scullery and laundry. The house's main door, at street level, was not directly above the basement entrance and was open to view from anywhere on the terrace. The gate that offered access to the basement level, however, was on the corner of the building, where it was bounded by a service alley.

Hyde told the cabbie to stop in the street some distance from the townhouse. He also ordered the Black Maria, along with the uniformed officers, all armed with long staves, to wait out of sight around the corner.

Dempster and MacCandless, who had travelled in the Black Maria, giving the uniformed men their orders as they came, now squeezed into the hansom with Hyde and Pollock.

"As you ordered, sir," said Dempster, handing Enfield revolvers to

Hyde and Pollock. The young detective sat looking at the revolver as if it were some object alien to his experience.

"You know how to use this?" asked Hyde. "You have had some basic training?"

Pollock nodded and slipped the revolver into his coat pocket.

"If this is indeed the meeting place for the Dark Guild," said Hyde, "and Cobb Mackendrick is their deacon, then we may be faced with desperate and violent men. As their aim is insurrection, there may be weapons in that address. We need to be prepared for all eventualities."

The light was dimming, and as they sat watching the building, an old man in a long coat and peaked cap, bearing upon his shoulder a short apex-form ladder and a long pole, made his way along the crescent. With slow and deliberate method, he stopped at each streetlamp. Without taking the ladder from his shoulder, the old man reached up with the long pole, flicked open the lamp's glass pane, pulled down the gas supply lever with the pole's small hook and lit the mantle with the flame of the spirit lamp that tipped it. One by one, the lamps flickered into life, marking his unhurried progress with pools of light.

When the lamplighter drew near the cab, he looked in without curiosity. His face was as old as stone and as impassive, but Hyde saw his eyes narrow slightly when they set on him. The old man nodded acknowledgement and moved on, casting light as he went.

"Old Lugh," muttered Hyde.

"What, sir?" asked Pollock.

"What? Oh, nothing. Lugh is the old Celtic god of light."

"I wonder how much longer he'll be lighting gas," said MacCandless. "With this big electric arc lamp experiment along Princes Street and up the Waverley and North Bridges."

"The main thing is Old Lugh has helped us see our target better," said Hyde. "Look..."

As they watched, several men arrived. They were of different ages, types and class, but all cast an eye up and down the crescent before turning into the service alley and descending to the basement. None was Cobb Mackendrick.

Hyde turned to Pollock. "I want you to walk past the building without stopping. Have a look down to the basement door, come back on the other side of the street and report on what you have seen. Do not turn up into the alley—just see what you can in passing."

Pollock nodded, and Hyde could sense in him an electric thrill. This had, after all, been entirely his idea.

When he came back, Pollock was even more animated. "We're definitely on to something, sir. The emblem on Dr. Porteous's key fob . . ."

"The Janus figure?"

"Yes, that—the brass door knocker is the same design. A double-faced Greek- or Roman-type head. You know, classical . . ."

"The motto—is that there too?"

"No sir, but the head design is almost identical, except it is modified to hold the hammer bar of the door knocker. There's something else. Through a ground-floor window I think I saw one of the men who entered by the basement. I don't think the basement has been converted to a separate apartment but is still connected to the rest of the building. It's just that they're using it, rather than the ground-floor street door, as the main entrance. Which would suggest . . ."

"That they want to enter and leave without attracting attention." Hyde finished the thought. He turned to MacCandless. "Tell the uniformed men to ready themselves. The Deacon and his Dark Guild are in for a surprise visit."

"Should we not wait to see if Mackendrick turns up?" asked MacCandless.

"Mackendrick is lying low—and as young Pollock has pointed out, this is the one place he will think we do not know about. We are unlikely to see him on the street, but he may well be hiding in the building." Hyde paused for a moment. "All right, let's go."

43

"Come and see, Elspeth," the voice repeated. "There is so much I have to show you. Great and wondrous things such as you could never imagine."

"What is this place?" demanded Elspeth. Her voice, unused for so long, sounded high, tremulous and creaking. "Why should I come with you? Why should I trust you when you brought me to this place against my will?"

The darkness-hidden man laughed—a low, ugly laugh—but the sound of it came from a different direction, as if he had silently moved around her. Elspeth turned desperately towards it.

"You brought yourself here, Elspeth," he said. "The will and the motive were your own. Come and see."

"Who are you? Why are you doing this to me?" she sobbed.

"You already know the answers to those questions, Elspeth." The voice came from yet another direction and again she desperately twisted around to face it.

"They await your discovery, your remembering," he said, and once more she spun around to the voice's new origin. Elspeth now realized she had lost all sense of the direction whence she came.

"I don't understand!" She pleaded to the dark, to the infinite void around her.

It was like an exploding sun.

After so long in the dark, the light that burst into being seared her eyes and stabbed bright shards of pain through her head. It dimmed, but its yellow and white ghosts continued to disorientate her, dancing before her dazzled vision. After a while, she realized the sunburst had simply been her captor striking a match before setting alight a torch, which he now held aloft. He was some fifty feet ahead, his back to her. He wore a long frock coat with a high collar and a shoulder cape, of a design that had not seen fashion for sixty years, and, when he turned, his features remained in the shadow of a tall, wide-brimmed top hat.

The torch blazed above his head and for the first time she could see the ground beneath her feet, black cobbles, sleek and worn flat as if by centuries of use. But that was all she could see: the red-gold blaze of the torch cast a pool of light that illuminated her, her captor-guide, and a disc of paved ground; no wall, no building, no roof revealed itself.

"I will be Virgil to your Dante, Elspeth," said the stranger, and his voice seemed vaguely familiar to her. "I shall be your psychopomp. You are Pilgrim and I Companion."

"Where are we going?" she asked.

"You will see . . ."

The stranger walked on, holding the blazing torch high. Elspeth remained unmoving, fearful. However, as his torchlight retreated and the darkness began to close in on her once more, she reluctantly set out to follow him.

44

Instead of walking past the front of the house at street level, and alerting the occupants of their presence, Hyde led the detectives and uniformed officers away from their target and around the block, so that they came around the back of the terrace and along the service alley.

Peter MacCandless eased up the latch of the iron gate and pushed it open, pausing as the metal creaked in faint protest. Hyde drew his revolver and led the others down the steps to the basement door, gesturing for them to remain quiet and avoid lingering in front of the barred basement window. The recessed area at the bottom of the steps was small, and the detectives and uniformed men were bottlenecked into its meagre space, some still standing on the steps that led down from pavement level. Hyde knew that, to retain the advantage of surprise, they could not loiter where they stood.

Frazer, a uniformed station sergeant whose proportions and robustness had been fashioned in the open spaces of the Highlands, stepped forward at Hyde's bidding and prepared to shoulder in the door.

"Wait . . ." Hyde placed a restraining hand on the Highlander's arm, as a thought occurred to him. He could now see the brass door fixture that Pollock had described, and it was, indeed, the same design as Porteous's fob, only modified for its function as a knocker.

He reached into his coat pocket and removed Porteous's fob and key.

The key fitted the lock. Hyde slowly and quietly turned it, then nodded to Frazer.

The door flew inwards and a wave of black-uniformed policemen surged through into the basement. Two large men, obviously functioning as doorkeepers, turned suddenly and in surprise, only to be silenced before they could call out by the truncheon and staves that rained in on them from the invading constables.

"Upstairs!" commanded Hyde. Revolver in hand, he bounded up the undressed stairwell that led from the basement into the remainder of the house.

They came up into the main reception hall, the walls of which were a deep crimson, against which contrasted the white plaster cornicing and the four marble statues, copies of classical sculptures, that decorated it. One of the sculptures, Hyde noted in passing, was a head and shoulders of the Roman god Janus and had clearly served as the model for the design on the key fob. Something about the look of the place jarred with Hyde, but he did not have the time to work out what. There were six doors off the hall and he directed two men to each.

"Peter, William, you take the room to the left front. Iain, you come with me."

Hyde and Pollock burst into the main drawing room of the house. Four men stood up suddenly, startled by the appearance of the detectives. Hyde saw they were shocked and very afraid. Two of the men were little more than youths, one of whom made a whimpering cry at the sight of the policemen's guns. Even with his mind racing and his eyes scanning for weapons or any other danger, Hyde knew there was something not quite right. The men looked almost as if the arrival of the police had been a shock, but not entirely unexpected.

"Edinburgh City Police," he shouted, and one of the younger men jumped. "Place your hands above your heads and keep them there and no one will come to any harm."

Again the younger man whimpered, the older men looking crestfallen. There was no resistance here, not even defiance—simply resignation.

MacCandless and Dempster came in behind them.

"We have secured this floor, Captain Hyde. The constables have seven men in custody."

"Have them secure these as well," said Hyde, nodding to the four men in the room. "Iain, Peter—with me."

He led Pollock, MacCandless and two uniformed men up the stairwell to the next floor; a long, wide hall with bedrooms off. The first door he tried was locked, and he aimed a kick at it, sending a jolt of pain through his injured arm. The door flew open and revealed two men in their thirties, both of whom were struggling into their clothes. The bed behind them was unmade.

It all made sense to Hyde now. *Duo in unum occultatum*: two natures hidden within one. The duality that Samuel Porteous had kept hidden from the world had nothing to do with splits in consciousness; nor were any of these men bound by political ideologies—and they were certainly not the Dark Guild. Their brotherhood was founded on different ground.

"Take these downstairs with the others," he commanded. Three more bedrooms revealed similar results. Eventually they had eighteen men in custody, including the two doormen, gathered in the townhouse's drawing room; but no Cobb Mackendrick.

"Where is Cobb Mackendrick?" Hyde asked the assembled men, who simply stood in frightened, mute response. "Where is Cobb Mackendrick?" he repeated. "I know you believe yourselves to be in deep trouble, but what I am investigating is a much, much more serious matter. I know Mackendrick has been hiding here, and if you do not yield his whereabouts, you will all find yourselves charged with obstruction of a murder investigation."

"Now listen here, Inspector . . ." One of the older men had clearly regained something of his composure and attempted to assert himself. He stepped forward and was immediately pushed back into line by the Highlander sergeant.

"I am not an inspector, I am a superintendent," corrected Hyde, "and former holder of the Queen's commission. Do you have something to tell me?"

"I am an advocate and I believe your breach of these premises is—" He broke off as Hyde took a step towards him, a gesture that, like so many of Hyde's, was filled with unintended threat.

"Where is Mackendrick?" Hyde again asked, this time more quietly.

The man said nothing, but tilted his head almost imperceptibly upwards, his eyes towards the ceiling.

"Constable Pollock, Station Sergeant Frazer, with me, please."

Hyde led them into the hall and up the stairway. "Keep it quiet, gentlemen," he said as they ascended. "I believe our quarry is in the attic."

They reached the uppermost level, a small square hall capping the stairwell. A tented glass cupola crowned the space, set some fifteen feet above, indicating that the void of an attic wrapped itself around the cupola's recess. There was a single door, with no lock, off the access hall. Hyde indicated for his men to remain quiet as he slowly opened the door, revealing a set of undressed wooden stairs rising into the dark of the attic. He removed his pocket lantern from his coat and led Pollock and Frazer up the stairs and into the roof space.

The attic was in near-total darkness. The angle of the roof was broken on the side that faced to the rear of the house by three evenly spaced skylights, which in the darkness of the night offered no illumination. Both Pollock and Frazer switched on their lanterns and scanned the attic. It was the full size of the house's footprint, broken by wooden pillars and beams holding the roof in place.

The three policemen spread out, scanning the loft space with their lanterns. Several pieces of furniture were in storage under dustsheets, but otherwise the space was open.

"Put your revolver away, Iain," Hyde ordered, and slipped his own into his coat pocket. "We're not dealing with terrorists or anarchists here." He stood up in the cramped space, still scanning the attic with his lantern.

"Mackendrick," he called out. "We know you are hiding. There is no point. This is Captain Hyde, Superintendent of Detective Officers of the City of Edinburgh Police. I want to ask you some questions. Come out of hiding and make yourself known."

There was silence. "Mr. Mackendrick, I advise you—"

Something large and heavy slammed into Hyde, its full force hitting his shoulder and arm and sending him crashing onto the attic's boarded floor. Simultaneously there was a deafening noise: the strangest clattering, jangling and ringing from whatever had collided with him.

"Captain Hyde!" Pollock yelled, and ran over to him. Hyde eased himself up to see that a grandfather clock, free of its dustsheet shroud, lay disembowelled on the floor beside him, its brass pendulum, chains and weights spilled like entrails.

He leapt to his feet in time to see a silhouetted figure at the far end of the attic clambering through a thrown-open skylight.

Hyde and the two policemen ran towards it, making the skylight only after the figure had disappeared through it. A dustsheeted cabinet sat beneath the roof light, and Hyde climbed up and out onto the roof, sliding down its angle until his feet came to rest on the crenellated stone edging that girded a foot-wide leaded gulley. He stood up and saw the figure running, with little care of falling, along the roof's edge.

"Mackendrick!" he shouted. "Stop!" He ran after his quarry, who now navigated his way around a chimney stack, pressing himself flat against its face. Hyde realized that the fleeing figure intended to run the length of the terrace, finding his way down to the ground through some other house. He heard Pollock and Frazer at his back.

"Take great care," he ordered. "Catching him is not worth anyone falling from this roof."

With a speed and ease that defied his heavy-set build, he continued along the edge, reaching the chimney stack. The leaded gutter came to an end where it broke to accommodate the chimney and Hyde, like the prey he pursued had done before him, had to press himself flat against the face, arms outstretched, his feet probing the six-inch-wide ledge that ran across it. He saw Pollock's face blanch as he reached the chimney and spotted Hyde's precarious position.

"Don't attempt this, Iain," he said. "Get back down onto the street and watch for him coming out somewhere else. Frazer, you take the alley at the rear."

Hyde pressed on. His boot leather struggled to maintain purchase on the slim edge, and twice his foot slipped, threatening to send him hurtling to the ground three storeys below. Eventually he reached the other side of the chimney and regained the foot-wide leaded gulley. He looked along to where the roof edge again broke for a chimney, but could see no sign of Mackendrick. He could not understand how his quarry could have navigated the next chimney so quickly, and leaned sideways as much as he dared to look along the next stretch of roof edge. Still no Mackendrick.

He looked up at the slate tiles and it was then he saw him. The fleeing figure was silhouetted against the night sky, walking haltingly and unsteadily along the apex of the roof, swaying slightly with each step, arms held out at his sides, like a hesitant tightrope walker.

"Mackendrick!" yelled Hyde. "For God's sake, man, you'll break your neck. It's not worth it."

The figure ignored him and continued its precarious progress along the roof, Hyde easily keeping pace with him. He realized, however, that Mackendrick was using the apex as a way of circumventing the chimney stacks.

"Wait," Hyde called. "I only want to talk to you—we are not interested in whatever activities occur at this address. Believe me, I have bigger—and much more dangerous—fish to fry."

The figure silhouetted against the sky paused in its halting advance along the apex. Featureless in the dark, Mackendrick turned his head towards Hyde.

"How can I trust you?"

"Because I give my word, as a gentleman and a Queen's officer."

The figure on the roof laughed. "And that is supposed to reassure me?"

"If not that, then my word as a friend of Samuel Porteous," said Hyde.

"You? A friend of Samuel?" asked the figure.

"It has become clear that I indeed did not know him as well as I could have, but I do believe he counted me as a friend. All I want to do is talk."

"And that is why you smashed your way into the club mob-handed and armed?"

"We were expecting something else. It was my fault. I had no idea of the real nature of this place. Please come down so that I may talk with you. I just want to understand what happened to Samuel."

The silhouetted figure hesitated for a moment, then bent its knees as it prepared to make its descent.

It happened in a second, but Hyde felt time stretch. As he had bent down to start his descent, Mackendrick had reached out a hand to steady himself on the roof's apex. His boot slipped as a slate dislodged itself and went skidding down the roof, shattering against the low, crenellated edge.

Cobb Mackendrick fell sideways, his hands clutching vainly at empty air as he, too, plunged down the tiled angle of the roof.

45

Again Elspeth found she had lost all track of time. They had walked so long, but she did not know how long, and still she had followed the stranger and the beacon of his torch. Had she slept while she had walked? Was such a thing possible?

As they had walked, she had kept the distance between them constant, so that she might escape into darkness should he seek to seize her.

Still there was nothing other than the cobble-rippled pool of light surrounding them, no other feature revealing itself to illumination; yet Elspeth made no enquiry of the stranger who led her, and he uttered no word as they made their progress.

After a long while, she more sensed than saw that solid forms were taking shape in the shadows around them as they walked, the light from the torch not quite reaching them. Eventually the vague forms revealed themselves to be buildings: tenements, the looming flanks of which became perceptible in the lamplight. Elspeth counted eight storeys, but there could have been more hidden in the torch-unreached dark above them. Soon the tenements closed in on them as they came to a descent of stone steps, leading into an even narrower alley. It was a typical Edinburgh Old Town close, but not one she had ever seen before. No light came from within or without the buildings, no sun nor moon relieved the darkness above.

The man in the top hat and frock coat remained ahead of Elspeth, the blaze of his torch still the only illumination.

"This is the city beneath," he explained. "The city lost. The city of the dead. They sealed it off, then built over it. It was the great plague, in 1645—they shut up all who lived here and left them to hunger and die in the diseased dark. Their bones abandoned and their souls forsaken, they remain here still."

"Why have you brought me here?" asked Elspeth. She was so afraid, terrified. In the narrowness of the alley, the flaming of the stranger's torch made shadows dance against the towering walls of the tenements, and pirouette around the skull-socket eyes of the dark, glassless windows.

"This is not our destination, my dear," said the stranger. "This is only our path, a way station on a greater journey. We have far to go, you have much to behold. Have no doubt that all will be revealed to you. You will see and understand the truth. Its terrible brightness will burn your eyes, its clarions will shake your bones."

46

As if time itself had slowed, Hyde watched as Mackendrick tumbled and rolled down the steep angle of the tiled roof. The low mock-battlement edge, he knew, was neither high enough nor substantial enough to prevent Mackendrick plunging over the edge and onto the stone-flagged back yard of the terrace. The three-storey fall would be more than enough to kill the man.

Hyde ran forward and leapt at the falling figure. They collided just as Mackendrick reached the roof edge and Hyde seized his coat. The impact slowed Mackendrick's fall, but not enough to stop him rolling over the edge. Hyde was now lying prone but twisted in the gully, clutching Mackendrick's coat with both hands. The weight of the falling man wrenched his shoulders and arms, and a trenchant pain sliced through muscle and sinew as the wound on his forearm reopened.

Without letting go of his prize, Hyde scrambled onto one knee and braced his other foot against the edging. He knew that the crenellated boundary, though fashioned in stone and cement, had been designed for ornament, and had not been intended to bear two men's weight.

Mackendrick, his feet dangling above the drop, looked pleadingly up at Hyde.

"Get a handhold!" shouted Hyde. "I'll pull you up as far as I can, but then you have to grab the roof edge and pull yourself up." His arms were aching from the effort, and he felt the inside of his right shirt sleeve wet with blood from the reopened wound on his forearm.

Mackendrick did as he was bade and managed to loop an arm around one of the mock parapets. Hyde readjusted his grip with one hand, then the other, till he had a firm hold with both on the other man's coat collar.

"Get ready," he said, his words hissed through clamped teeth. "When I pull, you pull. Now!"

Hyde gave a roar of pain as he hauled at Mackendrick with all his strength. Mackendrick hoisted himself upwards and scrabbled for a handhold with his free hand.

There was a cracking sound, and Hyde saw the cement along the base of the stone that bore most of Mackendrick's weight had started to fissure. He braced both feet against the roof edge and hauled.

Mackendrick hooked an ankle over the edging and rolled into the gulley and safety.

Both men settled for a while, their backs to the tiles, catching their breath. Hyde winced at the pain from his arm and could see his right hand was blood gloved, crimson black in the night.

"Captain Hyde!" a voice shouted up from below. "Captain Hyde—are you all right, sir?"

Hyde looked down into the shadowed gloom of the back yard below and only just discerned the stout form of Frazer, the station sergeant, looking up at them. From the service alley running along the back of the yards, he could hear the sound of urgent footsteps and could see dark forms running to join the Highlander.

"I'm all right," he said. "And I have our man. But neither of us is in a state to negotiate our way back. Have ladders brought to get us down."

While they waited, Hyde turned to Mackendrick.

"Why did you run? Why did you fear us so?"

"I can equally ask, why are you armed?" asked Mackendrick. "Why was such force used against unresisting men?"

"We thought your *club* was a meeting place for the Dark Guild—about whom I believe you know much."

"The Dark Guild?" Mackendrick laughed bitterly. "You have not, by any chance, been talking to a man from Scotland Yard called Melville?"

"Why do you ask?"

"Melville is an Irishman turned against his own kind. A Saxonized Celt who has sold his soul to the idea of Empire. You are a policeman, he is not. He is a spy and a torturer; at best an enforcer of a political status quo who blackens the reputations of all who threaten the balance of the British Empire. It was he who put these ideas in your head, was it not?"

Hyde turned to Mackendrick's silhouetted profile, ebonized by the night. The outline of his dense curly hair and beard, along with his aquiline nose, reminded him of the Janus figure used on the key fob and door handle, except here, captured by the night and circumstance, there was no second aspect.

"This has nothing to do with Melville," he said, wincing with the pain from his arm. "I was attacked in the street by men I believe are connected to the Dark Guild. I also believe Samuel was murdered by someone directly connected to your associations. Henry Dunlop, the photographer for whom you posed, has been found murdered—"

Mackendrick, his form still silhouetted, turned to Hyde. "What? Henry is dead?"

"His throat was cut and he was posed in front of a Highland scene. As if this was not enough, I then discover that you and Elspeth Lockwood were both models for his Scotian heroic portraits."

"Henry was a friend of mine," said Mackendrick. "I cannot believe he has been murdered."

"My concern also lies with your fellow model. Elspeth Lockwood has been missing for several days now and I fear for her safety."

"Elspeth is missing?" asked Mackendrick.

"So you also admit to knowing Miss Lockwood?"

"Not through Henry Dunlop. If she knew Henry, then I was unaware of their acquaintance." The darkness deprived Hyde of his usual cues to the veracity or mendacity of the statement, of the demeanour of the face behind it.

"But you do know Elspeth?" he repeated.

"I am assuming you know the answer to that already," said Mackendrick, "given the clumsy attempt at infiltration of our group by your boyish colleague. Yes, Elspeth is a passionate nationalist and has occasionally assisted at our meetings."

"How did you come to know her?"

"She attended one of my gatherings about two years ago—just sat quietly in the audience, near the back, but I recognized her of course. The Lockwoods had been very much in the public eye after the death of Elspeth's brother. I think that event had a profound effect upon her and she began to question her values, personally, socially and politically. I did not see her again for two or three months, until Frederic held a soirée for my group in his house in the West End. He then introduced us personally."

"Frederic Ballor?"

"Yes." There was something about Mackendrick's simple affirmation, something in its tone, that caught Hyde's attention, but again the gloom deprived him of an expression to read.

"You know Ballor well?"

"At one time we were close. No longer."

"Why no longer?"

"Frederic has other amusements to distract him now. His affections flutter from one to another like a butterfly. Moreover, I found him to be a charlatan and a dilettante. His beliefs, spiritual and political, are not genuinely held: they are more means to an end, schemes to be exploited for profit. Though I believe they were not always so."

"Oh?"

"That eyepatch—it is not an affectation. As a boy, he was blinded in that eye by a blow delivered by a laird's man."

"Ballor is a Highlander?"

"He was. His father was a *fear-taic*—of the tacksman class. One of the last. As intermediate landowners, the tacksmen were hit even worse than the crofters by the Highland Clearances. Frederic's family was evicted but, like most others, their chieftain adhered to the principal of *dùthchas*—the bond of blood, kinship and land—and acknowledged his responsibility to fund the passage and settlement of Frederic's family in the New World. That was why the potato famine in Ireland was so much worse than in the Highlands—in Ireland, absentee English or Anglo-Irish landlords did not give a damn for their tenants, while in the Highlands, landlord and tenant were bound by kinship."

"Ballor did not accept this?"

"He saw what was coming. He saw that the ancient feudal lords of the *Gàidhealtachd* would want to ape the manner and style of living of their English landowning equivalents, which they could not afford through the traditional ways—so they would turn soil to profit and replace kinsmen with sheep. Frederic and other young bloods—he was little more than a boy at the time—turned to resistance. There was a confrontation, and he was struck down by one of the laird's men."

"And that is what cost him his eye?"

"He has the eye still, but it is blinded, shot—like a black marble. But from what I could gather, there was more damage done than that."

"Meaning?"

"For more than a month, Frederic lay in a half-world somewhere between consciousness and coma. He was nursed through the most savage fever and came out of it changed. He told me—without sorrow or sense of loss—that the person he had been had died. All that he had been was lost, but he had gained some form of clarity. He still felt rage at the society that had betrayed his family, but that rage was altered. He told me that after the fire of that fever, and all the dreams that came with it, his fury had crystallized into something cold, dead and hard. But it was *his* rage—Frederic Ballor's rage, not that of a Highland youth poleaxed by a laird's man's cudgel. One Frederic had died, another had been born."

"Two personalities in the one body . . ." said Hyde, more to himself than Mackendrick. "For him to share this with you, you must have been . . . *intimate* with Ballor."

Mackendrick laughed at Hyde's forced delicacy. "Frederic is a man of boundless appetites and curiosities. And yes, I thought we were intimate—but that was my folly. Frederic is incapable of any deep connection with another human being. I thought his sharing his history with me was a sign of trust, of intimacy. It was not. He just needed to talk about it at that particular time and I was convenient—I was simply *there*. I could have been that grotesque servant of his, or a hansom driver, or someone with whom he shared a bench in Princes Street Gardens. There is no depth to Frederic's affections or acquaintances. His is a heart in perpetual winter."

Hyde thought for a moment, easing his injured arm onto his lap, the blood now adhesively wet and cold in the inside of his sleeve. He looked out over the dark clustered roofs and narrow streets of Stockbridge, columns of smoke rising from evening chimneys, yet darker against the dark sky.

"But you and Samuel Porteous were intimate . . ." he said eventually.

Mackendrick sighed in the dark. "We were. For some years."

"Was Samuel involved with Ballor?"

"No," said Mackendrick. "Indeed, I am unaware of them even knowing each other."

"Are you sure of that?"

"I am sure of nothing when it comes to Frederic Ballor. But I think I would have known if Samuel had been acquainted with him."

"And this society of yours—whatever you call it—Samuel was a member of that as well?"

"The Janus Club, yes."

"A secret society . . ."

"Secret because we're forced to be so. The Janus Club offers a place of safety, a sanctuary, in a hostile world. A place where gentlemen may enjoy their friendships away from the parsimonious and judgemental gaze of society. More than that, distant from the threat of violence and persecution."

"When you say 'friendships,' you speak of unnatural inversion?"

"I speak of friendship and love. Of acknowledging a duality of nature that our place and time criminalizes. Scotland, which so prides itself on its sense of justice and the sovereignty of its legal system, remains the last country in Europe to have the death penalty for homosexual acts. And you wonder why we are so secretive, why those men you have arrested are in fear of their lives?"

"That's ridiculous," said Hyde. "No one has been executed for that in over fifty years."

"But the law remains, and these men face years—perhaps even life—in prison. Each one of them has learned to hide his true nature and present a falsity as verity to the world."

"*Duo in unum occultatum*," said Hyde.

"Two natures hidden within one. Yes. The motto of the Janus Club."

"And you would meet Samuel here, at the club?"

"It was a place where we could be ourselves and true to our real natures."

"So you are telling me this had nothing to do with the Dark Guild?"

"We all spin fictions, Captain Hyde. The Dark Guild is the stuff of old myth that Superintendent Melville of Special Branch has spun into present-day fiction."

"Why would Melville invent a secret society?"

"To demonize any legitimate interrogation of Scotland's place in the British Empire; to besmirch those whose patriotism is differently defined. But I didn't say the Dark Guild doesn't exist. If it does, then I doubt it has anything to do with Special Branch's invention. It might be just another of the more than a hundred secret clubs and societies, like our own Janus Club, that exist in Edinburgh."

They were interrupted by the sound of voices below, and the clatter of ladders being extended.

"We shall resume this conversation later, Mr. Mackendrick," said Hyde. "I hope your candour will continue."

"You gave me your word that my fellow members of the Janus Club would go unprosecuted, that you had no interest in them. I will tell you all I can on that condition."

Hyde was about to answer when the top of a ladder rose above the edging before them, with the sound of a heavy-footed ascent, and the custodian-helmeted head and burly shoulders of Frazer, the station sergeant, appeared.

47

They walked on, he leading, she following. Still she had not been able to gain a good look at his face. Whenever he turned in her direction, which was seldom, the held-aloft torch, the sole source of light, cast his features in the shadow of the wide brim of his top hat.

They continued to navigate a warren of alleys, closes and constricted streets, exposed as they walked in the small pool of light from the torch. The deserted tenements crowded around them, tight and towering, giving Elspeth the feeling she was walking through some deep and narrow ravine. Every now and then, she would hear the faint ghost sounds of that other, so-distant Edinburgh, grey and solid under a milk-white sky, and her yearning threatened to overwhelm her.

They came into a small square. Still the stone structures around them impended darkly, clustered tight around the square and its ages-long-dry fountain. The light of the torch revealed that everything—the fountain, the cobbled square, the narrow pavements that framed it—was coated in a patina of grey-white dust, like soiled frost on the dark stone.

"Wait a minute," said Elspeth. "I know this place. Or I know somewhere very like it. How can that be?"

Her guide did not answer. There were five alleys that led off from the square, and he took to one, which closed like a mouth around the torch's light. The square was plunged into darkness and Elspeth ran after him.

After a while, an unpleasant odour swelled in the air, first faint, then growing in intensity with every step. The light from her guide's torch seemed to dim, and a pale green halo formed around it. Elspeth felt the air, thick and acrid, catch in her throat and nostrils. Something now rippled over the cobbles at her feet as she walked: a smoky grey-green mist, ankle-deep and carpeting the ground.

They reached a junction and suddenly the smell intensified into a putrid stench, causing Elspeth to catch her breath and fight back her rising nausea. It was a vile, rancid smell that was at once both acidly bitter and sickeningly sweet. Visible in the faint, flickering light of the torch's flame, Elspeth discerned a side street declining steeply from the corner, its ground becoming lost where the street, and those that lay beyond it, had become inundated. There was no doubt that the black, greasy water that had flooded the lower end of the street was the source of the miasma.

"It is bog waters from the old Nor' Loch, that most vile and miry slough," said her guide. "That which was not drained a hundred years ago found its way here into this reservoir of corruption. They used to tie witches together, you know—tied them thumb to toe, then rolled them down the hill and into the cess of the Nor' Loch. Or they would confine in weighted crates those guilty of incest and throw them in. There they would drown in water polluted with slaughterhouse waste and human sewage and all manner of foulness. The fruit of murder and suicide, too, would sink its rotting way to the bottom of the loch. What floods this place now is the distillation of all that mouldering corruption, all that pollution."

"Why are you showing me this?" asked Elspeth, struggling to keep down the gorge that rose in her throat. "Why do you bring me here?"

"To show you the other nature of this city, of this land, of this people. To show you what lies beneath and beyond and before. This is the place that made you, Elspeth Lockwood, shaped you from shadow and light. But our adventure has only just begun. There is so much more to see . . ."

48

Cobb Mackendrick was taken to Torphichen Place stationhouse, where he was confined to the cells, awaiting further interrogation. In the meantime, Hyde was returned to the Royal Infirmary, where his arm was examined, re-stitched and re-dressed. The bandaging this time was tighter and more extensive, bound beyond the elbow to restrict movement, and Hyde was forbidden to make any use of the arm for several weeks.

The duty physician was a tall, meagre man in his fifties whose long grey face gave the impression that a lifetime's aversion to the habit had rendered it permanently incapable of smiling.

"You have tendon damage," he told Hyde, as if his diagnosis was a disapprobation, "perhaps permanent. Whatever harm was originally done has been exacerbated by your lack of care."

"I shall be more cautious in the future, Doctor," said Hyde.

"I recommend you are, Captain Hyde. If that wound were to become seriously infected, you could very easily lose your arm."

Willie Dempster was waiting for Hyde in the infirmary's admissions hall, his ever-serious face further clouded with concern.

"I'm fine, William," Hyde reassured him. "Just a little sore and weary."

"I have Mackinley waiting outside to take you home," said Dempster. "I dare say a good night's rest will be welcome."

"It would indeed, William," said Hyde. "But first I am for the stationhouse. You can go home and get some rest yourself."

"I'll come with you, sir," said Dempster. "If you were to take ill or injure yourself further, then I would not want to face Dr. Burr."

Hyde smiled. "Am I to take it that you are revising your opinions on female physicians, William?"

"Whatever her chosen profession, Dr. Burr is a formidable woman." Dempster indicated with an outstretched arm to the hospital exit. "She gave us all a dressing-down when she discovered that we had allowed you to injure yourself further. I would rather face a drunken Cowgate mob than incur her displeasure again."

"I know what you mean, Sergeant Dempster," said Hyde with a smile as they made their way outside to the waiting carriage. The night air felt cool and soft on his face. Mackinley saluted him as he approached.

"I should further point out that Dr. Burr is also a most insistent lady," said Dempster as he held open the door, revealing Cally sitting inside. "I'll ride with Mackinley," he added tactfully, and left Hyde with Cally.

"You need not have come at such an hour," said Hyde when they were alone.

"I told you before, consider me your personal physician until I can be sure you will not do yourself permanent damage. Whatever were you thinking, gallivanting around on rooftops?"

"I assure you there was little gallivanting. I was pursuing a suspect."

"And you have no uninjured junior officers capable of pursuit and less likely to end up in the infirmary?"

"I shall be more careful in the future," said Hyde meekly. He paused for a moment. "I do appreciate you coming to check on me, Cally."

"Clearly someone has to. I will see you home and then we will discuss this again in the morning."

"I'm afraid I have something at the station to which I must first attend—"

"Edward!"

Hyde held up his hands. "I will only be there briefly, I promise. Then I shall go home and rest." He knocked for Mackinley, who slid back the hatch. "Can we take Dr. Burr home before we go to Torphichen Place?"

"You shall do no such thing, Constable," said Cally. "I will wait for Captain Hyde at the station till his business there is concluded." She turned defiantly to Hyde, her expression set firm.

"Very well, Mackinley," he said with a sigh. "You had better do as Dr. Burr instructs."

—

There was, Hyde thought, nothing more cheerless than a police station at night. Torphichen Place stationhouse was silent and bleak, its cream plaster wan and green tiles dull in the light of its gas lamps. The night pressed oil-black and sleek against the high windows and cast Hyde's face and form back at him, contrasting starkly with the grace of Cally Burr's reflection.

It was late now and only Station Sergeant Frazer remained behind the high oak counter. Frazer's red-blond eyebrow raised almost imperceptibly when he saw the young woman doctor enter with Hyde.

"I thought you would have been off shift by now," said Hyde.

"And I you, sir," Frazer lilted. "I decided to stay on till the gentlemen from Stockbridge were processed."

"And have they been so?"

"Just as you instructed, they have all been cautioned, their details taken and released without charge. Only Mr. Mackendrick remains in the cells, again as instructed, sir," he explained.

"He will have had time to reflect on his situation," said Dempster. "But as for letting the other men go—are you sure there was not enough evidence for us to bring indecency charges?"

"I think the experience will have been chastening enough for the Janus Club to disband forever," said Hyde. "In any case, we have bigger fish to fry and Mackendrick may be of great use to us."

"Aye," said Dempster thoughtfully, "that's as may be, sir, but I still think we should have hung on to such fish as we did catch tonight. The inverted nature and practices of these men will not cease, and they will simply find some new place to carry on their perverted ways. What was going on in that place was not just against the laws of the land, but those of good Christian conscience and of nature."

"At the best of times I have little appetite for prosecuting grown men for what they do in private if they harm no other—and at the moment we simply have no time for such distractions."

"But they indeed do harm, in my opinion," said Dempster, his expression unchanged. "Harm to society. And not just in my opinion, but in the opinion of the law."

Hyde sighed. He was too weary to enter into a debate with Dempster, whom he knew to be both an elder in the Church of Scotland and a member of the Masonic lodge. "Whatever our respective views on the issue, Sergeant Dempster, we have more pressing matters with which to attend: two murders and a disappearance. And Mackendrick's cooperation may be essential." He made for the stairwell. "Where's Constable Pollock?"

"He is still here, sir," said Dempster. "He has locked himself away in the collator's office with the materials seized from yon private detective's residence."

"I see," said Hyde. "No further information on Farquharson's whereabouts?"

"None of which I am aware, sir."

Hyde looked across to the stationhouse clock: it read a quarter past ten. The day had been long, exhausting and painful. He straightened himself up, aware of Cally's scrutiny.

"Are you sure I cannot have you taken home," he said. "I may be some time."

"I shall wait for you," she said firmly. "Otherwise you will spend half the night here when you should be recovering."

"Very well." Hyde turned to Dempster. "Could you please conduct Dr. Burr to my office and perhaps see if some tea could be arranged." He turned back to Cally with a smile. "I must go now and talk to my companion in my rooftop gallivanting."

Hyde asked Frazer to bring a metal mug of tea down into the basement cell-block.

"Yes, sir," replied the Highlander station sergeant, who then paused awkwardly.

"What is it, Frazer?" asked Hyde.

"As I said, I processed the details of all of the gentlemen from the Stockbridge address. One of the younger men . . ." Instead of completing the thought, Frazer handed Hyde an occurrence sheet with the name, address and other details of one of the men arrested. "I have not entered these details into the day book. I thought you would want to see them first."

Frowning, Hyde took the occurrence sheet from Frazer and examined it. He looked up at the sergeant, who responded with a raised eyebrow.

"I see," said Hyde, folding the sheet and slipping it into his waistcoat pocket. "You did the right thing. I will attend to the matter."

Once they had descended into the cell-block, Hyde instructed Frazer to open the door of Mackendrick's cell and leave it open.

"For the meantime," Hyde said to Mackendrick, "you are here as our guest. The imperative for your custody is protection not detention."

"You believe I need protection?" Mackendrick sat on the edge of the low, narrow bed, looking every bit as weary and beaten down as Hyde, but a flame of defiance still flickered in the emerald-green eyes. Nonetheless, he took the unsweetened and milk-less tea.

"All I know is that everyone with whom I have sought to talk about these murders has become added to their number," said Hyde, with his free arm pulling from the corner the three-bar wooden chair, the only other furniture in the cell, and sitting opposite Mackendrick. "I told you no lie when I said Samuel Porteous was my friend, and I need to understand why he met such a despicable end. If those involved suspect you can offer the police some intelligence on the matter, even if you are unaware of its significance, I believe that places you at risk. And, if you are honest, you sought to sequester yourself in the Janus Club for the same reason, not simply to avoid my company."

"And those you arrested at the Janus Club—you promised me they would not face prosecution."

"I have kept my side of the bargain," replied Hyde. "They have been released from custody. Their names and addresses are now a matter of record, however, and I strongly advise you disband the club with immediate effect—there are those who would pursue prosecution with great vigour. Added to which, your members—or such members as we found tonight—have lost their anonymity. Now for your side of the bargain . . ."

Mackendrick nodded resignedly. "I know of no sane reason why anyone would do that to Samuel," he said dully. "Which leads me to believe that whoever did it was insane."

"What about Samuel's associations? Did he have any knowledge or involvement with the Dark Guild?"

Mackendrick gave a bitter laugh. "You are like a dog with a bone,

Captain Hyde." He sighed, then said with exaggerated weariness, "I do not know if such a society truly exists, as I've said before. And Samuel certainly would have no knowledge of it if it did."

Struggling with his one sling-free arm, Hyde took out his notebook and flicked through its pages until he found what he sought. He held it open for Mackendrick to see. "This mark, the one drawn here, do you recognize it?"

"Of course I do: it is a triskelion, though it has only been known by that name for the past fifty or so years. It is the most ancient of Celtic marks, found from Celtiberia, through Gaul, to the ancient Celtic Tocharians in western China. The truth is it is perhaps much, much older than even the Celtic races: it is a common motif in petroglyphs on menhirs, dolmens, and the like. Why do you ask?"

"Have you ever seen it used as a tattoo?"

"No, I cannot say that—" Mackendrick checked himself, his expression suddenly illuminated. "No, wait, I have seen that as a tattoo—a small and discreet tattoo. One of the men who came to the meetings, a rough-looking sort . . ."

"With something like a sabre scar on his face?"

Mackendrick looked surprised. "Yes—yes, him. He came with a group of others, sometimes two others, sometimes three. I never did like the look of them, they made me uneasy."

"Why?"

"It was a feeling more than anything. They held back from the meeting, never seemed to be engaged with the speakers or the others attending. The only thing they seemed interested in—unpleasantly so—was Elspeth." The thought galvanized Mackendrick's entire demeanour. "Oh my dear God, now that you mention it, they were only ever there when she was there and they were always watching her. It must have been they who took her! They are your abductors!"

"Calm yourself, Mr. Mackendrick. I need you to focus on these men, particularly the sabre-scarred one. How do you know he bore the triskelion tattoo if, as you say, it was a discreet mark?"

"We had to move benches and I asked for help. He stepped forward—reluctantly, mind—and lent a hand. It was then I saw it, when his sleeve hitched up."

"And you never saw the same on Henry Dunlop, the photographer for whom you posed?"

"No, I never saw— Wait, Henry had the mark?"

"He did, but the tattoo was cut from his flesh after he was murdered. But let us return to these men. Can you describe them?"

Mackendrick did as Hyde asked and gave surprisingly detailed descriptions of each of the men. Hyde struggled with his left hand to scribble the descriptions, but had to give up. "I will fetch someone to take notes . . ."

"No, wait," said Mackendrick. "I can do better than that. Please give me your notebook."

He began sketching, one face per page. As they began to take form, Hyde recalled that Mackendrick the agitator by conviction was an artist by training and profession.

"One advantage of being a painter," explained Mackendrick, "is the acuity of one's visual memory."

When he had finished, he handed the notebook back to Hyde. He had sketched three faces: the first was the man with the sabre-scarred face, whom Hyde recognized right away as the colour sergeant from the castle; the second was unknown to him.

He took a long time to examine the third, despite the fact that he had also recognized him instantly. It was the man who had followed him from Cally Burr's home and had stabbed him. Who had also borne the triskelion tattoo.

"I don't understand," said Mackendrick. "What is the significance of the tattoo?"

"I have every reason to believe," said Hyde, "that it is the mark of the very brotherhood you deny exists. I believe this is the mark of the Dark Guild."

49

Hyde replaced the notebook in his coat pocket. In its sling, his arm ached and felt heavy; his head hurt from its injury, from the length of the day, from the angry buzz of conflicting ideas and facts that bustled around within it. He wished he could take a powder to ease its insistent throbbing, but he knew he needed to keep as clear-headed as possible. Mackendrick had effectively identified the colour sergeant from the castle as one of Hyde's assailants: why was it that Hyde's friend, Brigadier Allan Lawson, had failed to recognize a member of his own garrison?

"Let's return to Samuel's death," said Hyde. "You say you know no reason any sane person would murder him in that manner, yet we have a connection with some secretive criminal or political group, whether it calls itself the Dark Guild or not. Why do you think it was the work of a madman instead?"

Mackendrick sighed, resting his elbows on his knees and cradling the metal mug in his hands. "Because madness and the mad were Samuel's business. Because it is the explanation that makes most sense. He was thoroughly professional and never discussed any of his cases with me, save one—and even then only in the general, never the specific—but I believe that patient is Samuel's murderer."

Hyde ignored the cold dread that blossomed within him. "And what did he say about this case?" he asked.

"That he was dealing with the devil. Nothing less. All he confided in me was that his patient possessed an insanity more monstrous than any he had ever encountered. I know Samuel was afraid. Terrified."

"Did he give you any indication as to whether this patient was confined at Craiglockhart or Craig House Asylum?"

"Neither. That was the strange thing: Samuel confided in me only so far, but he did tell me that he had a special arrangement with this particular patient, who called at his home."

Hyde felt the chill of his dread intensify.

"Are you sure about that? Not at his private consulting rooms?"

"I am sure. He said that this monster came to his home, and that was why he was so afraid. He felt exposed."

"And how many patients did he see at his private address?"

"He only ever mentioned this one patient. None other."

"If this patient was so monstrous, then why did Samuel agree that they meet alone and at his home? Or why did he not seek counsel from others in his profession?"

"From the little detail he did confide in me," said Mackendrick, "whoever this patient was, the true scale and nature of the madness was not evident when Samuel first agreed to the sessions. Samuel was very professional and loyal to his oaths—for him to agree to see a patient at his home—in secret, almost—was such an unusual arrangement that I suspect he was treating someone known to him, an acquaintance perhaps."

The chill now coalesced into a cold, hard mass in Hyde's chest. He took a moment to gather himself.

"Did Samuel hint that he may have been carrying out some kind of experimental treatment? Particularly on this patient?"

Mackendrick shrugged. "That I cannot say. But I remain convinced that if you discover the identity of this patient, then you will discover the identity of his killer."

Hyde stood up. "I think we both need rest. We shall continue tomorrow morning."

Before returning to his office where Cally waited, Hyde called into the collator's office and was surprised to see young Pollock still at the desk, surrounded by box files and leather-bound notebooks.

"How goes it with Farquharson's papers? Anything to report?"

"Nothing so far," said Pollock. "It would appear that he was a meticulous man and kept detailed notes of all his cases. Most were matrimonial, others commercial—companies seeking to prevent employee theft and to prosecute when prevention failed, that kind of thing. There were, however, others that were criminal cases where the victims did not want our—I mean by that the police's—involvement."

"Blackmail?"

"It would appear so. The strange thing is, I have yet to discover his notes on Elspeth Lockwood, which I thought would be the most current and active investigation—indeed, his most exigent. I have still to make inroads into his backlog of cases. I am obviously working my way through from the most recent. Hopefully, I will uncover something soon that relates to his surveillance of Miss Lockwood."

"What is this?" Hyde picked up a metal document box.

"I've put that to one side for the moment, sir," explained Pollock. "It would appear to be unrelated to his investigations—personal stuff, more than anything."

"Mmm . . ." Hyde nodded and flipped open the box. There were several personal receipts, letters and legal documents. Sitting on top of them was a small silk-covered box, which he opened.

"Iain," he called to Pollock. "Did you see this?"

Pollock laid down the papers he had been inspecting and came to where Hyde examined the contents of the box.

"A medal?" he asked.

"The Kabul-Kandahar Star," said Hyde. "Our man Farquharson served in Afghanistan, it would appear."

Hyde lifted the box with the medal and set it to one side; he riffled through the documents beneath, eventually lifting out a photograph mounted on postcard. Three rows of soldiers, dressed in pith helmets, tunics and heavy kilts, sat in stone-faced imperial certainty as they gazed at the lens. A warrant officer stood at either side of the seated ranks. A printed legend along the bottom read: *The Heroes of Kandahar: 92nd Gordon Highlanders.*

"Look, sir," said Pollock and pointed to the soldier standing on the right, his arm bearing the chevrons of a sergeant. "Is it my imagination, or does that look like . . . ?"

"No, Iain," said Hyde. "It is not your imagination." He turned the card over. There was no indication of the photographer or studio, but a suspicion was growing in Hyde's mind.

"It would appear, Constable Pollock," he said eventually, "that we now have a name to put to our Hanged Man murder victim."

—

Before returning to his office, Hyde arranged for Pollock to go to James Lockwood's home, taking a copy of the post-mortem photograph of the Hanged Man.

"Apologize for the late hour," said Hyde. "Ask him to confirm the dead man is his investigator, Farquharson. Then go home and get some sleep."

"If you don't mind, sir," said Pollock, "I'd rather come back and finish going through Farquharson's papers. They are of even more importance now."

Hyde smiled. "Very good, Iain."

When Hyde returned to his office, Cally Burr was clearly alarmed at how pale and drawn he looked.

"You are running yourself into the ground, Edward," she admonished. "You clearly have taken on too much after—"

"It's not that," Hyde interrupted her. "It is not that at all." He bade her retake her seat and told her about Farquharson being the Hanged Man, then talked her through all that Mackendrick had told him about Samuel Porteous's mystery patient. The *only* patient he saw at his home.

"The only patient he told Mackendrick about," she countered. "For all we know he may have seen three, four, or however many patients there. As Mackendrick has said, there was only one patient that he knew about, and he only knew because Samuel was so alarmed by the case."

Hyde shook his head wearily. "Samuel's journal, or what remains thereof, suggests two patients at most, and it could be interpreted that it is only one patient with a dual identity. How can you be so sure that it was not I? Perhaps I suffer from this Alter Idem Syndrome that Samuel was researching and become this monster during my periods of lost time?"

"You know that's not the case—remember how worried you were that you had had something to do with the Hanged Man murder, only to discover you had been visiting Hugh Morrison's mother in Dean Village. Trust me, Edward, you are no split-identity murderer."

"How can you be so sure?"

"Because I believe I understand you more than you understand yourself. And, at the moment, you are too tired and pained to think straight. It is time for you to go home."

Hyde was about to protest but gave way, convinced not only by Cally's emphatic urgings, but also the clinging, opaque exhaustion that had wrapped itself around him and settled into his bones.

Cally accompanied Hyde home and tended to the dressing on his head, leaving his arm as the hospital had bound it. She also insisted he take another of the powders and get a good night's sleep.

"I shall make some tea," she said. "When did you last eat?"

He told her and it reawakened her ire. "You must eat regularly, Edward. You need your strength not just for your investigation, but for your recovery. I shall make you a sandwich."

It grew late and Hyde felt the weariness begin to claim him. Cally recognized it and made to go.

"You are welcome to stay," he said awkwardly. "I mean, I know you have to be guarded about your reputation, but I have rooms enough to spare and it would save you the incommodity of travelling home so late."

For a moment the same cool, unreadable gaze returned to her demeanour and Hyde cursed his clumsiness.

"I'm sorry, I meant no disrespect . . ."

"I know you didn't," she said, and the frost thawed from her. "If you show me a suitable room, I shall make it ready."

They breakfasted together the following morning. Cally enquired about the quality of Hyde's sleep and what pain had been there on awakening. He replied that he had slept well and had awoken refreshed. There was an awkwardness between them, brought by the fact that she had spent the night in his servant-less home. But there was something else, a new level of intimacy that went unspoken. Furthermore, Hyde enjoyed having the relentless routine of his solitude disrupted.

"I take it you consider me in sufficient health to attend my work?" asked Hyde over their breakfast.

"Providing you do not over-exert yourself," replied Cally. "And that you do not work longer than a normal day. What plans have you?"

"Today I intend to find out why someone investigating Elspeth Lockwood's association with Frederic Ballor was murdered in a ritualistic manner," said Hyde. "Today I intend to expose Frederic Ballor as the Deacon of the Dark Guild."

50

They had agreed that, for the sake of appearances, Cally should not be taken home by Mackinley in the same morning police carriage that had taken Hyde into his office. Instead, she should wait until after Hyde had left before quitting his house. He had told her he would arrange for a hansom to pick her up and take her home. All she need do, he had said, was to make sure the door was locked behind her on her departure. It had been an oddly awkward exchange, a vague embarrassment hanging over a conversation that made it sound as if they had been conducting an illicit affair.

That, perhaps, would come, she thought. Cally could not quite explain her attraction to Hyde, but her faith in him was total: she had never known anyone more devoted to good. Yet Edward Hyde was such a strange, enigmatic creature. And vulnerable. There was something deep inside the man that bled unseen, some great sorrow that he shared with no one. Such that he had shared with her was remarkable, and she was determined to help him find some resolution, some healing. Alone in his house, she felt tempted to investigate: to pry into the private corners of his life, better to understand the man she was becoming ever more closely involved with. But she would not; to do so would be a betrayal of the worst kind. He had already shared so much—it was up to him how much more he chose to share, and when he would share it.

She had just fixed her hat in place when the bell rang. Cally swung open the main door and saw that, as promised, Edward had arranged a carriage for her: a brougham waited open doored at the kerb and its driver, cap in hand, stood indicating her transport with outstretched arm.

"Captain Hyde sent you?" she asked, and he nodded silently.

As she walked to the waiting carriage, she was struck by the very odd build and appearance of the driver: abnormally short but stockily built, with the strangest colouring and features. Furthermore, he used only silent gestures to conduct her to the carriage.

Almost as if the man were a mute.

Part Four

IN THE SHADOW OF
THE DARK MAN

51

As they walked, Elspeth clasped her hand to her nose and mouth to mitigate the foul miasmic stench that seemed to intensify with every step. She maintained her distance from the stranger in the top hat as he led the way, his torch still held high as beacon and sole illumination. The globe of light it cast around them was their entire universe and Elspeth remained on its edge, the pitch-blackness always just at her back. She did not know which to fear the more: the robust dark behind or the fragile light ahead.

She noticed that the stranger spoke less now, turning only occasionally to check she was still there, following him. His silence as he walked with purpose unnerved her more. The shadowed buildings that flanked their way grew less frequent, eventually disappearing on the left. The stench now was overpowering and she realized they were on a path that ran along the edge of the sunken pond. The torch's light stretched out over its flat surface and Elspeth could see its waters—if such concentrated and putrescent foulness could still be described as water—and its unmoving, black and grease-slicked surface fumed with the same nauseous green mist that rippled at her feet as she walked.

As they passed, she noticed a large dark form out in the pond, at the very periphery of the torch's light. Like an abandoned ship adrift in the slough's mire, a black-walled and broken-roofed cottage sat alone. Elspeth started when she thought she saw dark movement in its vacant windows, but reassured herself it must simply have been the play of light and shadow. Again she was aware that the silhouette of the cottage awakened some ghost of recognition, as if she remembered the place but had forgotten the remembering of it.

This subterranean realm seemed unbounded. She wondered at the scale of her discovery: the number of streets and alleys, the count-less habitations. She had known about the closes and wynds buried beneath the city; everyone knew the stories, but none suggested any-thing of this magnitude.

It was impossible.

They began to ascend, the path rising steeply and there were no longer buildings on either side. Elspeth was relieved that the stench through which they had passed seemed bound by gravity, and as they climbed, they rose above it.

Her guide halted suddenly, as did she in his shadow.

Without turning to her, he laid the torch on the ground and struck another lucifer, which burst into phosphorescent brilliance. He took a rag from his frock coat pocket and set it ablaze before tossing it side-ways, to his left. Elspeth expected it to land on the ground next to the path, but it continued to fall, briefly illuminating the chasm into which it spiralled. She gave a gasp when she realized there was a cliff edge in the dark immediately to the left of the path. No more than two false steps and she would plunge to her death. She watched in horror as the burning rag continued to fall, fading from view without finding the chasm's bottom.

The stranger bound a second rag around the torch to bolster its burning before once more holding it aloft. He turned to Elspeth, his face again in shadow.

"Such is the nature of this place," he said, and walked on.

"Why do we go farther into this darkness?" asked Elspeth, desper-ately. "What is it you want to show me?"

"You will see," he said without turning. "And I have arranged for another to join us. She will be with us soon, then we shall all see such wonders. The darkness will be dazzling. It will reveal all to your eyes."

52

It was a season-debated day. In the grey, regulated squares, terraces and crescents of the New Town, nature had been allowed little sway, but in the barred and gated green spaces that punctuated its Presbyterian grammar, the trees had borne autumn's palette for a month now. Approaching winter, however, contested the point by sending a hand of chill wind to shake the less resolute leaves from quivering branches. As the police carriage taking Hyde to Torphichen Place passed by Princes Street Gardens, he saw their grounds were already shawled in philomot russet and yellow.

He wondered what revelations about these cases would unfold, what discoveries would be made, by the time the last of the leaves fell. He thought of Cally, and of a future beyond the police, and wondered what changes would occur in his life before new-budding spring took its turn to debate the season.

It was in the mid morning that Chief Constable Rintoul arrived unannounced at Torphichen Place, his expression set hard. Hyde happened to be in the reception hall when Rintoul walked through the main door, a newspaper folded and tucked under his arm like a swagger stick.

"May we talk in your office, Captain Hyde?" he asked without ceremony.

"Certainly, sir," said Hyde, and led Rintoul up to the stationhouse's top floor.

"You decided not to press charges against Cobb Mackendrick, I gather," said Rintoul as they both sat, the chief constable declining the offer of some refreshment.

"I did," said Hyde. "He cooperated with me as much as he could and there is absolutely no hint of there being any subversive activity."

"No, indeed, I believe the activity conducted at this so-called Janus Club was not subversive in the political sense. However, it would appear to have been morally subversive and criminally prosecutable . . ." Rintoul unfolded the newspaper and set it before Hyde.

The *Edinburgh Expositor* carried on its front page the same head-and-shoulders photograph Mackendrick had used for his own flyers. The banner headline declared: *SOCIETY PORTRAITIST AND SCOTTISH NATIONALIST AGITATOR ARRESTED IN DEN OF PERVERSION.* A sub-headline beneath Mackendrick's image read: *UNNATURAL AND IMMORAL ACTS PERFORMED IN SECRET: CITY POLICE FAIL TO PROSECUTE.*

Hyde sighed. "I rather suspect Special Branch has achieved its aims. Cobb Mackendrick is ruined—no one in society will want to employ his painting skills, and his political views are now so tarnished with scandal that none shall wish to be seen to share them. The Empire—and the Union, for that matter—endures by going unquestioned; this affair has silenced a questioner."

"That is as may be, Edward, but I am unhappy that Mackendrick and these other men were not prosecuted. Thanks to the editorializing of the *Expositor*, the City Police are seen to be weak on this kind of immorality. I think we need to revisit this matter."

"I gave Mackendrick my word, Chief Constable."

"You cannot be held to your word when its beneficiary is a sodomite pervert and criminal."

Hyde gave the resigned sigh of a man compelled to a recourse he would have preferred to avoid. "I had other reasons."

"Such as?" asked the Chief Constable.

Hyde reached into his vest pocket and pulled out the folded police occurrence sheet, handing it to the chief constable. "The details on this note have not been entered into any other record, sir. It was Frazer, the station sergeant, who thought quickly and sequestered this from the others."

Rintoul examined the sheet, his expression shifting to one of resignation. "Thank you, Hyde. I appreciate this."

"When Frazer saw the surname, he thought it best to—"

"My nephew," said Rintoul. "My brother's boy. In every way a decent lad. A good lad, but . . ."

"I think we are too quick to judge on these matters," said Hyde. "In any case, the issue is done with. But it might be best that we take any other investigation no further, in case—"

"You have made your point," said Rintoul, without bitterness. "I believe you have had a breakthrough in the Hanged Man murder?"

"We have a face and a name," said Hyde. "Donald Farquharson."

Rintoul's reaction was delayed a moment, then his face lit up with recognition. "Is that not the private investigator James Lockwood hired?"

"It is—we are working on how the two things connect. I'm afraid it promises no happy resolution to Miss Lockwood's disappearance."

"Damn," said Rintoul. "I—"

They were interrupted by a knock on the door. A weary-looking Iain Pollock entered without being invited, but checked his progress when he saw Hyde with the chief constable.

"Sorry, sir," he said. "I did not mean to interrupt, but . . ."

"What is it, Constable Pollock?" asked Hyde.

"I have finished going through the papers we retrieved from Farquharson's apartments. He seems to have collected copies of property transactions, all carried out on behalf of Elspeth Lockwood."

"Anything notable?"

Pollock beamed. "Elspeth Lockwood purchased a number of properties throughout the city and beyond the burgh's boundaries, all acquired for their rental income. It was quite a portfolio: mainly apartment buildings in the New Town or on its fringes, several properties in the Old Town, and a few commercial properties. One of those commercial properties is the land in Leith on which stands the hall used for Mackendrick's meetings. Another property that stands out is a dockside tenement, also in Leith—unlike the rest of her portfolio, it is little more than a slum, and I assume its potential profit lies in its demolition to make way for warehousing."

Hyde read Pollock's expression. "All right, Iain, spit it out—you clearly have something else to share."

"The property that stood out for me most of all was acquired a little over a year ago. A large country house and its policies recently purchased in Lothianshire." Pollock pulled a single document from the bundle he carried and placed it on the desk in front of Hyde.

"Elspeth Lockwood is the registered owner of Crunnach House. Frederic Ballor is her tenant."

Once the chief constable had gone, Hyde turned to Pollock as they stood in the stationhouse's reception. "Inform Sergeant MacCandless and Sergeant Dempster and get them to assemble a team. We no longer require a warrant—we are searching for Elspeth Lockwood and Crunnach House is under her ownership, if not her occupation. We are perfectly entitled to enter her house while searching for her. What does James Lockwood have to say about this? Was he aware she had bought the house?"

"I have yet to speak to Mr. Lockwood, but from Farquharson's notes, it would appear that his daughter had her own money, inherited from her mother, as well as a substantial allowance from her father. She had been building her property portfolio since gaining her majority."

"What is it, Iain?" Hyde read the young constable's frown.

"It's just that . . . I hope you don't mind me saying, sir, but the journal that was uncovered at the Porteous murder scene was incomplete, had pages missing. I get the same feeling about Farquharson's papers. There is no mention of his surveillance of Miss Lockwood, nor any details of her contacts. I believe that at least one, perhaps two working notebooks have been removed from his lodgings. It gives me an uneasy feeling . . . that whoever took those notebooks is the same person who has abducted Miss Lockwood and murdered both Dr. Porteous and Farquharson. There is some secret central to them all."

"I believe you could be right, Constable Pollock, and it is time we found out what that secret is. We will raid Crunnach House as soon as we assemble the men."

Hyde had been so engaged in his conversation with Pollock that he had barely noticed the small, untidy boy who had entered the stationhouse and walked up to the front desk. The boy was so small that Frazer had to lean over the counter to see him. It was only when Hyde heard his name mentioned that he turned.

"You have something for me?" he asked, frowning.

"Yes, sir." The boy looked at Hyde, an expression of sudden apprehension on his unwashed face. He held an envelope out at full arm's stretch, and Hyde took it.

The envelope was written in a clear, graceful hand: *Strictly Private and Most Urgent: Superintendent Captain Edward Henry Hyde, City of Edinburgh Police.* Something small bulged in its bottom corner.

Hyde opened it and fished out the object that had caused it to bulge: a large ring studded with emeralds and sapphires. A polki ring. A ring he recognized instantly. He took out the letter and read it.

> *Dear Captain Hyde,*
> *Please find enclosed a ring that I am sure you will recognize as belonging to the half-caste beauty upon whom you have so fixed your affections. You seek an audience with me, and I shall grant it. You know where to come and you know to come alone. I will give you until nightfall, then I will send you the beautiful golden finger that bore this ring. If you have not come by the first light of the morrow, I shall send you her pretty head.*
> *If I see any other police officer approach, Dr. Burr will greet your arrival with her dying breath.*
> *If you do come alone, then I give my word I shall release Dr. Burr unharmed. It is not her life I seek to take; nor is it her presence I seek to remove from the world. In return for your attendance, I promise to reveal unto you all the truths you have sought.*
> *We have knowledge of the Otherworld, you and I; it sets us apart from others. We have both seen into the shadows of that place, of our own souls, so you know it is no idle or empty threat when I say this:*
> *If you do not do exactly as I ask, I equally promise you I will reveal to Dr. Burr all manner of dark and glorious entertainments before she welcomes the release of death.*
> *Yours in expectation,*
> *The Deacon*

"Who gave you this?" Hyde turned to the boy with such vehemence the latter took a step back, startled. Hyde grabbed him by the shoulder. "Tell me, boy!"

"A gentleman," said the terrified boy. "He called me over to his coach and handed me this note and gave me a penny to deliver it here."

"What did he look like?"

"I didnae see him that clear," said the boy. "I'm sorry, sir, but he was in this coach and I couldnae see his face. He had a top hat on wi' a broad brim and it hid his face."

"Very well," said Hyde. "You may go."

The boy turned to leave, then checked himself. He turned nervously to Hyde. "Like I say, I couldnae see the man that clear, but his coachman—he was a funny-looking sort, sir."

"What do you mean, funny-looking?"

"Like a dwarf, but no' a dwarf, if ye ken what I mean. Too tall for a dwarf but too short for normal, like. Eyes wide apart, too. I dinnae ken why, but I think he was a foreigner."

53

For a moment, it seemed to Cally Burr as if she had been dreaming, and now lay in the borderlands between sleep and wakefulness. Slowly, so very slowly, her mind unravelled itself from the clutching fingers of whatever it had been they had injected into her. Her gradual ascent from the depths of unconsciousness meant that her reason recovered before she had time to panic. Eventually, she was awake, yet all around her remained dark. The ground beneath her was hard and cold, and the air hung damp upon her.

She tried to make sense of her confinement: she was clearly below ground level—a basement or a cellar.

Where that cellar lay was beyond her calculation: she may still be in Edinburgh, she may have been transported far outside the city. She remembered now what had happened: the strange, mute coachman had guided her to the waiting brougham, but someone had been lurking in the closed and shuttered cabin. Hands had been put on her and she had been forced to the floor of the carriage. Before her rage had ignited and she had gathered the wherewithal to fight back, there had been a stabbing feeling of a hypodermic needle in her neck, then the chill invasion of liquid into her bloodstream.

The darkness had come then. Not this dank, clammy darkness in which Cally now found herself; it had been a deep, velvet blackness where time had been lost. She may have been confined and unconscious for hours, for days.

Had this, she thought as she gathered her wits, been the fate that had befallen Elspeth Lockwood?

She sat upright. The drug's echo resonated as a yellow nausea in her chest and throat, but she remained still, taking slow, easy breaths, until it faded. She mastered too the panic that now began to rise up and threatened to consume her. Fear, she knew, would be her strongest gaoler, the most effective impediment to her escape. The key to her freedom, on the other hand, would be her reason. Cally Burr had been an outsider all her life, a child of Empire with conflicting heritages; but more than that, she had been set apart by the combination of her gender, the power of her intellect, and the force of her will. It was this combination that would unlock her confinement.

As a physician, she understood the mechanics of the eye; that what seemed a total darkness would often yield as vision accustomed itself and magnified the most meagre source of light. She remained still and scanned the black curtain drawn across her perception. The darkness was almost total; almost, but not completely unyielding. She got the impression of shapes: greater and lesser darknesses in the blackness.

Her handbag.

The thought struck her: she had a box of matches in her handbag. If her captors had tossed the bag in here with her, and she could find it, she would have some source of light. She padded the stone floor around her, fingers seeking out her bag. After a while, she found the hat that had become dislodged from her head. With that discovery came at least one small advantage: with urgent fingers she sought and found the hatpin that had secured the hat to her hair and lodged it in her jacket collar. It was not much, but it was at least a form of weapon.

She continued her fingertip search, moving with as much measure as the blinding dark would allow in an ever-widening circle, tempering her urgent searching with cool method.

She reached a wall, blunting the arc of her search. She would now follow its course and determine the dimensions of her confinement. After a while, she felt something cool, wet and sticky beneath her hand.

She lifted her fingers to her face and sniffed at the wetness. She recognized the cupric odour immediately.

Blood.

54

Peter MacCandless read the note first, then handed it to Willie Dempster. They exchanged a look once the latter handed the missive back to Hyde. Iain Pollock, who stood by the door, had already read it.

"Do you want me to assemble the men?" asked MacCandless. "We can be at Crunnach House within a couple of hours and tear the place apart if we need."

"You've read the note," said Hyde. "The first sign of a police presence and Frederic Ballor will murder Dr. Burr. We have no idea how many are involved with Ballor and this Dark Guild of which he is deacon. There has been at least one occasion when they have had someone watching the station. For all I know, the Guild may even have informers within the City Police—it would fit with the Deacon—with Ballor—seeming to know our intentions."

"Then what, sir?" asked Dempster.

"We don't have the luxury of time. I need to leave now to get there before nightfall. But I have a favour to ask of you both. An unreasonable favour that you must feel free to decline."

Pollock and MacCandless again exchanged a look. "Name it, sir," said the latter.

"As we know from our previous visit, it is impossible to approach Crunnach without being seen, certainly in daylight. I will have Mackinley drop me at the ruined gatehouse and make my own way from there. I must assume that my arrival, and Mackinley's departure, will be monitored. What I am asking is that you come with me, hidden in the carriage. After I am dropped off and Mackinley departs, I intend that he slows down once out of sight of the gates, and you both leap from the carriage and make your way, across country and out of sight, back to the gatehouse. By then it should be dark and you can make your way around the back of the house and across to the stable block, without being exposed on the brow of the ridge."

"We'll do it," said Dempster.

"What about me?" asked Pollock. "I want to help."

"And that you will," said Hyde. "I need you to take a uniformed man and investigate these addresses Farquharson uncovered. While we search for Dr. Burr, I want you to make sure that young Miss Lockwood is not confined in one of her own properties."

"But—"

"It is your case, Iain," interrupted Hyde. "You can help by finding Miss Lockwood and restoring her to her family."

"Yes, sir."

"What about you?" asked MacCandless.

"I do not intend to walk meekly into my own ruin," said Hyde, "but nor do I intend Cally to suffer for my errors. They will see me approach from the dule tree direction, with which compliance I seek to buy Cally vital minutes. When I start to pass by the Dark Man standing stone, I will dodge down into the depression. If I time it right, then the falling night will buy me vital minutes, any observer unsure if I have deviated from the path or not. Hopefully you will both be in position by then. I will arc round to the west side of the house and gain entry, while you do the same from the east. We will all be armed with service revolvers, but also take truncheons with you—if you encounter early interference, then it would be well to deal with it as quietly as possible. If you do hear shots fired, make your way towards them."

Hyde paused, his heavy face set hard and resolute. "I have one more thing to ask, and it is the greatest demand I can make of you. We must cut the head from this beast before it strikes Cally: if you encounter Frederic Ballor at any point, do not hesitate—shoot the man dead on sight."

55

One thing to which Iain Pollock had become accustomed was the disdain for his youth and ambition displayed by many of his older colleagues.

He had often sensed that both MacCandless and Dempster were irritated by Captain Hyde's clear willingness to entrust important matters to such a young and inexperienced officer. That, to a certain extent, he could understand: they were highly experienced detective sergeants and he a probationer detective constable. What rankled with Pollock, however, was the patronizing attitude of some of the older uniformed constables, who sneered at his enthusiasm and ambition. He thought of most of these older constables, who were self-described as "senior men," as time-servers: making no progress, achieving no promotion or merit since recruitment and coasting their way to retirement. He was therefore irritated when the duty uniform sergeant assigned Constable Bob Thomson, a corpulent, rheumy-breathed forty-seven-year-old time-server, to accompany him to Leith to search the properties on Farquharson's list.

In keeping with protocol, they called first into the Leith Burgh Police to explain their mission and to pick up an officer from that force to accompany them. The young constable assigned to them was, thankfully, more engaged with his role.

The door of the first property they inspected yielded to one of the skeleton keys, numbered and stored on a large metal loop, that Mac-Causland, the Leith constable, had brought with him. It revealed itself to be a small warehouse—more of a general-purpose building stripped of all ornament and fittings to allow the installation of racks of shelves, all of which were empty. There was a small office at the rear of the property, and Pollock and the Leith constable searched the desk and cabinets without profit while Thomson idled about in the warehouse. Their search revealed nothing.

"Where now?" asked Thomson wearily when they emerged into the daylight.

Pollock re-examined the list. There were five properties on it, all of which had sat uneasily in Elspeth Lockwood's otherwise practical property portfolio.

"Well?"

"There's one that fits least of all," said Pollock. "The slum tenement on the shorefront. Why should she buy a place like that?"

"You really think this lady might be confined in a property she herself owns?" asked the young Leith constable.

"There is but one way to find out," said Pollock decisively. "Let's head to the shorefront."

There was nothing wrong with instinct, Hyde had once told him. It was just something you knew, but did not yet know you knew it. As he stood with the two uniformed constables outside the smoke-blackened, shambling tenement that gazed through grime-glazed eyes out over the oily waters of the port, Iain Pollock's instincts screamed at him that he had reached his goal.

This was not a place where goodwill extended to policemen, and they had been the subject of hostile scrutiny as they had stood on the cobbled pavement before the building.

"I would suggest we get on wi' it," said Thomson. "We havenae got all day."

"Do you have your truncheon with you, PC Thomson?"

"What, aye. Why—" He broke off when he saw Pollock, having made sure they were not being observed, remove an Enfield service revolver from his coat pocket and check its chambers before re-pocketing it.

"There's a quarterlight in the door," said Pollock. "Use your truncheon to break it—as quiet as you can—so we can unlatch the lock."

"What about the keys?" asked the Leith man.

"I think this is our place," said Pollock. "And these people have murdered before."

"These people?" asked Thomson.

"The Dark Guild. I believe that is who has Elspeth Lockwood. And they will not hesitate to kill a policeman."

"The Dark Guild?" Thomson scoffed. "That's just a load—"

Pollock ignored him and turned to the Leith man. "Use your truncheon on the quarterlight, PC MacCausland."

"I'll do it," said Thomson moodily. "Just remember who's the senior man here . . ."

They were very quickly into the hall. Thomson had broken the window with a tap of his truncheon, easing the shards out with fingers protected by his handkerchief. Pollock had looped his arm in, unlocked the door and slipped into the hall.

The sounding alarm of his instinct continued to jangle at his nerves as he made his way into the gloom of the hall. The late-afternoon daylight did not accompany them into the building: it was dark, dank and the patina of soot and grime that dressed the windows dimmed the light from outside. Pollock turned off the hall and into a room so dark it could already have been night.

"Police!" he called. "Is there anyone here?" The air hung musty and silent in response, yet Pollock felt a tingle in his scalp, as if there was some other presence lurking in the room's dark. He was aware of a gas mantle, naked of its glass shade, by his head. Turning the key, he heard the quiet hiss of gas; he sparked a match and lit the mantle.

"My God," he muttered under his breath as the flickering light wanly illuminated the room. He was aware that the other two policemen now stood at his shoulder.

"What does it mean?" asked MacCausland.

"It means we've found the right place," said Pollock.

Despite himself, he felt a cold dread squeeze at his heart as he took in the room. It was empty: not a stick of furniture dressed the place, and the windows were opaque with fire soot. It was the walls, ceiling and floor that commanded the three policemen's attention.

There were hundreds of them, thousands, perhaps: patterns that seemed to writhe and dance in the flickering light of the sputtering gas mantle. Some were two feet across, others only an inch in diameter, completely covering every surface, all scrawled onto the grey plaster and wooden floorboards of the room. It was clear that it had taken an enormous effort of time, and an obsessive effort of will and focus, to cover each inch. Most were etched in charcoal or black lead, while others had the nauseous red-brown hue of dried blood.

Whatever their colour, whatever their dimension, their pattern was the same. A design Pollock recognized right away.

The three locked spirals of the triskelion.

56

They continued to climb, nothing other than the path visible in the torch's light. Eventually the way levelled out and their footsteps began to resound more, as if echoing against the walls of some large cave. Fingers of jagged rock reached out towards the path's edges on both sides, reassuring Elspeth she was now safe from the abyssal chasm and confirming her suspicion that they were in a cave.

It soon became clear to her that it was more than a cave; instead a vast cavern, its rock walls soaring up into a high-vaulted roof, like some subterranean cathedral. Then it struck her: she could see the ceiling of the cavern, so far above them.

Light.

They remained in sepulchral darkness, but Elspeth was convinced she could see more of the cavern than the torch's flames could illuminate. There must, she realized, be some additional source of light, no matter how dim.

And that light could be coming from outside.

Her attention was drawn to the path's edges where the walls of the cavern came down to meet them. There were rows of small items, all of equal size and oblong in shape, arranged in ranks along the edge of the path on both sides. There were hundreds of them. Thousands.

She examined them more closely. She knew what they were: they were the Arthur's Seat doll coffins. That meant, she realized, that the cave they occupied was inside the body of Arthur's Seat. That in turn meant she was close to the light, to a way out, to escape.

But again she was troubled by the scale of everything. Surely this cavern was too vast, the tiny coffins too numerous. She remembered the tale from when her mother had still been alive—when her mother had still been well—and Elspeth yet a child. Her mother had taken her and her brother for a picnic in Holyrood Park, on the slope of Arthur's Seat. It pained Elspeth to think of that bright childhood summer day and how her mother had told them both legends and stories about the magical Arthur's Seat. She had talked of the time before the Scots came to the land that now bore their name; of the stories of *Y Gododdin*, the Welsh Old North, when Camelot had stood on Arthur's Seat and King Arthur had sat here in command of his Briton and Pict knights. In childhood's bright summer, it had thrilled Elspeth to think that Arthur slept in some hidden cavern beneath the Salisbury Crags, perhaps even in Arthur's Seat itself.

It had been then that Elspeth's mother had also told of the coffin dolls. In the eighteen thirties, her mother had explained, a group of small boys had been rabbiting on Arthur's Seat, and in their search for burrows had discovered the cave. In it, neatly arranged in a row, were miniature coffins, each less than four inches in length and carefully crafted from wood. In each coffin lay an equally carefully crafted effigy of a man, dressed in cloth cut into miniature robes from full-size garments, the features and garb of each man different from that of his neighbour.

When they had been discovered, all kind of dark speculations had surrounded the origin of and intent behind the figures. Most commonly accepted had been the belief that they were poppets—the work of some Edinburgh coven practising effigy witchcraft. Another theory said they were the likenesses, carved in hazel, of members of a secret society, a dark guild of Edinburgh warlocks who had assured their immortality by creating and hiding their deaths in effigy. Others attributed the poppets to the workshops of the luspardan—the race of underground dwarves whom the Irish knew as leprechauns. Compared to that of their Irish cousins, the reputation of the luspardan in ancient Scottish legend was one of far greater malevolence and quickness to take offence. Many feared the theft of the poppets from the underground Celtic Otherworld would bring down doom onto Scotland's capital.

But Elspeth knew there had only been seventeen coffins with figures found, and they now resided in an Edinburgh museum. There were hundreds here—perhaps thousands of deaths in effigy—arranged in serried rows on either side of the cavern floor. As her guide led her through the cave, his torch seemed to bring them to brief, flickering life, and she could swear she saw carved faces change from impassive to scowling, from blank to glaring.

"How can this be?" she entreated the stranger, but her guide walked on, mutely.

There were more coffins, more poppets, as they progressed through the cavern. Elspeth scoured the direction whence they had come, searched above her, peered into the dark on either side, in a desperate search for a glimmer of daylight from the world beyond. If this was indeed the Arthur's Seat cave, then they were so close to an exit. But all she could see was darkness—a darkness that she could swear rippled and writhed with the shadows of tiny figures reanimated once out of the light, small wooden hands reaching out in the dark to clutch and seize.

Her last hope diminished when the path they followed declined, and the cavern walls closed in, so that they now walked through the suffocating embrace of a long, tight tunnel. Elspeth cursed her lack of courage: if she had acted with more conviction earlier, she would have struck out on her own, away from the stranger's guiding light and into the dark. Only then, so close to the surface as they must now be, could she have seized her chance to find the light of the world, or at least perish in the dark on her own terms.

The tunnel's decline steepened, its walls narrowed, its roof lowered. Elspeth now had to hunch over to traverse it. The torch carried by her guide was forced lower, and she noticed that he no longer turned to her, presumably because his face would be cast in light, rather than the shadow of his hat's brim. Every step seemed to bring the tunnel's confinement closer, and she felt a claustrophobic panic surge in her chest. Again she thought about turning around, ascending the descent they had made and returning to the cave of dolls.

Suddenly, they were at the tunnel's end.

The mouth of the passage opened out onto a vast cavern. It was the size of a cathedral, Elspeth realized. It was impossible.

"It astounds, does it not?" said her guide. "And we do not yet see its full majesty. This is what I wanted to show you, this is the realm you and I share, but at different times. This is the truth that waited to be revealed. Behold!"

He took his torch and swung it with full force, throwing it into the cavern. It traced a bright arc through the darkness before landing in a ditch filled with a black, tarry substance. Elspeth guessed it was pitch, for when the burning torch touched it, it burst into flame. The ditch ran along the cavern's sides, and flames coursed their urgent way along it, setting the pitch ablaze, then split into two directions when the ditch divided. Then four, then eight . . .

Eventually the entire cavern was illuminated by the criss-crossing of the burning channels, and Elspeth held shielding hands before her eyes.

"Do you see?" asked the stranger. Elspeth did not answer, still shielding her eyes from the sudden brightness after so long in the gloom. He walked directly towards her and she struggled to adjust her vision so she could see him.

By the time her eyes adjusted to the light, he stood directly in front of her. For the first time in their travels together, Elspeth could see her companion's face.

Suddenly, a shrill, screeching sound, like a banshee's wail, resounded through the vast cavern, and Elspeth realized it was the sound of her own screaming.

57

Ahead of him, at the opposite side of the depression, Crunnach House stood lifeless and dark, not a single light showing in the black eyes of its windows.

Hyde stood for a moment on the crest of the hillock, beneath the branches of the dule tree. He knew from his previous visit that this spot was the most clearly visible from the drawing room windows of Crunnach House. He paused there for a while, the very last of the low, cloud-muted sun at his back, ensuring his compliance with Ballor's demand was witnessed.

He then made his way at an unhurried pace along the coachway to the house.

After about five minutes, he reached where the path arced around the bowl of the depression in which stood the Dark Man menhir. Night had all but fully fallen by now and he silently thanked the sky for the winding sheet of cloud it wrapped around the half-moon. The path itself dipped slightly and, while not completely out of sight of the house, it afforded Hyde the opportunity he sought. He crouched low and turned sharply from the path and down into the depression. Once beneath the line-of-sight of Crunnach House, he sprinted across to the menhir and concealed himself behind it, catching his breath. He cursed as the moon shook free of its cloud shroud for a moment, casting its wan light across the scene.

As he prepared to make his break across the depression to its other side, his attention was drawn, as if by hypnotic force, to the obsidian-smooth-and-black surface of the standing stone. Like a tattooed man, it was covered with writhing cup, spiral and circle petroglyphs. This close, and despite the dim light, he could see one pattern dominated all others, the same pattern that had dominated his thoughts for three weeks: the intersecting triple spirals of the triskelion.

There was something about the standing stone that seemed familiar to Hyde, something about the situation he was in. With that sensation came another, that of unreality, that everything here was false, that he was false. A panic rose in him with the recognition of the prelude to an episode.

"Not now," he muttered. "For the love of God, not now . . ."

Already having removed from his head his hat and the white bandage that bound his wound and would have given away his presence, Hyde shrugged off the coat he had draped over his shoulders. Using his left hand, he took first the Enfield revolver, then the short detective's truncheon from his coat pockets. He tucked the revolver into his left jacket pocket and hung on to the truncheon. For a moment, he considered removing his sling, but he calculated that the arm was useless to him bound or unbound, and at least the sling held it close to his body and out of harm's way.

He ran on, taking advantage of the depression's cover, only crouching low again once he reached its far rim. The moon once more was dressed in cloud and he felt confident again of his concealment—though he knew that, by now, however many of Ballor's men awaited him at Crunnach House, they would begin to wonder as to why Hyde was not now approaching the main door.

A ragged tangle of bush and heather afforded some cover as he made his way around to the flank of the house. He scanned the gloom for figures, but if anyone lurked in the shadows waiting for him, they remained safely cloaked in shadow.

He had no time to hesitate. Still crouching low, he sprinted across the open ground until he was himself pressed into the wall and its shadows. He tried each of three ground-floor windows, all of which refused to yield. Edging his way along the wall, he came to a corner. There was still enough light for him to see that a door, presumably to a store or scullery, stood blankly inviting him forward. He had just taken a step when he heard the scraping sound of a boot on the gravel. Hyde dodged back behind the corner.

The footsteps grew closer and Hyde tightened his grip on his truncheon.

58

The smell of blood lingered in her nostrils and Cally pushed down the instincts it awoke. She forced herself to think as a physician and explored with one hand the extent of the blood. It yielded to her fingers as cool, not cold. This blood, she realized, had pooled on the cold cellar floor, gathering in the crevices between the flagstones, but still bore the fading ghost of a body's temperature.

It was blood freshly spilled.

She explored further, leaning with one hand against the wall, her other tracing the outline of the blood's pooling. She jumped back. Her fingers had come to rest against something solid.

Cally froze, and heard the sound of faint, rapid breathing.

"Save . . . yourself . . ." The entreaty was little more than a whispered gasp. A man's voice. There was no doubt in Cally's mind that she had found the source of the blood.

She gathered her wits and knelt beside the man, whose outline became barely perceptible to her. She ran her hands over his body: he was sitting, legs splayed, his back leaning against the wall of the cellar. Her blind exploration revealed the source of the blood: a chest wound that still bled profusely. When she applied light pressure on the wound to slow its haemorrhaging, the man coughed wetly. She pressed the back of her other hand against where she had estimated his cheek to be: his skin was cold—too cold even for this damp, unheated cellar— and clammy. His breathing remained shallow and rapid, with a rattling to it.

She knew that what little life remained in her invisible companion was fading.

"Stay calm," she said. "Help will be here soon, I'm sure of it."

"No . . . help . . ." he gasped. "No hope . . . Save . . . yourself. You must . . . get out . . ."

She searched through the man's pockets, seeking a handkerchief with which to form a pad and staunch the flow of blood. She found one and pulled it out; with the action, something else was pulled from the pocket and rattled as it fell to the floor. She picked it up and shook it close to her ear: a metal matchbox. She set it to one side on the floor beside her and folded the handkerchief into a pad, pressing it against the wound.

"Can you hold that there?" she asked. "And press as hard as you can. I'll get some light so I can—"

The man seized her wrist with surprising strength. In the dark he leaned towards her and hissed: "The Beast, the Deacon . . . back soon . . . You have got to get away. Forget about me. You have got to tell the truth. Passageway up . . . steps . . . secret door. Opens into the armoire in the hall . . ." His grip and his voice weakened at the same time. "Revolver . . . Drawer . . ."

He fell silent for a moment, as if gathering in the dark the last, tattered shreds of his strength. "The Deacon . . ."

"The Deacon?" she urged. "Ballor? Is he here?"

In the cold dark, the unseen man gave something like a sigh; his grip on her wrist loosened and his cold fingers slipped away. Cally felt for a pulse in his neck, but there was none.

She was alone again, and with that the darkness seemed to deepen, become more oppressive. She picked up the matchbox and struck a lucifer. The cellar was small and stone walled, with boxes and crates. Upon one crate sat a paraffin lamp. She lifted the glass chimney and lit it.

The lamp's light was poor, but enough for her to make sense of her surroundings. The man whose dying minutes she had shared remained sitting splay legged on the floor, his back propped against the wall.

She could see now the extent of his blood loss and it seemed he sat in a crimson throne, the wall and floor around him glistening.

Cally Burr had never met the man, never seen him before, but she recognized him from Edward Hyde's description. He sat, his mouth slightly agape, his expression empty, the anaemia of his complexion emphasized by a thick shock of raven-black hair; and by the black silk eyepatch that shielded one eye.

Frederic Ballor.

59

Detective Sergeant Peter MacCandless had served with all manner of men during the course of his fifteen years of service in the City of Edinburgh Police; tonight, as he edged his way towards the ruins of a remote gatehouse, he could not think of anyone he would rather have with him than Willie Dempster.

Where MacCandless acted on impulse and instinct, Dempster relied on reason and method. Tonight they would need both. And that was not the only reason for MacCandless being reassured by his friend's presence: Dempster had night sense, as beat men called it: that innate ability to perceive danger, to track fugitives in the black-shadowed closes and wynds of the city when others were blinded by the darkness. It was not simply an acuity of vision in the night, it was the ability to stretch every sense into dark corners and intuit what sought to hide in them.

Another reason MacCandless was glad of Dempster's company was that the latter, prior to his police service, had served in the army. The skills needed for the bizarre and desperate enterprise upon which Hyde had set them demanded as much military as police skills.

As arranged, once out of sight of the gates, Mackinley had slowed the coach to walking pace long enough for them to slip out of their concealment and into the ditch that lined the unmetalled roadway. From there they had crossed the strangely alien and desolate heath, crouching low in their advance towards the ruins of the gatehouse. They made a wide circle of their approach, cutting through gorse and heather, and by the time they reached the ruins, the sky had bled the last of its light and only a cloudy moon remained to illuminate their way.

MacCandless watched for a while to ensure there was no one to see them, then made to cross the main carriageway, but felt himself roughly pulled back into the gorse and rubble of the ruins. He turned angrily, but saw Dempster pressing a finger to his lips in a gesture of silence before pointing to the gateless stanchions. It was only then that he saw a dark figure stood guard, watching the roadway from the shadows, barely distinguishable but detected by Dempster's night sense. MacCandless nodded to Dempster, who pointed a way through the low, scruffy undergrowth, also indicating that he should go ahead of him.

Their progress was slow, the bracken and whin concealing them from sight but threatening to crackle and rustle with every movement. Each foot forward involved carefully and silently pushing entanglement from their path. MacCandless turned regularly to ensure Dempster was still close behind. After what seemed an age, they were far enough from the gatehouse and its sentinel that they dared to move across open ground.

"We must hurry," whispered MacCandless, "Captain Hyde must be close to the house now."

Eventually, they reached the service bridleway that led around to the back of Crunnach House, which now loomed lightless and black against the night sky.

"Over there!" Dempster pointed to a set of long, low buildings that sat a little apart from the main house: the stables and their objective.

MacCandless was already on the bridleway when something clearly caught Dempster's attention. He hissed: "Someone's coming!" and gestured frantically but silently for MacCandless to cross to the other side of the drive and take cover in the ditch running along its side, while he himself ducked back into the bushes.

MacCandless dashed across and dropped into the ditch, drawing his truncheon, ready to ambush whoever came their way. Then he heard it: the sound of a carriage coming towards them at speed. He sank lower into the ditch, shielded by a ragged clump of grass, and watched the horses and carriage, reduced by the night to a dark geometry of shadows, as they thundered by. The driver was a small man, but was silhouetted by the night and had his coat collar pulled high around his neck and his top hat pulled low, denying MacCandless a good look at him. He must be the odd servant Hyde and Pollock had described, he thought as he watched the carriage swing round and out of view behind the stable block.

After the carriage was gone, he strained the night for the sound of anyone else approaching, but there was none.

"Willie!" he hissed across at the bushes on the far side of the bridle-way, but could see no sign nor hear any sound of Dempster. "Willie!"

He waited a few seconds, then called out again, as loud as he dared. Still no answer came and he decided, with great unease, that Dempster must have found another route to their goal. Time was passing and they had to get to the house to support Hyde. Left with no other option, MacCandless crouched low and pushed on alone, ascending the incline of the embankment towards the stable block.

Keeping his head and shoulders down as he ran, he gained the shelter of the gable wall of the stable block without detection. Pressing his back against the rough stonework, he first scanned the direction whence he had come, seeking any sign of Dempster. A dread bloomed in his gut that something had befallen his colleague: that perhaps the sentry at the derelict gates had come back toward the house and had discovered the detective. But if that had happened, he thought, surely some form of alarm would have been raised.

The most pressing issue, however, was that Captain Hyde must have got into position by now, and MacCandless needed to make his simultaneous approach without detection. He glanced round the corner of the stable block and saw the small coachman stride towards the main house, leaving the coach and horses to be attended by another. He dodged back behind the corner. The man at the coach stood between him and the house. He would have to be dealt with, and quietly, as Hyde had instructed.

Again he searched the shadowed landscape for Dempster. What had happened to him? Once more he peeked around the corner and checked on the man by the coach. He had moved around to the other side, between the carriage and the stable block, and was now temporarily out of sight of the house. It was MacCandless's best chance: he would have to act without Dempster.

He slipped his wrist through the leather loop of the lignum vitae truncheon and gripped the ridged handle tight. Moving as lightly and quietly as possible, he crossed the yard to the rear of the carriage, then eased his way along its flank until he was close to the unsuspecting man, who still presented his back.

Something—a stone or piece of grit—crunched quietly as Mac-Candless took his final step and the man began to turn. MacCandless brought the truncheon down with as much force as he could manage onto his head, but the blow glanced off the side of his skull and most of the force was absorbed by his shoulder. The man was fully turned now and, though stunned, grabbed at the detective, who now saw he was locked in combat with the sabre-scarred fellow Hyde had described. This was a battle-hardened type, and MacCandless knew that if his opponent recovered his senses fully, he would not be a match for the ex-soldier.

He struck at him again, but the sabre-scarred man, beginning to recover himself, blocked the blow. He made to cry out, but MacCandless viciously jabbed the truncheon at his throat, just above the sternum notch. Taking advantage of his opponent struggling for breath, the detective swung the truncheon twice, both blows striking home hard, first on the right ear, then above it on the temple. The man made a strange half-moan and sank to his knees. MacCandless brought the baton down hard onto the crown of his head. There was a sickening crack and the man fell senseless onto the gravel.

MacCandless looked around, rooted to the spot, his pulse thundering and breath laboured, while he checked that no one had heard the sentry's strangled cry and now came to his aid. There was silence. He looked down at the man at his feet, who lay silent and in an unnaturally twisted pose, and a great fear rose in MacCandless that he had just killed a man.

Taking hold of the unconscious sentry under the armpits, he dragged him into the stable block. Reassured when the injured man made a low moaning sound, MacCandless dropped him into one of the stalls. He took his handcuffs from his pocket and fastened them on unresisting wrists. He cursed that he had nothing with which to gag the man, lest he stir and cry for help, but he estimated that he would remain senseless for some time.

Taking a few breaths to steady his nerves, he made his way back out of the stable block, checking no one had come from the darkened house. He had only taken a couple of steps when someone emerged from the shadows and grabbed him by the shoulder. He spun around, raising the truncheon high, ready to strike, then lowered his arm when he recognized who had accosted him.

"Willie!" he said to Dempster. "Where the hell have you been?"

60

Ballor's face, paled by death and the bleak, meagre light of the paraffin lamp, seemed luminous, like some sickly moon gazing out at Cally in sallow malevolence from the dark of the cellar. It made no sense. Her thoughts jangled, refusing to yield to any coherence, as if they were pieces from several separate jigsaws jumbled together. This was who Hyde believed to be the Deacon—which he clearly was not.

She gathered herself. It was only a matter of time until whoever had struck the fatal blow into Ballor's chest returned. Cally was, she knew, of limited use to her captor. She was bait, she realized that now: bait to snare Hyde. And when Hyde came, and come he would, he would be looking for the wrong adversary, seeking the Deacon with Ballor's face, setting him at a disadvantage and rendering him vulnerable. She had to warn him. But first she had to escape this cellar.

She knelt by Ballor's body and went through his pockets once more. There was nothing, other than the matches, of any use to her. She used the lamp to examine her confinement. There was a stout door to her left, the only way in or out. Taking the lamp across to it, she examined the door. It was solid oak, rough hewn but robust and completely devoid of a lock or handle. It did not yield to her urgings and she ran her fingers around it, tracing its edges.

Cally squatted down to examine the bottom edge. There was a gap large enough along the door's sill for her to slip her fingers through and grasp it, revealing it so thick there was no chance of breaking it down. She shook it in desperation and fury and was rewarded with a rattling sound halfway up its leading edge, where the lock should have been. She shook it again and realized that what she heard was the rattling of some kind of latch on the door's other side. There was no way of opening the door from inside the cellar, and she cursed her luck.

A thought struck her: the hatpin. Pulling it from her collar, she gripped its bulbous jewelled end and eased the point through the gap between wooden door and stone jamb, sliding it upwards. Eventually it came to rest underneath the latch on the outside. She pushed upwards, keeping her grip on the pin firm. She pushed again, focusing all her strength and will into fingers that ached from the effort, but the latch still would not yield.

Cally replaced the pin in her bodice collar and lifted the lamp once more, scanning the cellar for something more robust to tease the latch free of its housing. She examined the crates in the corner. They were mostly wine crates, the wood too thick to slide between the door and its stone frame. Casting them aside in her fury, she exposed two smaller trays, shallow, lidless and less robust, of the kind used for fruit and vegetables. She lifted one up and dashed it against the wall, picking up a broken slat.

She sighed her relief when the slat slid into the door gap without jamming. She pushed upward, again without success, unable to overcome the weight or resistance of the latch. Taking a deep breath, she pushed again. This time she felt some movement. Teeth clenched and the skin over her knuckles stretched taut and white, she pushed one last time and felt the latch free its housing. She pressed her shoulder against the door and it swung outward.

Holding the lamp ahead of her with one hand, clutching the hatpin with the other, she found herself in a narrow, low-ceilinged passageway. The walls were stone dressed but the floor was earthen, and the air in the passage hung moist and fusty with the odour of stale, damp soil and age; Cally had the unpleasant thought that this must be what a grave smelt like. The way was thankfully short and she found herself at the foot of a flight of stone steps. She climbed upwards, illuminating her way with the lamp until she reached the final step, which formed the base of another door, this time made of lighter wood and with a small knob handle.

The door pulled inward and she found herself in a cubicle, large enough for her to stand upright, with a set of drawers to the left, a hanging rail to the right, and double doors ahead of her. She eased

294 · CRAIG RUSSELL

them open and found herself in the main reception hall of a large house that sat in darkness. She could now see that the armoire with its false wall was a disguised doorway to the cellar, just as Ballor had described.

She remembered the words he had forced out, carrying some of the last of his life with them. Revolver. Drawer.

She set the lamp down and opened the drawers. The top was empty save for a large leather-bound volume with a Gaelic title embossed into it. Ignoring the volume, she continued to search and the second drawer revealed her prize: a short-barrelled revolver and three boxes of ammunition. She remembered the lessons her father had taught her in their brief time together in India, and she broke open the revolver and checked the cylinder. It was loaded.

Snapping the breech shut, she snatched up two boxes of ammunition and cursed her outfit's lack of pockets as she stuffed them into the bodice of her jacket.

Taking a deep, cleansing breath, Cally stood for a moment collecting herself, calming the rage that threatened to consume her. She then picked up the lamp in her left hand, the revolver in her right.

She could see now that the main doors of the house, which she realized must be Ballor's residence at Crunnach, lay open to the night beyond. Escape lay that way. Freedom and the chance to find help.

But Edward was coming, if he was not already there. Death would meet him wearing an unsuspected face. She knew how remote Crunnach House was from any source of assistance; she had no knowledge of the area, and might set her course deeper into the wilds and away from vital help.

She forced herself to think, but knew that indecision and hesitation here in the hallway could very quickly undo her escape.

She would go outside, seek some cover to survey the house and hopefully intercept Hyde's approach. It was not much of a strategy, but it was the only course she could see.

Cally had just set the paraffin lamp down on the hall table and was about to blow out its flame when a noise, far above her in the upper floors of the house, reached her.

She pulled back the hammer to cock the revolver and, leaving the lamp on the table, slowly made her way up the stairs.

61

"What in the name of all that is holy is this all about?" asked Thomson, whose flaccid face was etched with unease as he took in the maniacal scribblings that covered every inch of every surface.

"This has nothing to do with anything holy," said Pollock. "Quite the other." He took the Enfield revolver from his coat pocket. "We have to search the other rooms."

The sense of unease intensified as they made their way through the rest of the tenement. Lighting a mantle in each ground-floor room as they went revealed walls, floors and ceilings decorated with the same obsessive repetition of the triskelion pattern. The experience was echoed on every floor, all the rooms of which were empty and naked, save for the increasingly dense triple-spiral motifs that seemed to writhe and dance in the flickering gaslight. With each floor the scrawling, spidering artwork became ever more maniacal, ever more demonic; it was as if their ascent through the building represented a descent into hell.

The largest space waited for them at the very top of the building: the attic was a single room the width and depth of the whole tenement, beneath the steep-pitched rafters supporting the roof. There was the least light of all here: the daylight outside had all but faded and the windows that faced out to look across the port were small and almost opaque with soot.

As he stepped into the attic, Pollock knew instantly and completely that whatever dark secret lay at the heart of Elspeth Lockwood's disappearance, this was the place where they would find it. Like the others, he could smell it in the air: that unmistakable, nauseous odour that every policeman knew. The smell of human death.

"Jesus God," said Thomson, who clasped his handkerchief to his mouth.

There was no gas mantle here, but Pollock found, next to where the stairs opened out into the attic space, a metal tray laden with six thick, cathedral-style candles, all of which had seen service. He lit them all, leaving three in the tray, passing one to each uniformed constable, finally taking one for himself.

Light and shadow danced across the angles of the roof, the gable ends, the floor. Even after what they had so far witnessed, all three men were unprepared for what they found here. Again, everything was covered with shapes and patterns. Once more, the triskelion motif was everywhere, but here it was dominated by another repeated image: the three policemen stood under the gaze of a hundred eyes, the irises black spirals, the sclerae blood red. On the far gable a huge figure had been described in black paint that had been daubed and smeared on the wall by hand, rather than painted with brush. The head was almost completely filled with a single red eye.

But it was the object in the centre of the room that, as if magnetized, drew the policemen towards it. As they approached, taking careful slow steps, they struggled to make sense of it. Small—slightly bigger than a man's fist—and formless, it sat on an old, dusty wooden plant stand. As they drew nearer, they could each see the object was dark red and black, its surface rippling as if alive, its edges strangely fuzzy.

Pollock was first to reach it. He re-pocketed his revolver and, like Thomson and MacCausland, clasped a handkerchief to his mouth and nose. This small object was the source of the foulness in the air, and when he waved his free hand over it, the rippling black surface briefly became a buzzing dark halo of flies before resettling on the lump of putrefying flesh.

It was, Pollock realized, a human heart.

He ignored the sound of the Leith constable retching behind him. This, he knew, was the heart cut from the Hanged Man, the private detective Farquharson. For a moment, the three policemen stood silent under the gaze of a hundred blood-red eyes and a daubed monocular monster. Eventually Pollock turned to MacCausland, who was still recovering himself. "Go—get others."

Pollock stood staring at the rotting heart, seething with flies, and heard the sound of MacCausland's running footsteps on the wooden stairs, the street door being flung open, the desperate blasts of a police whistle. He turned and walked back to where Thomson stood, the older policeman gazing at the daubed, scrawled and scribbled maze of patterns on the walls, clearly coming to terms with the fact that in his career he had not, after all, seen all there was to see.

It was as he made his way to Thomson that one of the floorboards shifted slightly beneath Pollock's feet. He knelt down and traced the outline of the loose boards with his fingers, finding a notch at the end of the one that had moved beneath his boot. Taking his pocketknife out, he eased its blade into the notch and levered up a square section of boards.

"Bring your candle over here," he commanded Thomson, who complied, clearly having abandoned all idea of exerting seniority. Pollock placed his own candle on the floor next to the opened hatch. He could see there were three bundles concealed in the void, and pulled out the largest first. It revealed itself to be a leather roll pouch, fastened by two buckles. He unbuckled the pouch and rolled it flat on the floor. Two blades glittered in the light of the policemen's candles. Pollock and Thomson exchanged a look.

"It looks like you've found your murder weapons," said the elder constable.

"I rather think the murder weapon is the one that is not here," said Pollock. "Look—this strap has held a third dirk in place."

He recognized the smaller knife as a *sgian-dubh*; its neighbour was a battle dirk of the same pattern but longer bladed. Both weapons had ornate hilts of antler or bone decorated with carved Celtic ropework, capped with flat, round pommels in the design of a small targe. Highland weapons.

He slid the flattened roll pouch to one side and took out a second bundle, this time three black notebooks tied together with red ribbon. He recognized them as the same type that Farquharson, the private detective, had used. The third bundle was a collection of papers bound in red ribbon. He set them on the floor, untying the ribbon that held them together. Tilting the first page to the candle's weak light, Pollock could see it was filled with rows of small, meticulously neat writing in blue ink. He began to read, for the first two pages struggling to make sense of what it was he was reading. The pages seemed non-sequential, as if some were missing, and the language was in parts extremely technical.

Medical.

Iain Pollock felt the back of his neck tingle as the significance of what he held struck him.

"My God . . ." he muttered as much to himself as to Thomson, "these are the missing pages from Dr. Porteous's journal."

"The man with his eyes cut out?" asked Thomson.

Pollock nodded, reading on, his youthful brow furrowed as he sought to understand Porteous's notes and observations. He felt like an intruder, a voyeur, as he read what the psychiatrist had to say about Captain Hyde's condition.

It was on the sixth page he read, just as MacCausland came bounding up the ramshackle wooden stairs, bringing other Burgh Police constables with him, that understanding came to Pollock. He stood up suddenly, clutching the page and letting the others fall.

"Oh God," he said. "Oh God, no . . ."

"What is it? What is wrong?" asked Thomson.

Pollock turned to the uniformed man. "We have got to go. We have got to get to Crunnach House, now!"

He turned to leave, but Thomson grabbed his arm. "What is it? What did you read?"

"Porteous has written it all down here—all the details of his treatment. I cannot believe it. Oh God, I cannot believe it." He gazed at Thomson with eyes wide and wild. "I know who killed Farquharson and Porteous. It was the Deacon. But the Deacon is not Frederic Ballor." He took his watch from his pocket and looked at it. "Hyde is at Crunnach House already. I have got to stop him. I have got to stop Hyde before he gets to Elspeth Lockwood . . ."

62

Hyde braced himself to act. The footsteps grew nearer and he pressed himself into the shadow of the wall, his uninjured arm raised and ready to strike with the truncheon.

The man turned the corner and Hyde hit him hard on the side of the neck, then a second blow to his temple as he dropped. It was over in an instant and the man was unconscious before he hit the ground. Hyde turned him onto his back and recognized him right away. He still bore the bruises from their earlier encounter and his right arm was heavily bandaged: it was the assailant Hyde had so savagely beaten; the one whose knife attack had deprived Hyde's own right arm of its function.

With his left arm, he dragged the man into the shadows' concealment and made his way back around to the side of the house. The moon had freed itself of its cloud shroud and cast its light across the landscape, defining a clearer geometry of light and shadow. Hyde knew he needed to gain entry to the house before another sentry detected him. He did not know, of course, how many of Ballor's men waited for him inside. He replaced his truncheon in his pocket. From now on, any confrontation would be dealt with at gunpoint.

He prepared to make his way towards the scullery door but hesitated as the same strange sensation again began to take hold of him. Once more everything around him felt false, ethereal and otherworldly, as if governed by the implausible physics of a dream. He looked up at the sky and found the moon now seemed encircled by a multitude of concentric halos, as if its light echoed through the firmament. The dark of the night no longer appeared to Hyde as simply blackness, but as a rippling, textured ocean of dark velvet colour: deep greens and blues, ultramarine and violet. He looked up at the looming dark mass of

Crunnach House and was consumed with the overpowering sense that he had stood here, in this place and at this moment, a thousand times before, and he would stand there a thousand times more; that time was folding in on itself and consuming him in its infinite corrugations.

"Oh please God," he muttered to himself, "not now. I cannot lose time now . . ."

He felt a chill like no other course through his body at the sound of it: the same high, shrill, raw wailing tearing the night with sharp, juddering, ragged edges. The same sound he had heard at the Water of Leith, the sound of a banshee's keening.

It's not real, he told himself. *Get a grip on yourself man, it's not real.*

He tensed suddenly as he detected someone moving in the shadows. The shape did not so much step out of the darkness as take its form from it. The small figure walked on the gravelled way, its footsteps silent, stopping ten feet from Hyde.

The small, tattered and earth-soiled figure of Mary Paton, the Bairn in the Witch's Cradle, looked up at him and pressed a small index finger to her lips. "Shh . . ." Hyde heard her say, though her lips did not move, "it is coming. It will hear you. *Cù dubh ifrinn* is coming."

He squeezed his eyes tight shut but patterns of light zigzagged their way across the curtain of his eyelids. When he opened them, the apparition had changed form—was taller yet still small, the expression no longer blank but one of terror. He recognized her as Nell McCrossan, the mill girl who had run into Hyde the night the Hanged Man had been discovered.

"Did you hear it again, sir?" she asked him. "The *bean-nighe*? Did you hear the *ban-sìth* call you?"

"Not *now*!" he hissed, his jaw clenched. He again closed his eyes and took deep breaths, pulling the cold, cleansing night air into his lungs. When he opened them again, the apparition was gone, the universe once more solid and real. It would not stay so for long, he knew.

With an enormous effort of will, Hyde forced himself to focus. He crossed to the scullery door and tried the handle. It was locked, but the door was not particularly robust and it yielded to his left shoulder.

He was inside. He drew the revolver from his pocket and made his way into the heart of the house.

—

Hyde eased his way into the scullery, moving with as much stealth as his injuries and the disorientating effects of an incipient episode allowed. He must, he knew, be quick. Were he to have a full-blown absence seizure, he would be completely at the mercy of Ballor and his men. An episode now would prove fatal, not just for him but for Cally Burr and Elspeth Lockwood.

He found his way to the main hallway. There was still no sign of anyone within the house and everything lay shrouded in shadows cast by a paraffin lamp that sat on the hall table. He saw that the doors of the armoire had been flung wide, and he picked up the paraffin lamp to examine it. He was surprised to find that the back of it had been a false wall and a passageway stair led down to the darkness. He cursed as he remembered his previous visit to the house with Pollock, and how Ballor's arrogant composure had slipped when Hyde had asked to see inside the armoire. Had Elspeth Lockwood been confined underground, with Hyde and rescue only a few feet from her? He stepped through the armoire and into the stairwell. He took a few steps down, and the lamp's flickering light revealed a door at the bottom, unlatched and thrown open.

Hyde could see that if anyone had been confined there, they were no longer. Nevertheless, he decided to examine whatever lay beyond the door. He had just taken another step when he heard a sound somewhere distant behind him, a noise like a woman crying out.

He turned and made his way back into the hall.

63

Cally pressed her back to the wall as she climbed the stairway with measured steps, her eyes always cast upward, the gun held ready before her. There was little light: a few of the wall candle lamps had been lit, and she scanned every shadow for hidden danger. The landing of each floor was empty and dark, and the only light of any note she could see was at the very top of the stairwell.

She paused for a moment, thinking she had heard someone moving below her, on the ground floor. She looked down but could not see anyone, the paraffin lamp still on the table leaching its anaemic light into the reception hall.

She continued her ascent towards the attic, encountering no one, hearing no further sound from within the house. Where were her captors? What game was being played here? Such had been the silence that she was startled by a sudden knocking noise.

She had now reached the third floor of the house and the sound had come from a room off the landing. As with the stairway and the other landings, someone had lit candles in the wall sconces—not enough to illuminate, but sufficient to avoid immersion in total darkness. Her arm was shaking from the weight of the gun and she now braced her grip with her other hand, both arms outstretched. The sound, she estimated, had come from the corner room. She gave a small jump when she heard it again, something between knocking and rattling. She inched towards the room and saw the door was slightly ajar. With the toe of her boot, Cally kicked the door open, using just enough force to swing it wide but not so much that the door would crash against the wall, alerting others of her location.

No lamp nor candle was lit in the corner room, but it had large windows on both aspects and the vague moonlight from outside showed her it was a disused bathroom. The floor was coated with dust, as was the bath, sink and toilet. She jumped again at a sound—louder and more immediate this time. She sighed at the realization that it was nothing but trapped air seeking escape from the pipes.

She moved across to the window. From this elevation she could see the whole shadowplay of the landscape: the silhouette of a vast tree sitting on a hill opposite, the clumps of bush and gorse like black cankers on the valley's arcing lip. In the centre of it all lay the bowl of the depression, deep in the blackest of all shadows, as if liquid night had settled in its depths.

She heard another noise. It seemed to come from the floor above, this time faint—so faint that she feared it had been a ghost conjured by her imagination. She left the bathroom, crossed the landing, and began to climb the final flight of stairs.

It was clear that the attic rooms off the undressed wooden landing had been servants' quarters. As with the other landings, candles had been lit in their sconces, but here the illumination had been enhanced by a wall-mounted oil lamp backed with a reflective escutcheon. This, she realized, had been the source of the increased light she had seen from downstairs in the hall.

Was it a sign that she would encounter her captors here? Cally tightened her grip on the revolver and moved across the landing, wincing at every creak or groan of the floorboards.

The first of the attic rooms, a corner one beneath a conical roof, showed signs of occupation: a small bedroom, brushed clean and its few furnishings and personal items neatly arranged. There was, however, no sign of its occupant.

The other rooms were similarly empty, but unlike the first, they showed signs of dusty desuetude. That left only one other.

The last room was in the corner of the building opposite the one occupied bedroom. She calculated it sat directly above the disused bathroom she had searched on the floor below.

As she approached, she noticed its door was ajar, and she could see a key in the lock. Holding the revolver in her right hand, she silently removed the key with her left: Cally Burr had no intention of having the door locked behind her when she entered and finding herself once more a prisoner of Crunnach House.

She stepped through the door and found herself in a large tower room. Scanning it for occupation, she swept it with the revolver held in her outstretched arms. When she was satisfied she was alone, she stepped farther into the room.

It was a box garret with a vast window filling almost all of one wall and part of the roof. Half of the room was lit by the moon shining through the panes of the window, the other half in darkness. She could see from the items arranged on the moonlit trestle table that this was an artist's studio. A huge canvas sat propped against the far wall, almost filling it, but it lay in shadow beyond the moonlight's edge and Cally could see nothing of its subject.

There was no one here and there was no point in tarrying. Cally began to suspect that the noises that had drawn her up through the house had been nothing more than the sounds from the underused pipework.

Hyde was not here, and she must find him before he fell into the trap set for him.

She reached the door but paused, for a moment drawn to look back at the huge canvas, veiled in shadow. For some reason she felt she had to expose its subject to the light. As with the rest of the house, there were no gas mantles in the studio, and she searched around for some source of illumination. On the trestle table she found a four-branched candelabrum and used Ballor's matches to light its candles.

Picking up the candelabrum, she took it across to the painting and held it forth. She had to sweep it across the surface, its pool of light insufficient to illuminate the whole painting. A naked giantess strode across a landscape, crushing forests beneath her feet, a scarf of cloud around her throat. Cally saw that, as she strode, huge rocks tumbled from her leather bag.

The light of the candelabrum did not fully reach the titaness's face, and Cally placed the revolver on the floor, lifting across a chair upon which she could stand. Balancing on the chair, holding the candelabrum aloft, the woman's features were exposed, the oil paint still glistening, as if only recently applied.

"Oh my God . . ." Cally whispered to herself as she took in the face—a face she knew—and tried to understand its significance.

She had not time to step down from the chair, nor regain her revolver, when she heard movement behind her.

64

"Can this be true?" asked Rintoul. He clutched the siderail of the coach cabin as it thundered through the night, the two waggons filled with City of Edinburgh and Leith Burgh Police constables following behind it. "I can scarce believe it."

Iain Pollock sat beside the chief constable, the papers recovered from beneath the floorboards of a Leith slum resting on his lap.

"I still find it difficult to believe, sir. But it is all here in Dr. Porteous's notes. One patient, two personalities, one of which was gentle and good, the other the worst kind of monster. Which is why Dr. Porteous called it the Beast. His theory was that stories of the Celtic Otherworld heard in childhood were the basis of the fantasy world into which the Beast would retreat while the dominant personality ruled. The Beast built its own Otherworld deep in a divided mind and convinced itself that it had been around since the beginning of the Scottish race. A creature from Celtic myth trapped in the world of the living."

"*Cù dubh ifrinn . . .*" muttered Rintoul.

"Sir?"

"Nothing. What else did you find at the slum?"

"The remainder of Farquharson's notes. From what I've been able to see so far, Farquharson was murdered because, in his investigation of Elspeth Lockwood's relationship with Frederic Ballor, he stumbled across Ballor's blackmailing operation. Ballor would have Henry Dunlop photograph revellers at his drug- and sex-fuelled occult ceremonies. They were most often naked and in compromising positions, posed by Dunlop while they were stupefied by the drug potions Ballor supplied. Farquharson was on the point of exposing the operation to the police, and Ballor as the mastermind."

"Except he was not." Rintoul's face was set hard in the dim light of the coach lamp.

"Indeed not," said Pollock. "And when Farquharson realized the truth of who the Deacon was, and the madness that lay behind the Dark Guild, his fate was sealed."

Rintoul looked out at the darkening beyond the coach window, his own weary reflection cast back to him. "How long till we get there?"

Pollock checked his watch. "At least another hour, sir . . ."

65

Hyde stood in the hall, motionless, silent, listening for the sound of a woman crying out again. Had he imagined it? Had it been another ghost conjured in the dawn of a seizure?

He crossed over to the morning room, where he and Pollock had questioned Ballor, taking the paraffin lamp with him. Before he entered, he remembered the large windows that looked out over the Dark Man and the Lamentation Tree far beyond. If his enemy was outside, carrying the lamp into the morning room would expose his position. He set it down on the floor in the hall, next to the door. In any case, he decided, he would need his hand free for his revolver.

He made his way through the moon- and shadow-dappled room, pausing when he thought he heard movement somewhere high in the house, but when he could hear no more, he continued with his exploration. Where was everybody? Where had they hidden Cally?

He entered the next room, which he remembered from their previous search of Crunnach House had a second door onto the service corridor. Again, the room lay dark and empty, silent. There was a sound: not in the room but from the servants' corridor. Hyde crossed the room swiftly and silently, taking position next to the door and pressing his back to the wall, his revolver raised and cocked. The door opened and a silhouetted figure stepped into the room. Hyde was about to bring the butt of his gun down on the figure's head when it turned to face him.

"William?" He lowered his revolver.

"You gave me a turn there, sir," said Dempster.

"Have you come across any of Ballor's men?" asked Hyde.

"There's one on guard at the gate, and Peter dealt with another who is now tucked up in the stables."

"Where is Peter?"

"He'll be somewhere around the back of the house," said Dempster. "We split up to look for you."

"Where is Ballor?"

"That I cannot say—I do know that his weird coachman is lurking about somewhere."

"And Dr. Burr? Any sign?"

"Sorry, sir. I fear this might all be a wild goose chase—some kind of distraction."

Hyde sighed.

"Peter has a theory, though," said Dempster, "that they may be hiding down in the depression out there. Down by the Dark Man standing stone. It is the only place around here that offers them any chance of concealment. If they are not in the house, then . . ."

"But I came that way," said Hyde, "taking cover at the Dark Man. There was no one there."

"Perhaps there is now. I see no other place. I think we should . . . Are you all right, sir?"

Hyde had leant back once more against the wall, his knees bending a little. It would be soon, he knew. Another reality was superimposing itself on his world, and soon the authentic and the counterfeit would merge before he became lost in an absence seizure.

"I am fine," he lied. "It's just my head . . . the wound. Listen, if anything happens to me, if I should become . . . *unresponsive*, I need you to find Dr. Burr and get her to safety. Is that clear?"

"Yes, sir. You can rely on me," said Dempster.

"There's a cellar," said Hyde, forcing himself to focus, "entered through a concealed doorway in the armoire in the hall. Perhaps they are down there. Come with me."

Out in the hall, he picked up the paraffin lamp and carried it over to the armoire. The doors were closed.

"What is it, Captain Hyde?" asked Dempster.

"Did you close these doors?" asked Hyde.

"No, sir. I have not been this way." Dempster stepped forward and swung open the doors. "You say there's a passage to a cellar?"

"Yes," said Hyde. "There is a false back."

Dempster entered the armoire and pushed at the back wall. He ran his hands all over it, seeking out a catch or lever, then knocking on the wooden panel. "There is no door here, Captain Hyde. Are you sure you saw one?"

Hyde made to protest, but suddenly could not remember why. He looked over to the wall, at a picture he used to recognize, the history of which he had at one time known, by an artist whose name he had forgotten. A naked man floated in the air, surrounded by malevolent, tormenting figures in conical hats. As he looked at the painting, the figures began to move, their grimacing faces contorting; the floating man began to twist and writhe.

"Captain Hyde?" A distant voice he knew he should recognize but could not uttered a name he knew he should know but did not.

As the electric storm of a full-blown seizure surged through his brain, all sense of who he was, where he was, and why he was there became lost to him.

Once more, the otherworld of Edward Hyde claimed him.

66

Cally instantly recognized the short, squat figure that stepped into the attic studio as the coachman who had been one of her abductors. When he had posed at her home as a hansom cabbie, Hyde's description of Ballor's strange Cagot servant had not come to her mind, Cally never expecting that Salazar would turn up at her door.

But now she knew exactly who he was.

She looked down at the revolver on the floor by the chair on which she stood, and the Cagot followed her gaze, reading her intentions. With a grunt she threw the candelabrum at him, leapt from the chair and reached for the revolver. However, Salazar was already sprinting across the room, and dodged the thrown candelabrum.

Cally had just snatched up the gun when the Cagot's small but dense form slammed into her, sending her flying backwards into the canvas. The flames on the candelabrum had been snuffed out by the violence with which she had thrown it, and this side of the studio was once more in moon shadow. Salazar scrabbled on the dark floor for the revolver, but Cally had recovered herself and aimed a kick at the Cagot's flank. It made contact, but the restrictiveness of her skirt had taken much of the force out of the kick. Nevertheless, Salazar rolled sideways on the dark floor. Surprisingly nimble, Ballor's manservant sprang back to his feet. Cally made a run at him out of the darkness, but checked herself when she saw that the Cagot had the revolver in his hand, its barrel pointing in her direction. Cally cursed out loud, in anger more than fear, that her life was going to end in such an ignominious manner. She also was infuriated that she had let Hyde down: that she had not been able to warn him of the trap into which he would soon walk, if he had not already.

For a moment she considered a desperate rush at the small man, but then Salazar did something strange, something unexpected.

The Cagot pressed a finger to his lips, signalling for Cally to remain silent. He then pointed into the darkness at the shadowed canvas and slowly shook his head.

Then, with slow, deliberate movements, he turned the gun around in his hands and held it out to her, butt first.

She took the gun and aimed it at him, but Salazar held up his hands and again pointed to the painting, to the face once more hidden in shadow. He gestured for Cally to follow him and moved across to the window. He pointed down into the depression. Cally could see that the Dark Man menhir at its heart was illuminated, surrounded by a ring of blazing torches. They were too far away to be distinguishable, but she could see a group of people moving around the standing stone, appearing and disappearing in the flickering pools of light. She turned to the Cagot, who gestured impatiently.

Though denied words, he eloquently communicated that if they did not act, and act now, some dread thing was about to happen.

67

The air was cold on his face. That was the first sensation of which he became aware. For a while, that was all there was to his world: the cold air on his face.

Another world lingered for a moment, that otherwhere he had occupied. In that fading other place, there had been a wide glen framed by mountains and the ground had shaken as if with a giant's footsteps. He had looked up and had seen the face of the giant. He knew he had recognized the giant's face, had known its name, and that the knowledge had terrified him. The memory of it tantalized, just beyond reach, faded further, then it was gone.

One world yielded to another and with it came forgetfulness.

Hyde took a moment to make sense of his surroundings. The air was cold on his face because he was outside. A shape loomed blackly above him and he realized he was back at the Dark Man standing stone. There was light now: a circle of torches, staked into the ground around the Dark Man, illuminated the scene, but Hyde was alone.

How had he got here? He remembered coming to Crunnach House in the coach, MacCandless and Dempster crouched in the footwell. He had come to save Cally. Had he saved her?

That was all his injured memory would yield to him.

He knelt facing the Dark Man. He felt panic rise from deep within when he saw the glistening object on the menhir's concave shelf, rivulets of blood finding their way over the edge and running down its stone body.

A human heart.

Cally . . . he thought.

He looked down at his hands. He no longer wore his sling and he saw that both hands were covered in blood. Blood that was not his own.

"Oh God, no . . ." he gasped. "Oh God, what have I done . . ."

He looked around desperately. He looked towards the drumlin hill upon which stood the Lamentation Tree. The hillock, too, had been encircled with torches. The horror and dread threatening to burst within him, he could see the yew tree's gnarl-knuckled branch, pointing like an arthritic finger. He could see something hung from it. A body. Now he knew from where the heart had been freshly ripped.

"God forgive me," said Hyde. "Oh God forgive me . . ."

Like a man blind or drunk, he stumbled to his feet and staggered towards the Lamentation Tree. His mind raced, thinking of all of the occasions during which he had lost time, small moments that, when combined, became a monumental darkness. In that darkness, he now knew, he had been the Beast. He had killed Porteous, his friend, he had killed perhaps countless others. He was the Beast, he had hidden in that monumental darkness, even from himself. He was *cù dubh ifrinn*.

He had just reached the circle of torches around the Lamentation Tree when a figure stepped out into the light. It was Dempster.

"Willie," said Hyde, desperately. "Thank God. You have to take me in, you have to stop me."

"That's exactly what I intend to do," said Dempster, and Hyde saw he held his service revolver aimed at him.

68

Dempster waved the revolver, indicating the direction Hyde should take: towards the Lamentation Tree. He did as he was bade and stepped through the circle of torches. He could now see the body that hung from the branch, upside down, the ankles bound by rope, the chest rent open.

"Oh no," said Hyde. "Peter . . ." He recognized the dangling corpse as MacCandless and felt guilt at his relief that it was not Cally Burr's body that hung there. He had done this, he thought, that other part of him had done this. But with his arm injured, he could not have done it unaided. He turned to Dempster.

"We have to be careful, Willie," he said. "There are others."

"I know," said Dempster, his face strangely blank. He nodded up to the tree, and Hyde turned.

"Allan?" Hyde asked, confused by the appearance of his friend Allan Lawson on the hillock. He was flanked by two other figures. One was the scar-faced colour sergeant from the castle. The other figure stood mute, staring blankly out over the scene.

"Miss Lockwood!" said Hyde. "Are you all right, Elspeth?"

"She cannot answer you at the moment," said Lawson. "She is temporarily *elsewhere*."

"You?" said Hyde incredulously. "You are the Deacon?"

"You remember when I was your commanding officer, Edward? Do you remember the things we did to keep people from claiming what was rightfully theirs back from us? What they called me?"

"They called you *Jaanavar*," said Hyde. "The Beast."

"Exactly. And I deserved that name. What I did—what *we* did—was monstrous. We were monsters in India who came home to Scotland and shortbread and tea. But the real monster was the idea we served. You saw what was done, Edward. You were part of what was done, in the name of Empire."

"I don't understand, Allan," said Hyde. "You *believed* in what the Empire stood for."

Lawson nodded, gravely, then turned to study the trance-bound profile of Elspeth Lockwood before turning back to Hyde. "I was shown the falsity of the identity into which Scotland invested itself— the hypocrisy and the duplicity of everything we stood for. I saw the schism between these small, insignificant Atlantic islands and the monster of Empire they have become, plundering and raping a quarter of the world. Stealing from peoples who have no idea of the riches their lands hold. Crushing those who question their subjugation." He shook his head. "It is what happened to our own people, the Celts, at the hands of another empire. At least the Romans had the honesty to slaughter us. The British Empire bought our soul with plunder and baubles. I saw in India that that was how the Empire thrived, by getting those it subjugated to collaborate in their own subjugation. Like us, like the Scots. That's when I saw the truth of the whole thing."

"So all this," Hyde waved a bloodied hand in the direction of Mac-Candless's hanging corpse, "this is all *political*?"

"No, not political," said Lawson, "*spiritual*. There is meaning in what we do. Purpose. I lead men who served with me and who have seen the truth of their identities."

Hyde turned to Dempster, who stood with his revolver still trained on him. "You too, William?" Dempster nodded. Keeping his revolver aimed at Hyde, he pushed up the sleeve of both jacket and shirt to reveal, halfway up his forearm, the triple spiral of a triskelion tattoo.

Hyde turned back to Lawson. "So it is the sign of the Dark Guild," he said bitterly. "And you are its deacon."

"No," said Lawson. "You still don't understand, do you? I am not the Deacon. The Deacon exists locked within the mind of another, don't you see? I would have thought you would have worked that out. The Deacon has to be summoned, has to come to the surface."

Hyde again looked down at the blood on his hands. He was about to say something when he heard a deep breath being taken. Then a voice said:

"No, Captain Hyde, have no fear, it is not you who is my host."

Hyde stared disbelievingly at the source of the voice.

"It was I who summoned you here," said Elspeth Lockwood.

69

The scorched-black effigy of Edinburgh sat beneath the lightless stone sky, the channels of burning pitch the only illumination. This, she knew, was a place that had known the passage of Balor of the Piercing Eye—this was the Edinburgh she had briefly seen excoriated by the demon's burning gaze. It had not been a hallucination—it had been a premonition, a mantic glimpse into this wider, deeper hell to which she had been destined.

Elspeth looked around her, at the hellscape Edinburgh that surrounded her, at the woman dressed in male attire who wore Elspeth's face.

"What is this place?" she begged. "Where are we?"

"This is our mind," said the other Elspeth. "This is our version of the Otherworld—the hell we created for ourselves. The hell in which you tried to confine me. You forced me here, into the darkness, but when you needed me—oh, when you needed me, you let me come to the surface. But now I am going to live in the light always, and you will reside here. It is my turn in the light."

"I don't understand," Elspeth sobbed. "How can there be two of us?"

"There always has been," said the other. "And you knew about me, just as much as I knew about you. It was just you refused to allow yourself to believe. You pushed me down here, into the depths. But when you needed me, you let me out. Like with Joseph."

"What about Joseph?"

"You know. You know what we did—what I did for you, for us. You can see it, remember it, I know: the confused look on our brother's face when we pushed him from the roof of the store. He fell to his death so Lockwood's would fall into our hands."

"No!" Elspeth sobbed desperately, sinking to her knees. "It's not true!" she protested, but a memory took vague form in her mind: Joseph's face, eyes wide, frightened, confused, and so terribly sad; his outstretched arms as he fell silently to a cobbled death. "You did that! You did that, not me! You are not me!"

"We are each other. We are both and we are neither. But our halves are unequal: I am so much greater than you. I possess all our will, all our ambition, fortitude and strength. But what is more—so much, much more—is that I am the part of us that is eternal. Because I have been so deep in our mind, navigating the infinite spirals of our memories, I carry the memory of our people, of our race, from the beginning of our time. You have small dreams, small ambitions. I dream the dreams of an entire race.

"Yet despite my greater strength, my greater and ancient wisdom, you have been my gaoler, confining me here in the dark. But now it is I who will confine you. This . . ." the other Elspeth waved her hand to indicate their hellscape surroundings, "this will become your residence. You will become the confined, I the confiner."

Once more, the arched welkin of the stone-vaulted sky rang with the banshee cry of Elspeth's screaming.

70

Hyde could see it right away: the deference Lawson paid instantly to the emergence of Elspeth from her trance. He had no doubt now who the Deacon of the Dark Guild was.

"Where is Dr. Burr?" asked Hyde. "What have you done with her?"

"She will be with us soon," said Elspeth. "Then we shall conclude our business here."

"And Ballor? Where is he?"

"Frederic is dead. I kissed his lips and severed an artery and let him bleed because he wanted to bleed me. He became greedy. He began to feel that, as he organized the ceremonies and supplied the context for blackmail, he should receive greater remuneration for his efforts. He also became ambitious. He manipulated Elspeth—I mean the *other* Elspeth—knowing that my time in the waking world was limited. But I grew stronger, spent more time in control, pushed the other, weak Elspeth into the dark vaults of the mind we share. She is there now, lost and afraid. I intend that she remain there."

Hyde laughed. "Listen to yourself," he said. "You are mad, insane. There is only one Elspeth Lockwood, one mind. You are just pretending to yourself that this Beast exists."

"Am I? Until a second or two ago you had the same belief about yourself. You feared that during your seizures some other, monstrous Hyde came into being. Are *you* mad?"

"I do not believe myself to be some kind of eternal spirit of my people. I do not comport myself as some demigod from the Otherworld."

"Is that what I am?" She looked at her companions. "Or is it just that because I have been trapped so long in the dark depths of a mind, I have connected with a memory—not of an individual, but of a people, of an entire race? Samuel Porteous believed such things possible. He believed two Elspeths inhabited the same body, the same mind."

"And that is why you murdered him?"

"Hubris, Captain Hyde. My hubris, not his. His sessions were mainly with Elspeth, but he always sought to tease me to the surface. To chain the devil, you have to face him first. I was careless and told him about my brother, Joseph—about how I pushed him from the roof so that I could take control of Lockwood's store. I told him how Joseph had looked so frightened, yet so sad, as he fell. Do you know, I believe he did not cry out because he did not want people to look up and see me. His last act was not to incriminate the beloved sister who was his murderer. Porteous told me that he believed that it was at that moment that the schism in my mind happened; that I had separated a part of myself from that event so as to remain guiltless. I told him that I had been there for much longer than that, constructing my own world in the depths of the mind in which I was confined. It was foolish for me to have told him about Joseph. He tricked me into telling, and saw that which I had sought to hide. He had seen too much, so I took his eyes."

"And Farquharson?"

"We dealt with Farquharson," said Lawson. "He was investigating Elspeth's connection with Ballor and found out about the blackmail. But the main reason he had to die was that he recognized Dunlop as the regimental photographer in Afghanistan. And through Dunlop made the connection with me."

"But it was I who cut out his heart," said Elspeth, and smiled. "I wanted it as a keepsake. It sits even now in my special place."

"And you, Dempster?" said Hyde. "How long have you been part of this?"

"From the beginning."

"So that is why there was no trace of the colour sergeant here," Hyde nodded towards the sabre-scarred man, "when you went through the duty roster at the castle. I sent the wrong man."

"Or the right man," said Lawson. "Things would have become difficult otherwise."

"You are all mad," said Hyde. "But that will not prevent you all from hanging. You *will* all hang, every one of you."

"No one here is going to hang," said Elspeth. "When this is all over, Dempster here will be the sole survivor of your little expedition to liberate Dr. Burr. He will confirm that when you and he got here, you took one of your *turns* and revealed your alter ego to be that of the Deacon. He will explain that he and MacCandless tried to take you into custody, but you and your Dark Guildsmen killed MacCandless, Dempster only just escaping with his life.

"By the time help gets here, there will be no trace of you other than the victims you have left behind. Your colleagues will put it all together: your episodes where you could not account for your actions; the fact that, by enormous coincidence, it was you who discovered Farquharson's body; your slaughter here of Dr. Burr, Sergeant Mac-Candless and Frederic Ballor, and your ghost-like vanishing into the night just as suspicion closed in on you . . ." Elspeth laughed. "The legend of the Dark Guild and its duplicitous Deacon will endure for generations—the name Hyde will forever become associated with the duality of human nature. You will become as famous, perhaps more so, as Deacon Brodie—you will be a new Deacon, a new demon for a new age. We will make sure no one ever finds your remains, so that your reputation will endure, become immortal."

Elspeth looked meaningfully at Lawson. "They will be here soon," she said. "It is time."

Lawson looked at Hyde regretfully, then nodded to Dempster.

Hyde heard the sound of a revolver hammer being pulled back.

71

Hyde spun around, ready to rush at Dempster before he had a chance to fire. But when he turned, he saw that the treacherous policeman held his revolver skywards, his other hand also raised. Standing behind him was Cally Burr, jamming the muzzle of a short-barrelled revolver beneath his jaw.

He also saw Salazar, the Cagot, move to snatch the gun from Dempster's grip and Hyde made to stop him.

"It's all right, Edward," said Cally. "Salazar is with us. Take Dempster's gun."

Hyde did as she commanded. Cally pushed Dempster towards the others, and now she and Hyde both trained their revolvers on them.

"Are there any more?" he asked.

"I couldn't see any, but that does not mean there are none. I suggest we get these ones locked up. I know a cosy little cellar."

"Put your hands up," said Hyde, but Lawson and the sabre-scarred soldier remained unmoving. Elspeth Lockwood glared at Hyde with an intense ferocity. "I will not repeat myself," he told them.

The high, screeching scream startled him. Elspeth Lockwood ran down towards them, an inhuman shrieking issuing from her. In that fraction of a second, Hyde questioned whether it really had been the sound of a Highland keening he had heard that first night, down by the Water of Leith. He hesitated, an instinct preventing him shooting an unarmed woman, and she was upon him, clawing at him, biting, scratching. He heard shots fired and realized Cally was exchanging fire with the others. He pushed Elspeth away and Salazar grabbed her. Hyde turned and readied to fire, but Lawson and the other man had disappeared.

William Dempster lay on the ground, staring unseeing at the dark sky. A bloodless hole in his pale forehead marked where a stray bullet had struck him.

"Take cover!" Hyde yelled to Cally. It was now an uneven contest. Salazar was occupied with trying to restrain Elspeth, and Hyde and Cally were facing two armed professional soldiers. He took the revolver in the hand of his injured arm and helped Salazar drag Elspeth away from the circle of torches.

"Let's get down to the Dark Man," said Hyde. "And kill those torches. We'll be in the dark and they'll have to come at us from the light."

They ran, Elspeth suddenly and quietly quiescent, and Hyde wondered if there had been another change in her personality. They reached the Dark Man, and Hyde and Salazar kicked over the torches and stamped out their flames. Everything became shrouded in shadow, the cloud-mute moon casting the only, weak light.

Suddenly Elspeth screamed—the same inhuman scream—and Hyde saw a blade flash in the moonlight. Salazar made a strangled sound and the blade rose again. Cally was nearest to them and Hyde saw her slash at Elspeth with the barrel of her revolver. It caught Elspeth on the temple and she flew sideways, striking her head against the shelf of the Dark Man standing stone. She fell into its shadow, unmoving.

Cally went over and examined her as best she could in the darkness.

"Is she . . . ?" asked Hyde.

"She's alive," said Cally. "But she has a serious head injury." She moved over to Salazar. He pointed to his arm, which had been punctured in the bicep. Hyde heard tearing as Cally ripped strips of cloth from her skirt. "Salazar's fine too. He's not bleeding much—his brachial artery seems undamaged. I'll fix this tourniquet, but they will both need hospital attention when we get out of here."

"That is if we do get out of here," said Hyde. "Lawson and his henchman know what they're about."

With that, there was the crack of a shot and a bullet thudded into the dark earth immediately to Hyde's left.

"Keep down," he hissed. "They won't risk a shot unless they get a good target. Elspeth Lockwood is like some kind of priestess to them and they won't risk hitting her. My guess is they'll try to come in close."

—

Dark minutes passed. There had been no further shots. Hyde scanned the encircling horizon of the depression's lip. The torches still burned at the Lamentation Tree and Peter MacCandless hung pale and motionless. On the drumlin opposite, Crunnach House remained an irregular shadow cut into the sky.

Hyde could see no signs of either man.

"Do you think they've gone?" whispered Cally.

"I doubt it. They want to see if we try to get back to the house or make a break for the main road."

Elspeth Lockwood moaned where she lay by the Dark Man.

"We have to get her to a hospital," said Cally. "Salazar too."

Hyde thought for a while, cursing their situation. "All right, let's make for the stables. Hopefully the carriage is still there. Can you walk?" he asked Salazar. The Cagot nodded in the gloom.

"Follow me and keep low." Hyde jammed his revolver into his waistband and picked up Elspeth in his arms. He felt pain shoot through his injured arm, but the girl was lighter than he thought. He wondered how so much concentrated evil could have such little substance to it.

"Wait here," he ordered when they reached the lip of the depression and the gravelled carriageway. "I'll go ahead. If anyone other than me comes near, shoot them."

The coach still stood by the stable block. Hyde made his way over to it, moving from shadow to shadow. He made it to the gable of the stables, then edged his way along its flank. He checked inside; the stables were empty, but he spotted the gleam of a pair of handcuffs on the floor. Picking them up, he saw they were engraved *Sgt P. MacC.* MacCandless, who now hung heartless and upside down from the Lamentation Tree, must have dealt with a guildsman here before walking unknowing into betrayal by his friend and colleague, Willie Dempster.

Moving back out of the stable, Hyde checked the horses and the carriage. All was fine. He would go back and get the others, and carry Elspeth Lockwood to the carriage.

They had both been moving by stealth, one along the side of the stable, the other along the gable end. They came face to face at the corner. For less than a second, Hyde and the sabre-scarred man looked at each other in surprise, then both rushed at his opponent before either had the chance to raise his revolver to fire. Hyde grabbed the scarred man's wrist, pushing his revolver upwards, while he in turn slammed Hyde's gun hand against the stable wall. Hyde's injured arm did not have the strength to resist, and the revolver fell from his grasp.

Grinning in triumph, the sabre-scarred soldier took a step back and raised his gun.

Hyde heard two shots and waited for the pain to explode in his body, but it did not. The scarred man leaned forward into Hyde, his breath hot on his cheek, then fell onto the courtyard cobbles. Hyde looked across and saw Cally Burr standing sideways on, her arm outstretched as if shooting at a pistol competition. She let her arm slowly come to rest at her side.

They heard the pounding of hooves approaching and looked up to see the police carriage and waggons making their way along the carriageway towards the house.

"Lawson?" asked Cally.

Hyde shrugged. She walked over to him and they both leaned with their backs against the stable, looking up at the brightening sky while they waited for the police to arrive.

72

It wanted to snow, that day, but, as was often the case in Edinburgh, the close-by and dark-lumbering, slumbering sea forbade it and a chill, steel-grey rain fell in its stead.

Cally Burr was waiting for Hyde when he arrived at Craig House. Dr. Galston, the director of the asylum, was a dour man of fifty who wore an expression to match the day's weather. Galston seemed intent on addressing only Hyde, and when Cally asked a direct question, the asylum director pointedly addressed her as *Miss* Burr.

"You have permission from Mr. Lockwood, I believe?" he said.

Hyde nodded and handed him the paper James Lockwood had signed, giving them leave to visit his daughter.

"Very well," said Galston, "but it will do you no good. Miss Lockwood is in a state of total catatonia: she does not react at all to any stimuli and probably is completely unaware of her situation or surroundings."

"Is the catatonia the result of her psychological state or the head injury?" asked Cally.

"There is no way of knowing that." Galston again addressed his response to Hyde. "It is immaterial, I would say."

"If it is the head wound," Cally took her turn to address her comments to Hyde, "then it is irreparable; if it is psychological, then it may be reversible."

"I really do not see there is much profit to be gained in you seeing her," said Galston. When neither Cally nor Hyde responded, he shrugged narrow shoulders. "This way. I have arranged for her to be brought to the dayroom . . ."

Without thinking about it, Hyde had expected to find Elspeth Lockwood wild-haired and dressed in some kind of hospital gown, but as they entered the asylum's dayroom, he saw her sitting by the picture windows, dressed in an expensive white mutton-sleeved blouse and black satin skirt, her hair brushed and gathered up. She looked for all the world like a gentlewoman at leisure, and he half expected her to stand up as they approached and offer them a hand in welcome.

But she did not. Elspeth merely gazed out through the windows, her eyes blank and unfocussed.

"We have come to visit you, Elspeth," said Cally, placing fingers under Elspeth's chin and gently turning her face towards them. The eyes still gazed blank and empty.

Before they had come, Cally and Hyde had agreed not to tell Elspeth about what had happened in the year since she had been confined: that Allan Lawson had been tracked down, and, cashiered from the army, had stood trial in a civilian court. The result of the trial had been that, one month earlier, Lawson had stood briefly in the cheerless brightness of a white room while a small, businesslike man had efficiently eased his passage to the Otherworld. Nor did they tell Elspeth of her father's declining health, a lifetime of grief longing for release.

Instead they sat with her for half an hour, asking questions without expecting answers, trying to coax out a fragment of a personality retreated into the infinite shell spirals of her mind. There was nothing left to learn from her, Hyde realized. There was nothing left of the demon who had murdered Samuel Porteous and aided in the murder of Donald Farquharson and Henry Dunlop. With great sadness, it occurred to him that neither did anything remain of the innocent, grieving part of her mind.

Duo in unum occultatum. Two hidden within the one. Except now neither resided in the vessel that was Elspeth Lockwood.

"How long will she live?" Hyde asked Cally as they were escorted by a wardress back through pale corridors to the main hall. "I mean, in that catatonic condition?"

"She is a young, healthy woman—at least her body is. She is as likely to live a normal span as any of us."

"My God, it is beyond contemplation. I cannot imagine being condemned to such an existence."

"For all we know, there is no intellectual function remaining," said Cally. "She perhaps has no emotion, no awareness, no internal life."

"But what if she has?" Hyde shook his head. "What if her mind is still there, trapped deep in the prison of her own body? Poor woman."

"You pity your friend's murderer?"

"No—I pity the tortured soul forced to share a mind with that murderer."

The rain had cleared by the time they stood outside the asylum. Mackinley waited with the coach.

"Can I drop you somewhere?" asked Hyde.

Cally looped her arm through his and smiled. "You may take me for afternoon tea, Captain Hyde."

Hyde returned her smile. "That would be my pleasure, Dr. Burr."

Elspeth looked around herself. The dark cavern with its stone sky and black, crumbling city was gone, and fading from her memory. The tormentor who had worn Elspeth's face, who had led her through labyrinthine horrors was also gone, and Elspeth somehow knew she was gone forever.

Elspeth remained in the same place, but it had been completely transformed. The whole scene was illuminated by golden sunshine from the revealed sky, bright and cloudless. The castle had become restored to its full form, the dust cleared from buildings and streets, trees and grass returned to verdant life.

From where she stood, she could see the Lockwood's building on Princes Street, and was surprised how little it meant to her, how unimportant and empty those distant ambitions had been. Much of that, she realized, had perished with the other Elspeth. She also knew that this was not the real world, not the real Edinburgh in which she had lived her life. But even that thought faded.

She frowned and looked up at the sky, thinking she heard someone speak from far away, far above her. Voices that had sounded sad in their appeals.

"What is it, child?" asked another voice, this time close behind her. Elspeth turned and wept with joy when she saw her mother, still young and beautiful, standing there. Elspeth's gentle brother Joseph stood at her side, his face free of the worry and sorrow it had borne so much in life.

"I thought I heard voices," said Elspeth. "I thought someone was talking to me."

"Voices? From the sky?" Her mother laughed and it was like the sound of river water sparkling and bubbling over stones. Elspeth laughed too.

Once more she looked around herself at the colour and brightness, then closed her eyes and tilted her head to feel the warmth of the sun and the cool of the air on her face.

"Come, Elspeth," said her mother, holding out her hand to her. "It is time to go."

"Is this the Otherworld?" asked Elspeth.

"No, child," said her mother kindly, "or perhaps it is. This is just the moment and the eternity before death. But there is nothing to fear."

Elspeth looked around her, at the city restored in her mind to the light, at the vast sky, at its brightness. "I know, Mother. I am not afraid."

"Come, child," her mother said again. "It is time to go."

With enormous joy in her heart, Elspeth Lockwood took the hands of her mother and brother and stepped into the great brightening of the world.

73

It was an otherworld: another country. Its inhabitants dressed differently, spoke a different language, possessed different ways, looked on him as if he were a foreigner. This was yet another divide in Scotland's personality and, paradoxically, it felt familiar in its strangeness. To Hyde, who had spent so much of his life in the manufactured granite and sandstone topography of the city, this place was more akin to the otherworlds of his seizure dreams than to that of his waking. Had she described this place to him? Had the old woman he now sought placed the furled idea of it in his head, where it had unravelled in his dreaming?

Three changes of train took him deep into the enfolding glens. There had been no hansoms at the remote Highlands station, but a ruddy-faced deliveryman had granted Hyde a for-a-shilling obligement and taken him as close to his destination as metalled highway would permit. Thereafter he made his stout-booted way along the narrow roadway, little more than a frost-limned path.

It was sunny but bitterly cold, winter lurking behind the clear bright shoulders of the mountains and cloud-paling Hyde's exerted breath as he walked the four miles to his destination.

He had expected it to be a village, or at least a hamlet, given that it was a place with its own name. It turned out, instead, to be a scattering of crofts on the sheltered east-facing flank of the valley.

Again he was discombobulated by the valley's unfamiliar familiarity. It was not the same as the strath through which he had walked in his dreams, but it nevertheless reminded him of it.

The Morrison croft was the third he tried. Flora Morrison had been sitting outside, on a chair by the door, disinterestedly watching as he approached. She stood up as he drew near.

"I'm Edward Hyde," he said.

"Aye, the Edinburgh policeman," she said in the breathy accent of the west Highlands. "I remember you."

"I'm no longer with the police," said Hyde. "But they have retained my services as an investigative consultant—and I have not ceased trying to prove Hugh's innocence."

"And why would you do that?" she asked.

Hyde frowned. He was about to say something, then checked himself. "Listen, Mrs. Morrison, I know we spoke before, but I have a form of epilepsy that plays tricks with my memory. I came all the way here because I need to hear again what it was you told me that night."

Mrs. Morrison stared at him impassively for a moment, then said: "You had better come in."

The old woman remained quiet for a time, looking out of the croft's small, square window with its thick, bubbled glass, and Hyde had the feeling that she was looking towards some place, some time, invisible to him. "So you do not remember, do you?" she said at last. "You have forgotten our conversation that night of the keening for my son, in Edinburgh."

"I . . ." Hyde sought simple words to explain his condition, his symptoms of wild dreaming, daylight hallucinations and amnesiac episodes. But as he looked at her, at her pale, intelligent eyes set in a strong, weatherworn face, he knew there was no need. "I lose time," he said. "I lost time that night."

The old woman nodded slowly. "Do you know of *cù dubh ifrinn*?"

"Hugh spoke of it. He said that was what killed little Mary Paton."

"It is a legend here," said the old woman. "A myth, you would call it. There was supposed to be a great battle in this glen between the gods and demons of the Otherworld. They say the mountainside split open and the hordes of each spilled out into the glen, led by Crom Dubh and his monstrous warhounds, and did slaughter to each other. After the battle, fearful of leaving a trace in the world of men, they cleaned up the battlefield and withdrew back into the mountain, closing it behind them. According to the legend, one of Crom Dubh's hellhounds was left behind, trapped in the world of men and possessed of an insatiable thirst for blood. It is called *cù dubh ifrinn*, the black hellhound.

"Some versions say that Crom Dubh left the hound here deliberately, to feed his own need for human sacrifice. Only a very few, mainly the old ones, believe the legend, but many believe it explains the presence of a real wolf, the last of its kind in Scotland, that hunts and kills in the glen. They say that the last recorded Scottish wolf—hunted down some hundred years since by MacQueen Pall a' Chrocain—was said to be as black as night. Some say *cù dubh ifrinn* is nothing more than the descendant of that beast."

"I'm sorry, Mrs. Morrison, I don't see—"

The old woman turned to Hyde, halting him. "I sent him from here. For his safety and the safety of others."

"Who?"

"Hugh, my son. This is the wisdom you had, but lost—what I told you that night."

"Why?" asked Hyde. "I mean, why did you send him away?"

"Let me show you why."

Mrs. Morrison stood up and led Hyde out of the croft. The sky was bright, but a blade of chill wind cut through the material of his clothes. She pointed up the mountain to where copses and willow scrub clustered together on a hillside otherwise naked of trees but mantled in the pink, purple and white of heather.

"You have to see." She led the way along a path that took them steeply up towards the mountain. Hyde was surprised at how swiftly she was able to pace up the incline. He stopped and turned when they were at the halfway mark; the croft and its widespread neighbours now appearing so small and insignificant, isolated in a vast and empty land. There were ghosts still populating the landscape, however: roofless crofts, long abandoned and turning moss green as the earth reclaimed their stone. He thought of generations lost to the Americas or New Zealand.

"It is not far now," said Mrs. Morrison, the only words uttered during the ascent.

She led him into the densest copse of woodland and the day remained outside as they were immersed in a green-shadowed twilight. There was no path here and the ground crackled beneath their feet. They reached the heart of the copse, where the trees were thickest. She pointed down into a shallow hollow between them.

Hyde looked into the hollow and understood.

"Hugh had the manner of a child, the open face of an innocent," said Mrs. Morrison, "but he had never known childhood and his soul had never known innocence. When he was a young boy, he would play in here amongst the trees. Too far from home for a child of that age and I would beat him for it, fearing that some evil would befall him here, some accident or injury. No matter how often I beat him, he would defy me within days, as if drawn to the trees by some dark force. So instead of beating him, I followed him here one day. But there was no evil to befall Hugh in the woods—*he* was the evil that befell others. He had made this place for himself."

Hyde gazed down into the depression. Like the nest or lair of some beast, someone had woven together branches and twigs as one might weave a wicker basket, but on a scale that must have taken enormous patience and will. A huge nest that sat in the hollow between the greatest clustering of trees. One could have walked right by it without seeing it.

He had recognized it straight away. Though larger, and worn and part unravelled by the passage of time, it was of exactly the same construction as the witch's cradle in which the murdered girl in Granton had been found.

"This was not the cunning of a ten-year-old boy," said Mrs. Morrison. "It was the devil's cunning. When I surprised him here, he just turned to me and stared at me with those big, empty, childish eyes of his. Just as he has looked at you, I can tell. And this was no den created in childish play," she continued without heat, as if all emotion had been burned out of her years before. "It was a small hell, set here in the silence of the glen. It must have taken him endless hours to construct it, and with the same patience he had decorated it with ornaments. The heads of just about every type of creature that flew, walked or crawled through this glen. And there were other parts, where animals had been torn asunder in torture. I knew then that he was lost. Yet whenever I spoke to him at home about this place, it was as if he genuinely had no memory of it. I destroyed his lair, but found it restored a few months later. I broke it up again, and again, but each time, with great patience, he rebuilt it, and each time he knew nothing of its existence when asked. As he grew, I learned to accept the Hugh I had at home—the simple, harmless Hugh—and did my best to forget that some other Hugh came to this place with black dreams in his head."

"And this is why you suspect he was guilty of the Granton murder?" Hyde asked. "Because of the similarity with the crib they found the girl in?"

"There's more to tell of this place," said Mrs. Morrison, gazing down into the hollow. "The reason I sent Hugh away was because a girl went missing from one of the neighbouring crofts. She was, in fact, Hugh's cousin, my late husband's niece, and Hugh used to spend much time with her, though he was years older. Every man for miles around helped search for her, poor wee thing. They found her here. In that lair. Or I should say it was Hugh, searching with the others, who found her here, laid out as if asleep."

"Just like at the quarry," said Hyde. "Was Hugh suspected?"

"No." Mrs. Morrison gave a bitter laugh. "That was the thing— because he had been the one to find her, and because he was so shocked by the discovery and fair struck down by grief, everyone looked else-where. Most believed that the poor bairn had been taken by an animal, a beast of some sort, and that this was its lair. And in a way, of course, they were right."

"So no one was held to account?" asked Hyde.

"They settled on it being a beast. As I say, some believe there are still wolves, the last of their kind, roaming the glens here. And, of course, it was only a matter of time before folk started to talk about *cù dubh ifrinn*, Crom Dubh's black hellhound. Sometimes a superstition yields more comfort than the idea of a murderer in your midst."

"No one knows the truth of this place? About Hugh's history here?"

"Only me. And now, you."

"Why did you bring me here?"

"To give you peace. So that you might know that no injustice was done."

Hyde stared down into the crib, so like the version in his dream, which had bound him with clutching wood fingers while a black devil hound had snapped its jaws shut on Mary Paton. The truth he had been told but his waking mind had forgotten revealed in his dreaming.

Samuel Porteous had been right all along: the answers had lain in his dream otherworld.

"Perhaps, now, Hugh's nature is other," said Flora Morrison in her Highland lilt. "Now that he is free of his evil nature and the good, innocent half commands the whole."

"Now?" asked Hyde.

"Now. Where he has passed to. In the Otherworld."

EPILOGUE

They sat for a while, after Hyde had finished his tale, both silent and staring out across the sun-sparkled water. Eventually, Stevenson turned to his friend.

"And your episodes?" he asked. "Those have ceased?"

"They have diminished in frequency," said Hyde. "I still occasionally lose time, but only for a matter of a minute or so. I still have the seizure dreams. But again less frequently."

"It is quite a story," said Stevenson. "Quite a story indeed. And one I'll wager you are glad has reached a happy conclusion."

"I am," said Hyde. "I have only one regret in confounding their plan to pin all blame for the murders on me."

Stevenson smiled, intrigued. "Oh?"

Hyde laughed. "I rather liked their idea of my name becoming eternally synonymous with the duality of human nature. It appeals to my vanity to be more famous than Deacon Brodie."

Stevenson held his friend in his gaze for a moment, then said: "I rather think I shall have to do something about that, Edward . . ."

ACKNOWLEDGEMENTS

As always, I am enormously grateful to my wife, Wendy, for all her support and for her suggestions, which have made this a better book.

For their enthusiasm and commitment, I would like to thank my editor Krystyna Green, cover designer Sean Garrehy, and Brionee Fenlon, Clara Diaz and Amanda Keats at Little, Brown; my UK and US literary agents Andrew Gordon and Esmond Harmsworth, Alice Howe and the foreign rights team at DHA; and Georgina Ruffhead and Joel Gotler, my film and TV agents.

Huge thanks also to my copy-editor, Jane Selley, and to Martin Fletcher.

ABOUT THE AUTHOR

CRAIG RUSSELL is an award-winning Scottish author whose books have been translated into twenty-five languages. His previous works include *The Devil Aspect,* the Fabel series of thrillers and the Lennox series of noir mysteries. He is the winner of the 2015 McIlvanney Prize, as well as the 2008 Crime Writers' Association Dagger in the Library prize. A former police officer, he lives in Perthshire, Scotland, with his wife.